MARVEL

A NOVEL OF THE MARVEL UNIVERSE

LOKI

JOURNEY INTO
MYSTERY

NOVELS OF THE MARVEL UNIVERSE BY TITAN BOOKS

Ant-Man: Natural Enemy by Jason Starr
Avengers: Everybody Wants to Rule the World by Dan Abnett
Avengers: Infinity by James A. Moore
Black Panther: Panther's Rage by Sheree Renée Thomas
Black Panther: Tales of Wakanda by Jesse J. Holland
Black Panther: Who is the Black Panther? by Jesse J. Holland
Captain America: Dark Designs by Stefan Petrucha
Captain Marvel: Liberation Run by Tess Sharpe
Captain Marvel: Shadow Code by Gilly Segal
Civil War by Stuart Moore
Deadpool: Paws by Stefan Petrucha
Guardians of the Galaxy: Annihilation by Brendan Deneen
Morbius: The Living Vampire – Blood Ties by Brendan Deneen
Secret Invasion by Paul Cornell
Spider-Man: Forever Young by Stefan Petrucha
Spider-Man: Kraven's Last Hunt by Neil Kleid
Spider-Man: The Darkest Hours Omnibus by Jim Butcher, Keith R.A. DeCandido, and
Christopher L. Bennett
Spider-Man: The Venom Factor Omnibus by Diane Duane
Thanos: Death Sentence by Stuart Moore
Venom: Lethal Protector by James R. Tuck
Wolverine: Weapon X Omnibus by Marc Cerasini, David Alan Mack, and Hugh Matthews
X-Men: Days of Future Past by Alex Irvine
X-Men: The Dark Phoenix Saga by Stuart Moore
X-Men: The Mutant Empire Omnibus by Christopher Golden
X-Men & The Avengers: The Gamma Quest Omnibus by Greg Cox

ALSO FROM TITAN AND TITAN BOOKS

Marvel Contest of Champions: The Art of the Battlerealm by Paul Davies
Marvel's Guardians of the Galaxy: No Guts, No Glory by M.K. England
Marvel's Midnight Suns: Infernal Rising by S.D. Perry
Marvel's Spider-Man: The Art of the Game by Paul Davies
Obsessed with Marvel by Peter Sanderson and Marc Sumerak
Spider-Man: Into the Spider-Verse – The Art of the Movie by Ramin Zahed
Spider-Man: Hostile Takeover by David Liss
Spider-Man: Miles Morales – Wings of Fury by Brittney Morris
The Art of Iron Man (10th Anniversary Edition) by John Rhett Thomas
The Marvel Vault by Matthew K. Manning, Peter Sanderson, and Roy Thomas
Ant-Man and the Wasp: The Official Movie Special
Avengers: Endgame – The Official Movie Special
Avengers: Infinity War – The Official Movie Special
Black Panther: The Official Movie Companion
Black Panther: The Official Movie Special
Captain Marvel: The Official Movie Special
Marvel Studios: The First 10 Years
Marvel's Avengers – Script to Page
Marvel's Black Panther – Script to Page
Marvel's Black Widow: The Official Movie Special
Marvel's Spider-Man – Script to Page
Spider-Man: Far From Home: The Official Movie Special
Spider-Man: Into the Spider-Verse: Movie Special
Thor: Ragnarok: The Official Movie Special

A NOVEL OF THE MARVEL UNIVERSE

LOKI
JOURNEY INTO
MYSTERY

AN ORIGINAL NOVEL BY

KATHERINE LOCKE

TITAN BOOKS

MARVEL

LOKI: JOURNEY INTO MYSTERY
Print edition ISBN: 9781803362540
E-book edition ISBN: 9781803362557

Published by Titan Books
A division of Titan Publishing Group Ltd
144 Southwark Street, London SE1 0UP
www.titanbooks.com

First edition: December 2023
10 9 8 7 6 5 4 3 2 1

This is a work of fiction. All of the characters, organizations, and events portrayed in this novel are either products of the author's imagination or are used fictitiously. Any resemblance to actual persons, living or dead (except for satirical purposes), is entirely coincidental.

FOR MARVEL PUBLISHING
Jeff Youngquist, VP Production and Special Projects
Sarah Singer, Editor, Special Projects
Jeremy West, Manager, Licensed Publishing
Sven Larsen, VP, Licensed Publishing
David Gabriel, SVP of Sales & Marketing, Publishing
C.B. Cebulski, Editor in Chief

Cover art by Stephanie Hans.

A CIP catalogue record for this title is available from the British Library.

Printed and bound by CPI Group (UK) Ltd, Croydon CR0 4YY.

PART I

FEAR ITSELF

ONE

ALL STORIES have beginnings.

The good ones don't have endings.

In every world, stories are told. By gods or mortals, it doesn't matter. Stories are currency. Stories are power. Stories are sustenance. Stories transcend.

Many millennia ago, I read a fairytale that began like this: Once there was where there was not.

This isn't a fairytale. Not strictly speaking.

So, it doesn't start like that.

It starts with birds.

You probably weren't expecting birds, were you? Settle in. I am the Teller, and even I found myself surprised by the events that followed. Even the unfeathered ones.

It starts with seven magpies. If you are lucky enough to live in a place without magpies, then here's the thing to know about magpies: they are tricksters. They're cleverer than most birds, even ravens and crows, small enough that they can fit into all sorts of places they shouldn't, and craftier than a fox.

You may see where this is going. Because magpies could only be called to one god.

Seven magpies looked back at the remains of the destroyed Asgard. Loki had brought chaos and destruction to Asgard, and it'd ultimately been his own ending. Even those who didn't feel for Loki, even those who'd been cheering for his demise, could still hear the echoes of his screams in their dreams. No one spoke about it, of course. There was nothing left for Loki except animosity.

No one knows what the magpies saw when they looked upon Asgard. Perhaps they were looking to see if Loki was truly dead. Perhaps they were waiting for a rebirth. Perhaps they were simply procrastinating, for the distance they had to travel was long and arduous. Seven took flight, but not all would make it.

The first magpie did not make it far before she was overcome with grief. Hollow bones can fill with grief and weigh a bird down like stones from her feet.

Every magpie's grief is theirs to carry.

The others fly on.

The second magpie left after days at sea. The magpie knew that oceans are endless, and all oceans are one. He remembered a distant shore where he'd left one who made his heart flutter. Grief can look like searching for lost love too.

A third magpie was lost to Alfheim, where he stopped to feed on the eyes of a fallen elf girl. She'd been torn apart like an overoptimistic dream. Magpies were scavengers and he couldn't bear to leave those eyes, so beautiful and open, staring up at an uncaring sky forever.

MAGPIES DO NOT LIKE TO THINK OF THEMSELVES AS SCAVENGERS. THEY THINK THEMSELVES ABOVE THE RAVENS AND THE CROWS OF THE WORLDS. THEY'RE CLEVERER, REMEMBER. AND SO THE OTHER MAGPIES CHATTERED DISMISSIVELY ABOUT THE THIRD, LEAVING HIM BEHIND IN DISGUST MORE THAN PITY. IT WOULD BE BEST IF YOU DID NOT TELL THEM THAT I CALLED THEM SCAVENGERS.

It was not long after they passed Alfheim that word reached the magpies that Thor had returned Loki to life, as a child.

The news struck the fourth magpie straight out of the sky. He plummeted to the earth and his final thought was, "What was the Odinson thinking?"

It wasn't often that the magpies said something so universal, but there was hardly a soul who didn't wonder the same.

Another magpie thought, "I'm sure he knows what he's doing." He didn't have time to convince himself before he was shot with an arrow while passing through Hela's Valhalla.

Collateral damage from Loki's misdeeds, I suspect.

The sixth died in Hell. It would be best not to dwell on this one too long. It is gruesome, even for me.

It is important that you know about all the magpies, because now you understand what the seventh magpie survived. You see the distance and the flight, the internal and external dangers that this seventh magpie overcame. The seventh magpie did not fly on to his final destination quite yet. He made some stops along the way but that is neither here nor there. The important thing was, he made it, at last.

He turned for home.

This last magpie, he could not stop thinking about Loki and the choices he made. Why did he destroy Asgard? A good question. He suspected there was a logic there that he didn't know. Maybe it'd make sense to someone else. Just not him. He didn't like to admit this as he was a magpie, cleverer than most.

When the magpie returned to Asgard, he found that the heroes had won, as heroes are wont to do. The magpie had missed the triumph and he was a little peeved about that. *They should have waited*, he thought, though he knew they couldn't. He'd flown for forty-nine days and nights, and seen worlds he'd never dreamt of seeing. He'd flown until he could fly no more. And now he was home.

He wished he was not the only magpie to deliver this secret, but the others had died or left him, and that was that.

The magpie fluttered into the window of a tower, ready to deliver the message.

But the young master Loki was not there.

AS FOR me, I came into this story because I was summoned. Because if a story goes untold, it hasn't truly begun. OR, AT LEAST, THAT'S ONE WAY TO TELL THE TALE.

I was summoned, because that's what foolish young gods do. They summon eldritch gods, the way they beckon their friends to come over and see what happens when they poke the alligator with the stick.

He poked me.

TWO

LOKI, DARK-HAIRED and bright-eyed, his jaw set in an all-too-familiar way, sat on a pile of rubble, scrolling through his phone with a frustrated twitch of his thumb. The comments section of his post was—well, just the way comment sections typically went. He'd posted a picture of himself in Asgard, throwing a peace sign.

> Lensman47: Awesome. What filter is that?

There hadn't been a filter on it. So, Loki said as much.

Lensman47 came back with a string of all-caps accusations, calling Loki a liar and a wannabe influencer. Three hundred and forty-two people had liked Lensman47's comment.

Only one had liked Loki's.

And it looked like a bot, so that didn't really count.

"Even people online think I'm lying," Loki muttered. "Why do people always assume that?"

A passing soldier spat on the ground. "You know why, you despicable weasel. What is that device, anyways?"

Loki scoffed, shoving the phone into his pocket. "I'd explain it to you, but I don't have all day."

He probably should have looked up before he said that. Because after he said it, and after he looked up, he reconsidered the tone of his voice. The soldier loomed over him, face darkening like a stormy sky.

"You helspawned lickspittle," the soldier growled. "You brought Asgard nothing but ruin and sent many good souls to the pits—I am going to break you in half and feed you to the—"

"Is there a problem here?"

A familiar, soothing voice. Jealousy warred with relief in Loki at the sight of Thor walking around the corner, his stride long and purposeful. Loki tried to push the feelings away, the envy at his brother's confidence and ease, the embarrassment that he still needed his brother's rescue.

"Lord Thor, he was disrespectful," the soldier stammered, trying to hold his position but clearly cowering in the presence of the God of Thunder.

A crowd gathered, people wandering by slowing when they saw Thor, and stopping when they saw the commotion involved Loki. They shifted, a murmuration of bodies, until they stood behind the soldier like a wall. Loki wasn't even sure that they knew they'd chosen a side. Maybe it was instinctual. Whatever was happening, they wanted to be facing him, not standing behind him. Even him in this form. Not some past-Loki. The possibility soured his stomach.

"I'm sorry," Loki interjected quickly before Thor could ask for details, and before the crowd decided he was at fault. "I wasn't thinking. And I'm tired and hungry. Hanger always makes me say regretful things."

Thor looked like a smile might twitch at the corner of his mouth. "And do you accept this?"

The soldier did not want to accept it. He wanted to pummel Loki or throw him from the highest height in the ruins of Asgard. That much was clear to Loki and everyone else who'd gathered around. But this was Thor, and the soldier knew better. He bowed his head, accepting the apology, and beat a quick retreat.

Loki scrambled to his feet, dusting off his clothes. Thor waved dismissively at the crowd and they dissipated, slowly, and then quickly once they realized Thor wasn't going to say anything more, and Loki wasn't going to provide more antics.

Only when they were gone did Thor sigh and set a hand on Loki's shoulder. "This will pass, Loki."

Loki frowned at his feet. "I don't know if it will. I'm not him. I'm me."

"They know, it's just hard for them to believe it. They will come around," promised Thor. He didn't have the right to promise it, but Loki felt his brother's need for justice and optimism come through in the words. He might not have the right, or the ability, to make it so, but he'd try. If not for Loki, for whom he was responsible, but because this was who Thor was, right down to his core.

And Loki appreciated it. He needed that right now. The way the crowd stood around, siding with the soldiers, not ready to leap in to defend Loki being held accountable even for his past self's crimes—that hurt. He belonged here. He wanted to be a part of Asgard.

"I know," Loki lied. It came easily. It slipped off his tongue before he realized it.

"How did you get that phone? It's Stark tech," Thor said, reaching and tugging it out of Loki's pocket.

"Merchants of Broxton," Loki said, gesturing vaguely in the direction of the Midgardian town. "I bought it."

He instantly regretted telling the truth. The defensiveness seeped from his words and Thor noted it. His brother's shoulders stiffened and he peered down at Loki suspiciously.

"And how did you pay for it?"

Loki did not want to lie again, even though the opportunity was right there. "With gold. They seemed pleased with the deal! I didn't rip them off."

Thor pursed his lips. "And how did you get the gold?"

"I got it off some dwarves." Loki could see the next question on his brother's tongue. "And before you ask, yes, we were gambling. See? I'm trying truthfulness!"

Thor pressed his fingers to his forehead. "Were you cheating when you gambled, Loki?"

"Okay, *yes*, but"—Loki raised his voice before Thor could interrupt him—"they were cheating too! Cheating was basically part of the game. I won unfairly, but in a game of who could win most unfairly!"

Thor looked as if he wanted to laugh, or cry, or walk into the sea. "I'm not sure I should approve."

"You know what's worse than cheating? The humans of the internet."

"Are you reading the comments again? Stark says the first rule of the internet is never read the comments," Thor reminded him.

"You know he reads all the comments about him, though," Loki pointed out.

Thor tilted his head, conceding the point. "The humans are a frustrating people. But they are good. They are better than they know. And by coming together, we will build Asgard anew."

Loki was a kid, but he was just as clever as always. Rather, he certainly believed he was. He knew that Thor was really talking about him when he was talking about the humans.

"Why *did* you buy a phone?" Thor asked, starting to walk back through the ruins. These had once been buildings, piles of rubble punctuated by columns that stuck up through the wreckage like flagpoles with no flags.

Loki scrambled through the boulders after him, wishing his brother's legs weren't as long as they were. Or rather, wishing that he, Loki, had the height to match his brother's stride. What was the point of being half-giant if one did not come out the *size* of the half-giants?

"I want to learn. Mostly, I've learned that mortals like to—"
He brought up a website and waved it in front of Thor's face.

Thor took one look and winced. "That is not appropriate for someone of your age."

"I knew that mortals liked to document everything pictorially but I did not realize that meant *everything*. I thought it was just their pets and their food, but it truly is *everything*," Loki said excitedly. "Like all sorts of things I did not know you could share."

"Just because you can doesn't mean you should," Thor said with a sigh.

They made their way to a road that wound its way along the river and up toward the fallen city. They stopped to look at it, and Loki felt pangs of regret even as he gazed upon a destruction he knew he did not cause.

The road swooped in toward main gates that had once stood taller than any of the most ancient buildings, but now those buildings were half-caved in, and the gates of the city had been utterly destroyed. Piles of stone and mortar. The rare and exotic plants that once grew alongside the gate wilted on their way to death. The only thing that marked the beginning of this once-majestic city was the narrowing of the road. Even from this distance, they could see people slowly sifting through rubble. They were no longer looking for survivors. Now they were simply trying to find the bottom of the destruction so they could rebuild. Wheelbarrows and wagonfuls of rock were hauled away. Dust clouded the city. Loki didn't need to be down there to know that everyone's faces were drawn and tired—people who had gone through a war, survived, and found it was still not over.

Thor must have read his mind because he ruffled Loki's hair affectionately. "You are not as wicked as those mortals on the Stark phone, I think."

"I'd have to try *terribly* hard to be that terrible," Loki agreed, relieved that his brother had broken the silence.

Thor slung his arm around Loki's shoulder. "They will learn, Loki, that you are you, and not past-Loki's choices. But it will take time."

Loki wanted to say that he didn't want it to take time. It felt like wasted time, waiting for people to figure out what he already knew. But he didn't argue with Thor any more than the average soldier did.

"I know," he said. And it was only partly a lie.

LATER, THAT night, when Loki arrived back in his room, he found a magpie perched in the window, its beady eyes fixed on him. It'd been waiting for him, he was certain.

"Hello, Mr. Magpie," he said cheerfully.

The bird opened his mouth and it sounded as if he were about to say Loki's name, but instead he exploded, a disgusting slurry of feathers and bird guts splattering on the walls, all over Loki, and worse, over Loki's books.

"Ugh," muttered Loki, flicking entrails off his chest. "Gross."

Where the magpie had sat was a key.

Loki couldn't help himself. Who could have expected him to?

He picked up the key and accepted its silent quest.

It took him a while to find the chest in the basement that the key unlocked, and when it creaked open, dust floating around it, Loki peered inside with a peculiar mixture of anxiety and excitement. The chest was empty, save for another key.

This was the best kind of puzzle. No one made puzzles like this anymore: the kind that took cleverness and brains and brazenness to solve. He took that key and followed its clues. One mystery led to another, a path through the city, through tunnels and into towers, to the dwarves, and the elves, and back again.

And when he realized where the magpie's clues were leading him, when he'd untangled the final rune of the final puzzle, when he watched the dot beneath the question mark on the page grow and grow until it swallowed the ground beneath his feet and he began to fall, he whispered, without any hint of deceit, "Oh. I know where I'm going."

IT ISN'T A LIE IF IT ISN'T THE TRUTH BUT YOU DON'T KNOW IT YET.

THREE

AS SOON as Loki said he knew where he was going, the ground dropped out from beneath him. What was once a tower, a pile of books, torn papers, a key, magpie feathers, and the night sky of Asgard became nothingness around him. He tumbled head over heels as if he were falling through space and time itself, swinging his arms and legs out wildly in the hope of colliding with something to grab onto.

Loki hit the ground with a *thunk*, dust exploding up around him. He lay on his back, wheezing for a second, before he rolled over and sat up. Light glinted off metal, illuminating a small eerie space around him. He could see no walls, no tunnels, no paths. Nothing except the spot where he landed, and a helmet with curved horns on a pedestal, a magpie perched in the center.

Part of Loki hummed with excitement when he saw the magpie. It'd brought him a puzzle last time, and he'd solved it. What would it bring him this time?

But last time he'd been in his own territory. In Asgard. In a city he knew and loved, even if it did not love him.

He did not know where he was now.

He did not know what kind of puzzle could be solved if he did not know where he needed to go next.

He rose slowly. "Hello, Mr. Magpie."

Again, he thought to himself.

Green meteors burst from the dark emptiness above, striking the ground around him. Loki threw an arm over his face to shield himself from the spray of rocks. The heat blistered his skin.

Loki, cast in green fire, loomed above him, nearly as tall as the tower from which Loki had fallen. His face was familiar but not the face that Loki had seen in the mirror. It was chiseled and aged, cut by sharp lines where the younger Loki had only seen smooth and round cheeks when he'd washed his face that morning.

"I am Loki," boomed the Loki made of green fire. "Loki, whose whim brought Asgard crashing down. I am Loki, whose tongue was an anvil where the sharpest lies were forged. I am Loki, and I have things to say that you must know. I am Loki, who you must not trust."

So his past self had a flare for the dramatic. The green fire around the base of the Past Loki seemed like overkill, but Young Loki wisely decided not to mention that.

"What are the chances?" he said loftily. "I'm Loki too. We should be the very best of friends." He gestured around at the emptiness. "Where'd you bring me? What are you, precisely?"

"I am the echo of a scream. This room is hidden behind a whim, buried in a daydream, covered in bad thoughts and malice," said Past Loki.

"You could have just said you didn't know," observed Young Loki.

This was the thing with young gods. Sometimes they thought of something clever, and they couldn't resist saying it. The jibe slid from Loki's tongue as easily as lies.

Past Loki scowled at the younger one. "It is a place that Thor would never locate."

"I got that," said Young Loki, "from the 'covered in bad thoughts and malice' part. Thor would never."

"Would never *what*?" snapped Past Loki.

Young Loki shrugged, delighting in getting under Past Loki's skin. "He just would never."

"This place is my message from me to you," said the specter.

"I feel like you could have just sent a letter, a text, an email. This is a little dramatic, don't you think?" said Loki, glancing around. Then he shrugged. "Speak then, elder-self. I solved your riddle. I demand amusements."

"Amusements?" Past Loki repeated.

But Young Loki didn't want to explain amusements, or his tone, to this past Loki. He actually didn't even want to be entertained. He wanted answers. Because this Loki was the reason he existed, yes, but also the reason of *how* he existed. The reason everyone around him thought he was a betrayer, the downfall of Asgard, someone not to be trusted, someone who wasn't a good friend.

He straightened his shoulders. "Explain why you destroyed Asgard, but then sacrificed yourself to save it."

"Is that what you think I did?" A glint in the green fire of Past Loki's eyes clued Young Loki in.

He narrowed his eyes. "Maybe not." The words crystallized in his mind. He wasn't one to think before he spoke. Some things came by instinct. And he was speaking to himself. He ought to know. "If you wanted to live, you would have hidden yourself beneath the rug of the universe before the final blow was struck."

Past Loki's mouth turned up in one corner. The flames that encircled Young Loki rose, burned brighter. He was on the right path.

"You *chose* to die," he accused. "You wanted to die. That means you *needed* to die."

"And?" prompted Past Loki.

Young Loki frowned, stretching his fingers as he thought. "I don't know why, though."

"There is only one who Loki would sacrifice himself for," said Past Loki, gesturing at Young Loki.

Young Loki blinked. Being caught off-guard wasn't one of his strong suits. "You sacrificed yourself… for yourself?"

"Gods of chaos fall into a single trap: their capriciousness is its own pattern. They become predictable." Past Loki shrugged. "I wrote myself out of the book of death. I slipped predestination's noose. I would be found, or I'd find my way back. A new Loki. A fresh page with fresh ink to write a free future."

Past Loki had told Young Loki not to trust him, and Loki could feel that warning tug at him right now. He wanted to believe Loki. He wanted to believe his past self. But this sounded too believable—it tugged at our young protagonist's heart strings, his own desires and wants.

"You went into oblivion with nothing but the hope that there was something out there? Or that someone would show you the path home?" he ventured.

"It's as the people of Midgard say. Change or die," said Past Loki simply.

"And you'd rather die than not change," said Loki with quiet understanding.

"I'd rather be nothing," countered Past Loki. He straightened, a tower above Young Loki again. "*Thankfully*, it did not come to that."

"I should tell Thor of this. Or Odin," Loki said, trying to think of what their reactions would be. He corrected himself. "Definitely Thor."

"Yes, you should," murmured Past Loki.

Young Loki paced back and forth in the circle of green fire, ignoring the heat that blasted his face. "If I wanted to be *killed*, I should tell Thor. Thor couldn't keep them from my head. They'd think me part of some scheme or plan from beyond the grave."

"Hmmm," said Past Loki, making a noise of agreement.

Loki's head jerked up. "And they'd be correct, wouldn't they?"

He hadn't realized it until just now but in his truthfulness, Past Loki was telling him everything he needed to know. Young Loki spun on his heel to face his past self, "This *is* a scheme from beyond the grave!"

"Beyond their imagination, I imagine," said Past Loki lightly.

"What now?" asked Young Loki.

"Power corrupts. Therefore, you'll have little. You must become a new Loki, with naught but your wits to guard the Nine Realms." Past Loki pulled the green fire from the circle around him like a cloak, and the sudden absence of warmth made young Loki shiver. He was engulfed in the darkness once again.

"Soon they will be in peril," said Past Loki.

"Looming peril? Our specialty," said Loki dryly.

"They think we're the only one who can bring wickedness and treachery into the world. And they are wrong," said Past Loki.

"This is all very vague. If you're offering me advice, at least be specific about it," Young Loki countered, but his mind was whirling like a storm. Who was *they*? Asgard, he must be talking about Asgard. Loki wouldn't stand up for Midgard, would he? It seemed unlikely. And why would Past Loki help him? It seemed like a trap, a trick of some sort, a way for Past Loki to write his way into this story. But it didn't belong to him. Not anymore.

"If I gave you advice, you shouldn't pay any attention to it," chided Past Loki. "Knowledge is what I have and what you should take. Know the difference. I have lifetime upon lifetime of mysteries, packed into this spirit by your dead older self. But I can be whatever you wish."

Mentor. Advisor. Brother. Past.

Loki knew what he wanted. "What I wish," he said, stepping from the dark into the ghastly green glow of Past Loki's flames, "is to be Loki. To be myself, and not you." He threw up his hands at his past self. "You are done. You are gone."

Past Loki's face widened in surprise, green fire streaking through him into the air as light exploded around them.

Young Loki called, "You are now my Ikol, my opposite, my bird. You are an ear-whisperer and a worm-eater. You'll tell me what I want and nothing more."

Past Loki made an awful groaning sound, like an enormous metal door being slammed shut, and then he was gone, a helmet clattering to the ground, a black and white magpie flapping his wings as he alighted on Young Loki's arm.

Loki had said he'd be whatever Young Loki needed.

This seemed to be the safest way, the most trustworthy way, to gain that wisdom—without all the trouble.

"Let's go home," said Loki, trying to catch his breath.

"Yes, master," said Ikol, cawing softly.

Loki's smile grew on his face. "I like that."

FOUR

BEFORE THIS STORY BEGAN, BEFORE LOKI MET LOKI IN A PLACE OUT OF TIME AND RETURNED WITH ONLY IKOL ON HIS SHOULDER, ODIN HAD FACED AN IMPOSSIBILITY.

He knew that the Serpent would come for Asgard's destruction. He knew that the Serpent would bring his Dark Asgard to Asgard True one day in pursuit of all Nine Realms, and that he needed to prepare for this inevitability. The Serpent wanted nothing but destruction, and Odin was determined to protect his people and he'd do it at any cost.

Not everyone saw it this way. Not everyone saw the sacrifice of all of Earth and the mortals on it as an acceptable trade for preventing the Serpent coming here. Some didn't see the Serpent as a threat, or didn't believe him capable of what he threatened.

But Odin knew the Serpent's heart. After all, the Serpent was his brother. Long lost to the ravages of history and time, cut into a cruel shape by a life the Fates had kept separate from Odin, but his brother nonetheless.

AND THAT WAS WHAT KEPT ODIN AWAKE AT NIGHT. THAT WAS WHAT LED HIM TO CONSIDER SUCH EXTREME MEASURES. YOUNG

Loki, and all others in Asgard, found themselves in the aftermath of Odin's decision.

"This isn't right," Loki muttered, watching soldiers drag the Hel-Wolf to a cell to await a time when he'd be unleashed on Midgard.

It wasn't that Loki was particularly fond of dogs, or wolves, or beasts, but rather the part where Odin planned to unleash the beast on the people of Midgard. Midgard wasn't their true enemy. It was collateral damage, at best. Loki wasn't alone in thinking that condemning Midgard to death was no solution to the Serpent. Thor had railed against his father's decree, and now he too awaited his fate in a cell.

The Hel-Wolf gnashed at the soldiers soldering his chains to a wall.

"For this you will all bleed!"

His growls and threats were ignored. Still, Loki thought the Hel-Wolf was not making idle promises when he said, "For this, your sons and daughters will know murder."

To Loki, who had the precociousness of youth and prescience enough to see clearly, it seemed that those who created weapons of war felt obligated to use them, lest the effort be in vain. War begat war, it seemed, and Odin was mired deep in the effort.

"This isn't *right*," Loki repeated louder.

A warm, heavy hand clapped down on his shoulder. "Aye, Loki."

Loki glanced up, recognizing Galinn, a soldier who'd fought alongside Thor. He was young, but stubborn and traditional, and Loki had noticed how most of Thor's close compatriots had avoided him until now. To earn Galinn's agreement and regard thawed Loki's apprehension and he relaxed. Maybe if Galinn warmed up to Loki, the others would as well.

"Right?" he said. "To scour one realm undermines all the realms. What we plan is nothing less than taking a saw to our own arm." Loki glanced from Galinn to the other soldiers. "Thor's gone. It's up to us to help Asgard."

He was so eager, and so, so wrong.

Galinn's grin was wide and menacing, cutting his flushed cheeks and weathered skin like a crevice. "Aye, Loki. Thor is gone." Loki's eyes caught on movement and he saw Galinn's hand settling on his sword's hilt. "Thor is gone, and now we all know how we can help Asgard."

Loki thought of a few choice words that he'd learned from the comments section on social media, but he couldn't make his mouth say any of them. It was one thing to face the menacing hate online, and another to face it in person. He swallowed hard, turning his hands into fists to keep them from trembling. Last time someone had jeered at him, Thor had arrived just in time. But Thor was in a cell, and Loki was here. He leaned backward, away from Galinn, like distance was going to keep a sword from his throat. Not likely, in this rocky nook.

Suddenly, from over Loki's head, a fist swung into view, cracking audibly into Galinn's face. The air puffed out of Galinn with an *oof* and he staggered to the side, his hand leaving his sword hilt to catch his fall.

"I'm sorry, friend," rumbled a genial voice. "My fist appears to have accidentally found its way into your face."

One of Thor's confidantes, Volstagg, settled his other hand settled on Loki's shoulder. Loki didn't think Volstagg liked him much, but he was relieved as Volstagg said cheerfully to Galinn, "Please forgive me. This way, Loki."

He steered Loki away from the soldiers gathering around Galinn, who was scowling at Loki, like this too was his fault.

Loki wiped sweat from his brow. "Many thanks, Volstagg."

Volstagg dropped his hand from Loki's shoulder with a grumble. "I didn't do it for you, Loki. I'm fulfilling my oath to protect you."

"You made an oath to protect me?" Loki asked and then blinked. "Oh. Right. Thor. You made it to Thor."

This was not some great oath of honor, made on a battlefield or on the eve of war. It was one friend to another, when one was in jail, to look after the troublesome little brother. Loki didn't want to feel like the troublesome little brother.

"I'll be a slacker in the oath-swearing in the future," muttered Volstagg. He lumbered down the street, and Loki trailed after him.

"But don't you think it's true?" Loki said, jogging to catch up. Volstagg was a big man, with a bigger stride. "That we should help Thor?"

Volstagg ran his hand over his red hair and then down his red beard, avoiding Loki's gaze. "I can't believe I'm saying this, but you must be subtler in spreading dissent. Fomenting open revolt will not help Thor."

He was right, of course. Odin would throw Loki in jail as soon as Thor, if not sooner. He only needed an excuse.

But Loki was young, and naively confident in his subtlety. "So you're saying you agree."

Volstagg rolled his eyes. "Yes. But if you want to help him, you must find another way."

"Will you help?" asked Loki.

Volstagg wrinkled his nose and heaved a sigh so big it moved his belly. "Fine. But don't go telling anyone. I don't want it to look like I'm getting close to you. I've got a reputation to protect."

IT TURNED out that Volstagg's idea of helping was to introduce Loki to goats.

Two goats in particular. Apparently, Past Loki had convinced Thor to harness and tame the Lords of the Goats, Toothgnasher and Toothgrinder. It'd been a prank, and it had backfired spectacularly, because now Thor had a pair of indestructible goats who could go anywhere, and do most anything.

"I didn't think that one through," said Loki, surveying the goats.

"You rarely did," said Volstagg, though this was not entirely true. It was only a matter of Volstagg's perspective, as it is with all of us. "If you want to help Thor, you'll care for the goats."

"He just keeps the goats. And these godly goats just… stay." Loki couldn't keep the disbelief out of his voice.

"Well," Volstagg said, reaching up to a hook on the wall where a golden bridle hung. As soon as he picked it up, the goats sighed with a bleary *bleet* and lowered their heads submissively. Loki didn't have much experience around goats, but it didn't seem entirely natural behavior.

"Magic bridle?" Loki asked, raising an eyebrow.

"Magic bridle," confirmed Volstagg, his grin wide and toothy. "Made by the dwarves. It'll break the will of any beast."

"But there are two of them, and there is one of the magic bridle," Loki pointed out, feeling foolish even as he tried to make sense of why a bridle was needed for these goats.

"Aye," Volstagg said, hanging the bridle back up. "It was a problem for Thor, but not an insurmountable one. Toothgrinder and Toothgnasher are brothers, thick as thieves, thicker than blood. One would not bow while the other was free. So Thor—"

"—made them both wear it at once," Loki finished, seeing where the story was going. He looked back at the goats. "And it worked. Even when the bridle is off, their will is muted."

"Aye. Once the bridle is on, the effects are permanent. It is quite a piece of tack." Volstagg winked as he backed toward the stable entrance. "Their stall could use some cleaning, if you don't mind. I've got mead to drink, and their master is in jail. Which is probably also your fault."

It wasn't, strictly, Loki's fault. It wasn't *not* his fault either, since Asgard was only in this precarious position—with a war-mongering All-Father and a rebuilding city unprepared for coming war—because of his past self. Still, he watched Volstagg lumber out of the barn and shut the door behind him. The din of the city settled into a low hum outside these walls. The barn smelled warm, and like dung.

"Gross," muttered Loki. "This is not what I thought he meant when he said he knew how to help Thor."

A shadow flashed over the wall, spooking the goats, and Loki spun, on guard, only to see Ikol settling in a window. He rustled his feathers, his beady eyes sharp and uncanny.

"You must read between the lines."

Loki scowled at the bird. "Where have *you* been?"

"Observing," said the magpie.

"Your handiwork?" Loki retorted dryly.

Ikol glared at him with beady eyes. "Yours too, you know."

Loki gestured to the goats. "Tell me, with your infinite wisdom, what I'm supposed to do with goats."

"The wisdom you need is not for me to give," said Ikol loftily.

Loki stared at him. The magpie stared back.

Ikol flapped his wings, a bird's version of a show of reluctance. "Who is your enemy?"

He'd too many to count. On one hand, there were many who would want to be called Loki's enemies—Galinn and the others, for instance—who Loki wouldn't have counted as his enemies. There was Odin, who seemed completely immune to reason, to the point of threatening genocide to defend his people. And then there was the Serpent, the one who threatened not just Asgard but all the realms. All would suffer under the Serpent.

"The Serpent."

"And who is this Serpent?" asked Ikol, as though he was leading Loki to an obvious answer.

Loki frowned. "No one knows. You can't possibly know."

"I don't know, but that does not mean the answers must remain unknowable." Ikol hopped down the ledge and across the gate that stood between Loki and the goats. "The World Tree knows all."

The World Tree existed out of time and space, the connection between all Nine Realms, its roots and branches the pathways to the realms. Everything in the known universes and dimensions was connected through the Tree.

And at its base lived the Fates, three Norn goddesses.

If all was connected through the Tree, then that included stories. All history. All truth.

And to learn about the Serpent, he needed to go to the World Tree, to stand at its base, to get answers to questions he asked, and answers to questions he didn't think to ask.

"What answers could the World Tree have about the Serpent?" he asked. "How does this help Thor?"

"Three Nornish women sit at its base. Whispering secrets," said Ikol.

Loki was really starting to regret turning his past self into a bird of wisdom if the magpie didn't stop speaking in half-truths and riddles.

"So I must go to the World Tree," Loki confirmed. "How do I get there?"

It was a good thing magpies couldn't grin, because if they could, Ikol would have been grinning wider than the Rainbow Road. He hopped closer to the gate, fluttering his wings and startling the goats. Loki looked at the bird, then at the goats, and then at the bridle hanging on the wall.

"You've *got* to be joking," he said.

"I think you mean, 'You must be kidding,'" said Ikol.

RIDING A goat was not Loki's preferred method of transportation. Admittedly, goats do not rank high on many people's lists, though they are bright and curious creatures. These goats were sullen creatures, harnessed by a bridle that controlled them. Their will was not their own. And though they might have reached an understanding with Thor, they did not know this spry god of lies who directed them to follow a magpie to the center of the earth. They'd no reason to trust him.

Who did?

Ikol, perhaps. But magpies are capricious, intelligent creatures— entirely unknowable.

Loki, Toothgnasher and Ikol arrived at the edge of the cavern that led to the World Tree and the Nornish women at its base. A cascade of rainbow light, brighter than the Rainbow Bridge, splashed color on the walls of the cavern. The lights played on the walls, moving and spinning together.

Loki dismounted off the goat, awed by the colors. He'd never seen anything like it in his life. The Asgard he knew was blue skies over rebuilt ruins—there was nothing like the colors here.

He wanted to just sit, legs dangling over the cliff edge, and watch them for hours.

Ikol hopped over to him. "The preparations are complete."

Loki blinked and shook his head, pulling his attention back to where he was. Right. He needed to learn about the Serpent so he could fight it and save Asgard.

Loki tried not look afraid of the height when he walked to the edge of the cliff and looked down into the hole in the earth. He squinted as rainbow beams of light hit him in the face.

"I feel like it's an overstatement to say that preparations are complete," Loki said to Ikol, turning around to get the woolen rope he'd made from the coat of Toothgrinder, the goat he hadn't ridden down here. It hadn't seemed fair to shear the goat and *then* ride it.

"What else do you need to know?" Ikol fluttered up from the ground to his shoulder.

"What do I need to do down there?" Loki asked, looping the rope hastily around the goat's leg. He tossed the extra over the cliff.

Ikol didn't need to speak to communicate his disapproval.

"What? It's fine. I'll be able to climb that back up."

"Yes, you're known for your upper body strength, it's true," Ikol said dryly.

Loki scowled. "You didn't tell me what I needed to do down there."

"Survive," said Ikol.

Loki pressed the heel of his palm into his forehead. "Not comforting at all." He took a deep breath and set his shoulders back. "Well. Might as well go."

And then he threw himself off the edge.

FIVE

FIRST, YOU must learn the Serpent's story.

You are new here and, like Young Loki, lacking the context required to understand the enemy.

No one is born a Serpent. No one wakes up with evil in their hearts, destined to bring down the realms of gods. Before he was a Serpent, he was a boy. A boy of twelve, thirteen, what does it matter? Too young to know better, old enough for his heart to harden. Just about the same age as Young Loki himself.

The Serpent was a boy, a nameless one, with willfulness that hadn't turned to malice, curiosity that hadn't turn to cruelty. He roamed the realms freely, dreaming of the future. He'd be a knight. A hero. Something—someone—bold and brave, daring and true, admired and sought after.

Until one day, the leathery giant-hands fell upon him. Despite his struggle, they dragged him to the peak of a mountain under stormy skies. The giants reeked of sulfur baths and rancid food, a smell in which flies gathered and lay eggs that hatched into maggots. They dangled the boy over the edge of the cliffs.

"You gods think you live in the heavens!" they roared. "Let's see how you *fly*."

The Serpent had been silent when they took him. And he was silent as he fell, the wind rushing by, the enormous sky swallowed by the rocks beside him. He slammed into the earth below, bones breaking with sharp cracks.

Breathing hurt.

Moving hurt more.

Every time his heart beat, it struck a broken rib. The pain crisscrossed his body, drawing a map of pain.

He should be dead, truly. No one was designed to survive that fall.

But he wasn't dead. Instead, a terrible, deep thirst tormented him. This thirst could not be quenched by dew or rainwater or even the wines of distant Asgard. It was a thirst that drove him to splint his own limbs, setting bones that had been broken in his fall. He did the best he could, and though they were awkward and ill-formed, they did the job.

And while he wrapped rags around his makeshift splints, the boy had time to think. He had time to let the dreams that would never be fester in his heart.

Nothing good festers. Remember that.

He waited until nightfall.

His broken bones screamed, lightning lancing through his joints, as he belly-crawled, hauling himself by his elbows to the camp of the slumbering giants. He would not be deterred. No pain could slow him or stop him. He could see their sleeping forms, and that was enough incentive for him. They reeked of ale, sleeping like logs after gorging on drink and food, both of which had been denied to the boy.

He made his way to each of them, tearing out their throats before they could wake. The air was thick with the scent of metallic blood. It was the death he should have been given. Eternal sleep. But he'd suffered, and now he was going to pass suffering back in to the world.

He left one giant alive. And that giant woke to find himself surrounded by his slaughtered kin, blood and brothers. On the wall, the boy had written, *Gods do not live in the Sky. We live on Earth. And you do so at our pleasure.*

The man was no fool. He knew what he had read. He was in the presence of the Serpent, and he rightly feared him. Like all good sole survivors, he spread word about that night, and so the word of the Serpent spread.

All who heard the tale feared him.

Just as the Serpent wanted. He was in a story. He was the main character. Not the hero, but close enough.

SIX

THAT WAS not all Loki learned at the World Tree.

He climbed back up the stubborn goat's stubborn wool and flopped onto his back on the hot stone. Tears streamed down his face and he wiped them away hastily. He did not want to believe that the Nornish women were right, but they were.

What the Fates said had to be true. Didn't it?

He'd never wanted anything more than for them to be wrong.

Ikol hopped over to him and pecked at his cheek. Loki swatted the bird away and sat up, trying not to sniffle too loud.

"You know what you must do?" asked Ikol.

Loki could tell the bird saw his distress and was ignoring it, at least for now. He appreciated the kindness. He drew in a breath and hiccupped. "Yes."

Ikol pecked at him again. "Who are you?"

Loki wiped at his eyes again, swallowing hard to keep the tears at bay. There would be no time for tears. "I am Loki."

"Does Loki cry?" asked the magpie.

"But briefly," Loki said, his voice catching.

"So you know your path," Ikol said. A statement rather than a question.

"I know my path," said Loki, climbing to his feet. "And I know how I must do it. But this is beyond just me, and beyond just you, Ikol, wicked though you are."

"I am shocked that you think my counsel may not be enough," Ikol said.

"You know, I think it's alarming that I can't tell if you're joking or not," said Loki, swinging a leg over the goat. "Also, we'll need to find a new ride."

He was using humor to glide past the pain in his heart, he knew. And Ikol knew it too. But the bird was not always wicked and was sometimes generous. He flew ahead of the goat and let Loki pretend that he did not know what lay ahead of them.

THE FIRST thing Loki did was put the goat back in the barn where he belonged.

The second thing Loki did was go find Thor.

Thor was still imprisoned on Odin's orders, and so this involved climbing through a sewer system not large enough for full-grown adults, but with plenty of room for a scrappy kid. Especially Loki.

He wiggled through on his knees and elbows, scraping his way along on his belly until the tunnel opened up, widening where light came through grates, painting stripes on the tunnel walls.

It took several cells before he found Thor's. His brother sat dejectedly against the wall, legs in front of him.

"You look morose," said Loki.

"Loki?" Thor asked, looking up. For a brief moment, his face lightened. And then he frowned. "How did you get in here?"

"I need your advice," Loki said, scooting closer to the grate so he could pull his legs underneath himself. He brushed dirt off his shirt and trousers. "So I have come to see you."

"But how—" Thor began again.

"I really don't want to lie to you," said Loki. "I don't like it. So if you don't mind, could we skip the questions like *how* and *who* and *why*?"

Thor stared at him for a long second and then sighed, shoulders falling. His blond hair was greasy and clumped. He smelled. Loki decided not to tell him that because he could see his brother's dejection in how quickly he acquiesced and agreed to Loki's terms.

Loki brushed his own hair out of his face and took a steadying breath. "If you knew something bad was going to happen, what would you do?"

Thor snorted. "I would stop it from happening."

Loki would have rolled his eyes if it wasn't so serious. He fumbled over his words. "But what if it *had* to happen, because if it didn't happen, then something *worse* would happen?"

Thor hesitated and then sighed. "I'd make sure it happened."

"Even if it cost you everything?" Loki asked, his voice wobbling.

Thor bent down over the grate, frowning at his brother. "Yes. Even if it cost me everything. What are you planning, Loki?"

"What needs to be done, brother," Loki said, barely able to meet Thor's eyes. "All I need is a few good men."

"Loki," Thor said gently. "You're Loki. No good man is going to follow you."

"Then I'll have to lower my expectations," Loki said, forcing cheeriness into his voice. "I can make do with a few bad ones."

Before Thor could drill him further, Loki wiggled around and shimmied back down the tunnel. Thor bellowed after him, but Loki reached the narrow spaces, where he could not turn around, even if he were tempted.

A few bad men. That's what he needed. Bad was better than good. Good might question this too much, the act of letting— or making—something bad happen to prevent something worse from happening. Bad men just let things happen, regardless of the consequences.

He was in the prison already, so his next stop was easy enough.

THE HEL-WOLF was held in an entirely different type of cell than Thor. Thor's cell had sunlight, space, and he was not shackled. But the Hel-Wolf was a beast, a weapon that Odin intended on pointing at Midgard.

It was a good first stop, truly. The Hel-Wolf was neither good nor a man, so he fit Loki's specifications perfectly.

When Loki found him, the Hel-Wolf was chewing the bars of his cell and muttering curses to Asgard, Odin, and Thor between the absolutely horrific sound of teeth grinding against metal.

"Hi, little doggy," Loki said cheerfully. He'd learned quickly that the best way to get one's attention was through insults. "If I could have a moment of your time, I'd love to talk to you about a great investment opportunity—"

The Hel-Wolf growled.

Loki switched tactics and held up a key. "A great opportunity. How would you like to go free?"

The Hel-Wolf stopped dragging his teeth up and down the metal bars. He growled again, but this time, he said, "I'd tear out the hearts of all my wives for the privilege."

"Dramatic. Over the top. A theatrical flourish," Loki mused. "I like it. And I like you. That's what was I was hoping to hear."

He approached the jail holding the key carefully, keeping his voice and steps light even as his heart pounded.

Drool pooled and dripped from the Hel-Wolf's mouth.

"But I can't just *let* you go free," Loki said, like the thought suddenly occurred to him. "In exchange, you will serve me. Yes?"

The Hel-Wolf's eyes hadn't left the key. His grumble was reluctant, but there. "Yes."

"Promise? I'd ask for a pinky promise but it doesn't look like you have pinkies. Swear a binding oath on your very soul?"

The Hel-Wolf looked like he very much wanted to rip out Loki's throat, but he said through a slobber and growl of desperation, "I will serve you. May my soul wither to ashes if what I speak is not true."

"Love it," said Loki. "Appreciate it. You and I are going to do great things, pup."

He slid the key into the lock and turned it with an audible *click*.

The Hel-Wolf hurled his body against the door, throwing it open and slamming Loki back into a wall. The beast leapt from the cell, gnashing his teeth, his eyes glowing golden and fierce. Loki rolled, ignoring the pain in his side from where he'd smacked into the stone, and crouched in the shadows.

"My soul was cast to the fires before the placenta even slid from my mother!" roared the Hel-Wolf, clawing at rock and lashing his tail. "Where is that little morsel?"

Loki did not want to think about the Hel-Wolf's mother's placenta, vivid though the image was. He waited in the corner until the Hel-Wolf reached the window, still looking outward for him, oblivious to the trickster god behind him.

Loki leapt on his back and slid the bit of the goat's bridle into the beast's mouth, the very bridle Thor used to tame the goats and which allowed for nothing but obedience, according to Volstagg.

"Ha!" cried Loki triumphantly.

The Hel-Wolf screeched in fury, leaping through the window, crashing through stone and brick. The beast launched himself to the side of the prison, sliding down it with his claws dug into the stone, sparks flying. Then he surged sideways, hurtling through the air and clouds until he slammed into the ground. Loki's teeth clattered in his head but he gripped the reins tight as the Hel-Wolf sprang into the air again.

They plunged through air and land, falling from mountains and careening through the valleys, climbing the sides of buildings in the rebuilt city, and clawing their way through the clouds. Loki's ears popped and his eyes teared as the wind whipped them. His hands ached. But he did not let go.

And at last, the Hel-Wolf bent his head, coming to a stop on a mountainside. His sides heaved with exertion.

"No more. No more," muttered the Hel-Wolf, so low that Loki almost missed it.

"You tried," Loki said comfortingly. "It was at least a seven point eight on the effort scale. But you must understand. This bridle broke *goats*. Enormous, dung-depositing beasts of the most willful manner. A monster of the pits doesn't exactly measure up."

"You are a cursed demon," said the Hel-Wolf.

"There are many who would agree with you," Loki said.

"What would you have me do?" asked the beast.

"What I asked. Total servitude. I don't want to ride the goats anymore, and you'll serve my purposes much better."

"Yes, master," said the Beast, gnashing his teeth. "For as long as I live, I will only *think* about what a joy it'd be to bite you in half."

"I can live with that," Loki said with relief. "Okay! Step one complete."

Ikol landed on his shoulder, ruffling his feathers. "A Hel-Wolf? Loki. You shouldn't have."

"Only the best for my wicked bird," said Loki. "Now, Hel-Wolf, where do you think we're going next?"

"I dread to speculate," the Hel-Wolf said, his voice bitter and acidic.

"The clue's in the question," Loki said, patting his neck and ignoring the beast's growls. "Hel-Wolf. You're going home."

"We may not go to Hel yet," Ikol said with a grim clack of his beak. "Odin beckons you. Thor's been freed. Other prisoners reported hearing your voice in the tunnels before his door sprung open."

"Then Volstagg was successful," Loki mused quietly. "He's at least one good man. I'll have to tell Thor when I get back."

His heart clenched something fierce at that, pain like there was a blade between the chambers lancing through him. He pushed the thought away. He'd asked Volstagg for his help, reminding him that he'd sworn an oath to Thor to protect Loki, and one of the ways that he could protect Loki was by breaking Thor out himself, instead of Loki doing it. In exchange, Volstagg had asked the young god to promise him no more schemes.

Loki did not want to lie to Thor.

But lying to Volstagg came easily.

"Enough prattling," said Loki firmly. "Ikol, correct me if I'm wrong. Hel and Hell. Said the same, but quite different. One the dead, the other the souls of the dead. At least part of Hell is ruled by Mephisto. He's fashioned himself something of a Satan, hasn't he? Hel is Hela, who rules with her handmaiden Leah and her dead general Tyr."

The one thing that Hela and Mephisto have in common is Loki. Loki tricked both of them, in the past, and they care not that *this* Loki is not *that* Loki. He owes them a debt. They have unfinished business and neither Hela nor Mephisto are the type to forget it.

Loki was digging deep into his history lessons. "It's leased to Hela because she was banished from the Nine Realms and needed a place to store all the dead Asgardians, to keep them safe from the Dís—"

Ikol flapped his wings violently, striking Loki's face. "Don't say it! Say their name and they can come for you."

The Dísir, the ancient Valkyrie who consume the souls of the dead, after all, also had unfinished business with Loki. It seemed like everyone had unfinished business with Past Loki, and they were willing to make it Loki's problem.

"I tease," Loki said quickly, running a hand over the magpie's ruffled feathers. "I know. Do you think Hela knows it was my old dead self who actually controlled the Dís-folk and had traded temporary control of them to Mephisto in exchange for the lands in question?"

"And so she'd release her claim on your soul, so you could be reborn," Ikol reminded him.

"Details, details," Loki said, though those weren't exactly small details to Hela. "Past me just let the dead die forever to forward my own schemes. Cool. When people say I was 'conniving' they might be underselling it a little bit."

The Hel-Wolf dragged his claws along the stone. "When do I get to eat someone? My head hurts with all your godly prattling."

"Patience is a virtue," Loki said reassuringly, ignoring the Hel-Wolf's warning growl. "Your canines will be put to the task soon enough. Are you ready, Ikol?"

"I think the question is rather, are *you* ready?" Ikol replied.

"The board's packed, but I think I know my next move," Loki said. He climbed onboard the Hel-Wolf, who grumbled about the indignity of it all. With a kick, he launched them toward the gates of Hel.

SEVEN

THE STINK of sulfur and the heat of cracks in the earth's surface overwhelmed Loki as they landed within spitting distance of the gates of Hel.

Loki covered his mouth with his sleeve while Ikol tucked his head inside Loki's cloak hood. He tried to breathe shallowly. He remembered very little of his previous life and he didn't remember this: the stark landscape of cliffs and magma, steam rising into the air, and the dark stone rising up to swallow the sky.

"Stay here," Loki told the Hel-Wolf, who seemed unaffected by the stench and the heat.

The Hel-Wolf bared his teeth. "Just transportation, then? I could gnash you into bits."

"I'm sure you could," Loki said in his most soothing voice. He didn't need the Hel-Wolf blowing his one shot to get Hela to comply. "You might get your chance yet. Wait here."

At the gates of Hel, between two stone pillars which framed a narrow path between two magma lakes, was an enormous dog with glowing golden eyes, reminiscent of the Hel-Wolf creeping in the background behind Loki.

"Excuse me!" Loki called. Then out of the corner of his mouth, he whispered. "Name?"

"Garm," Ikol told him back.

"Garm, excuse me, hello," Loki called. "You are the keeper of these gates?"

The dog pulled at the end of its chain, eyeing Loki suspiciously. "I am the guardian of the gates of Hel, yes."

"Which makes you a Wolf of Hel, yes?" Loki asked pleasantly. "I had no idea there were so many of you!"

And with that, his Hel-Wolf launched from behind a wall of boulders, colliding with Garm in midair. The chained dog yelped in pain as the Hel-Wolf's teeth sank into its ruff.

"Have fun! Don't get killed!" Loki called back to the Hel-Wolf. "Be back soon!"

Fur flew through the air, singeing in the heat so the air smelled like burning hair and sulfur. Not an improvement over the previous stench. The Hel-Wolf didn't answer—but Loki didn't need him to. He only needed the distraction for that split second.

The flames of Hel turned colder as he walked, and the landscape bubbled less, then cooled, the red and orange magma freezing into hills of black rock. Sulfur drifted away, replaced by the distinct smell of a cold, damp wind. A castle rose up out of the black rock, imposing and stern.

It was not well guarded, though Loki supposed it didn't have to be. Everyone here, minus Hela herself, was dead. And who would come here for fun? Absolutely no one. Not even Loki.

Doing this because it's the right thing to do and Thor would do it, he reminded himself. Even spunky kids trying to do the right thing need to hold onto those talismans with clenched fists. It did not matter that Thor would not have done things *this* way—he would not be in Hel.

Loki slunk along the walls, sending Ikol up into the air to be his lookout.

Hela walked by, flanked by Leah and Tyr. Loki dreaded what Tyr might say to him, given the whole *dead by Loki's hand* business, but he was counting on Tyr being unchanged from the last time they met. The three of them seemed to be arguing. Hela glided confidently, face smooth except for her furrowed brow, the arm she lost to the Dísir missing below the elbow, but Leah and Tyr both wore faces of consternation.

Loki hadn't met Leah yet, but he liked her face. Her dark hair framed a pale moon face and her eyes gave away more than the rest of her expression did. She couldn't be much older than he was.

"You cannot do this, Hela," Tyr said firmly.

What he was referring to, Loki didn't know. He hoped Ikol might glean more from his vantage point.

"What do you say, Leah?" Hela asked.

"You have been hurt enough," Leah said, her voice so low that Loki had to strain to hear her. "You owe nothing to them and the Aesir owe you a debt they will never repay. I would strike alongside the Serpent. One master is much the same as another."

Strike alongside the Serpent! Loki nearly gasped. Hela couldn't think of allying with the Serpent, could she?

Ikol fluttered back to Loki's shoulder. "The Tongue of the Serpent is here."

So Hela was thinking of joining forces with the Serpent. And she wasn't just thinking about it, she was acting on it. An emissary of the Serpent was under this very roof. The Tongue wasn't just passing through and looking for a place to stay. Loki couldn't let this alliance happen.

"Hela—" Tyr began again.

"My duty, Tyr, is to the dead. What other option do I have?" Hela asked.

"I *am* the dead," Tyr replied. He stared at Hela, but looked away first.

"My decision is made," Hela said.

Tyr bowed his head. "As you wish, milady."

But when Hela and Leah continued down the hall, Tyr did not walk with them. He stood there, watching them, his hand on his sword's hilt.

"Tyr," Loki stage whispered.

With a speed that Loki had not anticipated, Tyr whirled, reaching out and grabbing the young god by the throat. He slammed Loki against the nearest wall. Spots swarmed Loki's vision and he gasped, kicking and scrabbling with his hands against Tyr's vicelike grip.

"Tyr!" he managed to garble. "I come in—I come in peace—*parley*!"

Tyr loosened his grip only a tad, just long enough to spit the words in Loki's face: "I'd rather ensure you never speak again."

"I come for Asgard!" Loki managed to cry out.

Tyr's hand jerked back and Loki fell to the ground in a heap. He gasped, rolling onto his back and pressing his hands to his throat. Every part of his body hurt. The former general leaned over him, his cold dead eyes glowing ferociously.

"What do you mean, you've come for Asgard?" Tyr growled.

"You're more threatening than the Hel-Wolf, I swear," Loki coughed. "We need Hela's assistance. But I understand she has guests of uncertain character. Does Hela stand with Asgard?"

He knew the answer to this, of course, but he needed Tyr to say it.

Conflict flickered in warring shadows over Tyr's face. He leaned back. "That is… also uncertain."

Loki pushed himself upright and leaned against the wall. "Okay, let's try this another way. Does *Tyr* stand with fallen Asgard?"

He knew the answer to this as well, and still needed Tyr to say it.

"I see there are two Serpents' tongues in Hel tonight," snarled Tyr. He stepped back and turned away, sweeping a hand over the smooth helmet he wore. "But yes. I—I do. I must. Hela must never know we've spoken."

"I understand," Loki said, relieved. His entire plan hinged on Tyr not telling Hela that they'd spoken. He grabbed hold of a crevice in the wall and hauled himself to his feet. The room spun but he was determined to ignore it. "Now. Tell me everything."

EIGHT

"TO HELL," Loki said, striding away from Hela's court back to the gates where Garm and the Hel-Wolf were hopefully no longer fighting. "We must move swiftly."

"What schemes have you played out in your head?" Ikol asked.

"A very good one," Loki said. "Now, shush. Tell me what I need to know."

"In your previous life, the lord Mephisto thought the two of you were cut from a similar cloth." Ikol dug his claws into Loki's shoulder to hang on as the god climbed over boulders and rocks on the path back to the gate. "So that's in your favor. Except, back then, you could hide your heart under your guile. You've got more heart and less guile this time. Your temperament isn't the kind that Mephisto likes, or respects. If he smells your scheme out—"

"He won't then, will he?" Loki said with more confidence than he had within. "Hel-Wolf!"

Garm and the Hel-Wolf were both alive, and seemingly friends now. Loki swung his leg over the Hel-Wolf's back and the Hel-Wolf tossed his head around wildly.

"Sssslaughter!"

"Next time," said Garm, "you needn't set him on me. I only prevent the dead from passing."

"Oh," Loki said, feeling foolish. "My bad. Sorry, Garm."

"Apology accepted," said Garm politely.

How she and the Hel-Wolf were the same species, Loki could not be sure.

He picked up the reins and the beast leapt into the sky, turning toward the glimmer of red on the horizon, where the heat slithered through the air.

Hell. Mephisto's domain.

The gates of this Hell were similar to the gates of Hel, but rather than fading away to cooled black stone and empty, gray corridors, Hell bubbled with frothy lava. It stank not of sulfur, but of desperation and despair.

He'd snuck into Hela's court, hidden from her, and accosted one of her generals. He didn't do that here.

Loki walked into the court of Hell, into Mephisto's reign, like he owned the place. He kept his strides long and languid, confidence oozing from every pore. Did he feel confident? Not even a bit. Did that mean he was going to avoid the topic altogether? Absolutely not.

"Mephisto," he greeted the Lord of Hell coolly. "Good to see you."

"Now, now, starting with the lies so quickly, so easily," said Mephisto, flicking his fingers in the air. Heat blew in through the windows overlooking the lava fields, cutting across Loki's face and making the young god squint. "What brings you to my humble abode?"

"Asgard's under threat," Loki said casually, as if he were remarking on the weather in Hell that never changed. "And I'm here for information. Tell me what you know about the Serpent."

"Not much, but enough to know you're in trouble if you're coming to me for advice," chuckled Mephisto. "He wants to usurp Old One Eye? I've heard that one before."

Despite Odin's recent poor choices, Loki was reluctant to agree.

Still, he shrugged, the very picture of nonchalance. "Maybe. Maybe not. We've yet to receive anything."

"The Serpent has dreams above his station. I think that's what it is," Mephisto said, relaxing back into his throne. "He wants expansionism. He wants success. He wants a world at his bidding. It is hard to fight men, or monsters, who are driven by ambition. They cannot be reasoned with."

"I'm not known for negotiating through reason, so I think we're all set there," said Loki. "If you have nothing more to add, I'll be on my way."

"You came a long way for little information, little godling," murmured Mephisto.

Loki spun on his heel to walk away. At the exact right moment, he said casually over his shoulder, "Oh, by the way, Hela's dining with the Tongue of the Serpent, and she's moving into Hell. A beachhead, if you would. Expect to see her in the neighborhood."

Mephisto shifted, a frown crossing his face as he leaned forward off his throne, a cobra ready to strike. "That won't do, that won't do at all."

IKOL LANDED on Loki's shoulder, chattering away. "I sure hope you know what you're doing, Loki."

He didn't. He was winging it. But even to his own self, he felt like he had to lie to move his scheme along.

"I do. One more piece to put on this chessboard."

HE BYPASSED Garm on his way back into Hel, but this time, he didn't sneak in. He didn't climb in a window or eavesdrop around corners. He ran right down the middle of the hall, trying to gather as much attention from bystanders as he could.

"Hela!" he called.

"Loki?" she asked, standing at her throne, frowning. "You are not welcome here."

I am trying *to rescue everyone. The Dísir. Thor. Asgard. Everyone we can. Is that welcomed?*

But he couldn't say that. He couldn't tell the truth, as much as he wanted to. "I bring dire news!" he gasped. "Mephisto plans to invade Hel!"

He was counting on Hela's one weakness. She didn't ask questions. She just acted. And sure enough, her face turned to fury and her hand tightened into a fists, green smoke twining around her fingers and up her remaining arm.

"No, this will not do," she snapped. "He has no right. The audacity!"

"He said the lease has gone on long enough," Loki lied. "I was there to find out more about a trouble with Asgard, and when I heard his plans, I knew I needed to warn you."

Hela was barely listening to him at this point. "I will not stand for that infringement on my property. Tyr, with me!"

She spun in a fast-weaving green wall of flames. But at the last second, Tyr stepped away. The flames evaporated and it was just Tyr, Ikol and Loki in the throne room.

"Loki," snapped Tyr, looking flustered and a little panicked. "This isn't what I had in mind!"

"It's genius," Loki said. "If I do say so myself. It gets Hela out of Hel for long enough for us to explore our options."

"What options do we have?"

"We need to find something that brings Hela and Mephisto together. Someone to hate, something they fear," Loki said. He was right, of course. A common enemy was the tried-and-true way to bring two furiously headstrong oppositional gods of their realms together. "And the Tongue of the Serpent will give it to us." He blinked and then made his face deliberately innocent. "That's the sort of thing I'm meant to say, yes?"

Tyr scowled at Loki and then made a *hrmph* that moved his shoulders. His jaw twitched and then he admitted, his voice low like it pained him to do so, "You know, this might just work."

Loki grinned. "I know. It's pretty genius."

"I wouldn't go that far," Tyr said. He gestured for Loki to follow him. "Come. I'll give you the lay of the land."

NINE

THERE WAS one more person that Loki needed to redirect, to give him time to find the Tongue of the Serpent. Leah hadn't been with her mistress, and Loki had been counting on that. So while Tyr walked him around Hela's fortress, Loki sent Ikol to find the handmaiden.

"You two should get along," he told the magpie. "Ikol, Leah, interesting anagrams, yes?"

Ikol flew off without another word, because magpies are not in the business of indulging gods who think their jokes are funny.

When Ikol returned, he had Leah in tow. Loki pretended to be anxious and distraught, playing the part he'd cast himself in. "Ikol found you!"

"Yes," said Leah dryly. "How can I help?"

She leaned against a stone pillar, crossing her arms. Her dark hair fell limp next to her face, and she pinned him down with her flat expression, her eyes flickering in suspicion. Still, even though she gazed at him like she'd throw him to Garm if her mistress would let her, she was ethereal.

Ikol landed on his shoulder, jolting Loki back into the present. He barely resisted shaking his head to clear it.

"I have dire news!" Loki told her, forcing urgency into his voice.

"You've already brought dire news, or so I've been told," Leah said.

"Direr news!" Loki insisted.

"Not a word," Ikol cawed softly.

Loki and Leah ignored him. Loki added, "It's news your mistress must hear."

The handmaiden's mouth twitched. "She's away. You just sent her away with your dire news. *I'm* running the fort now."

Loki gestured to the magpie on his shoulder. "Ikol saw something on our journey here that he just told me about. It's something your mistress needs to know. Surely a pretty girl such as yourself could help me out?"

"Pretty," echoed Leah.

She peeled herself off the stone pillar, walking across the space between them. Her shoes on the cold stone floor echoed in the chamber. Something inside Loki wanted him to back up as she advanced, but he made himself stand his ground. She sauntered up to him, brushing the back of her hand over his cheek.

Blood rushed to his face, giving him away.

Leah smiled, but it was cold. "Such pretty words from a pretty boy for a pretty girl. I feel something deep within me stir."

With a swiftness that Loki hadn't anticipated, she grabbed his shoulders and drew her knee up sharply between his legs. The breath burst from his chest in a wordless gasp, and pain turned his vision bright white.

"Vomit, I wager," Leah said, even though Loki couldn't hear her as he slid to the ground.

Loki lay on his side, wheezing and trying to catch his breath. He watched as Leah reached for Ikol who'd fluttered to the stop of a nearby pedestal, oddly reminiscent of when Loki first met him.

"Now," Leah cooed to the bird. "You and I are both pets of egotistical masters. We shall work together, yes?"

Ikol hopped closer to her, ever the traitor to Loki in his moment of pain. He fluttered his wings, almost bowing down to Leah as her fingers alighted on his head.

"Let's see what you saw," Leah breathed to the bird. She closed her eyes, and so did Ikol.

Leah's eyes opened wide with shock. She hid none of the emotion from her face this time, fear filling her expression. "Mephisto—he has the Dís—he has the soul eaters. Hela must know!"

"That's what I—" Loki began to say, but Leah was already gone, opening a portal with a flip of her hand and leaping through its icy blue barrier into the beyond.

He flopped back against the wall.

Ikol hopped down beside him. "Your older self had more skills with women."

"Shut up, Ikol," muttered Loki.

LOKI HAD connived to get Hela and Leah and Mephisto out of his way, and Tyr was in position to help him with the next stage of this scheme. Despite being a trickster and a god of chaos, Loki loved a good plan. All the best chaos was planned chaos—the trick was knowing who to let on to the plan and when.

That night, he set off down the cool stone corridors Tyr had shown him earlier. Hela's fortress was eerily still and quiet, and it unnerved Loki a little. Asgard was so busy, so full of people who could interrupt at any moment. The danger of being caught added a thrill to his mischief and he missed it here. But he also missed knowing that if things went wrong, Thor, or one of Thor's friends who had sworn to help Loki, would be nearby.

This place was empty. And he was about to consort with the enemy. There would be no help, if he needed it.

Ikol seemed to read his thoughts. "There's still time to turn back."

But that was a lie, and the god of lies knew it. He didn't answer his magpie, and the magpie didn't push the moment.

When he turned the corner near the Tongue's quarters, he stuffed his hands in his pockets, threw his shoulders back, and pressed cheerfulness into his voice.

"Hello, brave warriors! I would like to speak to the Tongue." He came to a stop in front of them. "If it's at all possible."

"What would you speak to the Tongue of?" sneered one of the guards.

Loki tipped his head up to the guard, keeping his face open and innocent. "Oh, you know. Treachery and the like."

Tyr had been certain that this plan would fail. But Loki knew something that Tyr didn't know. Creatures like the Tongue could not resist the lure of treachery, plots, and betrayal. It spoke to them on some deep, primal level. He knew this to be true, because he didn't think *he* could resist it if someone came to him and asked to speak to him on the subject of treachery. There were some things in his nature he could not flee. There were some things in his nature he did not want to change.

So Loki wasn't surprised when the guards glanced at each other, conferred silently, and then opened the great wooden doors. The hinges groaned as they opened, scuffing the floor, and Loki was delighted to see that the Tongue's rooms were as warm and cozy as the hallway was cold and dark. A fire blazed in the hearth, illuminating the room in bright, playful splashes of light and heat. The smell of dinner—a roast of some sort—lingered in the air.

The Tongue sat at one end of a long table. Maps and papers covered the surface, alongside a half-eaten dinner and a fork dripping grease onto a pile of documents marked with a seal. A guard stood behind the Tongue's tall chair, watching his back and the door on the other side of the room. As wide as he was tall, the Tongue's face was mostly a short, compressed nose, a wide mouth, and a forked tongue that could not be contained behind the rows of crooked, sharp teeth.

Neither the guards nor the Tongue saw the kid in front of them as any threat.

56

"Loki," drawled the Tongue. Spit flew off his lips. Loki did not wipe it off his face, though he very much wanted to. "I have heard of you. Your time was after that of the Serpent. But your deeds would do well in our more grandly, mythic age."

It was a ploy, Loki knew. But it was an effective one. There was a part of Loki that preened—he *could* be part of a grand, mythic age. But the Loki the Tongue had heard of was not the Loki who stood in front of him. And the Loki of now hadn't done anything of note for a grand and mythic age, nor did he think his predecessor belonged to that age either.

He was here for a different mission, and he kept that in the front of his mind. He flopped casually into a chair far too big for him, kicking up his feet and tugging his cape loose from beneath him to drape elegantly over his arm.

"I thought you'd be larger," the Tongue said.

"It's true that the size of my reputation dwarfs me in comparison," said Loki with a smile. "Still—you know me. That makes this so much easier." He gestured lazily. "I am extraordinarily evil and I want to destroy Asgard. Or something like that." He tilted his foot out of the way, playing nonchalance, to look at the Tongue between his feet. "You get the gist. I was hoping we could come to some kind of agreement."

Outside, he heard a distinct *thump*. The Tongue heard it too, pausing for a moment. Loki held his breath. Silence. The Tongue listened, then relaxed again.

"You are a liar," he said to Loki.

He could barely see the Tongue from where he sat. But he knew that more important than seeing the Serpent was the Serpent seeing him, casual and relaxed.

Nothing to see here, thought Loki. Aloud, he said, "Yes, lying is part of my charm. But does it matter? You came to Hel looking for an alliance."

The Tongue narrowed his gaze, forked tongue flickering. "Who told you that?"

Loki ignored him. "Why boring old Hela over charming, winsome me?"

If the Tongue could have rolled his eyes, he would have. But that was no more a part of his character as was visiting children in hospitals and volunteering at an animal shelter.

"Hela is full of duty. You are full of untruth. Who can say what reasons you have for being here?" He might have been a glob of green and tongue, yes, but the Tongue was not stupid.

"I could have many reasons," agreed Loki. "It could be jealousy of my brother."

The Tongue *hmphed* but something changed in his expression. He found this plausible. Loki saw the change and pressed his advantage.

"I could want old One-Eye's throne."

He did not want Odin's throne, or for Odin to hear him call him 'old One-Eye', but the Tongue wouldn't live long enough to spread that to anyone who cared. Behind the Tongue, a shadow emerged from the hall, looming menacingly. Loki did not move.

"It could be," Loki said suggestively, "the terrible lust I have for older men with serpentine tongues."

The Tongue sputtered. The shadow on the wall grew larger, larger than Thor or the Serpent himself on the wall. A glint in the dark hinted of steel drawn from a sheath.

Loki plowed on, sitting up with a grin on his face. "It could be that I said all of this to distract you."

Tyr appeared behind the guard watching the Tongue's chair, having already dispatched the one in the hallway. He snapped the guard's neck easily, and the man thumped to the ground.

The Tongue froze, his gaze meeting Loki's own cold one. Loki could tell the moment that the Tongue realized his mistake in taking the young godling for a fool, for a weak child, for a trickster not yet at full strength.

Loki said coolly, "You know what that noise is? The symphonic perfection of a spine breaking."

He might have gone a little far with that line, but it sounded so beautiful rolling off his tongue he couldn't resist. He glanced over the Tongue's head. "I wouldn't turn around, if I were you. Unless you wish for an encore performance with audience participation."

Tyr rested his sword against the Tongue's throat and Loki clambered up on the table, walking across it.

The Tongue's tongue flicked defiantly. "Neither you nor your thug can threaten the Tongue."

Loki thought it was kind of hilarious how Tyr's face scrunched up at the idea of being Loki's lackey, as though right now was the time to be peeved about the Tongue's insults.

"If I die," continued the Tongue, "My master will simply breathe me back into existence as easily as he will draw a scream from you."

Loki knew a thing or two about rebirth, though he wouldn't consider Thor his master any more than Tyr considered himself Loki's right-hand man.

"*If* you die," Loki repeated. He kicked over a goblet left on the table from dinner and it clattered to the floor. "I see your future, Tongue. It's knee-bound and tear-faced and bloody-lipped. I can see your eyes dancing at the end of meaty cords and your tongue sore-crowned in the belly of a beast."

The Tongue leaned back in his chair, pressing away from the table for the first time.

Loki took another step toward, nudging the half-finished dinner plate to the floor alongside the goblet. It splattered everywhere, droplets of grease landing on the Tongue's face. He flinched. Loki did not.

"You are in the hands of Loki. You are deep in the land of Hell. From where you will find yourself, you will not even be able to *see* mere misery. If you will gift me secrets, however, I will gift you the mercy of death."

He sank into a crouch in front of the monster.

"If you don't, then you will *truly* know Loki."

There was no use, thought the god of lies, *in knowing one's own reputation and not wielding it like a weapon to one's advantage.*

Tyr pressed the blade to the Tongue's neck, just enough for the edge to bite into green-tinged skin.

The Tongue rasped, "The scrolls' seal is released."

And the pile of documents unfurled, the wax on them broken at the Tongue's command.

"Inside you will find details of all the Serpent's plans for Hel." The Tongue's voice shook slightly, and Loki smiled at that. He was a fraction of the Tongue's size, had a fraction of his power. The Tongue had been welcomed here at Hela's court, while Loki had been explicitly told he was not. But now he held the reins, and the Tongue was at his mercy.

Loki straightened. "Excellent. Your death will send the clearest message to your master. There's more to fear than he."

Loki was not prepared for how quickly Tyr drew the blade across the Tongue's neck, and for the sudden, explosive burst of blood across the room. He yelped, barely getting up an arm to guard his face.

"Gross! You could have warned me."

"Warning you would have meant warning him. Besides, I have no love of torture," Tyr said, wiping his blade off on the slumped body of the Tongue. "The scrolls, Loki."

Loki jumped off the blood-soaked table and bent over, craning to find the scrolls the Tongue had mentioned. "That was a good line, though, wasn't it?"

"Which one?"

"More to fear than he," Loki said, a little annoyed that Tyr didn't immediately know which line was a good one. "Sometimes it's really fun to pretend to be a villain."

"For many people, you *are* the villain," Tyr reminded him.

"If he'd called my bluff, I'd have had to just hope he was ticklish. That was my backup plan." Loki picked up the unsealed papers and shuffled through them, turning to the fire for better light. He scanned them quickly. "Okay, here we go." He blinked at what was written. "Oh. Well. This is definitely worse than I thought."

TEN

WHEN LOKI showed up on the edge of Hel and Hell, at the precise spot where he intended for them to bicker over borders and alliances, Hela and Mephisto were trading barbed words over the Dísir—who rightfully belonged in Hel with Hela, and through the machinations of Past Loki were currently the property of Mephisto—and who was to invade whom. He almost wanted to suggest they take turns.

Loki hated to interrupt, but the sooner the better, before either of them stumbled into his role in that mess. And so he didn't hesitate to scramble up the rockslide leading to the outcropping where they both stood, Leah at Hela's side. The red rock stained his palms, streaks of red marking them up like blood, and the dust from his feet stirred up a toxic-looking cloud in his wake. Even with the noise of his approach, Hela and Mephisto didn't seem to hear him coming. Only Leah noticed, her arms crossed as she watched him, a small frown on her face.

There was really only one thing Loki *could* say as he reached them.

"Direst news!"

The look Leah gave him could have withered even Thor.

Loki kept going. "The Serpent doesn't care if you join him, Hela."

Hela blinked, surprised.

"He's already arranged an uprising."

"Uprising!" Hela echoed. She spun on her heel, dress and cloak flowing behind her. She stared at Loki, her gaze falling to the papers in his hands.

Scorching wind whipped around them, and far below them liquid hot lava rose and fell in waves. Now that he was up there, the outcropping they stood on looked narrower than he'd like it to be. It'd be a long way to fall into Mephisto's clutches, natural and unnatural.

Loki pressed the heel of his hand to his chest, trying to catch his breath and focus. "Yes. Among the dead."

Hela looked affronted, then her anger started to grow, a storm gathering on her face. "Impossible. No, their spirits belong to me. I'd know if there was rebellion fomenting."

"Here," said Loki, thrusting the Tongue's letters toward her. "These instructions are clearly aimed towards those planning to rebel."

Hela snatched the papers from him, holding them up to her face and squinting at them as she read. She growled and thrust them back at him. "I cannot fight an army without *and* within."

"And, as much as it pains me to say it, I cannot reclaim the kingdom from you before these plans of the Serpent come to fruition," said Mephisto, sounding genuinely disappointed.

Ikol landed on Loki's shoulder. This was his moment. Loki cleared his throat, reaching out to tug the Tongue's papers from Hela's hands. She stared at him incredulously as he rolled them up and tapped them on his palm.

"I realize that this border conflict is strictly between you two, but I think I can offer a solution. As an added bonus, we can teach the Serpent a lesson or two."

Explaining his plan to Mephisto and Hela went as well as

one could expect, though Loki thought throughout the entire negotiation that he was glad that he wasn't negotiating with Leah directly and she was only taking orders from Hela, for she had been the one to ask the most astute and pressing questions, the ones that made him both feel and look like a bit of a dunce.

A deal was struck to provide at least a modicum of satisfaction to both parties. Mephisto would help patrol Hel, the lesser hell in his opinion, with seven of his Dísir. If the Serpent was intent on provoking an uprising amongst the spirits, who better than the Spirit Eaters to counter it? In exchange, Hela would retire to her fortress and wait, neither moving against Hell nor the Serpent.

To Loki's means, she'd pledge both Leah and Tyr's assistance.

"And at the end of this," Hela reminded him, "you'll have other promises to keep."

He was trying to forget about those.

Sure enough, Leah and Tyr reluctantly followed Loki back down the slope.

Ikol scolded Loki privately as they slid down the rocks together, away from the outcropping where they'd hashed out a temporary peace. "What you offered to Mephisto is a princely gift, to say nothing of the other things you promised him. How do you expect to deliver?"

"That's for future Loki to figure out!" Loki said, brushing his hands off on his sides. "Plus, I have to keep Mephisto happy, don't I? He's got all the cards to reveal me and my past self's machinations to Hela. That'd ruin everything."

They navigated their way back through a tunnel, back toward Hela's domain and away from the fiery pits of Mephisto's realm. Loki felt along the wall as he wobbled his way through the dark to a cave. As they grew closer, Loki smelled a distinct, foul odor, like something wretched had retched.

In the dimly lit cave where he'd left the Hel-Wolf, the creature lay over the bodies of several already-dead, disemboweled further by the Hel-Wolf, who slurped up their entrails like spaghetti.

"Those are *souls*," Loki cried. "Hel-Wolf! You shouldn't have—"

"You forget. I am the Hel-Wolf," snarled the creature. "There is no *shouldn't*."

Loki did not see how the Hel-Wolf's Hel-Wolf status was relevant, but he couldn't hide his horror. He swallowed back the bile rising in his throat. "Right."

"What now?" Tyr asked, his voice a low growl.

The Hel-Wolf spat out a piece of a soul gristle, which stuck to the side of the cave, glistening in the low light. "We go and tear out the Serpent's spleen. Obviously."

Loki sighed. "Oh, Hel-Wolf. I'm sure in some corner of the universe, you're charming. But this war needs cunning. It's a war of subtle moves, not loud declarations."

"You know the next move," Leah noted.

Loki shrugged. "I know what's to come. There is a prophecy that Thor and the Serpent will fight one another, and slay each other. Thor will walk nine steps and fall, one for each realm. He and the Serpent are each other's bane."

"If there's a prophecy," Tyr said slowly, "then what are *we* doing?"

"There's prophecy, and then there's *wishful thinking*. There's prophecy and there's the divine equivalent of what the old say to the young to trick them into doing something stupid," Loki explained.

Leah and Tyr looked at him with blank expressions.

Loki tossed up his hands and took on a mocking tone. "And lo! It is prophesized that Loki shall eat his vegetables from time to time! Et cetera, et cetera. What I mean is—no one can know if this is prophecy or the universe needing to eat its vegetables. There's wishing and there's knowing."

"What do you know?" Leah asked.

"I went to the World Tree and came back with scratches and scars and precious knowledge," Loki said.

"Dramatic," said Ikol.

Loki rolled his eyes at the magpie. "Okay. I went to the World Tree and came back with precious knowledge, at least. So let me tell you about the Serpent."

64   When Loki told the story, he kept it to the bare details. A boy

in this world who'd been kidnapped, thrown off a cliff, left broken in a stone cell. He told the story dispassionately, aloof and flat, like he had no skin in this game. But he'd been to the World Tree and spoken with the Fates, and he'd felt like he'd been there, in that damp cell where the air tasted like the slime fungus that grew along the cave wall. He felt like he'd dragged his broken legs in their makeshift splints across the ground, and sank his own teeth into the neck of his captors.

There was something in the story that drew him to it. A boy, angry and hurting. Someone forgotten and discarded, seen as lesser and unimportant. He understood that.

He did not tell the others that. He only told them the straight facts, the solid rungs of this story.

He'd dream about it. Later. What it must have been like for that boy to tear out the throats of those men with his teeth. Like an animal.

At the end, he said, "There is no way anyone can defeat a god like that. So we must be distinctly cleverer."

When he looked up, though, Tyr's and Leah's faces were carefully masked horror and concern. Leah looked away, but Tyr stared him straight in the face.

"'Cleverer?' Easy for you to say, Loki, but what you speak of sounds like a reason to despair."

Tyr wasn't wrong. The Serpent had already wreaked horrifying damage on Midgard and the mortals there, damage they couldn't undo. But they could stop him from destroying Midgard and from bringing his hateful heart to Asgard.

"Not despair," Loki argued. "Not yet, anyways. I was told that I needed a few good men for this—and now I have them."

He did not explain that, as he'd been told no good men would follow him, he'd been looking for a few bad men instead.

"Then what is the next step in your cleverer plan?" Leah asked, rolling her eyes as she turned her gaze back to him.

"We need to get a few tools," Loki explained. "One's in Asgard. The other lies in Limbo."

"*Limbo*," Leah said. "Loki, you can't be serious."

"Asgard's easy enough," Tyr agreed. "But Limbo!"

"Limbo is where reality vomits dead demons and the soulless," added the Hel-Wolf. He blinked, snarling. "How do you expect to get to Limbo?"

Loki winced and shrugged.

The Hel-Wolf's eyes glowed. "No."

There was one other element of Loki's negotiations that he hadn't brought to Mephisto and Hela, mostly because it concerned them just enough that they'd be furious, and not enough that they needed to know.

The Dísir.

Seven of the soul-eating sisters would be patrolling Hel on Mephisto's orders.

But four of them would be accompanying Loki on his mission. In exchange, he would relinquish their debt to Past Loki. They'd no longer be tethered to the god of lies.

And now, they emerged from the deepest corners of the cave, their blades glinting in the dark, and they swung them towards the Hel-Wolf without hesitation.

"*NO!*" raged the Hel-Wolf.

Loki managed to grab a hold of the bridle as light flared bright, white, and hot around the soulless Hel-Wolf.

"To Limbo!"

And then the light swallowed the Hel-Wolf, Loki and Ikol whole.

ELEVEN

THE DESCENT into Limbo was nothing like Loki expected. They did not merely pass from one place to another. Rather, they hurtled through the air as if they'd been blasted, a meteor of uncommon proportions, Hel-Wolf and god and godlike magpie spun into a fiery ball that exploded into the side of a mountain.

Pain ratcheted through Loki's body and he rolled over, groaning. Dust filled his lungs and eyes and he coughed, rubbing his face blearily to no avail. Ikol hopped over to him, feathers askew, and began to preen, as if insulted by the landing.

Loki glanced around. At first, Limbo looked like any other mountain range. Vaguely Hellish—red dust, heat, red rocks, a dark sky that flickered with fiery shadows as if something raged war in its clouds. It was deathly quiet, though, save for the Hel-Wolf getting to his feet nearby.

"Limbo," Loki said, leaning against the cliffside and wishing he'd thought to bring a flask of water. "Not as impressive as I thought it'd be."

The Hel-Wolf shook his head, flinging dust into Loki's eyes again. "You know, Loki…"

Dread pooled in Loki's stomach. The Hel-Wolf's voice had that kind of tone that never meant anything good was coming for the young god.

"Hmm?" he replied.

"I swore to serve you as long as I lived," the Hel-Wolf said, stretching lazily, a smile spreading across his face, exposing his fangs. "And I've just had the life cut out of me by your soul-eaters."

Loki carefully pulled his feet underneath him, his fingertips pressing into the ground. "Ah. Yes. Details."

"Where does that leave us?" asked the Hel-Wolf, taking a step toward Loki.

Loki saw a crevice in the cliff and sprang for it.

The Hel-Wolf roared, lunging after him. Loki squeezed between two rocks, finding himself in a narrow passage that led up the mountainside. He scrambled on his hands and knees, desperate to grab purchase on petrified tree roots, boulders, anything. Rocks slid out from under his feet, giving way to his weight as he pulled himself up.

The Hel-Wolf roared once more, smashing through the crevice and snapping at Loki's heels. "I'm going to use you like a *straw*."

Loki hadn't appreciated the Hel-Wolf's colorful language enough while they'd been on good terms—as much as indentured servitude and trickery can lead to good terms. He supposed it didn't lead very far, given current circumstances.

"Who's the good boy now?" the Hel-Wolf snarled, bounding over a boulder and landing hard behind Loki, kicking up dust and pebbles. Loki kept running, panting, clawing at the ground with his hands as he climbed up an incline, trying to keep his balance on the loose stone and still move away as fast as he could. He didn't really care where this path took him, as long as it was away. And fast.

He glanced over his shoulder, seeing distance between him and Hel-Wolf. The dog was prowling, contemplating his way up the narrow ravine where he did not fit as well as Loki did.

"Hey, little doggy," Loki snapped back without thinking. He picked up a rock and chucked it far away. "Go fetch."

"I am the lord of hellfire," the Hel-Wolf howled, leaping up to scramble against the cliffside and pushing off again to land back on the path. "I cannot be stopped—"

Loki's blood curdled in his veins as he heard the Hel-Wolf cut himself off. Loki twisted, looking behind him. The Hel-Wolf was right there, jaws ready to tear him apart, but his eyes were no longer set on the godling. Loki turned back to the path, searching ahead of him in the darkness for what the Hel-Wolf saw, but he could see nothing.

Nothing, until it was too late.

The sky filled with fire, and it took Loki a moment to realize this wasn't just a sky full of fire, but that the fire had a shape. A fire demon, twenty times the size of the Hel-Wolf, sucking up the oxygen around them, the heat licking at Loki's skin. He was built like a bull standing on his hind legs, horns curling with flames, his eyes burning embers, a sword in one hand, and the other hand reaching for—

Not Loki.

The Hel-Wolf.

"Surtur!" cried the Hel-Wolf, desperation coloring his voice like Loki had never heard before. He lunged, trying to escape, but Surtur's fingers curled around the Hel-Wolf's body. The 'lord of hellfire' made a terrible scream, and then he was gone, swallowed into Surtur.

Loki could barely breathe. His hands trembled and his legs felt weak beneath him.

Surtur roared, thrusting his sword in the air. "All is consumed in the fires of Surtur! The more I feed, the more I grow! The more I grow, the more I consume!"

Loki knew he was coming back into himself when a small part of his subconscious whispered sarcastically, *yes, well, that is typically what happens when one eats. One grows, and one eats more, and one grows more.*

He managed to keep that thought on the inside of his mind.

He did, however, take a deep breath, and straightened to a stand from his hidden place between two rocks on the side of the mountain.

"Surtur! Hi. Hello."

He hadn't expected the fire demon to swallow the Hel-Wolf whole—he did feel a little bad about that—and he didn't expect for Surtur to turn toward him and growl, "*Loki*," with such vehemence in his voice that Loki shrank back against the rocks.

"*Loki*," Surtur repeated. "I know you, Loki! You are smaller, yet you do not deceive me!"

"I don't want to deceive you!" Loki cried, holding up a hand defensively. "I was concerned about your absence! I am merely *interested* in speaking with you!"

Surtur roared at him, putting two hands on his sword hilt. "Yes, but for some *scheme*! You may be small of stature, but your lies are as grand as ever."

"Listen!" Loki gripped the rock next to him for moral support as much as physical support. "Since Ragnarok came, I have returned from death twice. I wondered why you had not done likewise. It's not as if the Lord of Muspelheim is known for his tardiness."

Surtur's grip loosened and the sword came down slightly. Loki exhaled, but just a smidge.

"Odin trapped me here," Surtur said.

"I know," Loki said, keeping his voice low and steady.

"And now he's free," Surtur continued. "My Twilight can slice through space and time, but not from here. This place is without weight, without purchase. I am not strong enough."

"Yet," Loki corrected.

Surtur blinked at him. "I am not strong enough *yet*."

"Let me help you, I want to let you out," Loki implored.

For a moment, Surtur seemed to be considering it. And then his fiery brow furrowed over ember eyes, and Loki had just enough notice before Surtur brought his sword, Twilight, down on top of him, smashing into rock. Loki tumbled down the mountain, rolling onto his side and scrambling to his feet. He ran, looking over his shoulder as Surtur pursued him with thunderous feet.

"Not enough, liesmith!" Surtur roared. "I will be free in time! Those who do not run are my food. I consume demons around me. Soon I will be strong enough to fight my way through weak reality and home to Muspelheim!"

Loki tripped, somersaulting and landing on his belly. He groaned and rolled over to find Surtur looming over top of him. There was no more run in Loki. His body ached. His lungs were full of dust and pain spasmed across his ribs.

He closed his eyes. "And then what?"

"I will destroy the Nine Realms! Bright fuel of screaming! It will all burn! A final Ragnarok! Ashes! Nothing but ashes choking all!" Surtur bellowed, slamming his sword into the side of the mountain again. Pebbles and sand rained down around them.

Loki forced his eyes open and sat upright. "But starting with Asgard, yes?"

Surtur looked confused, Twilight hanging by his side.

Loki pressed on. "I'll give you Asgard. That's where I'll release you."

Surtur took a step back. "How would you do this?"

"Twilight casts a long shadow. Let me take it. I will carry it to Asgard. The link between the shadow and the blade cannot be broken. And similarly, between your blade and you. You will emerge from the shadow like a swimmer from a pool," Loki explained.

Ikol settled on his shoulder, surprising him. He'd lost track of the bird in the melee. Ikol chattered into his ear, "Had to use a water metaphor, eh?"

"Simile," whispered Loki.

"Smartass," said Ikol, but Loki could feel the bird's pleasure at finding him alive, and he was relieved, too, for his own shadow.

"But why should you?" Surtur growled, suspicion darkening his voice.

"I need the shadow for a purpose of my own," Loki said, forcing himself to his feet. "A sword's opposite is a powerful thing and a sword as mighty as Twilight's opposite is required for my little mission. And Asgard? Let it burn. Let Asgard burn. I've died for it once. Never again."

Ikol nipped at his earlobe but said nothing.

Surtur paced back and forth, thunder and smoke rising from his feet, fissures in the ground letting lava seep up. Loki carefully and slowly took steps backwards as the lava pooled, cooled slightly, and then cracked again as Surtur's pacing broke its fragile shell. For once, Loki had the good mind to be patient.

Finally the fire demon turned to him. "Swear it. Swear to be as ash if you do not speak the truth. Swear a binding oath. Swear so your existence will crumble if you do otherwise."

Loki put his hand over his heart. "I, Loki Odinson, of the blood of Laufey, swear to Surtur, on the price of being ash, and my very existence, that when you emerge from Twilight's shadow, Asgard as of old will be before you."

Surtur's growl was like thunder that rocked Loki's body.

He held out Twilight over Loki's head and Loki flinched, but the Lord of Muspelheim only said, "Take the shadow."

The shadow that spilled over the ground was too large to carry, as big as Surtur himself.

Loki winced. He needed Surtur to lower his blade carefully, and precisely, but without getting angry at Loki, which seemed like an impossibility. "Would you mind lowering it a bit? And tilting it that way, so it catches the light just so?"

Surtur growled again, but lowered his arm and sword, tilting it as Loki directed. Loki watched the shadow cast on the ground glint, turning ebony in the glow from Surtur himself.

"Ah, yes, perfect! Lovely! Thank you."

"There is naught of love from doom's own blade," intoned Surtur.

"You know, once you've burned the Nine Realms, you could be a poet," Loki suggested.

Surtur pointed at him. "Leave, before I think better of this."

He didn't have to say it twice. Loki took off, pulling the hood of his tunic over his head to protect himself from the heat and dust, Twilight's shadow in hand. Ikol flew ahead of him, leading the way through the dust clouds and red-hot ash that fell from the sky. Loki wondered if anyone had ever broken a promise to Surtur to turn into the ash that covered the ground.

Once they were far enough away, Ikol cawed, "When he discovers—"

Loki cut him off, "By then the task will be complete. We've got one tool secure. Let's not count our disastrous chickens before they hatch. Now that we're not dead… how do we get out of his place anyways? Odin did, so there must be a way."

Ikol clacked his beak in exasperation. "Follow me."

TWELVE

THE OTHER tool was not as difficult to acquire. As the others had suggested, procuring a tool in Asgard was infinitely easier than procuring one in Limbo. Loki merely slipped into the armory, descended several staircases deep into the bowels of the palace, and stood before a cell.

He explained the situation that faced him, that faced all of Asgard.

"Please don't cry," he begged. "It's unseemly. I wouldn't ask but only you have access. We need to steal it to do what I have to do. If I don't do it, then it's all for nothing."

He was laying it on thick, but here he didn't need cleverness. He simply needed to be a different Loki than everyone expected. Someone shy and genuine. Someone innocent, child-like. In truth, Loki reborn was somewhere between the one who convinced Surtur to give him Twilight's shadow, and the one who stood here, saying, "Thor said that if it needed to be done, we must do it, no matter what the price. No matter what it costs me. No matter what it costs you. We have to."

And it worked.

When Loki asked, "Are you with me?"

The voice in the shadows replied, "Yes."

And Loki's grin spread across his face. "Then we should act swiftly."

THE REST of the palace heard the blast. It'd be hard to miss. It rocked the very foundations of the buildings barely rebuilt from the last war.

Odin thought it was the Serpent, come for Asgard at last, but then his advisors told him the blast came from within Asgard. From within the armory.

By the time Odin and his advisors reached the bowels of the armory, Loki was gone.

Odin swore. "The god who took it will have to master the trick of living without a skin."

Loki, listening from the shadows, resolved to stay out of reach of Odin's blades.

WHILE LOKI made his way back to the cave where he'd left Tyr, Leah, and the Dísir, the tides of war and looming conflict had made everyone restless and prickly. The Dísir sat at the cave entrance, clustered together as they watched the sky.

"My arrows are itching," complained one.

"Kara, you'll need your shafts soon enough," murmured another, drawing her sword over a sharpening stone.

"I can always make more," Kara grumbled. She glanced over her shoulder. Leah watched her solemnly from within the cave, where she'd been since Loki disappeared. "Put one in her pretty little eye if she keeps staring at me."

"Boredom has left you as greedy for violence as Hlökk," Göndul observed.

And as if on cue, the most murderous sister raised her head and cried, "Let her shoot the arrow if she wants! There's no great harm. She can aim at mortals, if she wishes."

Göndul raised her eyebrow and gestured with the sharpening stone. "See?"

"I cannot stand that stench," growled Tyr from the back of the cave.

"Do you smell that, sisters?" asked Kara. They shook their heads. Kara turned to Tyr, her grin wide and toothy, a ghastly look on her face. "We smell nothing, Lord of War. You have a gentle nose."

Hlökk chimed in. "Tyr Gentlenose!"

"If you'd helped me," Tyr snapped, "we could have dug the Hel-Wolf a pit, but now he has a pyre for honor he does not have and we must suffer the stench of his burning body."

The Dísir looked at each other and shrugged, unconcerned with Tyr's quibbles with their situation on the mountainside.

"There's news," Leah said suddenly, making all four of the Dísir and Tyr startle. They'd forgotten she was there.

"Creepy child," murmured one of the Dísir.

Leah stood up. "There is revolution in Hel, as foretold." She sounded surprised, like she had thought perhaps Loki was lying. Fair enough.

"Where?" Tyr asked, his hand settling on the hilt of his sword. "Hela's subjects dare rise up?"

"Not hers. Ancient dead have risen from the oldest lands. War-dead of the Serpent from his forgotten war," Leah whispered. Her eyes were glazed over, as if she were neither here nor there, relaying information from one part of the realm to the next. "They are who would depose Hela, not the true dead."

Then she sucked in a breath. "The mistress is seized."

Tyr drew his sword. "Of course. The twisted sisters she bargained for are in the outer realms, patrolling the dead who would not rise against her. She is alone! We must go to her!"

"No, Tyr, she has called upon her Valkyrie. Hela wished us here," Leah said. She swayed, dizzy, and sat down on the stone. Though it should feel hot, it felt cold through her dress. "She would not thank us for disobeying her."

Tyr's mouth thinned and he slammed his sword into the ground and yanked it out again. The motion did nothing for his frustration, but the Dísir and Leah kept a safe distance. "Fine," he spat out. "We'll wait. But while Loki dawdles, Hela is in peril."

"Or are you scared, Tyr?" Kara cooed at him, stuffing her arrows back into her quiver and sauntering toward him. "Avoiding the Valkyrie? Are you scared of them like you're scared of us?"

The look Tyr gave her should have turned her to stone, if she was anyone other than Dísir. He stomped toward her, shoulders hunched, and with his size, the effect was intimidating. His voice was barely audible, a low growl that rose in volume and timber.

"I've faced you before, and since then I've seen far worse. I fear nothing."

Kara did not back down. She tilted her head up at him and grinned. "Nothing? Then say our name."

Tyr opened his mouth and Leah and the Dísir all stopped, watching him, waiting. The hulking soldier grunted and shut his mouth, glaring out of the cave and away from the murderous sisters and the handmaiden.

"Coward!" crowed Kara.

"Just because I have parted ways with fear," snapped Tyr, "does not mean I've parted ways with sense."

"TYR. SOUL-EATERS," Leah said, rising and moving to the edge of the cave. She gazed into the sky. "What is that?"

In the distance, a shadowed city rose on the horizon. The city was shrouded in darkness, and though there should have been daylight behind it, the sky around the floating city seemed to darken too, falling from a deep amber into a molten purple, the color of a fresh bruise.

"What *is* that?" Tyr frowned at the city, his hand going to his blade like he could strike it from the sky and make it fall.

"That," said Hlökk, sounding pleased at the onset of war, "is the Serpent's Dark Asgard. That's his city, a glimpse of what could be.

And if it's on the move, then the Serpent is making his own move to capture Asgard True."

"Odin will raze the realms rather than see that. And if he fails," Loki said, startling everyone as he appeared behind them, "then the Serpent's reign in Asgard will surely do the same. He already seeks complete destruction in Midgard. But, my dear friends, I have a different ending in mind for the Serpent's Dark Asgard."

He gestured behind him, and the Destroyer, large, glinting silver and metallic in the light, with laser red eyes, stepped forward.

"We're going to destroy it."

THIRTEEN

THERE ARE MANY PLACES TO START A STORY. HAD THIS BEEN LOKI'S STORY TO TELL, HE MIGHT HAVE STARTED IT HERE.

After securing the weapons he needed, Loki settled back into Asgard True. Defeating the Serpent needed to happen quickly, but it could not happen all at once. Different pieces needed to be placed on the chessboard, exactly when they were needed and not a moment too soon. He needed to be well-rested for the fight ahead.

But Loki could not sleep. He was troubled by the difference between the Loki he needed to be to get Mephisto and Hela and Leah and Tyr and Surtur all on his side, and the Loki he needed to be to get the Destroyer, and the Loki he wanted to be. The space between these points seemed so insurmountable, so distant, that he could not see them in the same universe. He'd wanted to rewrite his story, he'd wanted people to see him as *this* Loki, not Past Loki, but to accomplish what he wanted he'd had to resort to the same old tricks and lies and careful wordplay.

He did not know if the ends justified the means. That saying felt like something Past Loki might have said. And so he could not fathom it.

This is how Young Loki and I met.

He summoned me.

I came to the room, surrounded by green fire, a haphazard rune circle designed to keep me contained. It was a library in a stone tower, piles of books everywhere, cushions, overturned plants. It smelled like earth, burned herbs, and rain.

I had not been called like this in eons, summoned like a dog for dinner.

"WHO SUMMONS ME FORTH FROM MY ELDRITCH REALM?"

Loki stood on the other side of the rune circle, defiant in the way only youth can be, his face set stubbornly. "I do, but I will not say my name. Names confer power. I know that."

I stared at him.

He scowled. "Don't look at me like that. I'm not stupid!"

I stared because I am an eldritch god. That is what we do. We are not known to be emotive. Furthermore, it *would* be foolish to name himself—if I had not already known his name.

"THE QUESTION WAS RHETORICAL. I DO NOT NEED TO BE TOLD YOUR NAME. YOU ARE LOKI, AN ANCIENT SOUL NEWLY REBORN."

"And you are a Teller," he countered, like he wanted me to know I didn't hold all the cards, though, of course, I did.

"AND WHAT WOULD YOU HAVE ME TELL?" I asked him.

He blinked. His surprise was genuine, even if he tried to cover it with a scoff. "You don't know?"

I admit that my frustration got the better of me. If I had eyes to roll, I would have rolled them. "I DO. BUT YOU MUST ASK IT. THIS IS THE WAY OF TELLERS SINCE THE BEGINNING OF TIME."

He knew so much, and so little.

"You're overdue for a change," he said, his small superiority filling the space around us. "Change is good. I know this to be true. But I'll play your game."

It was not a game. It was merely the way of things. But Loki saw everything in the light of games, of play—things to be won and lost, lies and truth, black and white.

80   "Everyone around me knows me from my prior incarnation,"

he explained. "But I don't know *them*. And they don't know me as, well, me. They think they do, but they don't. I'm not the same as I was."

I waited. There was yet no question.

He seemed to realize this because the child straightened, arranging his legs so he was sitting cross-legged before me. "I would know what they are thinking and what they are saying, when I am not there."

"SIMPLE ENOUGH," I said. "WHERE WOULD YOU LIKE TO BEGIN?"

He began with Volstagg. Then he wished to know Sif's opinion of him. Neither regarded him fondly. But I admired him a little, for he jutted out his chin and soldiered on. He asked for Odin next. He did not call him father, but rather Asgard's king. And certainly Odin seemed to have no love lost for Loki.

Odin sat on his throne when Heimdall approached him to warn of the trickster god reborn. Odin had greeted Heimdall with a genial smile, but it faded as Heimdall made his case.

"What would you have me do? Have the boy put to death?" he asked.

"No," cried the soldier. Then he added, chastened, "But perhaps exile? To the outer world from whence he came?"

Odin scoffed, waving a hand dismissively. "It's too late for that. He's here now and he's our problem now, for better or for worse." Then he paused and added, "Even if I could exile the boy to some other land, his brother would go after him and bring him back. And then take up his aggrievement with me, personally. It would put a rift between the throne and its champion."

Heimdall hesitated and then lowered his gaze. "We would not want that."

Odin rose with a sigh, clapping Heimdall on the shoulder. "You forget two things. Loki is my son, even if he is not my blood relative. I cannot and will not abandon any son of mine. And secondly, Loki is young. You and I? We are old. We have experience and history behind us that he does not have. Should it come down to it, his youth and immaturity put him at a disadvantage."

Heimdall inclined his head. "As you say so wisely."

Odin grunted and shooed Heimdall out of the room. "Now leave me. I am weary of such conjectures."

The vision of Odin faded and we fell back into Loki's tower.

"Are you satisfied?" I asked.

"I didn't ask for fun and games," he protested. "I asked for enlightenment." He looked down at his lap. "And I am enlightened, I suppose."

I did not believe he should be without truth. I leaned forward. "Shall I show you Thor?"

Loki hesitated, and then shook his head. "I think not."

I admit, I was surprised. "I would have thought his confidences to be most valuable of all."

"I want to get to know my brother without the help of a Teller," he said simply.

I would have been touched, perhaps, by such honor and integrity—except for Loki's next move. He unfolded himself, standing up and then turning for the door, stepping over piles of books and clothes. "Thank you for your service. You may go."

The insolence.

The selfishness.

The *audacity.*

"Oh may I?" If I could sneer, I would have. "How very condescending. That is not how you dismiss a Teller."

Loki looked at me over his shoulder, haughty. "That is how *I* dismiss a Teller."

"You may think so, little master, but there is the issue of payment due. The price for telling a tale is a tale. And I choose yours."

The room blazed bright golden, and I unhinged my jaw, wide enough to swallow his story whole. I always *relished* the stories of youths, of the yearning for principle and optimism before the realms stomped them to smithereens.

Loki tried to run for the door. "I have no tale to give!"

"You are mistaken, little lordling." My magic stretched

past the silly rune circle and wrapped in tendrils around his ankles, his wrists, binding him to me. "YOU HAVE AN EPIC TALE. IT'S JUST BEGINNING. I CAN SEE IT STRETCHING INTO TIME..."

It tasted sweet and tangy.

"I WISH TO CONSUME IT, LOKI OF ASGARD," I rasped. "I WOULD CONSUME THE STORY BEFORE IT HAS FINISHED. THE PRICE OF YOUR TELLING IS YOUR FUTURE. I WISH TO MAKE A FEAST OF YOUR FATE."

"I deny you this price!" Loki cried valiantly. "You are contained in that circle!"

I was not. I stepped outside it, the room swirling with my magic, with my hunger.

He fought me, as they all did, twisting and shouting, demanding I let him go even as he was spun up in my magic, prey in a spider's web.

"THOR!" he bellowed at the top of his lungs.

I laughed. "YOU CALL FOR YOUR BROTHER? THE ONE WHOSE TRUE FEELINGS YOU WERE TOO SCARED TO LEARN? HOW REVEALING. HOW INTERESTING."

I reeled him in, relishing every spin, the magic flowing back to me and giving me a taste of what was to come. I would have his story, his fate, his future. It would sustain me.

"IT IS SUCH A COMPLEX TALE," I told him, rolling the flavors around on my tongue. "SUCH AN INTERESTING INTRICATE COMMINGLING OF CONFLICTING EMOTIONS: ENVY AND ADMIRATION, FEAR AND FEALTY, RESENTMENT AND RESPECT."

And I was so hungry.

My mouth opened. My jaw stretched.

A force slammed into me, sunlight on a hammer. A thunderous voice roared, "Whatever manner of creature you may be, flee or face the wrath of Thor!"

Loki had called to his brother, and to my surprise, his brother answered. The boy's hero-worship was based on more than mere fancy. I should have seen Thor coming but I'd been distracted by my prey. I should have swallowed Loki while I had the chance.

I could not fight Thor. I know my limitations.

I screeched, and let go of Loki, dumping him on the ground before I spun into nothingness, opening up a portal to whisk myself back to the eldritch realm. I was surprised by Loki—he did not dissemble as I expected. Perhaps he really had changed from who and what he was in his prior form. Or perhaps he'd gotten more subtle—trickier and cleverer.

But the story... you see, you are here. So you know, I still got the story in the end. My debt would be paid in full.

FOURTEEN

STORIES CAN have more than one teller.

And I'm telling this one. Loki believes the story is his alone, and I will let him believe that for as long as I need to. Because I have been waiting a for long time to put this story into motion, to set these characters around me on this journey.

What leaves home does not come home the same.

I'm not just talking about how you feel after a long night at the bar, drinking and throwing darts and playing pool and whatever else you mortals do when you want to forget your day.

Ask me why I'm telling you this story.

Ask me!

I'm telling this story because it is *my* story. No one's going to get the details right except me. The devil's in the details, after all.

This invasion by the Serpent? My idea. You heard right. My idea. I'm full of ideas, but this has to be top ten. Top shelf idea. Top tier. Brand name idea.

I was taking a stroll in the Marianas Trench and, as I passed the Serpent's eternal prison, I happened to muse aloud, *You know what might be a nice change of pace? You could break out. Summon the hammers of your wrath to terrorize the world in your name. Take over everything.* One of those afternoon musings, those ponderings and dreams that sometimes slip out, unattended.

How was I to know he'd take my advice? Surprising, right? I know. I agree.

And now someone's doing my job of making the world a miserable place, and the heroes—and the wannabe heroes—are all preoccupied, so my hands are idle. And you know what they say about a devil's hands and idleness.

The Serpent is a fear eater. That's what they call it. Fear eating. Fear soothes his soul and fills his belly. He stirs up fear in any realm he can reach—though Midgard's his favorite—and feeds on it, growing stronger. And he is growing stronger. Odin's scared of him. Scared enough that he's willing to burn Midgard, and any realm where the Serpent is churning up fear, to the ground.

It'd be funny, if it wasn't putting me in danger too.

I tried to get into the Infinite Embassy. Surely you've heard about the Infinite Embassy? No?

The Infinite Embassy sits at the top of Earth's cluster of dimensions—stop me if I'm losing you, but do try to keep up—overlooking everything. It was created by the Living Tribunal, the head judge, head honcho, the big cheese. Anyone who's unearthly-yet-of-Earth can visit.

I see where that's confusing. Yeah, it rules over your life but you can't reach it. Mostly because you're pretty limited when it comes to dimensions. Not the tribunal's fault, or the embassy's, really. I think if you work on that, they'd be open to hearing from you.

They say that all realities' embassies are one and the same. If you enter one, you can exit anywhere else, and any*when* else. I haven't tried it but it seems like a neat party trick. It just proves that gods and demons are just as likely to make up myths about things they know nothing about.

...

It's cute that you think the head judge is God. I like your optimism. Your naivete.

He's not god. He's just the biggest kid in the playground.

You're getting me sidetracked. Stay focused.

Anyway, anyone who's anyone is in the Infinite Embassy because of the Serpent situation, right? Big deal in these parts. As always, when things get heavy, the Council of Godheads are sitting at the top of the embassy and trying to work out what they're going to do. And I'm not allowed in because gods are judgmental bores and the tribunal's magistrati are sticklers.

The magistrati are the kind that read the owner's manual from beginning to end. For fun. It sits on their nightstand. A comfort read, basically.

I tried to explain that I wasn't just *a devil*. I'm Mephisto! They should know me. They should know who I am. It's not just that I'm unique among the demons: I have luxuriant sideburns, and I'm undoubtedly the most handsome of them all.

I'm capable. I can prove that.

It doesn't matter. I got all the hot gossip later. Tensions ran high, etc. etc. etc., yadayadayada. But the most interesting bit of gossip was that the Red King was nowhere to be seen.

Sky gods are shouting and the Red King is nowhere to be found? Chaos above, chaos below. So I checked it out.

Look, I just follow the party wherever it goes.

The Devil's Advocacy was packed. Hopping, even. For most here, at least, there's less to be actively furious about. It's really an excuse to hang out in Satan's throne room and mouth off. And who doesn't like to blow off steam on Satan's throne every now and then?

Let he among us...

Many have claimed to be the True Satan. Some have even managed to say it with a straight face. But none of them have tried it in that room. In front of that empty throne.

I've learned in my time that it doesn't really matter what you call yourself—it matters what others call you.

I've never done it. Called myself Satan, I mean. I wouldn't lie about that. I'd rather take a name I can defend.

No one's ever called themselves Mephisto. No one who lived to tell the tale, anyway.

Anyways, it was a real shock to the system to hear that Surtur was getting out. And that Loki was responsible for that. I hadn't expected that plot twist, but it's always nice when the regular program shakes itself up.

What should a demon do in days such as these? I'd personally suggest grabbing the remote, sitting back, and relaxing with your favorite Merlot.

There's more to come. This season's not over yet.

FIFTEEN

THOR WENT to face the Serpent, as the prophecy said he would.
Dark Asgard rose to try and ascend to Asgard True, and Thor would
not stand for that. Mjolnir rested in his hand. He was resplendent
in Odin's armor. Inwards, he was full of grace.

He was, after all, Thor. He was Loki's opposite in so many ways.
He was as ready as he could ever be.

It would not be enough. The Serpent was the God of Fear—
fed by a world's writhing. There was no way the God of Thunder
could halt the God of Fear.

Thor knew this.

The Serpent knew this.

And Loki knew this too.

But Loki had the Dísir, and Tyr, and Leah, the Destroyer, and
Twilight's shadow. Surely that'd be enough. There were many ways
to defeat evil, and Loki was determined to exercise every option at
his disposal.

The Dísir laid the first trap.

Where their name was spoken, they were called, and their swords
cut through the air, killing the Serpent's lackeys where they stood,

befuddled over the word written on a slip of paper. When the room was empty, the Dísir called for Loki, Tyr, Leah, and the Destroyer.

"Nice," Loki said approvingly, nudging the corpse of the reborn Tongue with his toes. "To Hell and back again, I see."

"One of them nicked me," lamented one of the Dísir.

"Whiny," commented one of her sisters.

"The Serpent's magic is ancient magic," Leah said. "They are not immune to your powers, but nor are you immune to theirs."

"It's fine," Tyr said. "We have the numbers to absorb some casualties."

The Dísir gnashed their teeth at him. "That bodes well," one said. "One day, Tyr, we will raid Hel again and you will be there. Our kisses will be sweet and bloody."

"This is very cute," Loki said, gesturing between the glowering allies. "I love the vibe here and I hate to interrupt. But we have things to do, places to go. Leah? Where are we?"

Leah opened up a map in the air, pulling green magic from one hand to the other, spinning it until it looked like a three-dimensional map of the castle. She pulled and pried until she found the exact corridor they were in.

"We need to get Twilight's shadow over here," she said, tugging at the map. "But between here and there are magic hordes of summoned frost folk. That's troublesome."

Loki liked the way she understated exactly how troublesome magic hordes of summoned frost folk would be. "So what would you suggest?" he asked.

She looked surprised, like she hadn't expected to be asked her opinion. "We could use a distraction."

Loki brightened. "Oh. My wheelhouse." He spun and faced the giant metallic warrior behind them. "My dear Destroyer. Act in a suitably eponymous fashion, if you would?"

He gestured to the path in front of them.

The Destroyer's eyes brightened and then began to burn, growing from glowing amber lights to lasers, cutting through walls, his fists curled into unstoppable weapons. He marched forward, thunder under his feet. His pace picked up until he was at a run that sounded as if the earth itself was cracking in half beneath them. The walls shook and the ceilings fell, and the Destroyer smashed through one wall, then the next, then the next, right until he reached the aforementioned frost folk. They attacked and he punched, slammed, and tore apart those who dared face him.

"By Odin's empty socket," breathed one of the Dísir.

"He's not available," Loki informed her. "Come on. Let's go."

They advanced behind the Destroyer, picking their way through the rubble left in his wake. Tyr fell in beside Loki, helping the boy over some of the larger chunks of wall and ceiling. He nodded ahead to the Destroyer in the distance.

"That thing's a beast. Shouldn't we face the Serpent with him?"

"No, not nearly enough power," Loki replied grimly. "The Serpent is not one we can face directly."

"Nothing can defeat this God of Fear," Leah agreed, hiking up her skirts and climbing over the stone.

The Dísir leapt ahead of them, climbing with fierce swiftness. As they crossed passageways, the Dísir dispatched those who countered them. Then Kara held up her fist, bringing them to a halt. She peered around a corner and shook her head.

"Armored Midgardians. Room full of them. Bring back the Destroyer."

Loki looked down the hall and in the distance, could see the Destroyer still fighting off frost folk. "He's busy."

"I've got this," Tyr said, standing up and striding toward the opening.

"Tyr!" hissed Loki, grabbing for the back of Tyr's cloak but missing.

Tyr stepped into the room, shoulders back and chest broad. He bellowed at the room full of armored individuals. "What are you doing here? Odin's weapon tears out the fortress's heart! And you lean here and wipe your sores?"

"We're the reserves!" squeaked a static radio voice.

"Aye!" Tyr roared. "And we're in need of reserves! You're now deployed! Go, go, go!"

Without questioning, the armored Midgardians straightened, and jogged clumsily out of the room on metal feet, toward the Destroyer and the rest of the battle, leaving the room empty.

Loki, the Dísir, and Leah stepped into the room, staring at Tyr.

The one-armed God of War shrugged. "The drawback of simple tyranny is that the fearful are easily led."

"Feature or a bug?" asked Loki.

"Deep philosopher," said one of the Dísir to Tyr. "We are blessed."

Loki had a sneaking suspicion that was the Dísir way of flirting.

"Where are we going, again?" asked another Dísir.

"The library," said Leah. "It should be right through there."

She pointed and they headed in that direction. The room was suspiciously empty and peaceful, like there wasn't a battle raging right outside its doors. Bookcases lined the warm wood-paneled walls, and in the middle of the room, a red carpet with ornate detailing on the edges lay with comfortable seating, candelabras glowing and flickering. If they weren't in the middle of a war, Loki would have liked to sit there and read a bit. Maybe Leah would join him.

"Wait—" Leah began, but Loki had already stepped forward.

The moment his foot touched the carpet, it blazed to life— the shape of a fiery emblem of a snake in the middle. A fire-person rose from the snake's tongue and ran toward the door. One of the Dísir shot an arrow at it, but it passed right through the form, and the fire-person disappeared around the corner. The fire snake on the floor of the carpet faded into a scorch mark.

"I fear that was an alarm," Leah said.

"Then we must work quick," Loki said. "Grown-ups!"

"I wish you would stop calling us that," complained one of the Dísir.

"Make barricades," said Loki, ignoring her. "Guard us. We will do the important hard work."

"Oh, and what will we be doing?" asked one of the Dísir dryly. But she joined Tyr and the others at tipping over bookcases and pushing them to block the doorways.

"Leah—" Loki said, but the girl was already setting to work. They grabbed all the books they could find, flipping them over and discarding the ones that were not the one they sought.

The pile of discarded books grew larger. They worked swiftly and silently alongside one another, ignoring the shouts and cries around them as the Dísir and Tyr cut and sliced the intruding enemy at every turn. Blasts rocked the room, and stone and dust poured down around them, but Leah and Loki stayed focused on their task.

Tyr hurried up to them, shaking Loki's shoulders. "Time is short. Our defenses are failing."

"Leah," Loki said.

"On it," said Leah, spreading her hands. Green magic leapt between them and enveloped the piles of books around them, her enchantment curling in searching tendrils through endless pages and covers.

"If you're going to use Surtur's child at a point before the next life," Tyr tried again, frustrated at being ignored, "now's the time!"

"Loki!" Leah cried excitedly. The green fire wrapped around one of the books. "This is it!"

Loki hurried over to her side, falling to his knees. "You're sure?"

"Positive," she said, breathless.

"Quickly, Loki," Tyr yelled. "The sword must be drawn!"

"Sword?" Loki pulled the book onto his lap. "You misunderstand, Tyr. Twilight is a sword. Twilight's shadow isn't. It is its opposite."

He pulled Twilight's shadow from his pocket. In the library, amidst the piles of books and discarded stories, the shadow glowed like moonlight, a feather quill shape, a pen and a blade both at once. Loki grinned at Leah across from him.

"And that's something considerably mightier than a sword."

SIXTEEN

YOU KNOW how this ends. If it's today, you'll know it from the news. If it's a hundred thousand tomorrows from now, you'll know it as legend. If it's later than that, you'll think it mere myth.

But it happened. You of all people know this.

So how is it that you still know nothing?

They were in the library, with Twilight's shadow, with Leah's bleeding arm held over a bowl—for Twilight's shadow only took blood—but outside, the war had not stopped. The final battles had not yet begun.

In Midgard, Dark Asgard drifted closer to the World Tree. When its shadow passed over this place, it'd be able to reach any of the Nine Realms. It would go to Asgard True first. But Odin had sworn he would not let the Serpent bring down his Asgard. He swore he'd do anything to prevent that. He did not, or could not, care if they'd later call him Odin the Betrayer or the Fall-Father-Usurper, because he only cared that he prevented the worst-case scenario. He was willing to burn Earth to a husk if it meant saving Asgard True. All of Midgard, sacrificed.

There were heroes on Earth who fought to turn the Serpent

back, to stop Odin's murderous path by stopping the Serpent's murderous path. This is, after all, a tale twice over of two brothers.

But the heroes on Earth could not stop the Serpent.

And Odin would not turn back from his choices, would not admit mistakes, would not risk failure—even on a path of certain doom.

So it was up to Thor. Thor would have to take the prophecy as his bride, and, to slay the Serpent, take nine steps for Nine Realms, then fall. And Thor would do this because Thor was a paragon of good in a world of evil.

But this arc would require the Serpent to be willing to play his part. And he was not. He would not be so accommodating to fate. He would not be struck down by something as pitiful as *prophecy*. Prophecy was but natural law, and there was no law that could lower the Serpent's head. He was as treacherous and poisonous as his namesake.

When the Serpent faced Thor, he felt nothing but contempt and loathing.

The battle was legendary, but there is more than legend. The battle was newsworthy but there is certainly more than news. The battle was tragic, and it was a tragedy.

The battle raged, and in a library, Loki wrote. He wrote furiously, the moonlight glowing quill that was Twilight's shadow flying across the page of the book held open on Leah's lap. She watched his face more than the words he wrote. She did not dare interrupt him.

There's a land beyond legend and news and tragedy. There's a land beyond truth, even. We live in that realm of mystery.

Loki raised the Surtur-forged nib, his work complete. He'd added to the biography of the Serpent. He'd given the Serpent a girl.

AT THE *bottom of the pit, where the Serpent lay in agony, he did not lie alone any longer.*

The girl came to him, dark hair and pale skin and a long green dress. She washed and dressed his wounds. She spoke kind words as she held a spoon of soup up to his mouth. She nourished him and cared for him. On the best days, she even made him smile. When he was healed, he looked for her. But she was gone.

Only her memory remained.

As the Serpent grew to his full power and majesty, he looked back on those days, not with fear, not with anger, but with wonder at the mystery of the girl with green eyes and a soft touch. Beneath the hide of the hard, scaled Serpent he hid an inch of vulnerability which he treasured and feared in equal proportions. That no other than he could recall.

○━━━━━━━○

WHEN THE Serpent faced Thor, he felt nothing beside contempt and loathing, but here—here is where the story changed. It does not end like you think it ends.

There was something else in the Serpent at that moment. Something from long ago. Something that had crystallized inside of him. A sliver of fear. Loki had said there was no way to defeat a god like the Serpent, but now he was no longer that god. He was not the god he was at the start of the story, or at the start at the battle.

The Serpent felt prophecy close around his throat.

We cannot change history.

But gods do not have history. They have story. They are made of the spaces between legend and tragedy, myth and mystery. And stories can always be rewritten.

○━━━━━━━○

LOKI SAT back. "It is done."

Leah wrapped her sleeve around her bleeding arm. "Good. I'll stop this bleeding." She ran fingers over her wound, magic sliding in and out of skin to stitch it up. "It seems so wrong to suffer such a small wound, when we were within moments of suffering such a large one."

"If it helps," Loki told her, "we likely wouldn't have suffered the large one. It'd be over too soon."

"Loki! Stop admiring your own work!" Tyr called. "Are you done? We have to get out of here!"

"Coming, coming," Loki said, scrambling to his feet. He slid the book of the Serpent back onto the shelf, safely, where it belonged.

He'd half expected the battle to be truly over when they finished their work, but it raged on. An explosion sounded in the next room, echoing in their ears. Tyr threw an arm around Loki, hustling him toward the opening that the Destroyer had made.

"Follow that path!" he shouted.

Loki gestured to Leah and the Dísir. "No delays, no distractions! Except for important staying alive business!"

"Back to form," Leah called to him, a small smile on her face.

He wanted to linger in that smile, but their work wasn't quite done yet. Halfway down the hall, he deviated from the Destroyer's path. "Come this way!"

"What?!" Tyr yelled. "Loki, no!"

Loki skidded to a stop. "Dark Asgard flies on engines powered by fear-stuff. I know where the engine room is."

Tyr's eyes widened and then he grinned, a fearsome thing to behold. "Let's blow them up."

Loki hadn't told his compatriots about the next part of his plan. They skidded into the engine room where glowing golden engines turned and chugged, keeping Dark Asgard in the air despite the damage done. It was still heading for the World Tree. It still threatened Asgard True and the rest of the realms.

"Those who can fight, do so!" Loki called, and the Dísir took their places, forming a perimeter. "Leah?"

"Portal," she said. "Got it."

She began to pull at strings in the air that only she could see, green spinning orbs glowing and growing at her fingertips.

"You read my mind," he called to her.

"I would never do that unless I could bathe immediately after," she retorted.

Loki knelt, pulling Twilight's shadow free again. *Here goes nothing*, he thought.

He held it aloft and cried, "Come, Surtur! Its shadow calls your Twilight sword! An Asgard is here for your consumption. I call you, Surtur!"

A howling wind flew up around them, sucking the shadow from Loki's hands, and it slammed, nib down, into the stone floor. Sparks flew up into the air, grew, and exploded, igniting the engines. The fireball's heat blasted Loki and the others back to the doorway to the engine room. As they looked up, the fireball took shape, and Surtur stepped from the flames.

"THIS IS NOT ASGARD!" he bellowed.

"I *live* in Asgard," Loki called back to him. "I would be a sorry god if I blew up my own home. Besides, this looks like a perfectly good approximation of Asgard to me. To whine would be most unseemly. You will see, I am not ash. I have not spoken a lie. You wanted energy? You have it here. The fire can consume a Dark Asgard as well as a light one. You're free. You can return home. Won't that be nice?"

Surtur's face loomed large over him, flares of heat and flame twisting from his head, singeing Loki's hair. Then Surtur admitted with a low growl, "That would be nice."

"Then, we're set," Loki said, bowing dramatically. "A pleasure doing business with you."

"FREE!" Surtur shouted, slamming his sword into the earth, which groaned and split around the sword, fissures appearing and spouting lava that hissed as it splattered around Loki and Leah.

"Now, Loki?" Leah whispered at his elbow.

He grabbed her hand and pulled her to the doorway where her portal glowed. "Yes. We leave now."

They leapt through the portal together.

Tyr stepped through the portal to safety. *One.*

Brün took her step to safety, smiling at Tyr, Lord of Battles. *Two.*

Göndul took her step, wishing it was many more steps, back to a time many moons ago. *Three.*

Hlökk took her step long ago. There was no step for her to take here. *Four.*

Kara waited too long to take her step. She fell through the portal, arrow-kissed. *Five.*

Ikol, who you might have forgotten about because the magpie had the good sense to stay out of the chaotic fray of battle, took no steps for he flew. He was nothing but a bird—why would you think otherwise?

The Destroyer took a step through the portal, and the spirit that guided it took one with it. *Six. Seven.*

Leah's step was a step across miles, but still counts as one. *Eight.*

Loki's step was the final step across the portal. *Nine.*

LOKI HAD expected relief when he stepped back into Asgard, the kind of relief that came with a job well done, even in grief. He'd done what he needed to do. There should be relief, and exhaustion, and peace. But none of that came. As soon as they were through the portal, Leah cried out, pointing past Loki to the mountaintop.

Loki spun on his heel, but he already knew what he'd see. He fell to his knees, watching two pools of light fall from the heavens back to earth, one distinctly Serpent-shaped, and one shaped like a god, shaped like a brother.

"Loki," whispered Leah. "What's that?"

That is the way of mysteries, the stories beyond tragedy and legend and myth. Sometimes fate laughs when she throttles hope's pretty little neck.

His plan was entirely successful, and that was the worst part of it. He bent over the dirt and heaved, but nothing came up. He remembered the tunnels beneath the prisons, peering up at Thor through the bars. What would Thor do if he had to let something terrible happen to stop something even worse from happening? He'd let it happen, he'd said.

And Loki had let it happen.

Worse, he'd orchestrated it.

He'd sacrificed his brother to stop the Serpent. Prophecy be damned, Loki had made sure that this would be the end of the Serpent, even if it was the end of Thor. He'd saved Asgard. But not Thor.

He sat on that mountaintop for a while, Leah sitting beside him to keep him company.

"I thought you said the prophecy was junk," Leah said finally.

"I said it was wishful thinking. The best we could have hoped for," Loki said, twirling a stick in his hands. He peeled at the bark, not even wincing when it stabbed his fingers. "This is what the World Tree told me. We fought for a chance to let Thor triumph. We had to do what we did, so he could do this."

"Die?"

Loki nodded miserably. "We fought for a chance for Thor's sacrifice to mean something. Without us, he would have died, and the Serpent would have won. At least this way, the Serpent lost."

"You fought for the chance for your brother to die," Leah said. There was no malice in her words, no hate or judgement. But Loki felt tears prick his eyes nonetheless. Guilt. Shame. Fear. Loneliness. They welled up inside of him. He swallowed, pushing the feelings back down.

"Yeah," he mumbled. "So I guess... I guess we won."

SEVENTEEN

THEY SAT up on the mountain long enough for Tyr to climb up
to them and then sit down next to them.

"What now, Loki?" he asked, gently.

Loki was content to sit on that mountain forever, just watching
the place where Thor died. He wished he'd had a chance to say
something to Thor, to tell him what he'd been up to before Thor
died. Instead, the last time he saw Thor was when Thor rescued
him from the Teller.

I BELIEVE RESCUED IS A STRONG WORD HERE, BUT GIVEN THE
CIRCUMSTANCES, I WILL RETREAT TO MY TELLER ROLE AND LIMIT
MY EDITORIALIZING.

He'd needed Thor, and Thor had come. Without a second
thought. He'd protected Loki.

Now who would protect Loki? From others? From himself?

No one.

"This wasn't easy to pull off," Loki admitted in the silence. "I
have debts to pay to some of the wickedest creatures in the realm.
I have freed one of Asgard's greatest enemies and facilitated the
death of our greatest protector. My people will still loathe me and

the grave holds the one who protected me. I'm not sure I know the answer to your question."

"You don't need to answer it now," Leah said with uncharacteristic generosity.

"Let's save the worrying about tomorrow for tomorrow," Loki agreed. He got to his feet. He looked at Tyr. "Does that sound fair?"

"Fair enough," Tyr said.

○————————○

IKOL HAD watched this from afar. He'd kept his distance—Loki hadn't needed his guidance, wisdom, collective experience over the last few days. And now he just watched. He could not bear to watch Loki this way. He didn't die to let Loki cry all the time, even if the boy was wiping his face off on his sleeve and calling it allergies.

Ikol took to the air. He returned to where his old-self started on the road that led here. A magpie is a bird unlike a raven. Ravens have thought. Ravens have memory. What does a magpie have? Mysteries and another word beginning with an M. And of the former, you have one too.

Loki, son of Laufey, adopted of Odin, had tied his brother to the altar of the future and passed fate the knife. That might be putting too fine a point on it—he was not so passive as this—but in essence, this was a choice Loki had made. To Ikol, it was ironic that Past Loki had longed for his brother's death and failed. It seemed strange and not coincidental that his relatively innocent younger self was the one who succeeded.

It was the motivation that struck Ikol. This younger Loki had done this to help Thor. Because he believed in the goodness of something and wanted to save something, rather than destroy it. And this action was unwinding the boy, unspooling him from within.

Even a simpler bird than Ikol could spot the irony.

Thor took nine steps and fell. Whatever the next step was for Loki, he'd take it alone.

Ikol suspected Thor might have gotten the better part of the deal.

102

LOKI WAS not the only one who suffered with his choices.

It had been Volstagg's consciousness in the Destroyer. It had been Volstagg that Loki had spoken to in the dark bowels of the armory. It'd been Volstagg who had said yes. He'd had access to the Destroyer. He knew how to pilot it. And he understood what was at stake.

And when they took the Destroyer's body back and stowed it away for a future date, Volstagg was left behind, back in his body, fully aware of what he'd done.

"No one must know of this," Volstagg said for the umpteenth time to Loki.

"Who would I tell?" Loki replied, frustrated. "How do you think that conversation would go? Hi, I'm Loki, I managed to get some leverage on Volstagg and he came and helped me defeat the Serpent."

"I helped you *kill Thor*," Volstagg protested, his voice wobbling.

"You allowed Thor to die. That's a big difference," Loki told him. It was the same thing that Loki was trying to tell himself. "Thor's death was necessary to save Asgard, and the entire world, and it's what Thor wanted. He *told* me! No matter what the cost, he would make sure it happened."

"I know, I know!" Volstagg cried. He surreptitiously wiped his eyes with his sleeve. "Why do you think I did it? Because he was right."

No one would say it was because Loki was right too. Not even Loki, so he couldn't expect it from Volstagg either.

"But necessity is a weak shield," Volstagg said, lowering himself to the ground. He drew his sword, halfheartedly turning it this way and that to see his reflection. "We sharpened the executioner's blade when my lord's head was on the chopping block."

Loki had nothing to say to that. They sat in silence for a long time, and then Volstagg hoisted himself up again.

"This victory is like a week's heavy drinking. There is a hangover you cannot hope to avoid. Stay away from me, Loki. I do not trust myself around you."

He strode off purposefully to some watering hole, and now Loki was well and truly alone.

Volstagg, for his own part, felt alone as well. He felt wobbly and unsteady in a world without Thor, uncertain of where he was left, morally, and frightened. More frightened than he'd been when the Serpent was alive and a threat to Asgard. He wished he'd talked to Thor about Loki's plan before it'd been set in motion. But it'd felt like there was no time.

There is always time, he thought.

He was nearly to the bar where he intended to drown his sorrows when he heard a familiar voice call out to him.

"Volstagg!"

Hogun, a fellow soldier, sat on a rock, chatting with another man Volstagg didn't recognize. They both leaned on their swords and Volstagg resisted the urge to tell them that they were disgracing the blade.

"It's good to see you, old man," Hogun said, giving Volstagg's shoulder a hard slap. "Where in all the realms have you been?"

"Odin had a mission for me." Volstagg mimed sealing his lips. "Top secret. Suffice to say, the right heads were cracked."

The other man cleared his throat. "Have you heard—?"

Volstagg fought to keep his voice steady. "Aye, a great loss. Good men died so we could live."

After a respectable moment of silence, Hogun put his hand on Volstagg's shoulder again. "Isn't that the way? Don't stay a stranger."

"I won't," said Volstagg, absolutely intending on staying a stranger. He needed space. Time. He didn't want anyone knowing too much, asking questions. Not yet. "But now I must get home to the little ones."

EIGHTEEN

WE ALL have stories that we tell ourselves to define our worlds, to justify our actions, to make sense of the senselessness.

Volstagg is no exception. His home: warm and cozy, blazing fire and furs draped over chairs, food to fill bellies, his wife's kisses, his clambering children—this was what he fought to defend. These were the people he thought of when he said yes to Loki's request.

But he needed to give them answers. They wanted to know where he'd been and what he'd done.

The youngest climbed on his leg and tugged at his beard. "Did you bring us anything, Father?"

"I brought you the greatest gift of all," he said with a twinkle in his eye. "A *story*."

"Tell us, tell us!" begged the children.

Volstagg looked over their heads at his wife and smiled. "I must be sure they've earned it, my dear. Have they been good little gods and goddesses? Done all their chores, cleaned their rooms, finished their studies?"

His wife pretended to think on it while the children shouted at her, reminding her of all the things they'd done to be good.

Carefully omitting all the naughty things they'd done that week—children create stories for themselves, too.

Then she laughed. "Oh go on. Don't deprive them any longer. Tell them your story."

The kids threw logs in the fire, grabbed pillows for the chairs, and covered the table in dried nuts and berries—their favorite snacks. They filled in the space around their father, hanging on to each other and him and the table and his words, eager.

He did not want to disappoint them.

"Very well, very well," he said, pretending to be forced into this story. He wanted this story as much as the rest of them. "I shall tell you about how your father, Volstagg, defeated the Serpent, *twice*!"

He started at the very beginning, before he was married, before children, when he was a young and strapping fellow.

"Back then, the Serpent, the Lord of Fear, ruled Asgard, and he was so terribly mean," he said, widening his eyes. "The children had to go to sleep at *sunset*."

His kids gasped, "No!"

He nodded gravely. "It was the least of his transgressions. He hoarded all the sugary treats as well. I wasn't about to let him get away with it."

"Did you punch him, Father?" asked his oldest son.

"You bet I did! Left hook! Right hook! The beating was something fierce!" Volstagg mimed the fight. "It was so fierce that in fact, Odin had to create a magic that kept everyone from knowing Volstagg's valor to spare his brother the embarrassment. The Serpent lay buried for a long time."

"The longest time," confirmed one of his children, pretending to know the story.

"Until some day last week, when a woman discovered his sleeping spot and woke him. She was a Nazi. And what do we say about Nazis, children?"

"Death to Nazis!" they screamed, falling over laughing onto his lap.

He scooped them all up into his arms. "That's *right*!"

He told them how the Serpent returned, fomenting fear and unrest everywhere he went. He told them how angry this made him. How angry it made Thor. He told them that Odin had built a machine to defeat the Serpent.

They asked him how it would and he carefully sidestepped the question. Some things are best left to the imagination.

"Didn't you slay the Serpent before?" asked one of the kids.

"No, I beat him, but I did not kill him," Volstagg explained. "Important distinction!"

He told them how Thor fought the Serpent.

He told them how Thor took nine steps, and fell.

The kids fell quiet. Volstagg regretted his decision immediately. He'd wanted to tell them of Thor's bravery, but he hadn't wanted it to feel like a funeral.

"The Serpent was defeated. But foes can return. Odin was busy being angry. He'd made his fancy machine for no reason at all. But I had an idea," he said, tapping his temple. "I had the idea to fry him in a frying pan!"

"You cooked the Serpent?" gasped one of his daughters.

"Right up! With an egg on the side!" chortled Volstagg. "Do you know what I did next?"

"You ate him!" the kids screamed with delight, falling over each other laughing.

"His actions were despicable," Volstagg stage-whispered, "But his taste was even worse."

The kids laughed and wrestled with each other, hyped up by their father's magnificent storytelling. He tickled them and lay on the floor, letting them climb up on his enormous belly and roll off him like he was the mountain. He did not want to get up. He didn't want to leave.

"Are we safe now?" asked one of his kids, sitting by his shoulder and braiding his beard.

He sat up a bit, pulling his son into his lap. "Yes. You are safe now."

LATER, AFTER he and his wife had gotten all the children to bed and the kitchen was peaceful and quiet, his wife said softly, "You don't have to lie to them, you know."

Volstagg stiffened. "They're just stories."

She sat down next to him, wrapped her arm around his and leaned her head on his shoulder. They faced the fire together, watching the flames leap and dance in the hearth.

"The world is not always good," he said finally. "I tell stories to make them feel better."

She squeezed his hand.

And he added softly, just loud enough for her to hear, "I tell stories to make *me* feel better too."

She kissed the side of his head and held him close.

PART II

FEAR-STUFF

NINETEEN

IT WOULD be easy to think the story was over there.

After all, Loki saved Asgard, didn't he? Wasn't that the whole point? Didn't he want to show the world that he was a changed god? And yes, the mortals of Midgard still suffered the effects of the Serpent—pain and suffering covering the Earth like a mourning shroud—but the destruction had been stopped. Loki had stopped it here in Asgard and there in Midgard.

But no one knew of his role in the whole endeavor. If they knew of his role in saving Asgard, then they'd know of his role in letting—no, setting Thor up to die. He'd saved Asgard, but not his reputation. In the end, he was still alone. Volstagg went home to his family, and Leah and Tyr went home to Hela, and the Dísir—well, we'll get to them. He didn't even have the Hel-Wolf anymore.

The goats didn't count. They served only as a reminder of Thor, which made Loki's heartache something deep and fierce right now. He didn't want to look his grief in the face. He wasn't ready for that.

So few of us are. Grief is its own mystery, isn't it?

So, no, the story doesn't end there. Besides, Loki made promises to Hela and Mephisto in order to use the Dísir, dispatch the Tongue, and prevent them from usurping his own machinations. Those promises were not all fulfilled. Not yet, anyways.

The Dísir called to him. They'd fulfilled their mission to him and he'd made a promise. Loki trudged up the mountainside to them, kicking at rocks along the path. They tumbled down the mountainside. Loki wished he could turn around and run back down the mountain, back into the warmth of the town, back to something familiar, and comfortable, if not safe. But the Dísir would find him, wherever he was. And there was no putting off this inevitability.

"You know," Ikol cawed to him. "We magpies have a saying for making promises that are hard to keep."

Loki was not interested in the saying. But he knew Ikol would share it anyways. So he kept trudging up the mountain, trying to catch his breath, trying not to let his face foreshadow what was coming.

"Flap around and find out," said the magpie to the silence.

Loki snorted. "You forget. I have one of those Stark-tech phones. That's not how the phrase goes."

"It's how it goes for magpies," said Ikol, a little primly.

When Loki reached the summit of the mountain, the air felt thin and sharp in his lungs. Or perhaps that was the guilt. Either way, he tried not to grimace when he saw the Dísir waiting for him. Brün and Kara glowered, like they could see the expression on his shadowed face. He'd pulled his cloak hood up, hiding his face the best he could.

"Today, we will be free of you," Brün said, drawing her sword. "We've danced on your leash long enough. It's time for you to fulfill your oaths and let us soul-eating sisters run free."

Loki nodded. "I know."

When rummaging through Past Loki's rooms, he'd found the oath necklace and known immediately what it was. Just as he'd known that the helmet would eventually be his, and to wear green on a regular basis. He'd kept the knowledge of its power to himself until it became clear that he'd need to waive the Dísir's debt to Past Loki's for his plan for the Serpent to work. He tugged their oath necklace free from his tunic and gripped it in his fist. With a deep breath, he yanked at it, snapping it. A bright blazing fire burst up around them and Loki threw up his hands to guard against the brightness of it, in stark contrast with the dusky sky. The fire coalesced, a crown settling from the flames, all aglow.

Brün knelt before him, bowing her head. Her shoulders quivered with anticipation. Loki tried not to let his hands shake, also with anticipation, before he set it on Brün's head and stepped back quickly.

"We can go! We're free!" Kara cried. "We—"

"Loki's betrayed us," Brün growled, her face slowly lifting in a most fearsome expression.

Kara nocked an arrow. "Oh, you—"

Fire burst around them, a sudden sinkhole to Hell, and arms reached out, grabbing for the Dísir's ankles and arms, whatever they could reach.

"We were supposed to be free!" screeched Brün.

"I have no claim over you," Loki retorted, his tone defensive. He muttered, letting the roar of the flames carry away his shame. "Unlike Mephisto."

"All we've done is simplified the matter of ownership," Brün said mournfully, lifting the crown from her head. It was hers no longer.

"We can run," Göndul cried, desperation clouding her face and words. "We can hide. In the dappled time of the World Tree. In a secret place. Somewhere. Anywhere!"

Loki's heart ached when he saw Brün shake her head. "It is too late, Göndul. It was too late even long ago. Do not shame yourself."

Göndul spun, screaming. "Run!"

She made it three steps before the flames from the sinkhole to Hell leapt out, swallowing her and her scream whole.

Kara shook her head. "We will remain what we've always been—wicked things made by wicked men and hated for being exactly how they left us."

Brün walked with her to the fire. She looked over the flames at Loki, who could not meet the eyes of those he betrayed.

"You betrayed us good and proper."

"I'm—" Loki started to say.

With a derisive laugh, Brün and Kara stepped into the flames together, swallowed whole like their sisters, right in front of Loki's eyes. In a blink, they were no more, and there was no evidence of them, or the Hell-sinkhole, except for a pile of ash.

"A long face for a victor," said Ikol.

"I feel sorry for them," whispered Loki, sinking to the ground by the ashes. He dragged his fingers through them.

"They are but tools and monsters," said Ikol.

"And we aren't?" Loki asked, shaking his head. "They get eternal pain. I didn't free them from that. I get a second chance. I'm just saying—it doesn't seem fair."

"Nothing about this is fair," said Ikol.

This was not something that the magpie, or his past self, would understand. It wasn't fair that no one knew of his victory, and no one knew of his failures over the last few days, so he could try again. And again.

The Dísir wouldn't know freedom for a long time.

Thor had granted Loki a freedom he wasn't sure he deserved, even if he didn't think he should be held to account for his past self's crimes.

Loki sat there for a long time on his knees, until the cold wind that whipped the summit had blown the ashes over the valley below.

TWENTY

LOKI WAS not the only one to suffer the fallout of the Serpent's rise and fall. This is, as I mentioned, the tale of two brothers. Though his brother nearly brought destruction on all the realms, and though he'd been willing to destroy all the realms to stop his brother, Odin was the one who carried his brother's corpse to where Celestial Asgard once stood.

He did not raise his gaze when he destroyed the Rainbow Bridge behind him. He would be his brother's keeper forevermore, a task he'd failed at when they were but children.

The fallen city of Midgardian Asgard rose again, home of the Aesir, though in Odin's stead, the Vanir ruled. Freyja, the gray imperial wife. Gaea, the bounty-giving mother of Thor. And Idunn, the youthful apple-dancer. Queen, mother, maid. They symbolize many things, not least the new. They ruled as the All-Mother. And they knew immediately that they needed to get a grasp on certain boy-gods in their midst.

The All-Mother summoned Loki to their throne room not long after he returned to Asgard from the mountaintop. He groaned from where he was flopped face-first on his bed.

"Can't they wait?" he grumbled into the pillow. "Odin never summoned me."

The messenger looked nervous at the doorway. "I—I don't—"

Loki sighed and rolled his head to the side. "I was joking. Mostly. I'll be there."

He just wanted ten more minutes to feel sorry for himself, and about ten more hours to sleep. But there was no sleep for the wicked, even if they were justifiably so.

For the Dísir, he had to be heartless. For the All-Mother, he needed to be playful, capricious Loki. He had to be a different version of himself for almost everyone he met. Like turning a crystal to catch and cast the light against the wall. Everyone looked at the way the light played on the wall. No one looked at whose hand was playing with the crystal.

The All-Mother's throne room in Asgard was nothing like the pomp and opulence of the All-Father's. Dark obsidian walls lined the windowless room. No art or sculpture or fanfare adorned the walls. The All-Mother themselves were the only adornment, sitting in their blue-white crystalline thrones in the middle of the room. At the foot of one, an ice-blue fox. At the shoulder of another, two eagles. The third only rested her chin on her fist, her hand on the hilt of her sword.

Loki had never seen the All-Mother rise. He'd never seen them fight.

And he hoped he never would. Everything about the space in that room, everything about their energy commanded power, respect, and all-knowing.

There was a reason that Ikol refused to accompany him inside that room.

"Loki," intoned one. "We would have you speak with us."

Obviously, Loki thought. "Yes, All-Mother."

"We hear you have information that would be helpful to us," said the one with the eagles.

"I have dire news," he said solemnly, the corner of his mouth tugging upward. If Leah had heard him use that phrase again, she'd swat him upside the head. And he'd like it. "From the land of the dead. Mephisto has the soul-eating sisters, and Hel is *in* Mephisto's lands. Hela fears the slightest devilish whim could send those who must not be named against her."

It really *was* so troublesome not to use the Dísir's name aloud. He knew some who wouldn't even think it. Still, *he'd* thought it, and nothing truly terrible had happened, so it seemed fine.

IT IS WISE TO ADD HERE THAT THIS WAY OF ENCOUNTERING THE UNIVERSE WAS UNIQUELY LOKI AND IS NOT ADVISABLE FOR READERS AT HOME.

The All-Mother sat back, so surprised that they did not bother to mask their expressions from Loki.

"Hela wishes to be allowed to return to true Hel, for the good of her people," Loki said. Then he pursed his lips and added, like he thought of it offhandedly, "I have to agree. I mean, think about it. It's bad enough to die. But to end up as the dinner of some soul-eaters…"

"Enough, Loki," snapped the one with the fox. She exchanged looks with the other two, and then raised her hand. "Very well. Hela's curse is lifted."

She snapped her fingers. Loki waited for lightning to crash down but nothing did.

"She can return to her ancient home."

"I can't wait to tell her!" Loki said enthusiastically. The enthusiasm wasn't faked. He was really thrilled to uphold one promise without feeling like he'd sold his soul to do it.

"Not quite yet," said another All-Mother in a sing-song voice. "We have more questions. We would be an inattentive All-Mother if we didn't."

Ah, Loki thought, followed by a series of swears that he'd learned from the internet on his Stark-phone. This was the all-knowing part of the All-Mother he had wanted to avoid.

"How go your studies?" asked one All-Mother.

Loki blinked. This was *not* the direction he thought they'd go in. "Ah, uh, well, they're fine? I'm learning lots and lots. I learned

Old Tongue for a puzzle. That was pretty great. I've also learned a lot about the internet, internet memes…" He paused. "I know what internet memes *are* for instance. It's a catchy idea. I try to make my studies as worldly as possible."

Surely they couldn't be mad at that answer. It was not technically wrong. Nothing that he said was a lie. He suspected that they'd hear it on his tongue, even one of his better lies.

"Are you well?" The All-Mother leaned forward, her voice gentle. "We understand that you are not well loved."

The pain in his heart. He wished Thor was here. "No, I'm not. But that's understandable. I have to prove myself. That's what Thor told me, anyways. If I was a villain for an eternity I must be a true friend to Asgard for another eternity. That's the only way to balance it out, isn't it? It's an intimidating task. But I'm not afraid to face it."

He was blabbering and he knew it. Ikol wasn't there to nip his ear and shut him up.

"Good," said the All-Mother. "I wish I could say it would get better. But you're right. It will be the task of a lifetime. You can always come to us."

He bobbed his head. "Thank you. I'll keep that in mind."

"That will be all," said the All-Mother with a dismissive wave of their hands.

Loki turned as casually as he could muster on his heel and started to stride out of the room. That hadn't been so bad, he reasoned. They hadn't questioned him on anything he—

"Oh, Loki. One more question."

His heart sank. He turned slowly.

The All-Mother sat with knowing smiles on their faces. "Why *did* you release Surtur from Limbo?"

"I… didn't… I mean, I wouldn't do… Why would," he stammered. Then he gulped and his shoulders slumped. "Ugh."

"Ugh," agreed one of the All-Mother, a smile on her face. The other two looked down upon him, firm-lipped and disappointed.

Loki approached the thrones again, his footsteps echoing in

the sparse throne room. He locked his fingers together, trying to stop from wringing them, but he wrung them anyways.

"The Serpent's stronghold had to be destroyed. I took a fragment of Surtur's sword to the city's heart and summoned its master," he explained. "Besides, Surtur would have escaped eventually. The Serpent would have destroyed us today."

"And so," began one of the All-Mother.

Loki cut her off, "Annihilation tomorrow is preferable than annihilation before lunch."

Bumper sticker potential, he thought. But he didn't want to explain bumper stickers to the All-Mother, so he wisely kept his mouth shut.

The All-Mother collectively sighed. "You haven't changed, Loki."

He winced.

"I take it you stole the Destroyer too?"

"Stole is a strong word," he protested. "Odin was going to use it against mortals. I found a better purpose."

"We know you did not pilot it," said the All-Mother. "Who did?"

He'd rather not add "betraying Volstagg" to his list of guilts, so he pretended to think hard.

"You know, I can't remember their name. Can't even remember their face! Wow, it's amazing what a long night without sleep will do to your memory, isn't it. My apologies, All-Mother."

"Odin said that he who stole the Destroyer would have to master the trick of living without skin," said the All-Mother severely.

"Wish I could, but absolutely can't," Loki told her. "It's one thing to betray a foe, but a friend? One who helped me save us all? That would border on knavish." He shrugged. "I'll have to learn the living-without-skin trick myself. I'll give it my best shot. I'm a famously quick study."

"He really hasn't changed," said one All-Mother to another, but this time, there was a smirk on her face. She turned to Loki. "Odin would have skinned you."

"Undoubtedly," agreed Loki.

"But we are different. In many ways. And I think we have different tasks in mind for Asgard's most errant child."

There was something about the way they said that that didn't sit right with Loki. He opened his mouth to ask some clarifying questions but the All-Mother leaned forward on her throne, her face severe.

"Go, Loki. Return when your business is settled. We will speak of your future, and ours."

When Loki exited the throne room and reunited with Ikol, the magpie asked him how it went.

"Started strong, ended on a foreboding note," Loki said, but he wouldn't elaborate to Ikol.

The All-Mother wasn't wrong. He had business to finish. But first, he had an appointment with his bed, and his pillow, and he was going to ignore all messengers for at least eight hours.

TWENTY-ONE

LOKI HAD no regrets about making Hela wait for him to clear some of his debts to her. The sleep cleared all of his doubts and some of his guilt. It was true, just like he read on the internet, that when one was feeling low, one only needed to drink water, eat, or sleep.

He made his way outside of the city to meet Hela on the borderlands. Though he was refreshed, Hela, Tyr and Leah looked anything but. Our young trickster god suspected they'd been pacing out here, waiting for him, since they'd parted ways on the mountain where Thor had fallen.

"Finally!" exclaimed Hela, throwing her hands in the air. She wore a dress that seemed to be as opposite to Leah's high-necked one as Ikol was the opposite of Loki, a shadow of him. Green smoke swirled around her, pluming up from the crevices: a path to Niffleheim and Hel, where they belonged.

"Niffleheim is all yours again, milady!" Loki said cheerfully. Hel was where it belonged, once again. "You needn't spend more time in that miserable little corner of Mephisto's domain any longer."

Hela blinked. She hadn't expected him to follow through. "You have done well, Loki. Considering."

The conditional *considering* seemed unnecessary, but this time, Ikol was on his shoulder and nipped his ear, keeping Loki's mouth shut.

"We will return," Hela proclaimed. "We'll need to prepare the dead for their exodus."

Tyr and Leah turned away from Loki and Hela, preparing to descend into Niffleheim. But to everyone's surprise, Hela raised her hand, halting everyone.

"Not you, Leah."

Loki glanced between Leah and Hela. Had he missed some part of his promise? What was happening here?

"You will stay," said Hela with a generous smile. "Assist Loki. He has other promises to fulfill."

Loki didn't know what to do with this information—not about the promises, he knew that part, but rather Leah staying—and he was certainly not about to humiliate himself by stammering all the questions flooding his head. So he did what he always did, or needed to do, when he had nothing else to do. He turned the crystal of his personality, sliding into his capricious character that he'd given the All-Mother yesterday.

"Don't worry, Hela! I'll take great care of her."

Leah threw daggers at him with her glare.

"We're going to have fun," Loki said, grinning at her. "I know a great place you can stay."

LEAH STOOD in the entry to the cave, staring down into it, her mouth dropped open. She spun to face him, her hands fists at her side.

"This is not a *place to stay*! This is a dirty hole in the ground!"

Not everyone found Loki as funny as he found himself.

"It has stairs!" he protested. "It's not just a hole. It's a cavern! A civilized one. Besides, what was I supposed to do? I didn't know that Hela was going to leave you here. I can't exactly walk you into Asgard proper. You couldn't just stay in my room."

He hoped she'd miss the flush on his face when the regrettable words left his mouth.

She glared up at the sky. "Not just couldn't. Wouldn't." It was clear that she didn't see another option either.

The cave had a set of stairs, used by herders in the past, Loki assumed, that led into the cavern. It smelled like damp earth, a little musty, but not as much like animal dung as it had when Loki first discovered it on the outskirts of Asgard.

Still, *not as much like animal dung* wasn't the strongest selling point he'd ever used.

Leah crossed her arms and sat down on a log, back to Loki. She sat ramrod straight, uncomfortable and angry. She looked out of place, in her emerald-green dress and golden circlet, in a depressing cave that was damp, dirty, and plain.

He hesitated, and slipped off his capricious façade. He *wanted* Leah to be happy here. His stomach churned. "I know it's not the best hole in the ground, but we can make it a great hole in the ground! I'll bring you rugs, and bedding, and food, and books, and—"

"Enough, Loki," Leah said, her voice choked up. "I'm my mistress's handmaiden. I'm used to my wishes and desires being ignored."

Loki swallowed hard, the dust from the cave stinging his eyes. "I'll try to bring food tonight."

"You must be pretty pleased with yourself," she called to him as he retreated up the stairs. "You played your tune and we all danced along. You didn't drop a note."

He coughed and turned back to look at her. She was still slumped over her knees, arms wrapped around her legs, staring deeper into the cave. He sighed.

"I've been many things, but mostly in the last few days, I've been lucky."

His response surprised her. She twisted to look back at him. "You're not what I expected."

He tried not to look so delighted by this, especially after the All-Mother said he hadn't changed. "I knew it! We're going to be B.F.F.s."

She blinked. "What's a B.F.F.?"

"B.F.F.!" he called, running up the last few stairs, buoyed by her compliment.

"Loki Laufeyson!" he heard her yell. "What does it *mean*?"

He grinned. He hadn't been lying to Hela when he said he'd take care of her and that they'd have fun together. They would. He'd make sure of it.

TWENTY-TWO

HAVING A drink with Nightmare was not precisely my idea of fun. Still, it was part of the job, and I like to think of it as *mentoring*. Makes the drinks go down easier. I stretched out on a red velvet couch, staring up into the abyss of Nightmare's ceiling, which was dotted with stars that I couldn't be sure were real. My empty goblet dangled absently from my fingers. I wanted to get up, refill it, but I couldn't be bothered. Seemed like such an effort when I was already going through this ordeal.

Nightmare, a demon tyrant of dream and all-together top-notch drama king, raged on the other side of the room. "The Serpent ripped me off! This is my land! This is my design! This is my home! My castle! To distill man's twitching neuroses into a sweet power-giving nectar!"

Now, I am many things, but tolerant of maudlin turns of phrase is not one of them. I was lucky that in the dark Nightmare couldn't see me roll my eyes.

Nightmare slammed his cup, full of glowing fear-stuff, onto the table. "This is *mine*. This Serpent drank from *my cup*."

To be fair, I could understand his rage. His jealousy, even.

Those were sins that I enjoyed and partook in often enough. Still, Nightmare was so... weak. "What do your fellow fear-lords say?" I prompted, for the nth time.

Nightmare slumped on his stool. "They say wait. I say strike. Strike before—"

"Before you're nothing," I replied, seeing where the fear-lord was going.

"Humans caught in dark dreams come to my kingdom from Midgard," whined Nightmare. "I draw my strength from the world screams. I should be feasting. But the Serpent reaped everything. He starved me!"

And he's gone now, I thought. *So figure out what you need to do to move on and just do it.*

"If it helps," I offered, knowing full well that it would not help, "I don't think he starved you on purpose."

"That doesn't help," pouted Nightmare.

I sighed and sat up, planting my feet on the ground. I really did need to refill this goblet. "The world's in pieces in the wake of the Serpent. Thor's dead. Midgard's terrified, though not razed like Odin wished. But everything's shattered."

"So?" asked Nightmare.

Dear *gods*, did I have to spell it out for this weak-willed lord?

"So," I drawled out, standing at last. "Go figure out how to pick up all the pieces."

TWENTY-THREE

THE CAVE was not grand, or warm, or cozy—but they made it so. Loki dragged furniture and rugs down the road, Ikol squawking indignantly about how they *didn't do this*, and with Leah's help, they made distinctions between a cave-living-room and a cave-bedroom. They built her up a library, shelves of boards on uneven bricks that wobbled but held books just the same. And as time went on, Loki thought she looked less and less unhappy in the cave. And Asgard grew up around them, a city spreading and rebuilding, the scars of war patched and sutured on bodies and buildings alike.

Some things, however, did not change. Loki was summoned back before the All-Mother before his first visit was even a distant memory. This time, he found the obsidian walls and the blue-ice thrones less intimidating. He sat on the floor in front of them, cross-legged and relaxed. Maybe he shouldn't have been, but he felt with Hela and Leah that he'd banished two shadows that had been hanging over his head. He felt clearer, freer.

Free just made him think of the Dísir, though. So he pushed that thought away too.

"A battle faces Asgard," said one of the All-Mother.

Loki startled. Hadn't they just finished a battle? How many battles would there be? "A battle?"

"*Change*," said the All-Mother. "While there will be many willing to pick up weapons for their causes, there are few in this battle who are discrete knives."

"And even fewer capable of putting the right word in the right ear, at the right time," added another All-Mother.

"You're our secret, sweetness," purred the third All-Mother, leaning forward to brush her knuckles against Loki's cheek.

He opened his mouth to ask a question, but they interrupted him. "But as much as we want to, we won't be able to explicitly protect you."

So if he was caught, they'd claim no knowledge over his actions. He wasn't so concerned about that, as he didn't intend on getting caught. He was much more concerned about what he could be caught doing. They hadn't gotten to that part yet.

"Equally, to do what you will have to do," said one of the All-Mother gently, "you must remain an outsider."

Loki's gaze fell to his hands in his lap. He'd worked so hard to be accepted as part of Asgardian society and now the All-Mother was telling him that he could not be a part of this world. He had to be apart, not a part.

"A secret weapon works best when it's concealed," agreed another All-Mother.

"The Queens of the Realm consorting with the destroyer of it?" said the first, saying what Loki feared the most. "Impossible. Our position will be tenuous. Your open allegiance would only make it moreso."

In a way, Loki deserved this: he had sacrificed so many others to protect his own secrets. Now he was being sacrificed to protect the All-Mother, and they'd bribed him by saying he could help usher change into Asgard. As though they knew how important change was to him.

"Of course, you're aware…" the All-Mother started to say.

Loki finally spoke. "That if I disobey or stab you or anything similar, you reveal that I freed Surtur and the Asgardian mob will play out the bloody yet popular pastime of Loki football."

That was why they'd wanted to confirm that it was him who freed Surtur. Blackmail.

As the god of lies and tricks, he should have seen that coming.

"Loki," admonished the All-Mother, but their tone was light. "We are the All-Mother. Do you truly think we would do that?"

Loki rolled his eyes. "Yes, I do."

Gaea stood, and Loki leaned back, surprised. He hadn't seen her stand since she took the throne with the All-Mother. He'd forgotten how tall she was; she towered over him.

"You are not of my blood, but not actually being my son doesn't change the way I feel."

"Think better of us," chided Freyja. "And we will think better of you."

Conditional, Loki thought again. It didn't seem right that the way they'd think better of him was by him thinking better of them first. They were the adults. Shouldn't they make the first good-faith effort?

Idunn handed him an apple. "For the journey."

WHEN HE left the chamber, Ikol flew immediately to his shoulder. "What did they want?"

Loki shook his head. He couldn't explain until they were safely back in his tower. Ikol waited patiently until they climbed all the stairs up to the three-sided ruined room with an open side facing the afternoon sky. Books were strewn everywhere still, messy from Loki's past adventures. Outside, a few snowflakes began to swirl. They turned Asgard into a fairytale.

I should bring some of these books to Leah, Loki thought absentmindedly.

He sat on the edge of the bed, fingers curling around the edge of the quilt that the All-Mother had sewn him. He'd never noticed that the tree embroidered on it was the World Tree until just then. He picked at a stray thread on the worn fabric.

Ikol hopped next to him. He twisted his head this way and that way, and then nipped at the same thread, not-so-accidentally catching Loki's fingers in the process. "So?"

Loki sighed. "They want me to be their spy."

The magpie's eyes were beady and bright. "Complications."

"I know."

"Loki, everything's already complicated enough," Ikol squawked.

"Oh, really?" Loki asked sourly, flopping backward on the bed. "I hadn't noticed."

"Odin almost killed everyone to stop the Serpent and the Serpent tried to destroy the world by controlling everyone through fear itself."

"We fixed that." Loki let his arm fall over his eyes. "Tuesday afternoon trifle."

"Okay, but to do that, we've got contractual obligations to Mephisto—who, may I remind you, *is the Devil himself*—Hela, and now the All-Mother that rules Asgardia in Odin's absence."

"Yes, I think that sums it up," Loki said, wishing for the first time that he hadn't made Ikol.

"And Hela's left her handmaiden with you to spy on you and ensure you won't forget her."

"Lighten up, Ikol. Nothing's a crisis right now," Loki said with a sigh. It'd be a crisis, eventually, but he wanted to revel in the brief respite from immediate threat of annihilation and imminent death.

"All will end in doom," intoned Ikol.

"That's the holiday spirit," said Loki.

It was, in fact, the holidays. And Ikol was not wrong. Loki had unfulfilled promises and contracts with those who were known for ensuring that contracts were upheld. And Leah was in a cave right outside the city because she could not come into Asgardia.

It occurred to him now that the All-Mother didn't know about

Leah. Not yet, at least. He resolved to keep this from them. If they never asked about her directly, then he wouldn't need to lie, he reasoned. Lies by omission weren't *really* lies. At least, not the way that Loki saw it. He could say to them, in the future, or himself, now, that he did it to protect Leah.

"It's so dark out," Loki muttered. The sun had set fast with this storm. The snow was swirling harder now.

"Yes, well, it's Yule," said Ikol. "The sun's reached the furthest point away from Midgard."

"It feels like it," Loki said sadly.

The magpie hopped on his chest and pecked at the pin that held his cloak to his tunic. "It is a dark season, Loki. But this is as dark as it gets. You must remember. The sun is returning."

Loki reached up and scratched the magpie in his favorite spot behind his head. "For the malevolent spirit of the dead Past Loki, you can be optimistic at the most surprising times."

"I always liked the season," admitted Ikol. "After all, nothing can wreak as much mischief as a well-chosen present."

"True. I have no present for her, but we could go see Leah," Loki said aloud. "I wouldn't want to be alone on the holidays."

Ikol wisely did not point out that Loki *was* alone on the holidays. Nor did he protest when Loki got up and pulled on his snow boots and heavier cloak, wrapped up a few of his favorite books for Leah, and called Ikol to his arm, before heading out into the snowstorm.

The walk through the city was easy enough. When he first started bringing things out to the cave, he'd been afraid of being followed, that someone would discover Leah. But what he discovered instead was that no one cared about Loki. No one paid him any attention. Thor wasn't there anymore to protect him, but Loki was keeping to himself and people preferred that, so they left him alone. It'd sting, except he could see how this kept Leah safer. And that, for him, was important.

He trudged through the snow out of the city gates and onto the road. The snow stung his face, little icy bits, and he could tell his cheeks would be wind-whipped red by the time he arrived. He was afraid the books might have gotten wet but he couldn't check now.

Ikol fluttered from his arm into the warmth and comfort of Loki's cloak and Loki wrapped his arms around himself, making a nest for the magpie, who snuggled down into his armpit.

"You should shower," Ikol squawked.

Did he stink? Probably from his anxious sweats when meeting with the All-Mother in the throne room. Loki desperately did not want to show up to Leah's cave smelling like body odor.

"Too late now," he said, his voice muffled by the storm.

The glow from the cave wasn't visible from the road, but as soon as he reached the top of the stairs, he could see that the fire Leah had built cast light and shadows on the enormous wall. Logs crackled in the hearth and the warmth of it made the cave feel like it was a different world from the snow outside. He stomped the snow off his boots before heading down the stairs.

Halfway down, he called, "I'm here!"

"I know," Leah said, her back to him. The cave was warm enough that she'd kicked off her boots and was curled up in her favorite chair—the only chair that Loki had managed to steal for her—her knees pulled into her dress. Her hair was down, loose around her face, and for once she wasn't wearing the golden circlet she usually had in her hair.

She looked up at him, and gave him a surprised, small smile. "I didn't think you'd come out in this weather."

"Well," he said, opening his cloak. Ikol flew out, cawing and landing on top of one of the makeshift bookcases of wood planks balanced on stones. "I brought you new books."

He handed her the pile wrapped in a blanket.

She unwrapped the books, running her fingers over the covers.

Loki swallowed and looked away. He spotted a box by the fire. "Oh. That's new."

"Hela dropped it off," Leah said absently. "It's for you."

132   "Well-chosen presents," Ikol cawed, hopping closer.

Part of Loki wanted it to be a gift from Leah. He'd trust it more from Leah, though he wasn't sure how she'd shop for him. He didn't know what to expect from Hela. He approached the box cautiously.

"Do you think it'll blow up?" he asked.

"I don't think so," Leah said. "This book looks good, thank you."

"It's one of my favorites," Loki replied. He sat down next to the box, reaching for the flaps. The box rocked a bit, like something inside it moved. His fingers froze on the edges of the cardboard. "Did Hela give you any hints?"

"Does she seem like the kind to give hints? Just open it."

He pulled free one of the cardboard flaps tucked into another, and before he could reach for the second, the box exploded into pieces. Loki flew backwards onto his rear end and coughed, dust and sparks from the fire flying.

A dog—no, a puppy, a very large puppy—charged around the fire, growling and snarling, snapping at the empty air. Loki stared at it, and then looked at Leah. She looked as shocked as he felt. She really hadn't known what was in the box.

"Death!" yelped the puppy. "Death to Asgard!"

Yes, this did seem like a gift from Hela.

"Murder, murder, murder!" growled the puppy. "Eat the Aesir's hearts!"

Ambitious sort, thought a dazed Loki. He reached for a letter that had fallen out of the box. He opened it and read it aloud to Leah.

> *You will remember you set your pet on me to give you time to sneak into Hel. You will also remember how you left us alone. We fought. And then we didn't. I guard the gates of Hel. I have no time for a pup. I understand the Hel-Wolf is now dead. It changes nothing. He was your pet. This is now your responsibility.*
>
> *Yours,*
> *Garm of Hel*

Leah watched the puppy, still screaming for murder, and said, "Well. If that's not the most effective spay and neuter advertisement I've ever seen."

Loki snorted. "Did you just make a joke?"

She shrugged.

"Death to Asgard!" the Hel-Pup yelped again. "I will gnash on your bones!"

"He definitely got his father's winning temperament," Loki said dryly.

"What now?" Leah asked.

"We can't keep it," Ikol said reproachfully.

"Was this not the well-chosen present you were imagining?" Loki asked him, grinning. The magpie's gaze was cold and angry. He did not like the puppy even when the puppy wasn't threatening his life. Loki shrugged. "Garm's right. It's my responsibility. It needs a name, though. I'm thinking… Thori."

"You can't be serious," Ikol protested.

"Thori," called Loki.

And against all odds, the puppy bounded back to him. "Roast your heart on this fire! Until it chars!"

Leah laughed, a sound that crackled like fire in Loki's heart. "Happy holidays, Loki. From Hel."

TWENTY-FOUR

IT WAS all well and good for Loki to be recruited by the All-Mother and befriend Leah in her cave and raise a Hel-puppy, but trouble brewed elsewhere in the world. It was the kind of trouble that stayed deep beneath the surface, waiting for the right time. Most of the warning signs wouldn't be seen by those who needed to see them, and when they saw them, they didn't see them as warning signs. They saw them as isolated events, not as interconnected elements of a systemic failure.

In a sub-basement of the Infinite Embassy, the fear-lords met. They met rarely, and even that was too much for most of them. Fear-lords, by nature, didn't get along. One might say that it was an inherent part of being a fear-lord. They sat on thrones in a dimly lit semi-circle, for they were not entities who enjoyed bright lights. They liked to chat and bicker, talk over and around each other, each convinced that their fear methodology held more weight than the others.

The Dweller, a creature of enormous brain capacity and eight long appendages, looked down on everything and everyone, even the eternal. He believed himself above them and beyond them. He was more than eternal: he was timeless. He was *endless*.

And so he was always the first to speak, and always had the strongest dismissive opinions.

"He was an amateur. A good showing but of no real consequence. His defeat was total. He is done."

He did not know why they were there discussing the Serpent, again. The Serpent had failed in his quest, and so he was uninteresting to the Dweller. Except as a corpse. If they were to discuss anything about the Serpent, he wished to know why Odin was allowed to spirit away the Serpent's body. He wanted that body. A corpse was a corpse, but that one was a good corpse. No one else seemed to care where the Serpent's body was.

D'spayre glared at his father, knowing that he was thinking about corpses again. How he wished he could dispatch his own fear-sire. But the time was not right, and that would be another story entirely. Mostly, he hated how he agreed with his father. The Serpent was not worth their time or energy. He was dead and it was over.

"I agree," he said. It pained him to deliver the words, but no one seemed to notice his agony.

The Lurking Unknown was the third fear-lord, angry and purple, small in stature but one who grew in the presence of those who recognized his power. He didn't agree with the Dweller and his fear-son. He rarely did. "It is an *insult*. He was no fear-lord. We should have faced him."

"What would that have accomplished?" asked D'spayre dryly. "Why would we face someone who was not a fear-lord? We would have legitimized him."

"We should have taught him true terror and destroyed him!" roared the Lurking Unknown.

"And you think you would have taught him true terror?" D'spayre snorted. "Unlikely."

The Lurking Unknown sputtered, spit flying all over his fellow fear-lords.

The Straw Man knew he was despised, and it freed up his options. He had no need to keep those around him friendly or amenable to his presence. "I agree with the little man with his conspicuously big threats. It is not about whether or not he was a fear-lord. He acted as though he was. He trespassed on our territory. We should have defended our domain. We failed. It sets a precedent."

Kkallakku was barely listening. Only one of its thirty ears paid attention to these meetings. It was a creature of necessity and instinct, the destiny of all things to decay. It sensed that it was its turn to speak, and so it took a break from feasting on the nagging dread of mortals to spit out, *"Thhhhtthhhththh!"*

Not even the fear-lords knew what Kkallakku said. How it defended its seat was beyond most of their comprehension. Not that they had any interest in asking Kkallakku that—better to keep things friendly and cordial, especially in so small a space, and with the other fear-lords not knowing exactly how Kkallakku worked.

Nox was the peacekeeper, as much as a fear-lord could be a peacekeeper. She hated that it fell on her shoulders. Of course it was on the woman's shoulders to be the polite one, the peacekeeper. "I think what Kkallakku is saying is that your lies are transparent, Straw Man. You argued so only to protect those mortals you are oddly protective of. That is what you desire. The question is what do *we* desire?"

Kkallakku made a noise that most of them took as a sound of agreement.

Nox continued, "And I suspect that you and I will never agree, in which case, unless anyone else has something to say, we should move on."

She waited for anyone to protest, but everyone lowered their gazes. Assent. She exhaled softly, glad that they didn't get into the weeds on this one. They moved onto the next topic on their agenda, which Nox had created, of course. The war had sown fear and seen fear harvested on an unprecedented scale. It demanded their discussion. It earned their jealousy. Still, the war was over, and what was done was done.

The seventh fear-lord, Nightmare, was conspicuously missing from the meeting. The other fear-lords did not note it. They did not question it. They did not think it of any great import.

This was one of those warning signs that they wouldn't see until later, with the benefit of hindsight.

TWENTY-FIVE

IN POLAND, a girl was having a nightmare.

She'd been having a nightmare for days. Her parents thought her ill, but they could not afford the hospital bills, so they sat with her, holding her hand, leaving cool washcloths over her feverish forehead, spooning soup between her lips and hoping she swallowed.

They'd wanted a daughter for so long. They'd prayed for her and for many years, it seemed they would not be blessed with a child. And finally, when it seemed almost too late, she arrived. She'd been an easy baby, all smiles and belly laughs, happy to sleep and happy to be held by whomever would hold her. She grew into a bright girl, and now a beautiful, talented daughter who danced and ran track and played the piano like she'd been born with her fingers on the keys.

They feared they'd lose her to this illness.

They thought that the time when children died of fevers had passed.

Downstairs, someone knocked at their door. Pounded, really. The father looked up from his vigil next to his daughter, across the bed at his wife.

"Go," he said, jerking his head toward the door. His wife was the sociable one. She knew everyone in the neighborhood. They were here for her, undoubtedly. Neighbors had been bringing by soup and bread and prayers.

She shook her head, gripping their daughter's hand as the girl moaned and kicked out, her feet trapped by the tightly tucked blankets. "I'm not leaving her."

Reluctantly, the father got up, went downstairs, and peered out the door. He did not recognize the man on the doorstep with a shock of red hair plastered to his face by the pouring rain. When had it started to rain? The father couldn't recall. Perhaps he hadn't heard the storm over his daughter's cries.

"We're not interested," he said, and started to close the door.

The man shoved a foot in between the door and the frame, holding it open. The father felt a flicker of fear ripple through his chest.

"I'm Daimon Hellstrom," the man said, his voice deep and gruff, his Polish passable but not native. He said his name like it should have sparked recognition in the father's mind, but it didn't. "I'm an exorcist."

The father's eyes widened.

Hellstrom pushed at the door. "You need me. Invite me inside."

"We didn't call an exorcist," the man managed to whisper. They hadn't, had they? How was he supposed to pay this man? If his wife had called one, she would have come downstairs. He'd never known an exorcist who didn't show up with a priest.

"Your daughter has been asleep for days," Hellstrom growled. "She's screaming. She's feverish. Invite me in. I only want to save her."

The father couldn't help it. He heard the words *save her* and he stepped back, pulling the door open. "What kind of exorcist are you?"

The man did not move from the threshold. In the glow from the living room light, the man's eyes burned red, like embers. He was taller than the father, as tall as the doorway. He'd need to bend to make it inside the house. But he still had not entered.

"There's two kinds of exorcists," Hellstrom said. "The ones who splash some holy water around, burn some incense, and have a little pray."

The father flinched at the way Hellstrom spat out *pray*. He wanted to protest. Tell him that prayer was important in this house. But he couldn't make the words come to his mouth. What had prayer done for his daughter these last few days?

"And then there's the kind who get rid of demons. I can help your child. Let me in." There was desperation in the stranger's voice. An edge. Something that sounded so close to desperate insistence that the father believed him. Believed this stranger would help. A demon. His child? Had a demon in her?

Upstairs, Petra screamed. *"The castle! The castle in the sky!"*

The father yanked the door back and gestured with his arm, but Hellstrom shook his head. "Invite me in!"

He had, hadn't he?

"Dark longings of the world!"

"Come in," he managed to say, and before he had finished, Hellstrom was bounding up the stairs, taking them three at a time. The banister broke under the grip of his hand as he swung around and charged down the hall.

The father didn't think. He ran up the stairs after Hellstrom, leaving the front door wide open. None of that mattered now.

His daughter arched off the bed, while her mother sobbed, reaching out for her.

"Citadel!" gasped Petra. *"Filling the sky! Filling us all!"*

Hellstrom grasped forward with his fingers, clutching at something that the father could not see. He grimaced as he tugged hard, leaning back against the weight of an invisible string.

"A throne!" Petra screamed, her body thrashing as it arched off the bed, a violent, unnatural shape to her spine. *"A crown! The castle!"*

Whatever Hellstrom held snapped and he staggered, hitting a

wall and a vase of flowers, knocking a photo of the girl at her first communion off the wall. The girl flopped back to the bed, unmoving.

The father could not move from his place at the door. He could not make his feet cross to his daughter's side. He watched his wife reach with trembling hands to touch her daughter's hair.

"No," whispered his wife. She scrambled onto her daughter's bed, hauling her into her arms. "No, no, no, no!"

Her chant became a wail, a siren, an unending howl.

The man felt weak. He looked to Hellstrom, standing with his head bowed. "You said—"

"It was too late," Hellstrom said, rain dripping off him onto the rug.

The man closed his eyes. If only he'd understood what Hellstrom meant by inviting him in. If only he'd just opened the door and said yes.

"It wasn't your fault," Hellstrom said, walking over. He put a hand on the father's shoulder. "It wasn't my fault. She was too far gone. It was some other bastard's fault. And that devil's going to suffer."

TWENTY-SIX

HELLSTROM FOUND a room at a motel in a quieter neighborhood on the outskirts of Krakow. It was rundown, discreet, and the bed did not smell of mouse droppings. It'd do, for now. He sat on the edge of the bed, rubbing a towel over his drenched hair.

He'd been too late for that girl. And others. Something sinister was at work here. In all his years (and there were many) he'd never encountered anything like this. All over the world, thousands of people were trapped in sleep, thrashing, feverish, unable to wake. They'd all been trapped in nightmares—some demonic possession keeping them from saving themselves. And he was but one person. He couldn't save them all.

He reached for his backpack, somewhere on the bed behind him, and dragged it to his lap. He rummaged around, past the granola bars and the infinite crumbs, past the spare shirt and the razor. He pulled out a soft black velvet bag that clicked softly. He held it for but a moment, then he tugged open the strings and turned the bag over in his palm. Bones fell into his hand. Small, sturdy bones, worn smooth and shiny from use.

Hellstrom set the bag to the side and studied the bones. Then he murmured, "Anyone who's about, listen. If you give me a bad lead, I'll hunt *you* down and drag you to *my* hell. And you'll have an eternity of screaming to ponder whether lying to me was that smart of an idea." He closed his fist around the bones. "Understand?"

Maybe it wasn't a smart idea to threaten the powers who could answer him. The ones in this universe who could help him chase down the perpetrator of this ghoulish virus infecting people all over the world.

But he didn't regret it.

He cast the bones in one angry, frustrated gesture onto the ground. They clattered, and then came to a stop. He bent over them, exhaling slowly to steady himself. He studied the bones and then grunted to himself.

"Interesting."

He gathered up the bones into his hands again, rubbing his thumbs over the slickness of their surface.

"There's a psychic and spiritual trauma on a global scale. No surprise there. That's what happens after a world war. Now, the problem is that it seems to be concentrating on some specific kids."

He didn't always talk aloud to himself, but right now, talking seemed to steady him. His anger dissipated. He felt more centered.

"I've been clearing out the heads of the ones I could find," he added. *The ones I'm not too late to save.* "But I've discovered what happens if I'm too slow. And that makes me wonder how many other kids out there I've missed already. That I never even knew about."

He rattled the bones in his cupped hands again.

"Who's at the heart of this?"

He cast the bones down on the bedside table and they clattered once again, noisily and aggressively, an unseen presence directing their motion. The map they fell on opened, slipped to the floor and unfolded. The bones wobbled until the map had opened completely and then they hopped, stacking themselves into a long pointer with soft clicks and clacks.

Hellstrom knelt next to the map, put his finger where the bones settled, and said softly, "Now we're talking."

TWENTY-SEVEN

LOKI DIDN'T know how he ended up in this wasteland with Thor, but he was glad his brother was with him. Around him, barren land, scorched as if there'd been a tremendous fire, stretched in all directions. The few remaining trees were dead, charred and scraggly. Their roots were exposed, spilling over cracked and dusty soil.

Loki's throat hurt. He was parched. Why hadn't he brought any water?

Thor was different than Loki last remembered him. He was taller and faded, as if the color had been sapped from him by this unending wasteland. Though his cape—red in Loki's memory but umber here—still felt as reassuringly thick and soft as Loki remembered it,.

"'Tis destiny, Loki," Thor was explaining as they walked. "We can't fight destiny. So we fight our foe instead. Are you with me?"

Loki had to agree that there was a certain logic. "Yes, of course, dear brother."

Loki found himself on his brother's shoulders. His brother was a giant. He was but a flea. How had he gotten up here? Why was he up here? Thor's hair flowed like a mane. Thor's voice sounded gravelly. Old. Unfamiliar.

Without thinking, Loki wrapped his arms around his brother's neck and jerked his hands in opposite directions, as swift as he could. Thor's neck snapped with an audible crack, and they both tumbled to the ground. Thor lay on his back, gasping for air. Loki scrambled to his feet, tears and dust stinging his eyes.

"Why, Loki?" Thor gasped.

"I had to," Loki managed to say, tears streaking the dirt on his face. "I had to! You had to die. I had to help. I did."

Thor's chest fluttered up and down. He could say nothing.

"It's for everyone's good," sobbed Loki, crawling on his hands and knees toward his brother. The closer he tried to get, the farther Thor seemed to be from him. "I wouldn't just do this because I was evil."

But in his mind, a small voice added, *would I?*

A great rumble came from the earth. The cracks of the dried soil, parched from fire and drought, began to widen. They swallowed Thor and Loki's scream, and from the dirt a vile, bony arm reached up. And then another. Loki scrambled backwards away from the crack but they were all around him.

"It's the D—" he started to say and cut himself off just in time.

"The Dísir," murmured one. Kara? He couldn't recall. "You can say it now. It's not so bad, being bad. Is it, Loki? You get the punishment you deserve."

She grabbed his ankles, dragging him to her, while another Dísir hauled him by his hair.

"We get to be together."

Loki bellowed, kicking and flailing his legs and arms as hard as he could, but he was no match for the soul-eating sisters.

The Dísir laughed and whispered, "We'll be together forever, sloughing skin in Hell where we—"

A searing pain raced through Loki and he scrunched his face up, shouting despite his attempt to grit his teeth.

HE GASPED and sat up.

The night air was cool against his skin. The room was dark. Wherever the wasteland was, it was gone. He blinked, and his vision focused. Ikol sat on his knee, head tilting, beady eyes assessing.

Loki touched his face and found a cut. He scowled. "Did you do that, Ikol? You could have blinded me." He wiped the blood off with his shirt sleeve. "Odin's gone but that doesn't mean Asgard's in need of a new Cyclopean presence."

"You were under attack," Ikol said, bypassing Loki's grumbles.

Loki closed his eyes, thinking of the wasteland, of Thor, of the Dísir. "I think it was just—"

"Spiritual. Mystic. Psychic. One of them. It's not acceptable. You wouldn't wake. I had to force the issue," said the magpie, hopping down off his knee but staying close.

There was something different about Ikol's tone. There was nothing judgmental or haughty, no hidden *I told you so* caught between words, no wisdom or knowledge. Short sentences. Straight and to the point. Things that Loki rarely was, even in his past self.

Something had upset the magpie.

Loki reached over and twisted the knob of the light, the glow filling the room. For a moment, he thought he might see the faces of the Dísir in the dark, grinning, all skulls and teeth and too-long fingers. But the shadows were empty. It was just him and Ikol.

"What were you dreaming of?" Ikol asked. "It'll be important. Dreams are always important."

Loki wisely decided not to tell Ikol that sometimes he simply dreamed of visiting a cheese factory and being hired as the taste tester for all the delicious cheeses.

He hesitated and then said, "I've had the dream before."

WITHIN MINUTES, he regretted telling Ikol about the dream. The magpie was relentless, pecking and squawking until Loki reluctantly got up, got dressed, and followed him out into the night. They slipped out of the city, making their way to the ruins of Dark Asgard, destroyed by Surtur and yet to be removed. It felt strange to be here. He'd spent so much time in the rebuilt Asgard and the cave with Leah that he'd forgotten there were parts of Midgard that still bore the scars of war.

"I still think we should have waited until morning," Loki called to Ikol.

Ikol cawed. "Perhaps. But dreams by night are a different thing to dreams by day."

But if we are in real life now, Loki thought, *why does it matter?*

He was paying so much attention to his footing on the uneven ground that he nearly ran into the branch that hung low over the trail. Ikol perched upon it, leaning down to nip at the hem of his cloak hood.

"This is *magic*, Loki," he chided, as though he could hear the young god's sulking thoughts. "Symbolism is important."

"What symbols? Rocks?" Loki gestured around them. "There's nothing here! Besides, the All-Mother and every sage and sorcerer and anyone they could find combed over this place looking for any remains of the Serpent or his power."

He kicked at a rock and watched it roll down a hill.

"These are just rocks. Magnificent and sinister rocks. But rocks nonetheless. Whatever power they had is long gone. And I could be in bed, waiting for the sun to rise."

"Perhaps. But it occurs to me that there's one place where the Serpent's Asgard is as powerful as ever." Ikol turned and looked toward the summit of the mountain.

Loki felt like he needed to sit down. He leaned against the tree, following Ikol's gaze. "Up there. Where Thor fell."

"You're not an entirely stupid boy now, are you?" Ikol took off, flapping into the night sky ahead of Loki.

Loki took a deep breath and started marching after him.

DAIMON HELLSTROM watched from above, unseen by the magpie or the god. "A kid," he murmured aloud to himself. It had surprised him that the bones led him to this empty ruin, but it surprised him less when he made out the shadowy figures below.

Not just some kid. Trouble. That was what walked below him.

He pooled up a fireball in his hand and launched himself off the cliff, throwing it at the boy-god below. The magpie screeched and the boy dove to the side. Hellstrom landed, his boots kicking up a cloud of dust.

"You're supposed to be *dead*, godling," snarled Hellstrom. "Here. Let me help."

"Oh *hell*," breathed Loki, his eyes wide.

It pleased Hellstrom that his face was the last that Loki would see before death.

TWENTY-EIGHT

PERHAPS IN the past, Loki had not been particularly good at knowing when he was bested. You could ask Ikol. He'd know.

But this Loki, our chaos child, knew a lost cause when he looked it in the face. And the man with burning ember eyes, hellfire-red hair, and inexplicably lacking a shirt seemed like the kind of guy who'd best Loki in a fight.

Gods do not lack a fight-or-flight response. They simply aren't good at picking the right one.

Loki ran. He scrambled up the mountain path, dodging behind enormous rocks and falling to his knees and hands more than once. Pebbles and stones slipped out from beneath his feet and he cursed at himself. He really had to stop getting into scraps on mountainsides. He needed to start having fights on nice solid flat pieces of land, in perfect weather, not in the middle of the night. He could barely see where he was going. His palms stung but he scrambled and climbed like a mountain goat over the false summit of the mountain top and higher, climbing to where Thor took his last steps.

He heard the firebolt before he saw it. It screamed through the air and exploded next to him, the heat singeing his hair and the burst of light nearly blinding him. Ikol tumbled through the air, wing over wing, and Loki reached out, grabbing him by a tail feather and a foot.

"Change of plans!" he yelped. "Hide!"

He wedged himself in a space between a half-scorched tree and a little hollow on the mountainside. He pulled his feet in beneath himself, dragging his cloak over his body and hoping that it'd disguise the shape of him.

Ikol squirmed on his lap, rearranging his feathers. "Grabbing me by the tail," he muttered.

"Oh, I'm sorry for saving your *life*," Loki hissed in response.

He bit back a yelp when Ikol nipped at his chin. He listened. The night seemed quiet again. No firebolts being thrown. No snarling, shirtless demon-men flinging themselves at him from cliffsides. But then he craned harder and realized it was *too* quiet.

It was utterly still.

Footsteps on the ground. Loki squeezed his eyes shut. It sounded like the man was walking around him, almost on top of him. It felt like he'd be pulled right out of his hiding spot—or fried to a crisp inside it.

He assumed the attacker held some spiteful grudge against Loki in a past life. Like everyone else, apparently. But Loki couldn't remember all these terrible things he'd allegedly done in a past life, which made it hard to get ahead of problems like this one. If he couldn't remember how he'd wronged this man, how was he supposed to resolve it? How was he supposed to wiggle his way out of this one?

It didn't seem fair that he'd die for a crime he couldn't remember committing.

The footsteps sounded farther away. Loki and Ikol waited, listening. It was quiet again.

"I think he's gone," Loki whispered to Ikol. "Maybe if I sit up, you could fly around and check?"

He opened the cloak, letting Ikol out first, and then he crawled out of his hiding spot in a half-crouch, straightening when he got free. His legs and neck were cramped. Ikol had taken to the sky already and Loki looked around.

"I think he's gone!"

"Not so fast, godling," came a low, dark snarl.

The man landed in front of Loki, dropping from a tree above, fiery trident pointed at Loki's throat. Loki shrank back against the rocks, hands flat at his sides.

"Look," Loki said. "I don't know you. I'm sure we can figure something out, though. I just don't think clearly when weaponry is pointed at me. Especially when it's on fire."

The man jabbed at him and Loki jerked his head to the side just in time.

"I know you're behind this," the man said, his voice menacing. "I followed you here."

Ikol screamed and divebombed the man but the man threw up a hand, shooting a fireball at the magpie, who dove out of the way. The trident never moved from where it had pinned Loki against the mountainside.

"Owning up now or later is what decides if you get first- or second-degree burns," the man continued. "The game's up. My sources led me to your sorry magical ass."

"I don't think you can call made-up conspiracy theories your sources," Loki said, cursing himself for never keeping his mouth shut. If he died and someone brought him back again— though who would without Thor there—the next Loki would have to pay for his smart mouth too. Like he was paying for Past Loki's choices.

"Make a decision, lordling," the man said, pressing the trident against Loki. The skin on his throat was starting to burn. Sweat dribbled down his forehead, stinging his eyes. He *did* need to make a decision. And fast. He just wasn't going to make the ones that this man wanted him to make.

"I wish I could, but I'm currently sprinting in the other direction, while this little illusion is swallowing all of your attention," Loki said. "I'm sorry we couldn't chat longer but I really encourage you to make an appointment next time. My schedule's so busy and if it's not on my calendar, it doesn't exist. You know how it is."

The man twisted, dropping the trident and searching for the apparition of Loki running in the other direction. But *now* Loki was running. *Now* he was sprinting. He ducked under the man's arm, giving him a little shove to send him off balance. The man grunted and Loki took off, running faster than he had when he was first being chased. His lungs burned but it was better than *him* burning, so he didn't care.

Behind him, the man swore.

"The 'quick, look behind you' trick?" Ikol cawed, catching up with him.

"It's a classic for a reason!" Loki panted. "Tried and true! Ol' reliable."

And then he was flying right off the mountain path. The searing heat of the explosion blew past him, and he was falling in slow motion. He slammed into the ground, tumbling head over heels right down the side of the mountain. Pain lanced through his body. Sound rushed into him: his grunts of pain, the sound of rocks loosed from the side of the mountain, tree branches that cracked and rustled as they gave way to his body. And then sound rushed out, leaving just a dull ringing in his ears as he came to a stop.

Everything *hurt*.

He rolled onto his back, gasping for air. Every breath felt like he was being stabbed between the ribs.

The man walked down toward him, through the path that Loki had cleared, taking long, easy strides. His fist gripped the trident wrapped in fire.

"Quit the act," he said firmly to Loki. "Stop acting like a kid."

"It's not an act," Loki gasped. He squeezed his eyes shut. He really didn't know how to get to his feet right now. Could he break all the bones in his body? How long would it take him to heal? "I can't do magic. I don't know what you're talking about. I haven't done *anything*."

This was not strictly true, but he definitely knew he hadn't done anything to this man.

"I'm Daimon Hellstrom. My father is the prince of lies. You don't get to feed me a line."

Loki wanted to say that he was going to challenge Hellstrom's father for the crown of lies, but his survival instinct kicked in and he refrained.

"I really can't do magic. I swear. Don't you think I would have fought back if I *could* do magic?"

"He can't," came a clear, steady, flat voice.

Loki could have wept in relief.

Leah walked up behind Hellstrom, her face serene but eyes annoyed. "It'd be easier if he could do magic but he's right. He's worthless."

Loki had never been so thrilled to be called worthless in his entire life. He couldn't help but grin.

Hellstrom bellowed and thrust the trident toward her. Fire burst from the three spikes, twisting and plaiting itself into a braid of fire that shot toward Leah. Leah stepped around him easily, planting herself between Hellstrom and Loki, and lifted her hand casually, like she was greeting an old friend.

Green fire burst up—a shield to protect her and Loki. The fire struck the shield and dissipated, crackling as it was absorbed by the shield.

"I, however, can do magic," she said simply.

"You are the best, Leah," Loki babbled with relief, slumping to the ground. "Like in all of the Nine Realms, the *best*. We should give you a medal or something. A trophy. An awards ceremony. How'd you know I was here?"

"The lamp in your room moved. I decided to investigate."

Through the pain in his body, Loki rolled over and sat up a bit, resting on his hands. "You *watch* my room?"

He didn't know if he was creeped out or a little intrigued.

"I don't sleep," Leah said.

"That's not what I asked."

"You owe my mistress," Leah retorted. "I have to be sure you will not renege."

"That's a seven-point Scrabble word," Loki said. "Renege. I am not going to renege any more than you're going to sleep."

Leah gave him a withering look. Loki was starting to wonder if withering looks were just Leah's way of showing affection. She was still holding the shield up between him and Hellstrom casually, like she could do this all night if she had to.

"I don't really care *why* you can't sleep—" Loki began.

"I watch over the dead. I have responsibilities," Leah interrupted him.

"Okay but it sounds like you're watching over me. I gave you my phone! You have access to the internet! You could be doing anything all night!"

"The internet is full of idiots," Leah said.

"...I'm on the internet!"

"Yes, and you're one of the idiots."

Hellstrom was just standing there, watching them with his mouth dropped open. He lowered his trident and the fire unwound from the weapon, withdrawing into his hands and arms.

"I didn't believe you two were kids, but now I do."

Cautiously, Leah lowered her shield. Never letting her eyes leave Hellstrom, she reached behind her with a hand. Loki grasped it, his gloved hand around her pale one, and she hauled him to his feet. She was stronger than she looked. He supposed she had to be, to be Hela's handmaiden.

"People are dying in their own nightmares," Hellstrom said. "My sources say you're involved."

"If your sources are on the internet," Loki said, "you heard what Leah said about people on the internet."

Hellstrom scowled. "I would not use the internet for sources."

"Then your other sources are wrong. Why would I be involved in that?" Loki asked. "Besides, if I was killing someone in nightmares, why would I give myself nightmares? Seems like I'd be defeating the purpose. Undermining myself."

"You're having nightmares?" Hellstrom looked surprised.

"That's why I'm up here," Loki said, avoiding Leah's curious gaze. "I had a nightmare about Thor and the Serpent. I thought coming up here would help me figure out why I keep having this dream."

"It sounds like the problems are linked," Leah mused. "It seems unlikely that you'd have nightmares *and* for Hellstrom to be chasing down nightmares at the same time."

Loki rubbed at his sore ribs. "We could team up."

"Team up?" Hellstrom looked at him blankly.

"If they're connected, we should work together. Like a team!"

Hellstrom and Leah both scowled. Hellstrom pointed and Leah's hands came up slightly, ready to defend.

"We don't know the issues are connected," he said.

Leah said, "Who were your sources?"

Hellstrom stared at her and then looked away, chewing on his lower lip. He was trying to decide if he could trust them, Loki realized. Then Hellstrom looked back at her. "Bones."

Leah lifted a single arched eyebrow. "Seems pretty definitive that the issues are connected, then. I hate to say it, but Loki's right. We should team up."

"Teamwork makes the dream work," said Loki. "There's a nightmare joke in here somewhere but I'm still working on it. Give me a moment."

"If we work together," Hellstrom said, "then you're my sidekick, at *best.*"

"Dying to further your own personal story arc? Love it. Heroic without all the trauma," Loki said. He tried not to think about the nightmare that brought him here, to the mountain where his brother died. It might be a little late to avoid all the trauma.

"I do too," Leah said dryly.

"You have somewhere we can talk?" Hellstrom asked. "We need to figure out where the overlap is."

"I know a great cave," Loki said, grinning.

Leah sighed deeply.

TWENTY-NINE

HELLSTROM WAS big. Bigger than Loki and Leah by far, and he made the cave seem small. He blocked out half the fire blazing in the hearth, and he didn't fit in the chair that Loki had filched and dragged up the road for Leah. He sat on the floor, cross-legged, his coat folded neatly next to him, drinking from a mug of something Leah had concocted. He looked like a pirate trying to pretend to be civilized, or a grown man playing tea-party.

But mostly Loki didn't like the way Leah couldn't stop staring at Hellstrom's chest. Bare. Broad. Scarred. She kept blushing as she chatted with him idly about Poland and wherever else he'd been. *Idle chatter*. From *Leah*.

Loki seethed. Not even at Hellstrom. At himself. For jealousy. How did Hellstrom do it? How did he make Leah *talkative*? Surely this was a teachable skill.

Leah wasn't the only one fawning over Hellstrom. They'd barely made it in the cave entrance when Thori had bounded up to Hellstrom.

Loki had started to make his apologies for Thori's language—

but the Hell-puppy did not curse at Hellstrom or wish death upon him. Instead the pup had looked up at him with baleful eyes that looked exactly like one of those viral videos on Loki's phone and said, "Master? Will you be my master?"

Everything Loki sought attention from seemed desperate to get it from Hellstrom instead.

"My old man's one of the Satans," Hellstrom was explaining.

"Why don't you stay in a Hell?" Leah wanted to know. "What brought you up here?"

"I tried the Hell thing," Hellstrom said with a shrug. "It just seemed like I was going to get lost in the shuffle. I'd just be another devil. It was the kind of job that really seemed like it could drag you down. I gave up my throne in Hell, gave it back to my dad, and he gave me a stretch of land. Something of my own."

"A respite," Leah said.

"A prison."

Loki snorted.

Both of them shot him a look and he hid his face behind his mug.

"I'm an exorcist," Hellstrom said. "When I find the devils that make people's lives hell, I send them back to *my* hell. Not some nice little spot where they've got friends in low places. This isn't a vacation. I can really make them suffer in my hell."

"Master," whimpered Thori. "Take me there."

Hellstrom rubbed the top of the puppy's head. "It's starting to work, though. The idea of being a victim is enough to keep some devils in line."

"You're so bad you're good," Loki said without thinking.

He looked up to find Leah and Hellstrom staring at him. Leah's face was pinched in a frown, but Hellstrom looked pleased. "Something like that."

Loki wouldn't call him aspirational, but in a different set of circumstances, maybe Hellstrom could have been a kind of mentor for him. A life coach. How to lean so far into your own nature that you nurture yourself into a better self.

BUT THIS ISN'T THAT STORY. HELLSTROM WAS NO LIFE COACH AND IF HE WAS, HE WOULDN'T HAVE THE PATIENCE FOR LOKI.

"So these sleepers," Loki said, turning over the question that he'd been thinking about the whole walk back to the cave. "They were all dreaming of the Serpent?"

"Or the Serpent War. And I've been trying to exorcise it."

"Successfully?" Leah asked, setting down her cup.

"Kinda." Hellstrom frowned, looking up at the ceiling and absentmindedly scratching Thori's ears. The puppy's hind leg thumped joyfully. "I've been able to exorcise this dark energy. It's not sentient. Not exactly."

The sentence, *it's not sentient, exactly*, was never reassuring. Never in the history of the Nine Realms did that sentence ever lead somewhere good.

"It's nasty. I've been quarantining it. That's the best I can do." Hellstrom shook his head. "I've never seen anything like it, to be honest."

Loki hesitated, and then scooted closer to Hellstrom. "What if that's what's in me? Maybe you can check."

"Loki," warned Leah.

Hellstrom nodded. "I can try. It'll give us some answers."

Leah looked apprehensive as Hellstrom settled on his knees in front of Loki, pressing his palms on either side of Loki's head. Loki closed his eyes. It felt strange. He hadn't hugged or touched many people since Thor died. And he thought that Thor might have been the last person to hug him at all. Hellstrom's touch reminded him of Thor. It was warm and comforting, even though the man was a devil (literally) and an exorcist, looking for something demonic and terrible inside of Loki's head.

Then there came heat and pressure, like Hellstrom was pushing his palms together, squeezing Loki's head out between his hands. Light exploded behind Loki's eyes but he gritted his teeth, pressed his fists into his legs, and made himself stay still.

He didn't want that nightmare. Not again. And if Hellstrom could take it away from him…

Abruptly, Hellstrom pulled his hands away and the pressure receded, leaving a dull ache in its place. Loki opened his eyes. Hellstrom was massaging his own hands, like the effort had hurt.

"There's definitely something dark and wicked in there. I just can't move it."

"Is it a brain?" Leah asked.

The corner of Hellstrom's mouth twitched. "No."

Leah looked away from Loki, disinterested. "Figures."

"So that's it?" Loki scrambled to his feet. "We're just going to leave it in me? Dark and wicked?"

"He's not a brain surgeon," said Leah. "What do you want him to do?"

"Well," Hellstrom said, sounding wary. "There is something else we could try. It's risky."

"I like risk," Loki said, feeling argumentative.

"If things go wrong," Hellstrom said, turning to Leah, "I'll need you to pull us both out."

Leah pushed up her sleeves. "I can do that."

Loki had a sneaking suspicion that if things went wrong, she'd save Hellstrom first.

Hellstrom dug around in his coat pockets and pulled out a small bundle of herbs that he untied and spread out. Leah bent over, watching him work. Loki had no interest in herbs, beyond wanting them to work for the ritual, but he watched anyways. He reached for Thori, but the puppy snarled, "Rip your spleen out and chew it up," so he sat back on his heels and just watched.

Ikol hopped up next to him. "Are you sure?"

"About the ritual? Better than nothing," Loki said, watching Hellstrom measure and spoon various herbs into a pot. It smelled like sulfur, and like dirty shoes, and like a slow-moving river on a hot summer day.

"That's not true," Ikol said, sounding worried. "Lots of things are worse than nothing. This could be one of them. So what if there's something dark in your head? You can survive nightmares."

Loki wrapped his arms around his legs. "You had to bite me to wake me up."

The magpie spread his wings and rustled his feathers. "True. But you just lost your brother."

Loki remembered what it was like in that dream. The Thor who wasn't Thor. He shuddered. "I couldn't save him in my dreams."

After that, Ikol fell quiet. He probably did not understand— he was a magpie and Past Loki, after all, so his understanding of these emotional tethers was not what Loki's understanding was— but he didn't leave Loki's side, and even tolerated Loki's nervous stroking of his slick black feathers.

It was a kindness of sorts.

"Loki, are you listening?" Hellstrom asked.

Loki had not been. The devil sighed.

"We can't get separated. That's just trouble. Do you understand?"

"Got it," Loki said. He wiped his sweaty palms off on his trousers and told himself that it was just the heat of the blazing fire in the cave.

Leah stirred the concoction in the pot and ladled it into mugs, handing one to Hellstrom that he passed off to Loki. He took the second mug and peered into it. It looked like brown sludge, and smelled like it too. But this would let Hellstrom into his head. This would make the nightmare go away.

"I'll dig into your subconscious trying to find the root of this dream," Hellstrom explained. "You're at the mercy of dreams, but dreams have their own logic, if you know where to look."

"Oh," Loki said with a frown. "That's the only way?"

"It's the only way," Hellstrom confirmed.

He could not keep living with these nightmares tearing him open from the inside out, but what if Hellstrom found his secrets? Secrets about Surtur and the Destroyer and Volstagg's identity and his role in Thor's death… But who would Hellstrom tell? Who would believe a son of a Satan? An actual devil? Not many people in Asgard ranked Loki highly, but he figured he probably ranked above Hellstrom—even with Asgardians.

"Whatever you do," said Hellstrom, "do not let go of my hand."

"It's time," Leah said.

Hellstrom and Loki lifted the mugs to their mouths and then in unison, began to gulp the disgusting concoction down. It didn't taste like anything at first, but then it burned, acidic and rancid, as it ran down Loki's throat. He coughed and gagged, setting the empty mug down in front of him.

The room swayed—the cave, it wasn't a room, it was a cave—it swayed and tilted. The fire grew and shrank, darkness taking over the edges of Loki's vision. Next to him, he saw Hellstrom bow his red head toward the fire, hands flat on his knees, palms to the ceiling. Like he was praying. The image made Loki want to giggle, but he couldn't. Heaviness pulled at him and he wanted to sink forward to the ground, letting his face hit the dirt. His arms were too heavy to catch him.

Leah murmured, "I'm so tired."

"Samesies," muttered Loki, swaying. Was he swaying or was the room swaying? He couldn't tell. He felt like he was in a hammock in a wind storm.

"I meant of you," Leah said. Her voice was distant now. She seemed far away. A speck of black hair and pale skin and green dress in the distance. He could still pick her out of any crowd.

"Meanie," he said, but there was a smile on his face when the deep sleep swept up and took him.

A hand reached toward him in the dark. He remembered Hellstrom said to take his hand. Not to let go or there'd be trouble. A low, melodic voice whispered, "*I will show you fear, Loki.*"

He took the hand.

THIRTY

THE WORLD twisted around and spun from nothingness into a flat prairie, grasslands as far as he could see, unfamiliar and vast. The hand he held stretched into an arm that stretched into the darkness beyond, and suddenly the tautness, the pressure that Loki had assumed was Hellstrom waiting to step through fell away.

Hellstrom's grip around Loki's hand loosened, and then dropped, heavy, and Loki glanced down just in time to see the arm swing from nothingness to point toward the ground, severed at the shoulder. He screamed, dropping the hand. It hit the ground with a thud, and immediately began to disintegrate. And crawl. Thousands of beetles, black and glossy, swarmed upwards. Loki swatted at them as they covered his arms, neck, face. Their legs scrabbled over his skin and he couldn't breathe. He wanted to scream but the beetles were at his lips, their wings fluttering against his skin as they tried to bore into his mouth.

He slapped at his skin, trying to brush them off, stumbling and running. He fell to his knees, gasping for air. The beetles scrambled across his skin, falling to the earth and streaming away from the stones jutting out of the earth around him. They looked like animals fleeing a wildfire.

Shaking, Loki stood up. Hellstrom was nowhere to be found. Had the beetles consumed him? Or had this been an elaborate plot by Hellstrom to trap Loki in a nightmare?

The stone was polished, marble, and Loki walked around to the other side, wondering if it had directions. He stood on a fresh mound of dirt, his feet sinking into the earth a bit. He started to shake as he read the stone. A tombstone.

Loki's Doing.

He fell to his knees, fingers digging into the dirt. He began to shovel it away. Thor? Was Thor here? Was he too late?

"No, no, no," he whispered, his breath coming in short sharp jabs as he frantically dug through the earth.

"All dead. All because of you," said a voice that Loki knew, and didn't know.

Loki scrambled to his feet, leaving dirty handprints on the tombstone. Behind him, the Thor of his nightmares, his face skeletal, like he'd been turned into the Dísir, loomed. Ten times larger than Loki ever remembered him being. Fires bloomed like blossoms. Pyres, as far as the eye could see. From the fire rose faces, not as they were before the war but in their last moments before death, wide-eyed and afraid, screaming and sobbing, clutching each other, and alone. So alone.

The pyres kept blooming until they didn't just stretch beyond Nightmare Thor's face, but surrounded Loki, closing off the paths, and pressing in on him. He could feel the heat of the flames scorching his skin, and the screams suffocated him.

"They are dead because of me. Because I let you live. Because I brought you back," shouted Nightmare Thor over the din.

"No," whispered Loki, sick to his stomach. "Not your fault." His, yes, but not Thor's. It could never be Thor's fault.

Nightmare Thor bared his teeth, eyes glowing like Hellstrom's. "I made mistakes. But this one is easily rectified, brother." He advanced toward Loki and out of thin air, Mjolnir appeared in his hands, cracked through the center, glowing orange and black.

"All you've ever done," Thor thundered, "is a trick. Whatever you're up to stops here. I never *trusted* you. I only loved you."

Tears ran down Loki's face. And he did not run. "I know. I know."

And it was true, wasn't it? Thor hadn't trusted Loki. He shouldn't have. Loki wasn't trustworthy. He'd connived for Thor's death. He'd plotted and planned and moved pieces on the chessboard. He'd used Thor's own words, Thor's own assurance that he'd do what Loki thought needed to be done too, as a shield. And he'd brought down so many others with him. Volstagg lived with that guilt too. Same with Tyr and Leah. He had tricked the Dísir, who would live unhappily with Mephisto. He had given Surtur Dark Asgard instead of the Asgard promised. He'd done terrible things.

"I only let you live because I was weak," Thor said, stepping closer. Each step was an earthquake under Loki's feet. "The dead don't have time for weakness, Loki. My weakness died when I did."

Loki fell to his knees again, hands pressed into the soft soil. *Loki's Doing.* He closed his eyes, letting the tears trickle to his chin and then fall to the earth. His brother was only good. Thor had never known how to be wicked or evil or villainous. He was who he was, and so was Loki.

"No," Loki whispered, hands curling around fistfuls of dirt. "No. That's not true." He looked up, gritting his teeth. "It's not true. I am not afraid. I am not a villain." He climbed to his feet and squared his shoulders. "I am not afraid of dying, brother. There are worse things than dying. If you're going to do it, do it. Make it quick."

The earth beneath Loki's feet trembled and the soft, upturned earth gave way. Loki fell, swallowed into a sinkhole, Nightmare Thor's face disappearing from view. Loki hit a river with a splash.

The river tasted like the herbal sludge he'd swallowed back in the cave with Leah and Hellstrom. Had that been real? Where was the cave? He didn't know.

Debris bumped against him and he clawed for purchase on the side of a metal ship that looked as if it'd crashed in this brackish water. He clung to it, trying to catch his breath. He couldn't climb the metal ship—he kept sliding down. He would have to let go eventually and let the river take him downstream.

"You were our leader," hissed a voice. Claws emerged next to him. The Dísir and their haunted, ghoulish faces appeared in the water. They drew their claws down his legs, digging into his ankles that hung below the water's surface. "You betrayed us. We trusted you and you led us to Hell."

You shouldn't have trusted me, Loki wanted to say. But all he could say was, "I'll make it right. Please. I can make it right."

"Promises, promises," jeered the Dísir.

"I'll save everyone," Loki cried out to them. "Please."

He didn't know who he was begging. He didn't think it mattered.

Kara laughed. "Look at you. You can't even save yourself. How can you save anyone else? Just let go, Loki. Join us. Damnation's lovely this time of year."

She sank her teeth into his calf muscle.

He screamed.

"Loki!" shouted a voice. A different voice. Not Dísir. Not Nightmare Thor. Someone else, calling for him from a distance, an echo reverberating through a tunnel.

He looked up at the sky, where the ship disappeared into bright white light that parted in a halo around someone familiar. Black hair. Pale skin. Green dress.

"Leah!" he shouted back. He wanted to warn her. To save herself. Get away. To not get pulled into the quagmire of his mistakes. "What are you—?"

"Saving you," she said. "Obviously."

She reached down and though she seemed impossibly small and far away, her arm stretched and stretched until she found him. He struggled, leg burning from where Kara had bit him, and reached back for her. Just before their fingers brushed, he recoiled. Would her hand turn to beetles too? What if this was a trick?

"Take my hand," Leah said impatiently. "Hellstrom lost the connection but you and I have a stronger bond."

He felt the words even though she didn't say them. *I trust you.*

He wrapped his hand around hers, felt the strength of her hold on him. "I thought that—"

"There's a powerful force at work in here," she said grimly, pulling him up into the sky. Or down the tunnel. Or close to her. He couldn't be sure. She'd seemed a mile away, but now the break in the sky rushed around him, shortening the space around them. She was far, and then, impossibly, she was right next to him. "We've got to get to the heart of your subconscious quickly."

He hadn't wanted Hellstrom in his subconscious, but he found he didn't mind the idea of Leah there. She already knew so much. What more damage could he do to how she thought of him?

"How do I do that?" he asked.

"Close your eyes," she said.

"Are you going to kiss me?" he asked, only half-joking. He had to break the tension. He had to find some opening in his heart that did not feel so afraid. Maybe she *would* kiss him.

She squeezed his hand so hard he yelped. "We do not have much time."

Later, he'd think, *that wasn't a no.*

But right then, he just closed his eyes and held tight to her hand.

They were spinning together, a gravitational pull hauling at them, but they held tight and refused to be pulled apart. The harder the forces tried to pull them apart, the harder Loki clung to Leah's hand. He was afraid he'd break her bones, but she didn't let go of him either. She didn't loosen her grip. She didn't shake him off. She held on tight as the world—universe—realms—tried to spin them apart.

And then, like it'd never happened at all, the spinning stopped. Their feet were still planted on the ground. He didn't dare open his eyes but he didn't feel dizzy. It was as if they'd won a battle he didn't know they were fighting.

"Good," Leah whispered. "Good job, Loki. You can open your eyes now."

THIRTY-ONE

LOKI AND Leah stood hand in hand on a bridge made of crackling brown lightning. It pulsed like it had its own heartbeat and stretched out into black oblivion. Below them, an abyss, and in front of them an abyss. The bridge was only a few feet wider than Loki and Leah standing side by side, and he wondered what would happen if he fell off, or if he was pushed off.

"What *is* this?"

"Your subconscious," Leah said, tugging him forward. They picked their way through the brown crackling lightning pulsing beneath their feet. It felt alive. It was not a smooth bridge like the Bifrost or anything else Loki had ever seen: it felt like tree roots— an overgrown path that climbed and slid along twisted fragments of Loki's mind.

"This has to be the source," Leah explained to him. "All these beams of light are feeding into your nightmares. You're a fascinating boy, Loki."

"Thank you. I'm sorry I couldn't make it more visually appealing," he said, huffing a bit as they climbed the bridge toward the black abyss. "I'm still working on my interior decorating skills."

"I know," Leah said, sounding like she wasn't winded at all. "Once we're at the top of the bridge, this spell should remove it from you."

She turned on top of a higher root of light and offered her hand to him. He took it and let her haul him up. The lightning heated up beneath his hands and he flinched at the burns on his palms. Leah looked unbothered.

"Thanks, B.F.F.," he said to her, brushing his hands off on his stomach. "You're the best."

Leah turned, surveying the distance they'd left to cover. "Of course. That's what B.F.F.s are for."

Her back was still turned to him, so Leah did not see Loki freeze. His motions slowed and he studied the back of her head, a frown on his face. Then he stepped toward her, put a hand on either side of her head and twisted, like he was unscrewing a large jar, and her head popped free of her neck. Her body fell off the brown bridge, right into the abyss. Sparks flew, catching on her dress, and she caught fire, turning white and brown and yellow as she spun into nothingness. He held her head in front of him.

His arms shook with the adrenaline. What if he hadn't been right? But he knew he had been. Even in a dream, Leah wouldn't be nice to him.

The Not-Leah head in his hands was hollow on the inside, like a helmet, with sunken holes for eyes. His gut told him what to do. It felt weird, but it felt too right to ignore.

He pulled the Not-Leah head over his own and in a muffled voice, he said to no one in particular, "Let's see what's going on inside here."

NIGHTMARE STOOD in a misty wood, his eyes glowing in the dim light. He approached the scrying pool in the grove. He liked the solitary nature of his work. He liked knowing that he alone among the fear-lords knew his worth, knew his potential, and was willing to take the steps toward seeing that future come to pass.

The Serpent was dead. Fallen in a foolish attempt to usurp the fear-lord throne. Still, Nightmare could appreciate what he'd accomplished. When the Serpent died, his harvested fear energies hadn't gone with him. They had washed across the world, sliding into minds and bodies unsuspecting. Nightmare knew the power in that energy once it was amassed. Fragmented across many people, it was nearly useless. But if he could harvest it, if he could consume it… he'd be unstoppable.

Fear-stuff gathered part to part, like to like, liquid slipping across a surface to swallow a droplet. Fear-stuff called to Nightmare as it gathered within people, clotting and sticking to the insides of minds and subconsciousness. Within people, there was no smooth surface to glide across—the fear-stuff stuck, gummy and tacky. Nightmare wanted a device, a tool, to scrape the fear-stuff from inside minds, like cleaning old caulk from a bathroom wall. He didn't care about the damage he'd do to the surface beneath, so long as it freed up the fear-stuff and channeled it into himself.

Nightmare was greedy and ambitious. He was also prone to dramatics and theatrics. He might have worked in stealth, but he didn't intend to stay in the shadows and hide his deceit and ambition from his siblings.

He snapped his fingers. "A crown."

No one heard him, of course. If words are spoken in a forest of fear, no one hears them. But still, Nightmare grinned at his own cleverness. Subtext was after all the greater part of dreams. He'd forge the crown of raw fear-stuff, siphoning dread into himself, and it'd make him more powerful than any fear lord in history.

The Serpent had dreamed, but not big enough.

Nightmare would not make that mistake.

He scraped fear-stuff from the afflicted dreamers, staying one step ahead of Hellstrom and delighting in the chase. It was a hunt, a puzzle and a game to find people Hellstrom hadn't found yet.

But it was a coup to find Loki. Loki sleeping and dreaming, full of more fear-stuff than any other dreamer Nightmare had found.

170 But it was hidden deep in the boy's subconscious. Nightmare couldn't just reach into the little god's mind and siphon off the stuff at the cost of his life. He needed to trick the boy into showing him to the heart of his subconscious, letting him past all the guards and gates of his mind...

He was almost there. Almost there.

Then, as if someone was narrating his life from the outside, Nightmare heard another voice in his head. A curious, cheerful voice.

"You're not Leah."

Ripped away from something he could almost taste.

Nightmare grasped at his head, leaning over the scrying pool. He fell to his knees. *Get out of my head*, he screamed. But he should have known that certain gods did not take well to direct orders.

He shoved at the sensation and voice in his head. The world wrenched away from him and he was no longer in the misty grove, standing at the scrying pool, but instead on a path made of knotted tree roots sparking with light.

He staggered to his feet. Loki stood a few feet away from him, the head of Leah disintegrating in his hands into dust that swirled and moved, like birds bursting from a bush into the sky.

"You trespassed against me. Me! The Lord of Dreams," Nightmare snarled, advancing toward Loki. "How dare you, boy!"

"Seems bold to call it trespassing when we're *in my head*," Loki pointed out, his tone infuriatingly calm.

"Your head is my domain," Nightmare said. "You cannot deny me my own kingdom."

"Can, will, did," Loki said. He grinned. And then he shouted over his shoulder, "Any time now, Leah!"

Nightmare screamed as he was wrenched free from Loki's mind.

All because Loki.

Woke.

Up.

THIRTY-TWO

LOKI SAT upright, groaning as he wrapped his hand around the needle and syringe that Leah had plunged deep into his chest, sliding between his ribs and his sternum.

"Rude," he muttered.

Leah sniffed, but Loki didn't miss the look of relief on her face as she sat back on her heels. She hadn't been positive it'd work. She didn't usually let things slip like that.

Leah played things close to her chest, mostly because of who her mistress was.

Loki sat for a moment, relishing the sight of Leah in a moment of vulnerability. If she hadn't wanted him to see it, he doubted he would. Even though he'd caught the Not-Leah in the dream by her niceness, he didn't think the B.F.F. status was as false as Not-Leah. Even if Leah wasn't ready to admit it aloud.

The cave seemed small, confined after being in his own subconscious. The vastness of that space—the emptiness, the loneliness—had startled him. He'd been tripped up by the tree roots of fear-stuff but distracted by the immense cavern inside of him. Did everyone have a subconscious like that? Was Leah's like that?

The cave felt stuffy by comparison. The smoke from the fire curled around the low ceiling before drifting out into the night air. Everything smelled like cinders and ash. The chairs he'd brought down here for Leah seemed tired and weary, like they belonged in the trash where he'd found them. It seemed insulting to have asked her to stay in this dark, damp cave with its smoky air and creaking, broken furniture.

Hellstrom paced by the mouth of the cave, his jacket flipping behind him to reveal more of his bare torso as he strode back and forth. Thori followed in his footsteps, nipping at his heels and trying to hang onto the back of Hellstrom's coat tails.

"What's his deal?" Loki muttered to Leah, yanking out the needle. He tossed it to the side. Leah sighed as she picked it up and recapped it.

"He thinks it's Nightmare," she replied, keeping her voice low.

His hands were shaking. He shook them out, trying to stop the trembling. Then Leah's words registered. Loki blinked. "How did he know?"

"So it's true?" Leah sounded surprised.

"Yes, but—"

"Oh that makes this so much messier than I thought it'd be," Leah said, frowning down at the needle in her hand.

"Focus, Leah," Loki commanded. He ignored the death look that Leah shot him. "How did he know?"

Leah looked like she wanted to be anywhere but there. "When he was wrenched away from you, he was dropped into a crowd of people who were just shouting at each other."

Loki narrowed his eyes. "What aren't you telling me, Leah? What were they shouting?"

"Just… random one-liners. Some guy just yelled, 'First!' over and over again. Sentences that began with, 'what about' and 'convenient to ignore'. Someone tried to sell him currency with weird names. Someone else kept pitching his podcast," Leah said. "It took him a while to realize that he was in a crowd that was just shouting out things from the comments section on that internet you love so much."

Relief made his legs shake harder but Loki exhaled a long breath. It could have been so much worse, but it wasn't. "He was dropped *into the comments section?*"

Leah looked increasingly miserable. "Yes."

Despite himself, despite what he went through and the dull pounding ache in his head, Loki couldn't help but smile at where this was going. "And he knew who was causing this, because...? Just say it, Leah."

She looked like she'd rather hurl herself off a cliff. She sighed heavily, like she knew what was coming. "He said that it was a total nightmare."

Loki lifted his head back, closing his eyes and smiling. It felt as gratifying as he thought it would. "That is the most beautiful pun in all the realms and I can't believe I got you to say it."

"You're going to be incorrigible now," Leah muttered.

He winked at her. "Was I not before?" He called up to Hellstrom, "So, you going to help us face Nightmare or what?"

Hellstrom stalked down the path into the cave and back to the fire, the dilapidated furniture, Leah, and Loki. Loki reached out to scritch Thori's head but the puppy snarled at him and followed after Hellstrom instead.

"Tell me what you saw," Hellstrom said.

"Jumping right into it," Loki observed. "No, 'Hey Loki, sorry we got separated after I told you that would be real bad,' or 'How was the trip?'"

Hellstrom stared at him and Loki quickly realized that Hellstrom might make funny puns that were hilarious to make Leah repeat, but he wasn't inherently funny and he did not think Loki was funny.

"Okay, fine." Loki sat back down again. "This Nightmare guy is very territorial, it turns out. He says that there's fear-stuff from the Serpent left everywhere. He wants to siphon it into *his* head but instead, a lot of it's going into my head. He can see the traces—oh boy, I'm getting giddy. Do you know what this means?"

"He's even more excitable than usual," Leah said, picking up the syringe. "What was in this?"

"Pure adrenaline. Enough to kill a rhino." Hellstrom's voice was flat and stern.

"I am not a rhino and I resent the accusation," Loki said, shaking his finger in Hellstrom's face.

Hellstrom batted Loki away. "Calm down, Loki."

"I *am* calm," Loki said, rubbing his palms together. "Nightmare's harvesting the fear-stuff. He wants to turn it into a weapon. Why do they *always want to turn it into a weapon*? Why is no one ever like, 'oooh, this shiny new mineral or energy source, let's build a rollercoaster'?"

"Loki," Leah said warningly.

Loki waved his hands, dismissing her tone. "Okay. I know. Focus. There's oodles of this fear-stuff in my head, and it's sort of pouring in there from people all over the world."

"The other sleepers," Hellstrom realized aloud.

"Yes," Loki agreed, nodding vigorously. "Fear-stuff calls to fear-stuff. Since I have a lot of it, the fear-stuff is coming here. Nightmare's going after the other sleepers. And as long as I don't go to sleep, he can't get my fear-stuff. Never thought I'd say this but it sounds like I should hold onto my fear-stuff. Hoard it, even. The problem is that when he's going after the other sleepers, he's kind of messy about it. He doesn't care if it wakes them or kills them when he steals their fear-stuff."

"And that's why it's impossible to keep up with him," Hellstrom said, his voice grim. "He's trying to get to them before their fear-stuff gets to you."

"Precisely. Which is why we've got to act fast," Loki said, getting to his feet. "Like we should be leaving right now."

"Loki," Leah said, her voice somber. "Are we just supposed to skate past this part where you said that having a chunk of fear-stuff in their head is killing people and you have the biggest chunk of the fear-stuff? Doesn't that mean—"

"You are so *depressing*, Leah. Can we worry about that later?"

Loki cut her off. "That's a future Loki problem, not a current Loki problem."

Leah looked doubtful, but she didn't push the subject.

Even through the adrenaline coursing through his body, Loki shivered. This was all his fault. He'd orchestrated the downfall of the Serpent and then what had he done? Nothing. Sat about feeling sorry for himself and how his role in the Serpent's death hadn't changed anything for him. And meanwhile, the Serpent might be gone—but the effects he had on the realms remained. Fear-stuff, from the Serpent, in all these people's heads. If the fear-stuff didn't kill the sleepers, then Nightmare would.

And Nightmare would kill him, if the fear-stuff didn't first.

Loki raked his fingers through his hair and turned his hands into fists, pulling hard at his scalp. Right. He wasn't worrying about that later. He was worrying about that now. But they didn't have time to waste. More lives than his were at stake.

THIRTY-THREE

IKOL WAS none too pleased to be left in charge of Thori while Loki gallivanted around Midgard waking the trapped sleepers. Hadn't he shown his worth when he'd woken Loki from slumber where Nightmare had nearly gotten him?

Needless to say, the magpie was anxiety personified. He needed to be with Loki right now, to make sure the little trickster god didn't mess everything up. If Loki fell asleep... well, the fear clot in his head would get him, Loki and all the sleepers would die, and Nightmare would win. But worse, the Serpent would win. All that work, all the dealing and scheming, the sacrifices, Thor's death... all for naught. A waste of time and cleverness. The Serpent might not be the one to reap the fruits of his labors, but he'd have the last laugh in the beyond.

The plan was simple. Hellstrom, Leah, and Loki would try to wake as many sleepers as possible before Nightmare reached them, or before the fear-stuff in their heads siphoned off into Loki's head.

The thing is, plans that look simple never are. Plans that look linear always end up looking like the flight patterns of panicked parakeets.

"I THINK we should call ourselves the Wakers," Loki said, jogging along the path of Hellstrom's magic into their latest sleeper's subconscious. He could see the sleeper at the end, a middle-aged man twisting and turning on a bed, gasping like he was starved for air, his arms strapped down. Next to Loki, walking with long and purposeful strides—under few circumstances did Leah *jog*—his reluctant B.F.F. shook her head.

"Just do your job," she warned him.

"We need a name."

"Why are you so obnoxious?"

"It's distracting me," he said without thinking, and deliberately avoided her gaze because he didn't want to see Leah look at him with sympathy. He'd grown rather accustomed to her scowl and disparaging, disappointed expressions. Pity, sympathy... He didn't want those from her.

But she didn't argue with him about the name after that.

"Hey!" Loki reached the man on the bed and loosened the straps on the sleeper's arms. "You gotta wake up!"

"No!" cried the man. "Don't!"

Loki ignored him. He knew that the man wasn't necessarily seeing Loki and Leah as they looked to themselves but rather pieces of whatever nightmare he was experiencing.

"I'm Loki, this is Leah. Ignore her face, she always looks like that."

"*Loki*," Leah scolded.

He hid a grin. That was more like it. Less pity, more scolding. He'd explore why he preferred that later.

Loki tugged at the man's arm, pulling him upright in his bed. "Trust me, this is imperative."

"What?" The man blinked. "I don't understand."

"It's hard to explain," Loki said, leaning backwards against the man's weight until he reluctantly stood on unsteady feet. "You got some bad stuff in your head and the gentleman in green wants to tear it out and turn it into a very powerful hat."

"Bathetic flourishes," Leah muttered.

"Explain that to me later," Loki said in an aside. He turned back to the man and pointed up.

Silhouetted against a night sky, Nightmare, dressed in green like Loki had said, crackled with purple light, grappling in midair with a shirtless Daimon Hellstrom. Nightmare dodged Hellstrom's fiery trident and snapped out his hand, the purple light flying out from his fingertips like arrows splitting in midair. Hellstrom spun his trident, blocking each of the arrows, and they exploded with sparks at the contact.

"The villain is Nightmare," Loki explained, trying to hurry the man down the walkway. "I know it's kind of hard to tell who's the villain up there but trust me, man with the purple lightning, villain. He's the Lord of Dreams. So this is kind of his home turf."

"This is a dream?" the man asked.

"Nightmares, dreams, basically the same thing," Loki said. "We're deep inside your own head. The other guy? That's Hellstrom. Long story but basically he's an exorcist. He's keeping Nightmare at bay and our job is to get you back across this bridge. As fast as possible."

The man was walking like he had lead feet, tripping over the roots of the bridge. He kept twisting to look at the battle happening in the sky of his subconscious. "This is real?"

"It's not *not* real," Leah said helpfully.

Above them, Nightmare cried, "How can you defeat me? I am dreams! Hope itself! Who can stand against that!"

"Propaganda, pure and simple," Loki told the sleeper. "I promise you that Nightmare hopes for nothing but his own power."

"I dunno," Hellstrom shouted back. "But I'm going to try fireballs. Lots and lots of fireballs."

Balls of hellfire rained down like hail in a tornado, setting everything around them ablaze and pummeling Nightmare farther from the man's subconscious.

"Great, that's the signal," Loki said to the man. "Ready to run?

We'll wake you up and take you to Waffle House. Bacon. Runny eggs. It's gonna be great."

"I don't want to wake up," whispered the man. "There's nothing left for me in the real world."

"I know," Loki said quietly. "I get that. I really do. But when things seem inevitable, you have to think that they may *not* be. Even when life seems a bad dream, you can think that it *is* a bad dream and you can wake up. That's what they can't take away from you. You get to choose."

They were almost at the end of the bridge now.

Nightmare screeched above them, "That's *mine!*"

"Okay, Leah!" Loki shouted.

Leah shoved the man the last few steps to firm footing on the other side of the subconscious bridge. The man fell to his knees.

Nightmare reached for them, his purple lightning crackling. Hellstrom chucked a fireball to intercept it.

"Loki!" yelled Hellstrom.

"We're aware, thank you very much!" Loki called back.

"First the Serpent steals my fear routine, and now you are! Norse gods are plagiarists!" yelled Nightmare.

"Been called worse!" Loki shouted.

"Loki," Leah snapped.

He turned just as her hands settled on the man's shoulders. The world spun, turning from dark to light, spinning faster and faster, the dark colors of the man's subconscious falling to the outside, bleeding outward and then disappearing. The spinning slowed, and then they came to a stop.

They stood in the man's hospital room, Leah and Loki side by side with Hellstrom and the man, upright in his hospital bed. All of them were breathing heavily. The curtains were drawn and it smelled like every Midgardian hospital room Loki had ever been in: a disgusting mix of cleaner and human excrement. The sheets were thin and scratchy and the machines next to the man blared alarms that went ignored.

A circle of flame that Hellstrom had placed around this man in Midgard still flickered, burning slowly.

"You promised bacon? Waffle House?" the man said at last, breaking the silence.

"He lied," Leah said. "He does that a lot."

Hellstrom swept his hair off his face with a tired hand. "Nightmare's onto the next sleeper. We have to go."

"Wait," said the man. "What am I supposed to do now?"

"Anything," Loki told him.

Leah tugged at his hand. "We have to go, Loki."

Hellstrom opened a portal gate. "Let's go." He stepped through.

Loki followed, exhausted. He just wanted to sit down, but Hellstrom wasn't going to let that happen. Not while there were still trapped dreamers. And Loki was afraid. Afraid that if he sat down, he wouldn't get up again. He was so tired he felt like he was nodding off as he walked. He tripped over the portal and staggered, barely managing to right himself.

Leah grabbed for his hand. "Loki, are you—"

She trailed off but he knew where she was going.

Loki waved her off. "I'm fine! I'm more worried about leaving Thori. Leaving him with Ikol? Not exactly the best of role models, you know. Never mind the fate of the world. I'm thinking about the fate of the furnishings with those two left to their own devices."

"Loki," Leah said, and the softness in her voice could break him.

He shook his head. "Yes, I know, it looks like I'm dying. I kind of feel like I'm dying. Don't worry. I can hold it together for a while. Just have to avoid falling asleep. And this is a *very* inopportune time for you to start showing concern, Leah."

"It's not concern," she said sharply. "You still have work to do for my mistress, you arrogant—"

Hellstrom stuck his head back through the portal, looking like a disembodied head. "Hey. Stop having a moment. We've got places to be."

Leah scowled and stepped through the portal before Loki. He did feel like death. He felt shaky and weak, and he was afraid that his hands were *actually* trembling. But his voice wasn't hoarse yet and he was still on his feet. He couldn't sit down yet. If he sat down, he'd fall asleep and that'd mean death.

He needed to keep going.

So he did.

THEY SAW a girl in Canada and a kid in Kuala Lumpur, and a mother in Astana and a prisoner in Kyiv and a fugitive in Rio de Janeiro. And each one was the same. Hellstrom did the ritual and they all stepped inside the sleeper's mind. The exorcist battled Nightmare while Leah and Loki raced across a shattered subconscious, found them, and brought them back to firmer ground where Leah could wake them up. They woke the sleepers and left to the next one. One after another, stepping through portals to new worlds and places, to new innocents.

And each encounter tore Loki apart. He kept dragging himself on, though, forcing energy into his limbs. If Thor was here, he wouldn't let anything stand in his way of saving the sleepers.

Exhaustion weighed down his words. He couldn't make his sentences as glib and light and optimistic as he did with the first, or the second one. His sentences slurred. Still, he did not sleep. He knew what would happen if he slept.

Leah gave him more worried looks. Hellstrom glowered more. Loki pretended not to notice.

But he noticed when Leah stopped calling Hellstrom Hellstrom and started calling him Daimon. He made sure to tease her appropriately. He added some third person narration in his head to their own adventures, *Leah, Loki and the Son of Satan save the day*, and laughed. It sounded like a tagline. Or a band name. He wanted to remember to tell Leah about it later.

If he got a later.

It took a few more sleepers for Loki to admit defeat, but he did.

Hellstrom opened the portal after their latest sleeper, and before Leah stepped through, Loki said her name, once, quietly.

When she turned, he was down on one knee. Not proposing, but because he couldn't stand up any more.

She touched his shoulder. "I can't do it. Daimon's exorcism rituals don't work on you."

He expected a quip. Something funny about how the exorcism requires a soul or a subconscious or a robust inner life to work. But none came. Just the light touch of her fingers through his tunic and shirt.

"I know," he said, looking at the floor. Breathing felt hard. His chest felt heavy. "Hellstrom's rituals don't work. But when I was in Nightmare's head, I saw how he performed his."

"That's dangerous," Leah said after a pause.

"Yes," Loki agreed. "Done swiftly, it'll kill. But I think you could do it. I think you could carefully and slowly cut out everything that shouldn't be there and leave everything that keeps me alive. You're detail oriented."

"I can't believe you're asking me for help," Leah said, kneeling next to him.

Loki wiped sweat off his brow. "I know, me either."

"Are you afraid? Of dying?" she asked.

"I didn't think I was," he admitted. "But I am. I don't want to die. I don't want anyone to die. Like, no offense to your mistress, but dying doesn't seem like fun. And the afterlife seems boring, hot, and tedious."

"No offense taken," Leah said.

That was how Loki knew he really looked like death.

"Doing this would risk all the sleepers," Leah said.

"We're not going to save all the sleepers," Loki said. "Playing hero like we have been is risking the sleepers. If we fail once, someone dies. If we get killed, they all die. If I die, they all die. So I think we're pretty much out of options at this point."

Leah chewed on her bottom lip. "We should pull Hellstrom into this."

Not Daimon now, Loki noted in a distant corner of his mind. "No. Leah. Please."

"We have to. He needs to know. He could help—and he's waiting for us," Leah said, looking toward the portal.

Daimon Hellstrom would stop them. He wouldn't get why Loki needed to do this now. And Loki couldn't do it anymore. He couldn't keep fighting. And he saw a path through this nightmare, so to speak, one that Hellstrom wouldn't like. Hellstrom didn't seem like the kind of fellow who was willing to think outside the box or lose a battle to win the war.

"Leah, your mistress ordered you to help me. Do your duty," Loki said, summoning a stern tone he didn't feel internally.

She turned from the portal, her eyes cold and furious.

Loki winced. "Leah, I'm sorry."

She cut him off, her voice ice. "Lie down."

Through the portal, Hellstrom bellowed, "Where are you two? We're ready. Answer me!"

For a brief moment, Loki thought Leah would answer him. But she did not. And Loki sank to the floor, lying on his back at Leah's feet. He felt sleep take him swiftly, as if it'd been waiting for the moment to sweep in, a thief in the night. Heat crackled around his head. His tongue felt thick in his mouth. He wanted to tell Leah *thank you* but he couldn't form the words.

He slipped under.

And then our little godling was at the mercy of Hela's handmaiden.

He had been right, of course. Leah was more than competent at this. Her eyes and fingers were deft as she sorted her magic through the mess of fear-stuff wrapped tightly around Loki's subconscious. She worked like a demolitions expert, sorting out the threads from one another and deciding which to cut and which to keep. She tugged and untied and pulled through. She plaited the ones she untangled so they wouldn't re-tangle. She worked as fast as she could, but without the speed and carelessness of Nightmare. She would not leave Loki for dead.

Behind her, Hellstrom screamed and threatened. Behind her, Hellstrom told her that people were dying because of her. Because of Loki's choice. And she hadn't needed to comply. She could have come up with a way to explain to Hela why she disobeyed. But she'd felt the compulsion of the oath between them, and she'd felt the choice, the split in the path of fate and destiny in the world.

As a rule, Leah did not backtrack. And she would not regret or relitigate this one, now or in the future.

When it was done, she let Loki's lifeforce settle back into his chest.

What was left was in her hands was black as coal, but illuminated with glowing threads of blue, like radioactive diamond bedazzling black stone.

"It's out," she murmured.

Loki woke with a gasp. His hands flew to his chest and she watched him sit up, breathing freely in a way he hadn't been able to do for a long time.

"It's so small," Leah admitted. "It looked so tremendous, so immense inside of you I thought that it'd be impossible at points. It's so light and yet, it feels so heavy."

Loki didn't want to look at it. "It's made of pure fear. There's a lot of fear and sadness in the world that can't be measured, but you can feel it in that."

Leah looked a little in awe with what she held in her hands. She held it up. "Now to quarantine it in Daimon's hell…"

"Wait," Loki interrupted. He scrambled to his feet, hand outstretched. "Hold on. Can you do a communication rite for me?"

THIRTY-FOUR

COMMUNICATION RITES worked a lot like Midgardian phones, and a little less well than Stark technology. There was a lot more crackling and interference than Loki expected, but it did the trick. He could see Nightmare and Hellstrom battling it out in someone's head, and this time, Hellstrom was losing. The sleeper wasn't waking. Loki and Leah weren't there to help. And the power difference between the Lord of Dreams and the Son of Satan loomed. Nightmare was growing more powerful.

"Hey!" Loki shouted to Nightmare. "Gotta minute? Need to chat."

"Busy, trickster," snarled Nightmare. "I will not be distracted."

Hellstrom heard Loki and swore with a collection of words that Loki hadn't heard strung together in all his adventures on the internet. It was almost impressive.

"I've got a proposition!" Loki shouted.

"You do not need to shout," Leah chided him. "He could hear you if you whispered."

"I don't feel like whispering though," Loki said.

Nightmare went on his usual spiel, which Loki was finding quite boring at this point.

"I am Nightmare, Lord of Dreams, and I am pursuing a dream—"

"Same," said Hellstrom, grunting as he dodged Nightmare's fire. "Thinking about crushing a little godling to death."

"You two can bond about that shared dream later," Loki replied. "Nightmare, I'm not trying to distract you. I've harvested all the fear-stuff from my own head." He held up the mess of dark matter laced with pulsing blue. It looked so much cleaner, brighter, purer out here than it had in his subconscious. "Thought you might be interested."

Nightmare tore his gaze away from Hellstrom and stared to the window above him, where Loki's face loomed. Loki held up the knot of fear-stuff.

Nightmare lunged for it, arms outstretched and eyes wide with hunger. Loki quickly yanked his arm back and launched the ball as far as he could away from him as Nightmare sailed through the communication portal Leah had opened.

"Leah!" cried Loki.

Leah knotted her fingers and snapped them apart, closing the window behind him. Nightmare was trapped here now, without Hellstrom, and out of the sleeper's head.

Nightmare rose, his scaly green raiment catching the dim light of the room. He'd sprouted bat wings since Loki last encountered him—he'd gained power. They were winning, but just by a fraction, and their lead was not enough. Loki could only hope his plan would work, and it was a gamble. He'd gambled with Asgard, and now he was gambling with all the realms.

"What's your game, godling?" snarled Nightmare, stalking toward them.

Leah and Loki backed up against the wall, shoulder to shoulder.

"I was in your head," Loki said lightly. "I know your plan. I know this is enough fear-stuff to make your hat."

"Crown," Nightmare growled, his clawed hands curling into fists.

"Pointy hat," agreed Loki. He tossed the ball of fear-stuff lightly in his hand and watched Nightmare's eyes track it. "If I give it to you, it means you won't need to rip it from all the other sleepers."

Nightmare lunged forward and Loki dodged to the side, his fingers tight around the fear-stuff, and Leah got out of the way just before Nightmare face-planted into the wall. They twisted, backing up, having room to navigate now. Nightmare spat viscous blood onto the floor and swiveled, his eyes glowing purple with fear-stuff.

"Deal," said the fear-lord.

"I haven't even named my terms yet." Loki tsk-tsked. "They all live. All of the sleepers. You get the crown and mastery of fear, et cetera, et cetera. Seems important to you. *But everyone lives.* Sound good?"

Nightmare ground his teeth. "Deal."

"We could have a party," suggested Loki. "Everybody Wins Party."

"No parties," snapped the fear-lord. "Give it to me. And Loki, I will know if even the smallest amount has been altered or poisoned."

Loki really hoped Leah hadn't taken it upon herself to alter or poison the fear-stuff. He shrugged, keeping his movements nonchalant. Relaxed. He needed Nightmare to buy this.

"Yeah. I know. It's pure, unadulterated fear, all balled up and ready for pointy-hat making." He gripped the fear-stuff in his hand, and then made himself toss it toward Nightmare.

Nightmare caught it with both hands, cradling it. His sharp-edged face suddenly softened. He almost looked like he was in awe. Or confused. Or maybe those were the same things for a fear-lord. "It *is* pure. Untouched. You're really doing this."

"We had a deal," Loki reminded him, keeping his heart rate steady, low.

"We did," Nightmare said. He opened a portal with one hand, his fear-stuff held in the other. "Have a great day. Pleasure doing business with you."

188 Loki could have wept with relief but he forced a smile onto

his face and waved a hand. "Bye. Hope we never have business in the future."

Nightmare stepped through the portal, long-legged and eager in his movements. And at the last second, just as Loki was turning to Leah, the fear-lord popped his head back into their realm. "Actually, here's a thought." He grinned. "What stops me from killing you to make sure you don't have anything else planned?"

"Rude," gasped Loki. "After all I've done for you? I mean, if you did that, word would get out. Leah would avenge me—"

"I would not," Leah said, her voice cold.

"But she could and would spread the word in the hereafter. Imagine how that'd go for you. It'd put a total damper on your dating life," Loki reminded Nightmare.

Nightmare looked to consider his options, and then smiled coldly, lifting his fistful of fear-stuff, aiming right toward Loki and Leah. "I can live with those consequences."

Loki held up a finger. "I wasn't done. The second reason is that Hellstrom's here."

It was a nice bookend. Thematic. Excellent touchpoint. The same way that Loki had distracted the Tongue long enough for Tyr to strike, he'd distracted Nightmare long enough that Hellstrom had quietly opened a portal behind him, stepping through with all the grace of a dancer and all the stealth of a spy.

Hellstrom slammed the fiery trident into Nightmare's back. The fear-lord howled in pain, purple light bursting around him and tangling with Hellstrom's fire. He twisted and leapt away, out of reach of another attack.

"Why battle when the war's won?" he crooned, holding the fear-stuff aloft. "The boy's just given me the keys to my black heaven."

Hellstrom froze, his eyes jerking over to Loki. He hadn't seen the transaction.

Nightmare wrenched open a portal from thin air and leapt through it, the fear-stuff tucked safely in his arms.

THIRTY-FIVE

HELLSTROM LAUNCHED toward the portal even as it was closing. "He's going to the dream dimension. We've got to stop him before he—"

To Loki's surprise, Leah stepped between Hellstrom and the shrinking portal doorway. She held up a hand, her face placid and serene. "You would storm his place of power?"

It was a fair point—Nightmare was a formidable foe when he was not in his home realm. In the dream dimension and with the fear-stuff he'd be nearly unstoppable.

"What other choice do we have?" Hellstrom bellowed, trying to shove her out of the way.

Loki caught Leah when she stumbled as Hellstrom lunged past, his hand out, but the portal closed too quickly, and he was cut off, standing in silence in the dark room. The whine of mortals' cars outside was the only signal that dawn, and rush hour, was coming. They could not stay here much longer.

"Hellstrom," Loki began. "You can go rescue the remaining sleepers. He won't go after them anymore. I have his word—"

"You tricked him," Hellstrom interrupted, his voice calm.

He still stood with his back to Leah and Loki. "That's the only explanation here. You tricked him. He's going to be furious when he finds out. But that wasn't the real fear-stuff."

"He would have noticed right away," Loki said softly. "I couldn't."

Hellstrom whirled, reaching out and seizing Loki by the throat. Loki gasped, flailing, his legs kicking out as his hands grasped at Hellstrom's. He tried to pry Hellstrom's fingers open but he could not.

"I should have killed you the moment we met," growled Hellstrom, voice cold despite the fire and flames radiating around him. "You made a fear-lord into a fear-king just to save your own skin."

"Wait," Loki gargled.

He wanted Leah to step in. He wanted Leah to explain to Hellstrom why Loki did what he did. That it hadn't been an impulsive move but a calculated one.

But Leah still held a grudge against him for being compelled to harvest the fear-stuff when she hadn't wanted to, so she stood by, arms crossed, watching Loki struggle. Her face was stoic.

"I've got a holiday home in hell, kid, and you're coming to stay," Hellstrom said, opening a portal with his free hand and marching toward it.

"Wait," Loki managed again. He struggled, kicking out, and pulled one of Hellstrom's fingers free. He gasped for the tiny bit of air the loosened grip granted him. "Banish me to hell if it goes wrong. But it might not."

Hellstrom threw him to the ground, letting go of his throat. He held the trident over Loki as Loki gasped for air, dragging himself onto his side.

"How the *hell* will it not go wrong? You gave him exactly what he wanted."

"I know," Loki said. "But I promise you—I did it to save everyone."

"He's incapable of saving anyone in a normal way," Leah said finally. "He has to do it in a Loki way."

Loki beamed at her. "See? Even Leah, who's pissed off at me, agrees I did it from a good place."

"I don't care if you're coming from a good place. I care what the outcome of your actions is," snapped Hellstrom.

Loki pushed himself to his feet, rubbing at his sore throat. "He's going to make the crown. You're not wrong. He's going to succeed at his pointy-hat trick. We're going to wake the last of the sleepers. And then we're going to make sure that certain people—certain *fear-lords*—know about Nightmare."

Hellstrom's face tightened, and then smoothed out to deliberate flatness. "You're going to tell the other fear-lords."

Loki smiled grimly. "I was told that the thing all fear-lords hate more than anything is one of them trying to raise himself above the others. So, yes."

Hellstrom scrubbed his hand over his face. "He's going to be a fear-king now. Or, he'll try to be. Do you even understand those consequences?"

"Why should we fight him when the other fear-lords can?" Loki countered. "Let them take care of their own."

It would work—if fear-lords were the kind to handle their problems in-house.

WHICH THEY WEREN'T.

WHEN THEY returned to Leah's cave, Ikol looked sick of Thori, and Thori bounded around in circles in puppy exuberance. He told Hellstrom he loved him with all the gnashing teeth in the world. He ignored Leah completely for reasons known only to Thori. And he threatened to rip Loki's kidneys out and feed them to the birds. All was still well and good.

Ikol fluttered over and settled on Loki's shoulder, preening the boy's hair. "Did you set out to do what you wanted to do?"

Loki exchanged a look with Leah. They'd found the fear-lords assembled in the sub-basement of the Infinite Embassy, which seemed like a place that Loki wanted to explore more when he had the time.

And Loki had been right. The fear-lords in all their navel-gazing, self-centered, egotistical bickering had been horrified to find out that Nightmare's inconspicuous absence from their meetings had been because he was plotting against them. He'd chosen to raise himself above his station, to attempt to rule over them and not solely his own domain.

Just as they'd despised the Serpent for his grasping ambition, they too despised Nightmare. But where they'd been unwilling to do anything about the Serpent, they knew how to fight Nightmare. They'd lived and served with him since before they could remember, and they cared not for the threat he posed to each of their dominions.

Loki had promised Hellstrom that Nightmare and his fear-stuff crown would pose no threat. And he was right. The fear-lords would be forever stuck in an infinite dance of in-fighting and squabbling amongst themselves such that all of the realms would sleep and breathe easier. After all, by nature, fear-lords were *ruled* by fear. Fear of losing power. Fear of losing place. Fear of being outplayed and outsmarted. Fear dominated them. Even more than it did Loki.

"Mostly," said Loki to Ikol at last.

"Is the fear-stuff gone?" Ikol pressed.

"Mostly," Loki said with a sigh. There was much he still needed to do. He knew the inner landscape of his subconscious now, and it was bleak. Bleak, but not hopeless. Not barren. "Nightmare will be preoccupied until further notice."

"Good," said the bird, satisfied. "When you're ready, the All-Mother will see you."

Loki grimaced. "Do I need to be ready right now?"

"Tomorrow's fine. It's good to keep the All-Mother waiting," said Ikol.

Loki lifted an eyebrow. "Is it?"

"No, but they'll survive."

Hellstrom and Leah were throwing bones—human bones—for Thori to fetch. They had been reluctant to appreciate Loki's maneuvering, but they'd accepted it, if only because the proof was in the pudding. Nightmare had not come back. The fear-lords were no longer in the embassy. They were causing chaos in some other dimension, but not one that bothered or touched the Nine Realms.

It would have been nice, Loki thought, if Hellstrom and Leah admitted that Loki had been right and trustworthy all along. But he wasn't going to push it. Neither of them enjoyed being tricked and betrayed and played, and he'd done a little bit of everything to reach this end game. He could understand their frustration.

"Time to go," Hellstrom was saying, standing up and gathering his coat—duster. He scrubbed the top of Thori's head and said to Leah, "The more time I spend around him, I wonder why I bother trying the good thing at all."

Leah nodded. "Trust me, I know."

Loki realized immediately that he was the *him* of that sentence, not Thori.

Hellstrom opened a portal that blazed hot and bright, almost nearly white flames sprouting from it. The flames roared with hunger, and in the distance, Loki could hear the sound of screams.

For a moment, he thought that the Son of Satan might disappear without another word, and he was a little sad at that. For all Hellstrom's headstrong nature, Loki liked him. He was a man of action. Narrow-minded sometimes in what that course of action could and should be, but at least he didn't dither about.

But then Hellstrom sighed. "See you around, kids. Hopefully not *too* soon."

He stepped through and closed the portal behind him. The crackle of the flames and the screams snapped shut along with the portal, leaving the cave eerily quiet.

Thori whimpered at the edge of where the portal had been. "Master?"

No answer came. Thori lay down, whining pathetically.

Loki glanced at Leah. "Is it too soon to say that went better than expected?"

194   A sudden blaze of light burst out of the fire, a Surtur-like figure

rising out of the flames, six feet tall and... shirtless? Fire-etched abs and a trident were the only parts of the shape that stood out.

"If this goes wrong, Loki, your head is mine."

With the pop of a burning log, the fire died down, returning to its warm, normal-height-flames status.

Loki exhaled a shaky breath. "That is a *horrible* trick. I want him to teach it to me."

Leah sighed, and Loki startled at the sound of it. It wasn't a tired or despondent sigh—the kind he was used to from her—but a dreamy, sad, lovesick sigh. She was staring into the flames like she hoped the disembodied abdominal muscles of Daimon Hellstrom might return.

Thori went to the fire and lay down next to it, whimpering. Loki thought he heard the puppy whisper, "Come back, master."

"What is *wrong* with the pair of you?" Loki cried.

"Bad boys," Leah explained. "Everyone loves a bad boy."

Loki gestured to himself. "I'm a bad boy!"

Leah rolled her eyes. "Not *actual* boys. Now, run along. I hear the All-Mother is calling for you."

WHEN IKOL had told him that the All-Mother had wanted to see him, Loki wasn't sure what to expect. He hadn't been reporting back to them as promised. He wasn't even sure they'd see the wisdom in his approach for handling Nightmare. He definitely did not expect to see them lounging around the Ruingarden, drinking wine and eating fruits. The last time he'd been before them, they'd stood in front of their throne, gazes calculating and cunning. They'd been intimidating and threatening, cruel in their own way and kind in another.

Now they just reminded him of other ladies in the Asgardian court. Unaware of the chaos outside of these walls. It bothered him a bit but he tried not to let his concern show.

"Well done, Loki," said one All-Mother. "I can only imagine the fear-lords' faces."

"They were *displeased*," Loki admitted, allowing himself a small smile.

The All-Mother smiled back, but it didn't reach her eyes. "I can imagine. However, strictly speaking, I don't believe the curtailing of Nightmare and the fear-lords was the mission we gave you."

"Fair," acknowledged Loki. "But I imagined that you would want him dealt with, would you not?"

The All-Mother exchanged glances. "Well. Yes. However—"

"And you wouldn't have wanted *your* fingerprints on it," Loki guessed.

The All-Mother looked uncomfortable. "Unlikely, it's true."

"So in a way, it was a problem you gave me and I enacted a solution without you ever getting your hands dirty," he said, keeping his tone light. Being called to the principals' office, that was one thing, but to be told that for the second time that he'd solved a problem but solved it in the *wrong way*? He hated it. This idea that there was a socially acceptable way to solve a problem and a not-socially-acceptable way to solve a problem. That they (the All-Mother, Leah, Hellstrom, everyone) cared more about how the methods looked to the outside, whether they were *appropriate* and *couth*, than whether they did any good in the world.

Loki cared more about doing good.

"So what's the problem?" he challenged them.

"Your unorthodox methods have turned heads," they said at last. "This isn't a problem. But we want you to be mindful—use your methods for good. And do not forget that not everyone wants the outcomes you wish for. You are sometimes too much a child, and more good-hearted than others may think. A little cynicism would do you some good."

"But that's not why we brought you here," one of them said. "We do have a mission for you. A specific mission. Have you ever heard of the Manchester Gods?"

PART III

THE MANCHESTER GODS

THIRTY-SIX

THE ALL-MOTHER looked at Loki and saw opportunity. Two birds, one stone, as the mortals say. (THOUGH THE MECHANICS OF THIS HAVE ELUDED ME.) They looked at the god of trickery and lies and treachery and knew they'd need to keep him busy. And they looked to the world and saw events playing out that required their steady hand on the rudder.

One might say that the All-Mother meddled, professionally.

And this time, their sights—all of them—were set on Otherworld.

It is not often that a story does more than touch upon the Otherworld. But this tale sits in it, digs roots into it, pulls in threads and starfire from other dimensions to seep into the very nature of Otherworld.

In some dimensions—namely Midgard—Otherworld is referred to as a pocket dimension, a piece of a dimension between other dimensions, a gateway, or a portal, or a passageway, an intersection. And like all four-way intersections, Otherworld sees drivers and storytellers who are capable of navigating four-way stops without trouble, and others who are not. Cataclysmically incapable.

Avalon exists in Otherworld, a kingdom and a well of ancient magic, a place where Celtic gods walk amongst the people, a place that shifts on the subconscious of the British Isles in the Earthly realms. It had once been so tightly connected that people passed to and fro without noticing the stone gateways that marked the boundaries between worlds.

Though it had not been that way for a long time, Avalon still leaned on the touchstones and places that grounded it to the British Isles. (THIS IS IMPORTANT. I WOULDN'T TELL YOU THIS IF IT WASN'T IMPORTANT. JUST BECAUSE I AM A TELLER DOES NOT MEAN I PRATTLE ON WITHOUT PURPOSE. REMEMBER THIS.)

The Celtic gods of Avalon enjoyed an unparalleled existence: no competition, and little of the strife that plagued the Asgardian gods. Their dimension was one of fairies and green knolls, of rolling hills and castles, moats and drawbridges, and the sound of hoofbeats on dirt roads.

They had little to fear.

LUCKY THEM.

And so when a god called Manchester rose in the North, they were unprepared. They'd never seen such a god before. He was made of metal, but he was not armor. His exterior was a dull, dark metal that did not gleam in the sun, and he creaked and groaned as he rose from the earth, breaking open that peaceful grass knoll and leaving upturned dirt smoking in his wake. He smelled sour, like sulfur, and heat rippled from him, like a fire.

Rumors spread ahead of him. And with rumors, fear. Even among those who resided in Otherworld, who were familiar with fantasy made real, this unfamiliar thing stank of the strange. To the fair, it reeked of the foul.

That fear was not seen or recognized by those who would protect Avalon. Where the king and knights celebrated the defeat of the Red Lord, they ignored the threat the Manchester God posed to them. And they did not care where the Red Lord went after his defeat.

A MISTAKE.

They did not believe that this slow, lumbering metallic beast climbing out of a crack in the earth was a threat to Avalon's peaceful existence. They should have crushed it when they had a chance, when one mere mechanical god could be defeated by horses and knights and lances. Before the others came.

It grew, this monstrosity. As it moved, it grew. It moved like a spider, quick and catlike, sideways and up and down and forwards and back with shocking nimbleness, one spindly leg after another, and the hulk of it grew wider and taller until it was the size of a castle.

Where it walked, the soil turned black. The underfolk could not breathe.

Oil, thick and black, rose to the surface and trickled down into the water, nauseating the surface with a glistening rainbow. The fish turned belly up, bloated. They tasted sour to the hungry who tried to eat them.

Where it walked, the sky turned red and black clouds gathered. Gone were the days of blue skies over green land and forests that changed color with the seasons.

The trolls and underfolk tried to fight, but they were no match for the Manchester God's many-winged Engels that fought and killed and turned the trolls into more brutal Engels. Then it spawned a new city, another sprawling monstrosity of metal and darkness and sulfur and oil. Birmingham, the first child of Manchester.

The war began in earnest now. But it was too late. The gods and lords of Otherworld attempted to meet at the table with those who brought the mechanical gods, but there was no room for compromise.

"We have no more need for gods," declared the representative from some distant land that had brought the Manchester God to Otherworld. He was ghostly pale, an apparition more than anything, with a tailored coat and a chiseled face set with determined, fiery eyes. "We control our gods. Your time of power has come to an end. The time of the Manchester Gods has begun."

No one in Avalon liked this idea—not just because they faced losing their own power. The world they loved was being torn apart by these Manchester Gods, by these mechanical beasts that tore up the land and poisoned the water and polluted the skies.

They were ill-prepared to fight. Otherworld ached from the wounds of many recent wars. And their people were weak compared to these new gods. They called for aid. And aid came. But aid was not enough.

That was when word reached the All-Mother of Asgardia.

The All-Mother heard their pleas, but stood firm. Otherworld would have to stand alone in this fight. It wasn't a popular opinion. The All-Mother stood steadfast behind a pact of non-interference.

At least, to the public they did. To their warriors they did. To all the gods of Asgard they did.

Save one.

The messenger from Otherworld returned, carrying the All-Mother's rejection of aid.

And the All-Mother called Loki to them.

They charged him with supporting the Old Gods of Otherworld, and with supplying them with information. They did not know much about these new Gods of Manchester and before the tides of power were clear, they wanted to remain publicly neutral. They'd deny him, if he were caught. A spy undercover in a foreign land.

"So you want me to support the Old Gods, because you say so, but to deny you say so if asked?" Loki clarified.

"Yes," said the All-Mother.

"I'm pretty sure I just heard you say that there's a pact of non-interference. I'm interfere-y. Famously so," Loki pointed out, frowning at them. "It's kind of my thing. My brand, if you will."

"Yes. You're a private citizen of legendary unruly character but in reality you're doing our bidding," said one All-Mother.

"I don't get it."

The All-Mother sighed. "Despite some periods of strife, the Celtic Powers are, cosmologically speaking, closely aligned with Asgard."

"I love when things are cosmologically speaking," Loki said dryly. "What does that even mean?"

They ignored him. "It would be in Asgardia's best interests for the Otherworld to be at peace."

No one had ever reached for Loki to be a tool of peace before, and in a way, the God of Lies was honored. Sometimes it did take trickery to maintain peace. A little white lie here and there between allies never did any harm. And it meant that someone saw his natural skills as a tool for good. Hadn't this been what he wanted? To be seen as an agent of potential good?

He grinned. "Mission accepted."

"You're supposed to be *undercover*," warned the All-Mother.

"Just call me Laufeyson," Loki intoned. "Loki Laufeyson. I'll take my milkshake shaken, not stirred."

The All-Mother sighed, but their smiles were gentle and appreciative. Idunn pinned a rose to his cloak, above his heart, and pressed a kiss to his forehead. Loki could tell from Ikol's fluttering wings up in one of the windows that he'd hear about this later.

"We have every faith in you," said Gaea.

"Go," said Freyja, "before we regret this."

THIRTY-SEVEN

LOKI HAD to drop Thori off with Volstagg for the time being—the Hel-Pup wasn't exactly great company for staying undercover—and, as he was leaving, he was relieved to hear the puppy threatening to murder all of Volstagg's children and the kids laughing and squealing with joy. He didn't like the guilt that plagued him when he left Thori behind. It wasn't helping the puppy's socialization challenges.

Leah only had one dress, it turned out, which was convenient because Loki didn't intend to pack any bags, and travelling across the Earthly realms was complicated enough without having to go through baggage claim.

As they deplaned at Heathrow, Loki handed Leah her scroll of parchment. She unrolled it in the slow-moving line.

"Diplomatic passport?" She scowled. "Did you make this by hand?"

"Hey, don't knock it. It looks official! I asked one of the librarians what one looked like and just copied it. It's like a free pass to chaos," Loki explained. "Did you know that Asgardia is a recognized state?"

"You didn't?" Leah asked. "This looks like it was made with crayon, Loki."

Loki ignored her. "Now, the All-Mother said there'd be a representative here to pick us up. Ah. Yes. That must be him."

Among the sea of mortal humans, a man taller than Thor or Odin stood stiffly, his horned helmet extending two feet on either side of his head and coming down over his forehead, a gold plate covering his eyebrows and nose. His eyes glowed an otherworldly silver. He held a piece of paper that clearly used to be a menu for a nearby Chinese restaurant, with LOKI scrawled across it.

"So much for inconspicuous," Leah muttered.

"I don't think that undercover necessarily means inconspicuous," Loki objected as they walked toward him.

"You wouldn't."

"Hail, and well met," said the conspicuous man. "I am Herne the Hunter."

"Do you hunt giants?" Loki asked.

Herne stared at him.

"Ignore him," Leah told Herne with a sigh.

The Hunter's shoulders relaxed a fraction, as if he needed someone to translate Loki for him. "Are you here to fight in the Great War?"

"Erm…" Loki glanced at Leah. "Probably not? But I am hoping to be useful."

It did not seem as if Herne knew of ways of being useful that did not involve being a warrior, but he accepted Loki's words with a deep bow that made Loki and Leah distinctly uncomfortable. They followed him outside where they crammed into a small black London cab, Herne next to the driver, who kept glancing in his rearview mirror with vague alarm. No sooner had Leah slammed her door shut than Loki lunged forward between the front two seats, grinning at the driver.

"Do you know the Queen?"

"*Loki*," Leah hissed, grabbing his arm and yanking him backward.

Ikol flapped his wings and cawed, nipping at Loki's ear. "You can't just ask someone if they know the Queen."

"Ignore him," Leah addressed Herne. "Loki is a genius of little brain."

Herne twisted to look at them both and then looked back out the windshield. "I see."

"Where are we going?" Leah asked.

"Otherworld is a reflection of the British Isles, like looking into a lake and seeing a reflection of the sky," Herne said. He sounded almost wistful, as if lost in memory, though he had undoubtedly been there this morning before he picked them up. "In places of power, you can cross over. To enter a home of magic, you must travel to one."

"Like…" Loki began. Leah elbowed him and he finished the sentence anyways. "Kensington Palace?"

Herne's eyes moved back to the road. "No. We will be leaving the city."

Loki frowned, glancing at Leah. "Surely there are places of power and import here in the city?"

Herne nodded. "Yes. But it would be foolish to cross over here. We'd appear in the southeastern corner of Avalon, beyond the wall of wailing mists, so we must skirt—"

"A safer route," Leah interrupted.

Loki slumped back against the seat. "Why does safer always mean boring?"

IT TURNED out, though, that the drive out of the city and into the countryside was beautiful. Idyllic, even. After the cave, and war, and underworlds, and fear-filled subconsciousness they'd spent time in over the last months, they were soothed by the sight of gray-blue skies that hinted of rain, the green fields dotted with sheep, the hedges made of overgrown bushes and old collapsing stone walls that ran on for miles. Loki and Leah barely spoke as the roads turned from wide highways into narrower roads, unmarked with lines, barely wide enough for two cars to pass without clipping the sideview mirrors.

It was a peaceful drive, gorgeous in an unassuming way, the kind of scenery that Loki suspected the locals took for granted, but he and Leah did not. He could tell by the way her eyes stayed transfixed on the world outside the little black cab that she felt the same as he did.

"I chose the scenic route to eat up time," Herne said without preamble as they turned off the main road. "Better to cross after dusk. Fewer tourists."

Loki had nearly forgotten he wasn't a tourist. He was here for a mission. Superspy undercover to do the All-Mother's bidding and ensure that the Old Gods had Asgardian support, if need be.

"Right," he muttered as they climbed out of the car. "Right. Focus, Loki, focus."

Leah shot him a look. "Has that worked before?"

"There's a first time for everything," he assured her. "I'm working on my positive affirmations." Loki looked around and gasped. "Stonehenge!"

The circle of enormous stone pillars, some upright, some toppled, some made into arches and some just towers, stood at the top of the hill, outlined by the fading light to the west. They were bigger than Loki had thought, and even more impressive.

"Yes," Herne said proudly. "A place of great power."

"I've wanted to see this place *forever*! Did you see that sunset photo on social media of Manhattan? They called it Manhattanhenge. It was cool, but this is the real thing."

"Of course it is," Leah said, tromping up the hill after him. "It's not like a replica would be a place of power."

At the top of the hill, they stood next to one of the stone pillars and Loki placed his hand reverently on it. "So cool. Sooooo cool."

"How do we cross over?" Leah asked dubiously. "I don't see a path."

Herne held out a hand to each of them and they took it. Ikol landed on Loki's shoulder, his talons gripping Loki's tunic tightly.

"It is but a step," intoned Herne, "if you know which step to make."

And he pulled them through the arc with one enormous stride, his foot landing thunderously ahead of them. The circle exploded into white light that spun through the arches and pillars, racing around them and weaving between them like a wild sprite, leaving long trails behind it. Then it sailed into the air in the center, and they craned their necks back to watch. It shot downwards, hitting the ground with such force it felt as if an earthquake had rolled through the earth. Loki stumbled but Herne's grip on his hand kept him upright.

A maze, like an illuminated labyrinth, lay on the grass, shimmering. The air around them was still, as if the stones were holding their breath.

"Now," Herne said softly, "it's time to take that step."

He took each of their hands in his own, and then side by side, the three of them stepped into the maze.

THIRTY-EIGHT

THEY STEPPED into the labyrinth and though the path looked narrower than three abreast, it accommodated them nicely. Loki expected some sort of lurch, some sort of sensation that he'd transported from one place to the next, but there was no such feeling. The grass was damp from recent rains and lush, like it hadn't seen hundreds of tourists' feet that day alone. The light glimmered as Herne navigated the path with them.

At the center, they stepped onto a stone that radiated warmth, drying their shoes which had grown damp with dew. Herne seemed to be waiting for a signal, and none came that Loki saw. But as the Hunter stood quietly, so did Loki and Leah. The trickster god itched with the desire to banter and tease or make some cutting sly remark, but he held his peace. Something about the stones around him felt sacred and special, a place of reverence and following the footsteps of those who knew more than he did.

His heart ached for Thor.

Abruptly, Herne said, "And now we walk the labyrinth again."

"What? It didn't work?" Loki said, his desire to hold his tongue evaporating.

Herne looked confused. "It did work. We have passed through to Otherworld. We must exit now."

Loki stared at him and then looked around. "We didn't go anywhere!"

"Reflection, Loki," Leah reminded him.

Herne gripped their hands again and they followed as he led them through the glowing light maze once more. As Loki walked it, he felt that this time was different to when they had walked into the center. The turns were different, dead ends where he expected open paths. And though they'd left at dusk, they arrived at dawn. The light rose in the east, glowing between the archways and stone pillars.

They reached the archway where they'd begun in the Earthly Britain, and Herne stopped there.

"Now we wait for your escort," he said.

They were being handed off to someone else, Loki realized. Who would come now? How did they know to come for Loki? If the All-Mother wanted to look as if they were not interfering, how had they set up Herne to pick up Loki? And how had they found another escort for them in Avalon?

He had questions.

He doubted that the All-Mother would deign him with answers.

"I'd like to keep you as an escort," Loki told Herne. "You're very calming. Like a very large elephant. Gentle spirit."

Herne stared stiffly into the distance. "That is not possible."

Loki wasn't sure if he meant staying their escort, or his gentle spirit. He found that many men of Herne's stature and command, especially those who hunted and fought professionally, did not like being called gentle spirits, but that was just the truth. He wouldn't lie about that. Herne had picked them up in this strange place and ushered them across the countryside, through a magical gate, and into their third realm this day alone. All without any calamity or chaos.

"Hail!" called a voice that sounded bright, young, and strong. It had none of Herne's deep timbre. It sounded quite a bit like—

A man rode up the hill, his big gray horse snorting with the exertion. They'd ridden a long way, Loki guessed, by the flush of the man's face and the horse's heaving sides. Unlike Herne, who wore the tunic and trousers of a man who spent long hours in the forest stalking prey, this man wore a suit of red and blue, skin-tight and marked with the red cross of a Union Jack over his chest.

"You're Loki!" the man exclaimed.

"And you're Captain Britain!" Loki cried back. "My brother's told me of you!"

"Your brother didn't need to tell me of you," Captain Britain said, his voice skeptical. "I'm watching you, you understand? I don't trust that you're here to do good."

"I am though," Loki said, realizing too late that such insistence didn't help his cause.

Captain Britain nodded to two ponies tied up a few paces away, where a parking lot had been in Midgard. This world truly was a mirror, Loki realized. A slanted dimension of Great Britain.

"You know how to ride, I presume?"

"Hardly," said Loki.

"Of course," said Leah.

Loki gaped at her. "Where are there horses in Hel, Leah?"

"I have been other places," she said primly.

Loki doubted that. That meant Hela had Hel-horses. He was determined to find them when they got back.

They thanked Herne for his service and companionship thus far and then, with his help, Loki and Leah climbed ungracefully aboard two shaggy ponies that looked as if they spent their entire lives running feral and had only been caught and tamed last week. Loki winced as he figured out how to sit in the saddle and picked up the reins.

Leah, however, sat gracefully side saddle, her skirts draped over her legs like she did this regularly.

Ikol tried to ride on Loki's pony's rump, but the pony swished his tail and humped his back, so the magpie screeched and took to the air.

Captain Britain's eyes followed the bird. "One lonely magpie's always bad luck."

"Consider me the second, then," Loki said brightly.

Captain Britain scowled slightly. "I don't think that makes it less bad luck. Time will tell." He turned his horse toward the dirt road and they began to trot in that direction. "Come. We have a ride."

Loki kicked his steed lightly and the pony grunted, but obligingly trotted to catch up with Captain Britain.

"So do *you* know the Queen?" Loki ventured.

"I know several," Captain Britain said, staring down the road.

"Several?" squeaked Loki. "How do you know several?"

"Time," said the Captain cryptically.

THE ROAD rose and then dipped down into a valley. Cottages made of gray stone and with thatched roofs lined the roads, and a mill stood where a creek trickled lazily through. Their horses slowed to a walk across a bridge, their feet echoing on the stone, and then they walked up the main street of the town.

It felt wrong, and it took Loki a moment to realize why. He reined his pony in to a stop. "Why is it so quiet? Where *is* everyone?"

It was morning. A town like this ought to be waking up. Busy. Stores opening and children in the street and people bringing their wares to the market. There should be the smell of chimneys puffing out smoke and bread baking and the ringing of bells.

Instead, there were no sounds other than hooves on packed earth and the soft snorts from their mounts. Not one sound. Not even birds.

"Most of the land has been depopulated," Captain Britain said grimly as his horse walked onward. Loki nudged his pony to catch up with the Captain. "People get lured from these quiet villages to the promise of these city gods. Manchester. Birmingham. We might have a new one by supper. How is that any future? What will happen to these towns?"

"And that's why there's a war," Loki said quietly. "To stop people leaving."

"To win," Captain Britain corrected him. "We have to win. For the people's sakes as much as our own. They don't know what they're losing when they leave."

As soon as they were out of the village, Captain Britain picked up a trot again. "Come, we have many hundreds of miles to go before we reach Camelot."

Loki gasped. "*The* Camelot?"

Captain Britain didn't answer and Loki nudged his pony faster to keep up.

"Hey. Wait. Is it the *real* Camelot?"

THIRTY-NINE

IT WAS, in fact, Camelot. Perhaps not the real Camelot, but certainly the real Camelot for the Otherworld. The castle rose between the hills, nestled into a valley where the road narrowed to one path—a drawbridge over the moat. The castle glittered white, a polished stone that they'd seen nowhere else in their travels though they had crossed through many towns and villages along the way. The roof was tiled in red clay, and arched windows dotted the castle's many turrets. It looked like a fantasy, like a perfect drawing of what a castle ought to look like.

"I think that we shall never more, at any future time, delight our souls with talk of knightly deeds, walking about the gardens and the halls of Camelot, as in the days that were," Loki said to Leah, his voice lofty. He bowed deeply.

She stared at him blankly.

"Tennyson!" he exclaimed. "'Morte d'Arthur'! Didn't you read it?"

"Loki," she said, her voice quiet. "Here, Arthur is still alive."

"Oh," Loki stage-whispered back with a wince. "That's terribly awkward, now, isn't it."

"So long as you don't bally well quote it beyond those gates," said Captain Britain, "we can forget it ever happened."

He rode ahead and Loki and Leah followed side by side over the drawbridge. Loki leaned over and said, "You *are* impressed I memorized that though, aren't you?"

"It's a little dramatic and over the top, so no, I'm not. It's exactly your brand," Leah said coolly.

Loki was pretty sure she was impressed and just wasn't going to admit it.

When they reached solid land on the other side of the drawbridge, Captain Britain dismounted, holding each of their ponies' bridles so they too could dismount. He promised he'd see them at dinner and then he led the ponies away, and servants in long cloaks emblazoned with a dragon greeted them, showing them into Camelot itself.

For all its windows on the outside, Camelot was still a stone castle, just like any other that Loki had been in: darker, damper, and mustier than it had any right to be. Everything felt old and worn: the divots in the stairs that they took up one turret to their rooms; the candle holders that fell, lopsided, out of the walls where the stone had eroded and left the metal weak.

On the other hand, their room turned out to have two enormous, canopied beds stuffed with down feathers and a fireplace with a fire already roaring in the hearth.

Loki flopped on the bed and sighed, grinning up at the red velvet curtains. "This is *much* better than the last adventure we went on."

"I'd rather a pocket dimension than your subconscious any day of the week," Leah said primly. She sat in a chair by the fireplace.

"I mean, the sheets are silken! The fireplace has a chimney, which even *you* have to admit is a *huge* upgrade from the cave." He spread his arms and legs out on the bed, making snow angels on the crisp white sheets. "Glorious."

"Loki!" Leah said sharply, her voice changing in a way Loki hadn't heard before.

He sat upright, expecting to see her under attack.

But she simply said, "My mistress has a message for you."

Her head jerked back, and her body spasmed, her arms going slack as she rose off the floor a few inches. Black, green, and white light exploded from her chest in tendrils that snaked up to the ceiling, climbing down the walls, and reaching for Loki. He shrank away instinctively.

When Leah spoke, it was not Leah's voice he heard, but Hela's.

"Your account with Hel is still red, Loki. You are in Otherworld. There is an opportunity to repay me."

Like he wasn't going to be busy enough here.

"The Dísir wound still will not close."

Loki frowned, pursing his lips. "That seems like Mephisto's problem, doesn't it?"

"They are Undead, and have taken a position as my shieldmaidens. The wound remains your responsibility. And remember, Loki, you of all people should know that it is easier to destroy than to create," Hela intoned, echoing around the room.

She didn't know how to fix the Dísir, Loki realized with surprise. She wouldn't admit it, but if she was coming to him, neither she nor the Dísir knew how to heal their wounds and break the final bonds.

"What would you have me do?"

Hela sounded peeved. *"You are in the land of magic. Among its greatest treasures is the Holy Grail."*

"You want me to go on a quest? I'm busy, Hela," he said with a sigh.

"This is your debt!" she snapped, and her anger made Leah's limp, floating body twitch in a horrifying way. *"It is your responsibility."*

He winced, holding up his hands up. "Okay, fine. Holy Grail."

"One sip from the healing cup is all I need," she whispered, her voice giddy. *"Make it happen."*

If he didn't, he'd never get home. And he never wanted to see Hela use Leah's body like that again. He hadn't even known this was possible. Hadn't even considered it. Could he use Ikol's body like this? He doubted it. Plus the magpie might remove his eyes for the trespass.

"Fine," said Loki.

And with an audible pop, the light and fire that filled the room with Hela's voice evaporated, and Leah's body came back to life with a gasp. Her feet hit the floor and she sucked in a breath, letting it out slowly like she was trying to regain her bearings and balance.

She eyed Loki.

He didn't know what to say to her. *Sorry, I didn't realize that putting off your mistress would make her body-snatch you and use you like a loudspeaker or a bullhorn to get my attention* didn't seem to cut it.

"Your mistress is scary," he said nonchalantly.

Leah rubbed at her neck. "My throat itches."

"We can ring this little bell for some tea!" Loki yanked down enthusiastically on a hanging cord. He turned back to her. "By the way, that was *me* levels of drama. 'My mistress has a message for you' followed by—"

He flung himself backwards, limp, limbs askew, chest to the sky, mimicking Leah's posture when Hela had spoken through her.

"It's not like I can choose when she speaks through me," Leah said sharply.

"Yes, but you could have been like, 'LOKI. I HAVE BECOME HELA, MISTRESS OF DEATH.'" He deepened his voice and threw his arms open wide.

A hint of a smile played at the corner of Leah's mouth. "I'll try to keep that in mind."

He flopped onto one of the armchairs by the fire. "See? Sometimes I have good ideas."

FORTY

THE NEXT day, neither of them were smiling.

A battle raged in the valley across the mountain range next to Camelot, and they rode over early in the morning to see what the war looked like.

It sickened Loki. As it would have sickened anyone with a heart.

The sky was reddish black above the valley, clouds of fumes and smoke hanging low in the sky. The cities—mechanical gods—lumbered onwards, expanding as they went. They were enormous, more than suburbs now, surely as big as the London Loki and Leah had left just yesterday. The forces of Avalon had built fortresses and wooden barriers in an attempt to slow the cities' approach, but they crashed through them. Oil dripped behind them, iridescent slicks where birds came to sip and perish. Gigantic trolls smashed rocks onto the cities, denting the metal and they stumbled, swaying, but did not fall.

Down in the valley, a man with silver hair and a golden crown thrust his sword into the air, bellowing a call that the wind swept away before it reached Leah and Loki. Above the fray, Ikol swooped and soared, taking in the sights and details in case there was anything Loki and Leah needed to know from the depths of the battlefield.

Captain Britain and other heroes of the Otherworld sailed through the air, delivering blows that sparked electric waves of purple and bursts of fire against the hull of the moving city. The city lurched and swayed, slowing to nearly a stop. It swung a few degrees to the north and toddled away on its mechanical legs, under attack, but still moving. Camelot was safe for now—but the rest of Avalon remained at the mercy of these mechanical beasts.

Loki turned away, hiding his face. "I can't watch. This is horrible."

Leah did not turn away. "Only the living think there's glory in battle. The dead know better."

He drew his knees up to his chest and wrapped his arms around them. He wished Thor was here, someone able to tell him that the battle was worth raging, and that sometimes the ends justified the means. But no one reassured him that the destruction and death and chaos in the valley below was worth it. That there'd be an outcome that satisfied everyone.

He kept his back to the valley, even as Leah stood serenely at the edge, her hands clasped behind her back.

Ikol returned, swooping down to land on Loki's shoulder. The magpie's feathers smelled of smoke and sulfur. "It's as bad as it looks from here."

Loki nodded glumly but didn't respond.

Ikol pecked at his cheek. "You're thinking, Loki."

Loki picked at rocks on the ground, drawing his fingernail against their chalky surface. It was ash, he realized. The chalkiness wasn't from the rock, but from the fallout from the sky above.

"I just think that there's got to be a better way to solve this war than whatever this is," he said, gesturing vaguely over his shoulder in the direction of the valley. "Hitting each other in the face with hammers. Clanking about and hoping for the best. We just need to find it."

"That's my boy," Ikol cawed.

Loki shot him a glance. "Sometimes when you say that, it doesn't sound like praise."

Ikol tilted his head, beady eyes staring at Loki. "Why not?"

Loki rolled his eyes. "You're Evil Me. If you're praising me, it probably isn't a good idea."

"Meddling in a war and calling it efficiency and smarts is always a good idea," Ikol said.

"See? Not comforting at all," Loki said, grunting as he got to his feet. He brushed the ash off his trousers and tunic. "Leah? You seen enough?"

"Enough for today," she replied.

They picked their way back down the valley path on the peaceful side of the mountains and followed the road back to Camelot.

As they reached the castle, Loki inquired about the Holy Grail and was directed to a woman in the courtyard garden. She was as tall as Thor had been, with wide-set blue eyes and soft reddish hair that fell in messy waves around her face. A silver circlet sat on her forehead.

"Lady of the Lake?" Loki asked cautiously.

She glanced at him, eyebrow quirking upward. "Loki."

It was probably not a good sign, Loki decided, that she knew him.

"You're the keeper of the Grail, yes? I was hoping to arrange—" he began.

She cut him off. "Nay, Loki."

"But I merely—" he tried again.

She shook her head curtly. "I said nay."

And with a swift turn making her white gown flip behind her, the Lady of the Lake strode out of the garden and toward the castle gates. No doubt to move the Holy Grail to a safer location.

"It's possible they know me too well," Loki said to Ikol. "Any chance you want to own up to that?"

"I had nothing to do with it," Ikol said, in a voice that very much suggested he had everything to do with the lady's response.

Leah was waiting back at their rooms. Loki washed his hands in the basin, trying to get rid of the ash stuck underneath his nails. "We'll have to figure out the Grail later. Your mistress really picks the worst times to make demands, you know."

"She won't wait long," Leah warned.

"I know but surely after the battle we saw," he said, giving her a meaningful glance and hoping she understood it to mean she should share what they'd seen today with Hela, "she'll give us a little time."

Leah pursed her lips. "Perhaps."

Ikol flew back in through the open window and landed on the edge of the bedspread.

"We've been summoned. For dinner. With Arthur Pendragon himself."

LOKI DID not often get summoned for dinner, much less by notables from history and fable like Arthur Pendragon. He was positively giddy as he bounced down the stairs of their turret and followed the procession of neatly dressed lords and ladies into dinner. Most wore long gowns in pastel shades, and the men wore white tunics with a red cross over their chain mail, long swords at their hips.

Long swords would not win the fight against what Loki had seen in the valley.

"Ah," he whispered to Leah. "Our plan to be inconspicuous has backfired immediately."

They were both the only ones wearing dark colored clothing and they stuck out like sore thumbs in the audience room. People stared and whispered, which bothered Loki much more than it bothered Leah, who seemed to float through the crowd ignoring those around her. Loki's face flushed with embarrassment.

A servant guided them to two chairs next to Pendragon. The legendary knight was a tall, strong man with a white beard and white hair, and one of those faces that always seemed to be looking for something to be angry with. He reminded Loki unnervingly of Odin.

They settled in their chairs, the chitchat in the room continuing before Pendragon stood, his chair scraping back noisily against the polished stone floor. The room fell silent and everyone looked to him expectantly.

"A hard battle today," he acknowledged in a hoarse, gravelly voice.

A murmur of assent rolled through the crowd. Loki frowned at the plate in front of him. None of the soldiers who fought were in this room. Who was Pendragon addressing? He was the only one in the room who had lifted a sword. How could the others agree?

"I have seen many things," Arthur Pendragon said with a sigh. "In Britannia and Otherworld alike. But I have never seen anything like this. We are under siege. Tyrant gods of modernity have begun invading our mystical land."

He made a fist, shaking it in the air.

"Although a path precludes other pantheons from joining us, the All-Mother sent us aid. And she sent us—*Loki*?"

Loki startled as Pendragon gestured at him, face dismissive and angry. Loki tried to smile at everyone around them. No one smiled back.

"And he came back to us... a child."

Loki raised a finger. "I prefer 'kid'."

Leah quietly reached over and pulled his finger down.

Pendragon barked a laugh. "The irony! It's these *young people* who are the problem! They don't care about our old ways!"

The crowd at the dinner table murmured and nodded in agreement. Loki squirmed in his seat.

"They just care about drinking—" Pendragon paused, glancing at Loki.

And, against all his instincts, Loki piped up, "Milkshakes."

"They just care about drinking milkshakes! And listening to noisy music!" Pendragon roared. After each item he listed, the crowd 222 at the dinner table cheered their agreement. It was like they were going into battle… against young people? As a collective? "Looking clever! Chasing clout! Getting clicks and likes!"

Loki leaned over and whispered to Leah, "How does he even know about that?"

"This is *war*!" Pendragon bellowed. "Kids today, they get a scraped knee and they go running to the doctor. We didn't have doctors in my day! We had barbers who would bleed you!"

"Is he suggesting we go back to those days?" Ikol cawed into Loki's ear.

"You know," Loki said, letting the din of the speech and the pounding of fists cover his voice as he turned to Leah, "if I'd known we came here to be lectured by an old man, I would have gotten takeout. Want to sneak out the back? I've got an idea. You're going to hate it."

"Say no more," she said, her hands around the edge of her seat.

"We turned out just fine!" Pendragon banged his fist on the dining room table. And so did the others, a chorus and drumming of fists and shouts. The complaints went on—a list that got flimsier by the moment—but people were standing and shouting, the volume and crowd growing raucous. Loki nudged Leah under the table and they carefully stood, taking advantage of their smaller stature compared to those around them, and made their way to the back of the room.

No one even glanced their direction.

No one noticed when the pair and the magpie snuck back out the kitchen door and up the servant stairs, back to their room in the turret.

FORTY-ONE

A CAB swerved a hard left, cutting a corner and nearly jumping the curb. Tires squealed against the wet pavement and splashed into a puddle, creating a wave that hit Loki and Leah like a punch.

Leah sputtered, her hair plastered to her face. "You're right. I hate this idea."

"You won't hate it for long," Loki said with confidence. His shoes squelched as he walked, following a bouncing green light that shone ahead of them, courtesy of Leah's magic. It led them down the streets of Camden, a lively neighborhood of London full of shops and bars and restaurants, and lots of brightly colored things that Loki would love to look at, if they had the time.

At the door to the pub, Loki tried to explain their situation to the bouncer, who was not thrilled with the lack of ID, their young faces, or their strange costumes. He kept asking why they were dressed like that, while Loki kept protesting that this was how people dressed now.

"You'll know who we're looking for," Leah interrupted before Loki could get stuck in a roundabout conversation. "Red hair. Intense eyes. Black coat. Not a fan of shirts."

The bouncer's eyes flickered inside the pub briefly. "If I take you to him, he has to claim you, or I'm kicking you out."

"Deal!" Loki exclaimed and held out his hand to shake on it.

The bouncer picked him up by the scruff of his neck like a puppy and grabbed Leah by the arm and dragged them in out of the steady rain.

The pub door slammed behind them and the smell of beer and who knows what else filled Loki's nostrils. He was hungry, he realized, because they hadn't stayed long enough through Pendragon's angry rants to eat.

"Think we could get some fries?" he asked the bouncer. The man grunted. Loki tried to remember the Britishism. "Chips?"

The bouncer dragged them through the pub to a corner booth. It was quieter back here. It smelled less like body odor and more like beer and... sulfur.

Daimon Hellstrom sat sprawled in an otherwise empty booth, his back against the window. He still wore sunglasses inside to hide his glowing red eyes, but he was unmistakably Daimon Hellstrom. Shirtless. Leather pants. Red hair that looked like it hadn't seen a clarifying shampoo in at least a dozen years.

"They say they know you," the bouncer said, holding Loki and Leah up like he was holding up a lost puppy poster. "We don't let kids in here."

Daimon seemed to slump a little farther into the booth. He sighed. "They can stay."

As soon as the bouncer left, Loki and Leah slid into the booth across from him.

He scowled and held up the glowing green light to Leah, who picked it up and tucked it back inside the pocket of her dress.

"I knew when I saw this you were tracking me. Didn't we agree to part ways and stay parted?"

"We've got a proposal," Loki said. "Hey, can you order us some food? We're starving. We skipped out on dinner with Arthur Pendragon."

Hellstrom opened his mouth, and then seemed to reconsider.

He closed his mouth and shook his head, gesturing for a waitress. She took their orders and disappeared back to the kitchen.

"I want to be clear," Leah added, putting her hands on the table, "that this is Loki's proposal—not mine."

"We came up with it together," protested Loki.

The waitress stuck a plate of fish and chips and mushy peas in front of them and both Leah and Loki dug in. Between mouthfuls, Loki explained the situation.

"Okay, Otherworld—you're familiar?" He continued on when Hellstrom nodded. "It's at war. The Manchester Gods are rising up. Apparently they're gods of a modern age? The details are hazy, but the facts are clear: people are dying. And people who aren't even people are dying. I think if I make certain moves, I can bring it to a swift, minimum-number-of-people-dying conclusion."

"Feels like I've heard this before," Hellstrom commented to Leah.

She nodded and bit into another forkful of greasy, battered fish.

"I can't do it by myself. *We* can't do it by ourselves," Loki clarified, elbowing Leah. "We're hoping that you might be available as a—what's the term?"

Leah swallowed. "Private contractor."

"Right," Loki said brightly. "Otherworld would be enormously grateful. They'll give you pretty much whatever you want."

Leah unfurled a map and other documents in front of Hellstrom and he slid them across the table, studying them.

"I don't get it. If this is on Otherworld's dime, why do you need me? They've got more posh mages than a certain magical wizarding school reunion."

"First," Loki said, waggling his finger. "You could be posh too, if you tried. No negative self-talk. No self-rejection. But secondly, yes, I know they do. We're looking for someone who is perhaps... more likely to fly under the Otherworld radar. I could do it, but I haven't the mastery. She could do it, but she hasn't the street smarts."

"I do too," Leah said, lifting her chin.

"No, you don't," Loki and Hellstrom said in unison.

"These still aren't details," Hellstrom said, taking a long swig of his beer.

Loki leaned over the table, using a chip—or french fry—to point out locations on the map. "Otherworld is connected to all the symbolic sites in the real world. Everything here is connected to there. Stonehenge. The Tower of London. Avebury."

"Yeah, yeah," Hellstrom said thoughtfully. "Buck Palace, Hadrian's Wall, et cetera. I know. This is basic sh—"

"Yeah, but these Manchester Gods are *also* part of the British subconscious," Loki interrupted him, excitedly. "I mean, they're not going to be connected to all these pretty places on pretty tourist maps, but they're going to be connected *somewhere*, aren't they?"

Hellstrom looked up at him. "You want me to make you a map of the Manchester Gods' counterparts in this Earthly realm?"

"Exactly," Loki beamed. "See, Leah? I told you he'd get it."

"Okay," Hellstrom said slowly. "And then what?"

Loki grinned, bouncing at the edge of the booth seat. "Nothing! That's the beauty of it. Leave the rest to us."

"Seems sketchy," Hellstrom said to Leah.

She shrugged. "Sketchy, but pays well."

He rubbed at his bare chin thoughtfully. He touched the map in front of him. "Can I take this with me? As an example?"

"Is that a yes?" Loki asked, holding one edge of the map.

Hellstrom nodded and Loki crowed with victory, trying to high five Leah and then Hellstrom, neither of whom returned the gesture. It didn't deter him. He grinned, sitting back.

"Yeah. Then you can take that map. Return it when you have the other one."

FORTY-TWO

THE THING about plans like this was that they required patience. And Loki, at least *this* Loki, was not a patient boy. He was eager, if not overeager, and eagerness undermined patience, chipping away at its foundation. If it wasn't for Leah keeping a lid on Loki's energy, the whole plan might have been blown to bits before it even got off the ground.

They didn't have to wait long. Two days previously, Hellstrom had called for Leah, who they'd agreed would return to the Earthly London to fetch the new map from him, the one that marked all the key locations for the Manchester Gods. It'd taken both of them, and a lot of trial and error, to figure out how to slip from this realm into Midgard. Herne had been right about needing to take the right steps and Loki was grateful that Leah had been paying attention. He certainly hadn't been. But then, Loki suspected Leah offered to run the errand not because she wanted to get into the habit of running errands for Loki but because she liked seeing Hellstrom. Shirtless, annoyingly handsome Hellstrom.

"Jealousy looks ugly on you," Ikol cawed when Loki watched her walk quietly up the road away from Camelot and back toward the stones to open a portal. After all, anyone might be watching from inside the castle, even in Loki and Leah's rooms.

"You're a bird," Loki replied.

In Otherworld, though, they did not know what the reportedly obnoxious, self-centered uppity kids were up to. As far as Pendragon was concerned, Loki could stay far away from the battle. In the same breath, he complained that this was just like kids these days, to promise to help and skip out when the going got tough.

"In my day," he grumbled to anyone nearby who'd listen.

They fought a fierce battle in the north, along the wall that kept the Highlands safe. The Otherworld gods and their armies fought to hold the wall, fighting with magic and arrows and swords and shields. The Manchester Gods lurched and sputtered uphill against the onslaught.

The sky reddened, then blackened with smoke. The fields lay barren, whatever greenery that had survived the Manchester Gods crushed under the boots of soldiers and horses. Pikes lay stuck into pieces of metal and the ground, the bodies of soldiers, Engels, underfolk, fair folk, trolls and more lay scattered, covered in mud, blood, and oil. Even as the mechanical city-gods pressed on, their fighters facing off against archers and swordsmen, flies swarmed to the fields. It smelled of rot and ruin.

"We must not lose the Highlands!" roared Pendragon, thrusting his sword in the air. "Hold the wall!"

"Hold the wall!" echoed the soldiers.

Then abruptly, the Engels and the cities slowed their movements. They stopped. The clanging that had filled the valley was suspended like a bell half-rung. Then, the enemy turned away. They retreated back down the hill.

Everyone on Hadrian's Wall—or rather, its Otherworld equivalent—stood up, watching the enemy retreat.

Pendragon was rattled. They'd been losing, and he knew it. Why had the enemy retreated?

Then on a nearby hill, a green doorway opened, a split in the world made in mid-air. Two figures, slim and dark-haired, stood framed by emerald fire.

"Loki," breathed Pendragon, "and his girl."

It was lucky that Leah didn't hear him say that.

Pendragon looked to the retreating enemy and then back to Loki. "What did you do?" he bellowed at the top of his lungs.

"Did it work?" Loki shouted back. He punched the air with a "Wahoo!"

He jogged down the hill toward them while Leah followed at a more leisurely pace. Ikol flew alongside Loki and when they came to a stop in front of Pendragon, the bird alit on Loki's shoulder. It was only the magpie's talons that kept Loki from bowing out of habit to the old king.

"Well," Loki said with a grin while all of the Otherworld allies gathered around him. "You know how *you* have important spots in the Earthly realms?"

Captain Britain's eyes narrowed. "Yes."

Loki snapped his fingers. "So do the Manchester Gods. Except they're down one."

The Old Gods gaped at him and then Captain Britain sputtered, "That's terrorism!"

Leah arrived just at that point and she tensed, glancing between Loki and those around him. She was always better at realizing when everyone around Loki was giving him distrustful looks than Loki was.

"It's not terrorism," protested Loki. "It's just blowing stuff up! I didn't *intend* to cause terror. No one was hurt! It was just a—"

"Unscheduled demolition," suggested Leah.

Loki looked relieved to see her. "Yes! Exactly. And you can un-unscheduled demolition them with the appropriate magics when this is all over. Until then, you won a battle you were probably going to lose."

"But why did you do it?" Pendragon asked, voice aghast.

"Because I came here to help, and your methods weren't

working," Loki said simply. "This way, we destroyed a place of power for them. This is as important as Stonehenge is to you."

They all flinched, and Loki knew that the old men who were stuck in their ways were starting to understand the significance of what he had done.

"I've got an agent looking for more sites to target," he offered. "Clifton Suspension Bridge in Bristol. Some guy with an awesome beard's grave in Highgate. The Cavern Club in Liverpool."

"No, not there," said Captain Britain quickly.

Loki and Leah exchanged a glance and then Loki offered Captain Britain a warm smile. "Of course. We'll cross that one off the list."

Captain Britain still didn't seem appeased. "You can't just go around blowing stuff up, Loki."

"We're not just 'going around and blowing stuff up,'" Loki said with more patience than he felt. "This is *leverage*. They know we can do this now. They'll be willing to come to the table. I think. But you must remember something."

"What?" said Pendragon, sounding a little shaken, and a little more willing to hear out the kid he'd lambasted a few nights prior.

Loki grinned. "They still don't know I'm working for you."

"How is *that* relevant?" cried Captain Britain.

"I'm a creature of mischief!" Loki replied, spreading his arms wide and proudly. "Interfering with a war like this is exactly what everyone expects. That's why I was sent, after all. So I slip them some information. Tell them what's happening. Tell them where you'll strike next."

"You'll need to make a cursory attempt to attack it. They defend it," Leah added.

"You're going to build your credibility in their eyes," said Pendragon thoughtfully. "A counteragent. A good ploy, if it works. I still don't know why you would help us." The faintest spots of pink arose on the king's cheeks. "Especially after the way I treated you."

Loki shrugged. "I like chaos. I'm trying to steer my chaotic nature in the general direction of universal good."

"Would they take this bait? Would they believe you to be a two-faced traitor? Why would they not believe you'd betray them in return?" Captain Britain wanted to know.

"Everyone takes the bait, because the bait is true. He is two-faced. He always has a second agenda," Leah replied quietly. "Everyone can look at what the Manchester Gods have done here and see the unearthly red fire that fuels their machines. The question is, are you willing to play a dirty game to win their dirty war?"

Loki waited as the Captain and Pendragon conferred off to the side with the other leaders of the Round Table. When Pendragon returned to Loki and Leah, his face was grim.

"We approve of your technique. Do not blow things up indiscriminately. We expect you to offer them information in exchange for leverage. Tell us where we must go."

THE PLAN was set. The bait laid out for the Manchester Gods. And a date for a meeting between Loki, Leah, and the creators of the Manchester Gods penciled into the calendars.

The Manchester Gods and their creators took the bait of the next attack by the Old Gods of Otherworld hook, line, and sinker.

Loki was starting to think he was rather good at this tricky-plotting-for-the-forces-of-good business.

FORTY-THREE

THE MEETING place was at Witton Park, a name that neither Loki nor Leah recognized. It took them to a village so small that if Leah had overshot it by a quarter mile, Loki was sure they'd never have found it at all.

The sky was gray and flat, the kind that seemed sure to rain and never followed through on the promise.

The village was small, just a few streets, the houses well maintained and gardens brimming with flowers along the hedges. Soccer balls lay freely abandoned and kids' bicycles leaned against the garden walls alongside the street. No gates were locked. This wasn't the kind of place where one worried about locking gates.

"Why *this* village?" Loki wondered aloud, lowering his hood. It was misting, slightly, but he didn't mind.

Leah pulled out a guidebook. "If you would let me consult my *British guidebook* that the merchant assured me is both comprehensive and inexpensive—"

"Those two things rarely go together," Loki interjected.

"I know!" exclaimed Leah with a shocking amount of emotion.

"He thinks I'm *stupid*. He tried to sell me a *Rough Guide*. I almost broke his finger. The insolence."

Loki held up a finger. "Do you smell that?"

Leah was paging through a guidebook that looked as if it weighed nearly as much as she did. "No, but I'm flipping to the Ws."

Loki sniffed again, following his nose like a dog as he turned a corner, away from the houses and shops, and stopped in his tracks. "You don't need to look for the Ws, Leah."

"Yes, I do," she said irritably, following him with her nose in the book. "Witton Park starts with a W, Loki."

"I think I figured it out," he said, gesturing to the glowing red train tracks in front of them.

"Oh," said Leah faintly. She closed the book. "Yes. Well. This seems like a clear sign."

The train on the tracks glowed red like the hottest embers, and it loomed larger than a normal train, drowning out the pastoral landscape around it. The engine hummed steadily and the whistle blew, loud and clear, steam hissing from the front of the train.

A conductor called with an eerie, detached voice, like he was calling from far away, "All aboard for Manchester."

"That's us," Loki said faintly. He moved first and Leah followed, and one after another, they climbed up the steps and onto the unnatural train.

The interior of the train seemed normal. Empty, but normal. The seats were worn bare at points, the fabric so thin that the cushion below was visible. They took a seat together, side by side, instinctively wanting to stick together.

They'd deceived Surtur and stopped the Serpent and fought Nightmare, but this was the most unnerved they'd been in their adventures together. IT WOULD MAKE SENSE, OF COURSE. THEY MIGHT NOT KNOW THE HISTORY, BUT I DO, AND THEY HAD EVERY RIGHT TO PAY ATTENTION TO THAT TICKLE OF THEIR INTUITION.

In 1825, Stephenson opened the Stockton & Darlington Railway. Twenty-six miles of track that connected Witton Park with Stockton. There were tracks before, certainly, but this was the first commercial passenger trainline. It was where steam met people and transformed them. The journey of the Age started here. And in this Industrial Revolution, all rails led to Manchester. The beauty and the wreckage, the promise of progress facing off against the reality of industry.

Of course, the two fearless children do not know this. They got on the train because it was clear they should. They intend to deceive the Manchester Gods. They are not concerned with whether or not the Industrial Revolution deceives them in return.

"What if someone asks us for tickets?" Loki asked Leah in a low whisper.

"No one's going to ask us for tickets, Loki."

"Why have us come here, if they were going to bring us to Manchester?" Loki asked. "Why not bring us to Manchester directly? It would have been easy enough."

"Power play? The ambience of an abandoned ghost train running on underworld fire?" suggested Leah.

"You're spending too much time around me, Leah," Loki said, stretching out his feet onto the seat across from them. "Tell me what your guidebook says about Witton Park."

WHEN THE train arrived, it was not at a Manchester that you or I would know. You could not go there by any other train. The green hedges, red brick houses, and gray skies of Witton Park had disappeared in exchange for an airy, empty train station with high arched ceilings, which made the train's hissing and clanking echo eerily in the stillness. A cool gray mist poured out from beneath the train and rose up, shrouding the other platforms and the sky from view. Everything was cast in gray and black, save for Leah's and Loki's clothes.

Loki jumped down the two steps from the train to the platform and offered Leah his hand. To his surprise, she took it. Her palm was sure and warm, and when she came down to the platform, he had to force himself to let her go.

He nearly asked Ikol to lead the way when a voice emerged from the mist.

"Welcome, Master Loki of Asgardia. Welcome, Miss Leah of Hel."

"How does he know who I am?" Leah asked in a low voice. "Everyone knows you. No one sees me."

But this figure, stepping out of the mist between two intricately patterned Victorian gates, had seen and known Leah too. Loki didn't like someone knowing more than he, especially when this man was here by a plot of Loki's own design.

The emerging figure was tall, with shoulder-length white hair, a furrowed brow, and a smile that did not quite reach his eyes. His collar was stiff and his coat hardened like a shell.

Like a shield, Loki realized. The man was forged out of metal.

"For your warning of the Otherworld attack, you have our thanks. I am Master Wilson," the man said, walking forward with a staff in his hand. The top curled over, like a snake, or a sun in the abstract. The latter, Loki thought, would be acceptable. Optimistic even. The former, a sign of sinister intent.

Maybe he was reading too far into it. Still, the fact that he couldn't tell what the staff's symbol was supposed to be bothered him.

"I'd prefer Mister," the man said, casually, like he didn't know Loki was distracted by his staff. "But it seems the gods have forced a position of power onto me."

Loki frowned at that. The gods did not force power onto mortals frequently. He doubted that was the reason.

"I am no man's master. That's very much the point," mused Wilson. He opened his arms wide. "Come. Follow me. Tell me why you shared such a fortuitous warning."

It sounded like the fake attack had been a success, then. Loki began to follow him as they walked down the platform's edge toward the entrance to the train station. The station remained unnervingly empty except for them and the glow of their train. The ticket office remained shuttered. The waiting room doors were shut. It looked abandoned, for all intents and purposes.

He realized he hadn't answered Wilson's question. "Mischief, basically," he said vaguely. "I'm all about mischief. Famously so."

Leah elbowed him. He was not selling this very well. He was *distracted*. Leah's hand in his hand. The train ride. The mysterious staff. He was very distracted.

He quickly covered his missteps. "And really, I just wanted to learn more. For instance, I was really wondering—"

"What in the Nine Realms are you?" Leah asked bluntly.

"Hel-puppies, Leah," Loki hissed. "You can't just ask people—"

"I suppose it's easiest to think of me as an unusual kind of druid," Wilson replied, his tone friendly and open, as though they'd asked him how he felt about coffee or tea. "Except instead of a fondness for ash and oak, I prefer steel. Steel, steam, and holy concrete."

He tilted his head back, face to the sky, his eyes closed and expression serene. He inhaled deeply.

"Have you lived here long?" Leah asked, not specifying exactly where *here* was, as neither of them knew.

"I found myself spontaneously come into being a couple of centuries ago," he said, a warm smile on his face.

"The opposite of spontaneous combustion," Loki said.

"Is it?" mused Wilson. "I don't know if it is." His staff clicked on the ground as he walked onward. It was a gear, Loki realized. Not a sun, or a snake. A gear. "I was a druid of the cities in a land with none. And that didn't strike me as *right*. I started to work on finding a way to correct that imbalance."

"I see," Loki said, thinking of the city he'd seen devouring the countryside.

"I call my beliefs 'urban pantheism,' but I've been known to be a little pretentious like that," Wilson added, almost apologetically. "*Pretentious*. A lovely word. Wielded like a weapon, a whip used to flick people with ideas above their station. But I do not have much time or tolerance for people being stuck at their station."

He paused, looking over his shoulder and past Leah and Loki at the train station they were leaving.

"Except train stations. Isn't it a place of beauty?"

It was, in its own singular way. The metalwork throughout the station curved and bent with such a natural flow that it reminded Loki of a river, or of vines. There was an elegance to the way that the paths of a mostly open space were made by the curvature of the walls, the arched doorways, the change of brick pattern. It was beautiful. Lonely, but beautiful. It didn't take much imagination for Loki to think of this place packed with people, with trains coming and going, the whistles of conductors and ticket inspectors.

Even this train that traveled through pocket dimensions had a sense of style. It was not strictly utilitarian.

"There's always a price for progress," Wilson said, as if he could read Loki's mind.

"Like the Red King's imprisonment?" asked Loki slyly.

Wilson shot him a look, walking them to the edge of a plaza. "There's no need to be so judgmental, Loki. The Red King is a monster. He lives to destroy. Why should he be free?"

"But it's clearly the Red King's energy that fuels your cities, and your train."

"Yes," Wilson said placidly. "Reparations for all the harm he's caused poor people. Do you know how many trolls died in his hands? The life expectancy of a troll child in the pits?"

"No," admitted Loki. He looked at Leah, and she shook her head. She did not know either.

"Does it justify what you are doing in Otherworld?" Leah asked.

Wilson frowned as they walked. His feet made hollow thuds as they crossed through the strange, vacant train station. "The common persons of Otherworld come to live in these city-gods for hope of a better life. The only reason those at Pendragon's court care is that there are suddenly fewer people to serve them dinner."

"I don't think that's fair," protested Loki. But was it? Pendragon hadn't talked about the people disappearing, the ones moving into the city-gods, which let the city-gods grow and expand their territory. He'd talked about the damage it'd done to the countryside where he loved to ride and hunt.

"Does anything strike you as 'fair' in a land of perpetual monarchy without a democratic leash?" Wilson asked. "Their only defense is this is how it's always been. We ask, how *else* could it be?"

Loki felt as if he'd been hit with a stiff wind strong enough to blow him right over. Wasn't that what he was trying to do with his life? Everyone saw him as how he'd always been. And he wanted to know how else he could be. That was what brought him here to Otherworld. That was what drove him to use his trickster nature for the greater good.

Wilson continued, oblivious to the war inside of Loki. "This is a war of ideas."

This is a war of self, Loki thought.

As they walked out of the station, the city sprang up around them, buildings tall enough to block out the light—if there had been any. Even at night, smog choked the stars and the moon, low-hanging clouds that puffed up from chimneys and stayed low over rooflines. The buildings were built in tight clusters, making the roads feel narrow and claustrophobic.

They followed the road until it widened, and the density loosened its chokehold on Loki and Leah and anyone who lived here. The mansion ahead of them had more space—and more air—than those who lived close to the train station.

As they walked up the steps, Leah asked what Wilson meant by the war of ideas.

"They say that Britain is fundamentally rural. We say Britain is fundamentally urban," Wilson explained. "Otherworld is the subconscious of the British Isles. But are fairies and fable the most important things that this island has contributed to the world? No. *We* introduced the concept of modernity and modern urban cities to the world. Manchester was the first city of the future, anywhere," Wilson said, thumping his staff on the steps as they climbed them up to the front doors.

He creaked open the front door and reached to a side cupboard, fumbling around in a drawer. There was a snap and hiss of a match being struck and then Wilson's face was illuminated as he leaned close to a lamp on the wall, sliding the match into the base. The gas lamp caught, illuminating the hallway. It felt like a museum, its paneled wooden interior and black and white checkered floor lined with endless rows of statues and paintings.

Leah and Loki followed Wilson in.

"There is no future in England's dreaming," said Wilson. "The world that led to that Starkphone you're so obsessed with started here."

"You can't have one without the other," Leah said, turning a slow circle with her head tipped back. Her green eyes were wide, drinking in the art and music and plants and architecture around her. A glaring difference from the cold, grayscale train station outside the door.

"Now is the time of modernity," Wilson insisted. "The war came because there was no choice. Our existence threatened the realm."

Loki opened his mouth to protest—tell him that there was always a choice, or that the Manchester God had risen first, threatened first—but then he closed it.

"They can have their dales and glens and all the leafy tedium," Wilson said dismissively, leading them up a grand set of marble stairs and gesturing to the next room. "They will think we devour all, but we don't care about their realms. All we'll do is… populate their skylines a little."

The next room held delicately carved statues of women draped in silk and furs, robes made of satin and sheen, somehow portrayed through marble and stone. It smelled like ash and sulfur, but it looked as beautiful as an untouched countryside.

"All we want," Wilson said quietly from where he stood in the doorway to the gallery, watching Loki and Leah explore, "is for an Otherworld that actually represents the nation it purports to represent. This realm's eternal past deserves to have a future."

Loki hadn't liked seeing the city-gods devour the countryside. But hadn't he seen both sides of Britain in the Earthly realm? Hadn't he flown into London and badgered a rough bouncer of a

240

Camden bar to let him in despite his age to find Hellstrom? And hadn't he loved the rolling hills of green and overgrown hedges splitting up the gardens of Witton Park? There was something alluring about feeling insignificant and small, one of many in a city, essentially anonymous. And something so healing about the quiet of the countryside.

He rubbed at his forehead, confused. He came here to trick Wilson, not be tricked. This was the mastermind behind the city-gods? Pendragon was fighting tooth and nail to keep Otherworld from this gentle druid and his metal coat?

"We can change," Wilson said. "The city changes us all. And change is good." His eyes traveled over and then fixed on Loki. "I thought that some gods would understand. I suspected that I'd find you in their number."

Loki and Leah stayed silent. Loki was too embarrassed to meet Leah's eyes, but he felt her gaze on him.

Wilson gestured around the room. "Stay as long as you like. When you return to Asgardia, I hope you'll bring an accurate word of our character."

And with that, he was gone. They were left alone in this art gallery, filled with precious and irreplaceable pieces of art.

"Now's the time to strike," Leah hissed after she checked the hallway to see that Wilson was truly gone. "We get to the Red King and free him. Ready?"

Loki yanked his arm away, striding away from Leah. "No. No, no, no." He gripped his hair in angry fists. Frustrated fists. He spun around. "I mean, I don't think I can. Can I?"

Ikol stood on his arm, alert and ready, but silent. Of course. Silent when it mattered most. Loki groaned and stomped over to the window. The roof lines collided into each other, becoming their own rapid rise and fall like urban hills, running until they reached the edge of the factories marked by the smokestacks reaching toward the clouds.

"I can't, can I?" he murmured, more to himself and Ikol than anyone else. "Oh, by Odin's sores, I can."

"You make no sense," Leah stated flatly.

He spun around hard enough that Ikol took flight to avoid being thrown into a wall. Loki's face was a picture of distress. Pink cheeked, wild eyes, hair sticking up at every angle.

"Leah," he whispered. "We're on the wrong side."

FORTY-FOUR

LEAH MADE Loki promise not to act rashly, and they both agreed that they needed to talk through the problem with a neutral third party. That being said, they didn't know many neutral third parties, so they went with a neutral-for-a-price third party.

They took Hellstrom out for lunch in Camden.

This time, they beat him to the pub. Midday, the pub didn't care if two kids were in a booth so they sat on the same side, drinking milkshakes, wishing their feet touched the floor.

Hellstrom slid into the booth with ease, his legs already up on the bench and his back against the window. "You got my pay?"

Loki winced. "No. Not really. But I have something better! By the way, do you not own shirts? I could buy a shirt for you. Or maybe we could talk about budgeting and setting aside a certain amount of this payment for shirts."

Hellstrom grinned. "No shirts."

Loki sighed. "Fine. No shirts. Thanks for coming, though. I wasn't sure you would. This is the Trio of Trickery and we're ready for our inaugural meeting."

"Call us that again and I'm leaving," Hellstrom said balefully. He switched gears when the waitress approached, ordered coffee, and called her doll. She blushed and scurried off.

"Trio of Trickery?" Loki sighed dramatically. "I know. It's a terrible name. I can't believe Leah suggested it."

"I didn't," Leah informed Hellstrom.

"To business!" Loki proclaimed. He leaned forward. "Britain's new gods are threatening to take over power in Otherworld from the Old Gods. The All-Mother tasked *us* with crippling the modern gods to help our allies, the Old Gods. What happens here affects all the realms. All-Mother says that the Old Gods' victory will mean a stronger Asgardia."

"And you got there with my map of the new gods' mystical power," Hellstrom said pointedly. "Which is why you should have a purse full of money for me."

"Your map was good. And then I laid a trap. Told the other side some key intel that we followed through on. They trusted me. They think I'm on their side. But actually I'm on the Old Gods' side. Kind of. But I don't think Camelot's going to pay you anymore," Loki said in a rush. Best to pull the Band-Aid off.

Hellstrom blinked. "Why the hell not?"

"Because we're switching sides," Loki said excitedly. "Change is *good*, Hellstrom."

"Switching sides?" Hellstrom snorted. "God of Mischief indeed. But I don't really care what side is which. *Someone* has to pay for my expertise."

"Leah, a little help here?" Loki stage-whispered.

"The new gods, the Manchester Gods, we think they're right. Loki thinks they're right," she clarified. "Who are we to stop modernity? It marches on, even against us. And now we must wait to reap the rewards and money. Time will be in our favor."

"That's a compelling speech, Leah," Loki whispered over the table. "But I think Hellstrom gets the message. Sometimes, change is good. Sometimes, the powers that be must be reminded of who gives them that power."

"And how are you going to use this newfound power?" Hellstrom asked, his voice salty and acerbic.

"Disguises and the old map. Not yours. We're going to destroy the seats of power of the Old Gods," Loki declared.

"Why?" Hellstrom asked, more curious than shocked.

"He made good points. Who amasses wealth and power, why people were invested in the status quo, and how sometimes, you have to back the druid to shake things up around here."

"No, I mean, the whole double-double cross scheme. Why are you telling me?" Hellstrom drummed his fingers on the table.

Loki made himself meet Hellstrom's eyes. Or at least Hellstrom's sunglasses. "Because I kept secrets from you last time. And I hated how that felt."

Hellstrom's lips twitched. "That's it?"

Loki shrugged. "I am Loki. I can only be Loki. But as much as they're able, I want people to trust me. Not because I need their trust to deceive them, but because I've earned it."

Hellstrom flicked a salt packet from one of the holders on the table at Loki. "You're a manipulative little brat. I trust you about as far as I can throw you."

Loki grinned. "Luckily that's a long way."

"You *are* tiny, and I *am* pretty damn strong," Hellstrom conceded.

"Are you ready for the best part?" Loki asked, bubbling with excitement.

Hellstrom's face fell. "Oh no. I doubt I'm going to like this."

And from behind their backs, Loki and Leah both withdrew their Guy Fawkes masks. The ghoulish face, white with pink, holes for eyes, a mustache that curled up at the end and a little strip of a goatee.

Loki tied on his own and hated the way his voice echoed, but loved the way that it sharpened his vision. He turned to Leah and gasped.

"Another one? Imposter! Imposter! Seize her!"

To his delight, he heard Leah laugh. He couldn't remember hearing her laugh before.

She touched her fingers to her face, delicate and smooth. "These aren't as comfortable as I thought they'd be. It's fun but not practical."

"No, it's *symbolic*," Loki corrected her.

He held out a final mask to Hellstrom. Hellstrom hesitated and then, to Loki's utter surprise, reached out to take the mask.

"Only because I think you two are liable to get yourselves killed," he muttered.

But Loki saw Hellstrom tracing the outline of the mask's features with reverence and curiosity. If there was anyone who ought to be blowing up Britain's finest things, it'd be Hellstrom.

THEY WASTED no time. Leah cut them gateways and portals from one place to the next.

They blew up Stonehenge.

The Long Man of Wilmington.

Hadrian's Wall.

Glastonbury Tor.

One by one, they tore down these symbolic gateways to the Otherworld, these wells and reflections of the Otherworld's presence. This time, they went into their path of destruction believing that change was meaningful and necessary, and sometimes the system had to be broken to fix it.

Loki wanted to banter and joke, but he kept his lips sealed tight. *I am become Death!* he thought, quoting Dr. Robert Oppenheimer. *Destroyer of the Otherworld. I am the Lightbringer.*

I am the Lightbringer, he repeated again and again after blowing up or damaging sacred places here in this Earthly realm, wondering what the effects looked like in Otherworld.

And despite believing he was on the right path, Loki felt guilt prick at his heart. He walked next to Hellstrom, just behind Leah who led the way. They chased the last bits of sunlight out to the west.

"I think this is the worst thing I've ever done," he said finally.

Hellstrom shook his head. "Betrayal? Really?"

"Thor's dead because of you and you think this is the worst thing you've ever done?" Leah asked dryly as they passed through a narrow copse of trees. "I don't know if—"

"*I've* ever done," he cut her off. "Not what past-me has done. You'll have to ask Ikol that."

"That's not what I was going to say," Leah said smoothly. She brought her mask up onto her forehead so she could see him clearly and so he could see her. "It was necessary and relatively kind, what you've done here. If Otherworld must fall, better it fall quickly. The loss of the Holy Sites will hurt the ancient regime as surely as a loss of the sites of the Manchester Gods would weaken them."

Loki blinked up at her. "Is this really happening?"

She scowled at him.

A grin spread across his face. "You agree with me!"

"Please," she scolded him. "Not so loud. People will think our bickering is just cover."

He laughed. "Wouldn't want that to happen."

"Exactly," she said primly.

"And we've both worked so hard to establish our mutual enmity," Loki said cheerfully. "Let the historical record show—"

"Enough, Loki," Leah said, but her voice was gentle, and he could almost hear a smile in her voice.

That was victory enough for Loki.

"That was disgusting and cute and I'm going to have to ask the two of you never to do it again," Hellstrom said flatly behind them.

Loki grinned as Leah opened another portal. He'd entirely forgotten that Hellstrom was there. What a delight.

FORTY-FIVE

THE OLD Gods of Otherworld did not understand what was happening. Everywhere Loki, Leah and Hellstrom struck, the Old Gods of Otherworld and the spaces around them—the Round Table, their grand halls, the battlefields and forts—were hit with little earthquakes that shook and rattled the roots of their power. They could feel it changing their magic, their defenses, and the walls they built to hold the Manchester Gods at bay. One earthquake was terrible, but not cataclysmic.

But this was not one. As the Long Man of Wilmington fell, Merlyn's Tower crumbled within Otherworld. When they blew up Hadrian's Wall, Castle Le Fay fell as if it'd been blown over by a soft breeze. Glastonbury Tor turned into the death of the Green Chapel, and when Stonehenge fell, so did the Starlight Chapel. When one icon fell in the real world, one would fall in Otherworld. Immediately and without warning. The fortresses and stalwarts of the Old Gods, the places where people sought strength and protection.

And they fell, like a house of cards on a breezy day.

The magic of this world—the power they held dear, all they

wanted to keep sacred—began to disintegrate. The footing beneath Pendragon, Captain Britain, and the others began to shift and collapse. They reached for power that was no longer there.

Around Pendragon's table, the lords and knights were panicking.

"The wall's been breached," bellowed Herne, shoving open the doors and bursting into the room without any regard for decorum or protocol. "The Manchester Gods have breached the wall! They will take the Highlands!"

"Fight back," snapped Captain Britain.

Herne glowered at him. "Something sinister is afoot. Our spells flickered. Our arms grew weak. And some men sobbed as a great weight fell upon our hearts."

"It's like something's sapping away our power. Leeching it away," Captain Britain hissed under his breath as he leaned over a map. "But how would that be possible?"

But Arthur Pendragon knew what was happening. He recalled the conversation with Loki just a few days prior. He remembered the map. He remembered their detailed discussion of places of power destroyed in the Earthly realms to weaken the places of power in Otherworld.

"Where," he spat out, "are they?"

Another rumble rolled through the room. Another place of power destroyed.

Herne looked pale beneath his armor. "Where are they *not*?"

This was not the way that the war was supposed to go. Pendragon had wanted the whole weight of Asgardia, a pantheon behind him. And the All-Mother had declined his request. They'd sent Loki, assured him that they had control over the God of Mischief, that he would work his chaos in their favor.

But the God of Lies had lied. Arthur had been double-crossed and made a fool.

He slammed his fist down on the table, goblets of wine jumping to attention and sloshing over. No one moved for napkins or to mop up the mess. They dared not breathe when he was in a temper, and they could see the fury building on his face.

"How could a boy-god and a girl move so fast?" he asked.

Herne shook his head. "It matters not *how* or *why*, but that they've made the path clear for our enemies. As our powers fail, iron tracks burst from the ground."

"If they bring engines here," warned Pendragon, trailing off.

"Bloody hell," muttered Captain Britain.

The Lady of the Lake had stood serenely off to the side, but at the hint of engines bringing more waste and ruin to the countryside, she stepped forward. "Merlyn, you too have been quiet. What do you sense?"

The wizard spoke when invited, and he had not yet been invited. He tilted his head graciously to the Lady of the Lake. "That disruption is only temporary. We can still rally. It'll take cunning," he said, turning to Arthur, whom he still saw as a boy-king from long ago. "And it'll take wit. But if we move swiftly—it is not too late."

"Partially correct," sneered a high-pitched voice in a timbre close to the whine of a machine.

Those at the table whirled and found an Engel hovering in the arched window. The Lady of the Lake gasped, and Herne and Pendragon took steps backward. They were not used to seeing the fair folk transformed like this, so far from their earthly beauty. This one had lost his ageless face, the lines around his mouth and eyes pronounced, his forehead and chin jutting forward. His body was contained in a spindly metal cage with mechanical wings that trapped his own natural ones.

They'd heard of this happening, of course, but they had not seen it with their own eyes. And there was no accounting for how this fairy became an Engel, be it by choice or by force, and they all knew that they could not trust the answer given, should they ask.

The Engel cackled. "It's not too late for a *treaty.*" His feet hit the stone of the open window and he crouched above them. Pendragon's heart wanted to flinch and cower, but he stood strong. This Engel was small. He could crush him, if he came down to where Pendragon could reach him.

"You have a simple choice," crooned the Engel. "Will there be peace in Otherworld?"

Everyone at the table tensed, the smoke of war filling the room around them.

The grin that spread across the Engel's face was cruel. "Or will there be ruins?"

THE ENGEL left them to their decision, and the men and women of the Round Table argued and fought with one another, but they all knew the moment that the Engel had flown to the highest room of Camelot, had breached their secret war room, that there was only one outcome. And that was how, a few days later, they found themselves standing on one half of the room, watching Arthur Pendragon unravel a treaty. A peace agreement.

It didn't matter what they called it. Everyone in Camelot knew what it was.

Surrender.

And Master Wilson didn't hide his glee as he pointed out to Pendragon where to sign.

Pendragon snatched the pen from Wilson's hand and grumbled, "Mere reading isn't one of your baleful inventions."

Wilson's smile did not change. Once the treaty was signed, he rolled it up and tapped it on the table triumphantly. "Thank you, my king."

Pendragon wanted to tell Wilson that he would never be Wilson's king. That he had no desire to have a subject like this one. But he kept his mouth shut.

"Your realms will be your realms. Your icons in the real world will be reconstructed. We'll arrange a parliament shortly. You'll certainly have representation there."

"I wonder if you have any sense of the magnitude of what you've done here," Pendragon mused, rising slowly to his feet. He leaned on his staff. A cane, to some. "You've brought down years of tradition and put in place this strange—"

"You say strange," Wilson interrupted. "We say 'the new.' It really is a matter of perspective." He turned away, and then paused, gesturing for Engels to bring forth two figures from the shadows. "Here are your two spies back. We were not so easily fooled."

Loki and Leah were shoved to the front of the room, into the spotlight, as Wilson walked away.

Captain Britain gripped their shoulders. "Did they hurt you, Loki? Leah?"

Loki lowered his head contritely. "No, Captain. We're well. Sorry. I wasn't much use. I can't believe we were caught so easily."

He glanced up to see that Captain Britain's face was pitying. He'd bought the lie from the little godling boy. But behind him, Pendragon's face was etched full of fury and betrayal. Loki's stomach sank.

Lord Arthur Pendragon knew. And he would not forgive.

LOKI WAS the first to speak as they trudged up the stairs to their room in one of the turrets.

"You couldn't open us a portal?" he asked. "To the room?"

"It's good for you to get your steps in," she said.

He pulled out his phone and showed her the screen. "I've gotten *plenty* of steps in. I think we could have opened a portal."

Leah sniffed. "This is why you're not allowed magic. You wouldn't use it responsibly."

"You don't know that," he protested. She raised an eyebrow at him. His shoulders slumped and he relented. "Okay. Fair. Did you see Pendragon's face?"

"Yes," she said, a frown on hers. "He knows."

"I thought so too. Think he'll tell the All-Mother?" Loki asked, dreading the answer.

"You don't think the All-Mother will figure it out?"

"You have a vested interest in me not getting into too much trouble."

"I do. Speaking of," she said. "You owe my mistress a debt. It's time to pay it."

"I know," he said with a yawn. "I've been putting it off. Can we do it in the morning?"

"I will hold you to it," Leah said, turning her face away from him, so he couldn't see her expression. It was a needless movement. He had been too busy looking at his feet on the stairs to see her face and the desperate sadness that had filled her eyes.

FORTY-SIX

FOR REASONS Loki didn't understand, Pendragon told no one of their plot and betrayal. Which meant the next day, when he asked Wilson to distract the Lady of the Lake, she was amenable to the druid chatting her up, instead of suspicious, and she did not see Loki, Leah, and Hela sneak off to the cavern where the Holy Grail was kept.

Which was why the boy-god now found himself leading the way down a set of stairs that did not seem like they'd pass safety inspection into a cavern where he'd never been before, pretending like he knew where he was going. Worse, his lantern only lit up the next step in front of him, so he was fairly certain throughout the entire descent that he was about to plunge to his death.

He couldn't decide if Hela, three steps behind him, would allow that or not. On one hand, he was pretty sure Hela wouldn't mind seeing Loki perish. On the other hand, pun intended, her debts would remain unsettled. Still.

"And here to your left, you'll see the infamous black abyss of Camelot!" he said cheerfully.

"And this was arranged *how*, exactly?" Hela asked.

Her footsteps behind him were annoyingly precise and calm. Their descent on crumbling, decaying stone staircases into utter darkness apparently didn't bother her.

"Wilson owes me," Loki said. He couldn't believe he was using his favor on this. But he could, in a way. He wanted to get out from under the debt of Hela. Mephisto. All the others.

"Who?" Hela asked.

"Paperwork," Loki said. "I filled out mountains of paperwork. Grant applications, visas, gate cards, background checks—"

"Ignore him, mistress," said Leah dryly from behind Hela.

"I intend to," Hela replied.

Loki's foot slid forward on smooth surface and his lantern caught the edges of a thin pool of water. They'd reached the bottom of the cavern. Loki swung his lantern around and there, in the center of the shallow pool on a pedestal made of grotesque bones, was a plain-looking silver goblet.

"Anyways," he said casually. "Behold. The Holy Grail."

It felt like the announcement should come with a choir of angels singing, or the tremendous ominous clamor of an organ, or foreboding background music laced with the voices of haunted children, but instead there was just the three of them, a shallow pool, a silver goblet, and silence.

Even in the lantern light, it was easy to see Hela's eyes glittering with desire.

She inhaled deeply and closed her eyes. "Well *done*, Loki. Your debt to Hel is repaid."

The arm she'd lost to the Dísir was cradled against her body as she waded through the shallow pool and lifted the goblet in the air. Hela tipped it unceremoniously to her lips and drank deeply. She slammed the cup back down and gasped as white light raced across her skin, and down her arm, filling in the gap where her hand was missing.

Loki glanced sideways at Leah, his mouth opening to make a silly remark, a quip, something witty that would drive her mad. But just as Hela's arm was wrapped in light, Leah was enfolded in a soft green glow. Bits of light broke away from her, floating upwards in the cavern, and in their place, they left open, gaping wounds on her.

"Leah," he whispered, glancing between her and Hela.

"Don't look sad," Leah said shortly. "I'm a handmaiden. Sacrifice is in my nature."

It hadn't occurred to him that the girl placed with him to ensure his debts were paid would disappear when the debts were paid. He'd thought maybe she'd go back with Hela and he'd have to visit. Make excuses. Lie.

He hadn't realized that'd she'd disappear. *Hand* Maiden.

He swallowed hard. "It was good knowing you, B.F.F."

More and more pieces of light were breaking off from her. She was disintegrating. Disappearing. His heart ached. He wanted to reach out but he couldn't make himself.

"Best friends forever," she said. "I looked it up."

"See?" he managed to choke out. "I told you it was true."

She reached for him then, a smile on her face surprising them both. "Thank you, Loki. I do appreciate the sentiment."

He reached back for her, but his fingers passed through her palm. Tears welled in his eyes and his chest felt so tight he was sure he'd explode.

"But did you ever really think it could be true?" whispered Leah.

And then she was gone. Thousands of pieces of light floating upward, like sparks into the dark sky of the cavern. Loki's whole being ached. There'd been so much more he wanted to say to her.

"The wound is healed. What was sliced apart is whole," Hela said breezily. She began to climb the stairs again, two at a time, ascending into darkness, both arms swinging by her sides. A natural movement, like all was whole and well. "Good to see you, Loki. You've grown up so much. Don't let Pendragon get you down."

And then they were both gone, and it was just Ikol and Loki staring at the Holy Grail.

"She was important," Loki said quietly.

"I know there was affection between the two of—" began Ikol.

"It was more than that," Loki snapped. He covered his face, mumbling into his palms. "It was more than that. *She* was more than that."

He hadn't been ready to let her go. There'd been so much more to say. To do. So many more milkshakes and so much more teasing. So many more silly masks and funny names for their adventures. He'd been naïve, he realized, but he'd truly thought it'd go on like that—forever, maybe.

He swallowed, his throat bobbing with pain. He wiped his eyes on the backs of his hands. The breath he took shuddered when it exited, but he didn't cry.

"Besides," he managed to say. "How am I going to explain this to Thori? I'm a single dog-dad now, Ikol."

IT WAS true that he didn't know how to break the news to Thori— not that the Hel-pup would care much—but freeing Volstagg from the snarls of the vulgar-mouthed puppy wasn't the first thing on his to-do list. No sooner had he arrived back in Asgard than the All-Mother summoned him to stand before them.

He hadn't been prepared for their fury.

It seemed that Pendragon *had* told *someone* about Loki's betrayal.

The All-Mother's rage was a palpable thing: sucking out all the air and filling the space around them, crushing Loki. They burned with fury, their words boiling over their normal, careful control. Even their faces, usually serene or at least carefully blank, were pinched in fury. Loki kept his head bowed contritely but bit his lower lip to keep his mouth from snapping back at them. Did they not know what this had cost him? How could they not understand?

In the bright light flooding in from the courtyard, under the clear blue sky of Asgardia, he found himself missing the battlefields of Otherworld, the red skies and smoke-filled air, the sounds of metal clanging and the despair of the Old Gods.

"Loki! Look at us!" commanded the All-Mother.

He raised his face to them.

One of them growled, "Do you have the slightest comprehension of what you've done?"

It took every bit of willpower he had to not bite back. "I did what you commanded."

The three of them scowled at him. "Under what circumstances is this what we asked?"

His voice was bitter, sullen. "I brought peace to the Otherworld. If you're unhappy with the results, you should have provided a more thorough commission."

They stared at him with thin, flat mouths and furrowed brows. One of them turned to the others. "This is what I told you would happen."

They turned to Loki again. "Loki, this is—"

He was tired. He was hungry. He wanted to sleep in his own bed and hug his own ungrateful puppy and cry over the loss of his best friend. And they were standing between him and all those things he needed.

"Listen, All-Mother," Loki said, interrupting them. "Our *new* allies sit in Parliament. They rule Otherworld and are good people. Bar their lack of political power, our old allies are perfectly fine. And most importantly, *no one is dying*!"

"Loki, you are not listening to—"

"No, All-Mother, you're not listening to *me*," he shouted back, stamping his foot. He hadn't meant to do that. It made him look younger and more childish than he already did. But he couldn't help it. His anger welled up in him and he curled his hands into fists. He tried to take a deep breath.

"I did this all for you. You have *no idea* what I've had to sacrifice for you and Asgardia and everyone. I don't expect or need gratitude. But if you don't want Loki to save you, don't ask Loki to save you! I can only do things *my* way! Here is peace—so I ask you, what's the problem here?"

He ended in a scream, something so feral he almost didn't recognize it as coming from himself.

The All-Mother exchanged a glance. Quietly, one of them said, "That will be all, Loki."

He'd been dismissed.

He wanted more from them, but right now, he'd take this. He'd get food. Maybe Volstagg had dinner to share. He'd get his puppy. And then they'd go home.

He nodded, turned, and left without another word.

FORTY-SEVEN

THERE WAS, in fact, a problem.

Wilson walked alone down a forgotten path. His face was grim and set, though the news he was to deliver seemed good enough to him.

He opened a gate that had not been opened in any memory.

He was no longer alone. He could not see the force on the other side of the gate, but he could feel its presence.

Wilson cleared his throat. "It is done. The land below reflects the land above. From your prototype, we've grown a harvest in Otherworld's fertile soil."

A gravelly voice intoned from the abyss, "And when will our debt be settled?"

"The god-spore tithe is being delivered as we speak," Wilson said, keeping his voice level and unemotional. He'd learned early in this partnership that was key. "We hope your own industrial revolution goes as well as ours."

There was a long pause, long enough to make Wilson's fingers curl into his dusty palm.

Then the voice spoke, "You misunderstand."

Wilson did not think he misunderstood at all. How could he?

He hesitated and said, "But these magnificent machines... you labored so hard to create them. What other purpose could they serve than the betterment of all?"

He was not prone to being an idealistic man, but when idealism found a foothold in him, he found it difficult to uproot. And he did not know yet that this was optimistic.

The glee in the voice on the other side of the gate sent a chill down Wilson's spin as Surtur stepped toward the gate emblazoned with fire.

"*Doom.*"

Perhaps, Wilson thought a little too late, it had been wrong to make a deal with the devil.

LONG AFTER Wilson left Muspelheim, Mephisto received a message. He unrolled the scroll and sat back on his throne, tossing one leg over the other casually. He began to laugh, a small chuckle that grew until he laughed so hard it echoed through every corner of Hell.

"Oh how glorious," he said with a grin. "How *delightful.* Of all the people to betray you, Loki..."

He smiled at the red sky, rolled the scroll back up and tossed it into hellfire.

"This is going to be so much fun."

PART IV

EVERYTHING BURNS

FORTY-EIGHT

THE ALL-MOTHER does not know all. Sometimes, they know too late what is coming, and this was one of those times. Had Freyja shared her dream with Gaea and Idunn earlier, perhaps they would have understood what she did not. But she hadn't. She'd thought it some dream about sisterly jealousy and petty squabbles.

It had not been just a dream.

Freyja had dreamt of her sister Gullveig, the steward of Vanaheim, a realm alongside Asgard at the World Tree. Gullveig had always been a little bit gullible, the younger sister always trying to keep up with the elder and more accomplished sister. She styled her hair like Freyja and wore armor, though Vanaheim was a largely peaceful realm. She wanted to be seen as the warrior that Freyja was.

In the dream, Gullveig sat on her throne, receiving visitors. Freyja stood to the side, waiting for her sister to acknowledge her, but her sister never looked her way. Instead, the Herald of Surtur approached, cloaked in a vibrant red cloak with golden trim, lavish and far more regal than anything the emissaries of Surtur had the right to wear.

He bowed deeply, deeply enough that Freyja knew he appealed to her sister's ego.

"Steward of the all-holy Vanaheim. The fires of Rebellion burn again. Vanaheim has another chance."

Another chance at *what*? Freyja had wondered, and the answer came to her softly, like a whisper. *Greatness. Power.*

The Herald's expression was sly. "Will you take a gift that Surtur offers you? Will you harness this fuel for Vanaheim?"

Gullveig wavered, her expression thoughtful but her forehead pinched with worry. Freyja wanted to reach forward, offer counsel, but she couldn't. Her feet would not move.

"My sister made a peace between Vanaheim and—" Gullveig began carefully.

The Herald dismissed this with a handwave. "Yes, yes, she did. But that was before you were born. Your sister's not one to keep her promises, and neither is Asgard. Did Odin keep any of those promises? Did Asgard?"

Think, Gullveig! We all know that not all promises made to find peace are meant to be kept, begged Freyja. But she could see her sister thinking about the Herald's words.

The Herald could see he was making progress too. He pushed forward. "You are vassals! You have spent your entire lives on your knees for Asgard. Old grudges and slights are still grudges and slights. Why should you forget the yoke?"

The court around Gullveig murmured, the people agreeing with the Herald. Gullveig tilted her head, her eyes scanning her people and taking their reactions into account. She touched her fingers together, tapping them lightly.

"We took Surtur's gifts before. We did not win. What's different this time?"

The Herald knew he had won her over. He struggled to keep the grin off his face. "Surtur does what Asgard never can. The Fire. It always changes. And the power he offers has already toppled one of the pantheon."

Freyja flinched to the side of the audience room where she

stood. What did he mean? Who fell in the pantheon? Surely he was not saying that… Otherworld? She fought to clarify her thoughts.

"I am saying you could say yes to change. Yes to the future," urged the Herald.

Gullveig's face shifted then, moving from thoughtful and unsure to something steady. Freyja reached for her but her arms would not move. Her stomach sank as her sister lifted her chin and said, "I say *aye*."

Freyja thought it was only a dream.

That is, until the next day, when Heimdall came to the All-Mother with a story of the Temple of the Union in Vanaheim burning. Burned by warriors, he claimed, warriors led by her sister.

THE ALL-MOTHER sent word to Loki to go to the World Tree, and despite how their last meeting had ended, he went as they summoned. He could not decide what was more alarming, the World Tree ablaze, or the familiar tall, blond man standing beside it, his red cloak brushing at his heels and the floor, his broad shoulders set with determination.

Loki pinched himself. He was not dreaming.

The light from the blaze was so bright he could not stare directly at its center. The flames rose as if they were being pulled straight up, hauled by some invisible force, and the sound was deafening. The crackle of the wood splintering and breaking echoed in Loki's chest. The flames licked into all the realms, and he felt the strange compulsion to go to his knees. To weep.

But Thor was there, and he was not weeping.

Loki had made the mistake of bringing Thori with him—Volstagg could not pet-sit, and the pup could not be left to his own devices. He was in some sort of Hel-puppy adolescence that resulted in the destruction of any room in which he was left unsupervised. The internet suggested that Thori was suffering from *separation anxiety* but Loki thought that Thori was more likely to be suffering from *separation jubilation*. Either way, the solution was to bring the puppy everywhere and apologize for his filthy mouth.

"The fiery tree cannot resist the cocked leg!" cried Thori, straining at the end of his leash as Loki let the puppy drag him toward the blaze.

"I don't think it's going to be that easy, Thori," Loki said with a cough. The fire burned smokeless, but still the heat seared his lungs.

"Did you name that puppy *Thori*?" Thor asked after a moment's pause.

Loki looked up at his dead brother, still in disbelief. "It was supposed to be an honor. A way to remember you."

"Death to the tree! My bark is the strongest!" howled Thori.

Thor looked down at his namesake. "I see."

"Should I ask about the tree or about you, first?" Loki asked.

"It's easier to explain the tree," Thor said grimly.

Loki looked back at it. "This isn't a good sign, is it."

"I see you've mastered the art of understatement in my absence," Thor said dryly. He clapped a hand on his brother's shoulder. "Come, let us find the All-Mother. I have heard whispers of war."

"You've been back what, twelve hours?" complained Loki. "How come you hear whispers of war before I do?"

THE ALL-MOTHER'S throne room was crowded. Every realm was represented, Asgardia in all its colors and shapes, everyone worried, everyone ready for battle. Faces were grim. Whatever jealousy Loki had felt at Thor's hearing the rumblings of war before him faded. Even in all the chaos of the Serpent and Surtur and Nightmare, he'd never seen the throne room this quiet, this still, this serious.

Some part of him wanted to hide behind Thor, but they'd summoned him, and they were unlikely to forget that small detail. Thor had no idea what had transpired, so he couldn't known how to read the expressions on the All-Mother's faces.

"Well met, Thor," said the All-Mother. "You have returned at an auspicious time."

"I was called," Thor said firmly. "I am ready to serve Asgard once again."

"Pyromania sweeps the Nine Realms," said the All-Mother grimly. "And Vanaheim has taken Surtur's gifts, again. Gullveig fuels the fires of rebellion. She is our sister, but she has made a choice here that affects all of Asgardia and all the realms. If setting the World Tree ablaze is her doing, then it is rebellion."

"The World Tree is where we made peace," Thor said. "This is where they make war."

The All-Mother nodded quietly. "Thor, choose men. But go swiftly. This cannot get out of control." Freyja looked to Loki and added, "Bring your brother. You will need him."

Thor nodded, snapping his heels together and he turned, hand on Loki's shoulder, guiding him to follow him out the door.

"This will be dangerous, Loki," Thor advised. "You should stay here."

"I know you're freshly back from the afterlife, brother, but you wouldn't believe what I've seen and done since you've been gone," Loki said confidently.

It did not land as he'd hoped.

Thor frowned. "What does that mean? What have you done?" The furrow on his brow deepened. "And why did the All-Mother say I'd need you?"

"Never mind, I'll catch you up later," Loki said hurriedly. "The point is, I think I can help."

Thor shook his head. "No, Loki. That's a command. Stay safe. A burning World Tree…" He shook his head. "Surtur's gifts? How did Surtur even reach Vanaheim and Gullveig?"

He turned away from Loki, walking off with all his questions, while Loki bit his lip. It didn't seem like the right time to tell his brother that *he* was the reason that Surtur was in a position to reach out to Vanaheim.

"I thought that Surtur would be happy with what he had," he said to Ikol.

The magpie flew alongside him. "What an assumption."

Loki scowled at him. "Come. We've got to find the best hiding spot."

ABOVE THE Temple of Union where peace had been forged in Vanaheim, Loki found a safe spot in the mountains where he could see the battle, but he was not visible to Thor—and thus a distraction—or bait for Gullveig to use for Surtur. He crouched there, watching the events play out, trying to make sense of it all.

Gullveig set fire to the temple, her warriors with torches chanting, *Let it burn, let it burn*, as they lit pyres underneath the holy site.

Thor, Volstagg, and a great many warriors of Asgardia flew through the sky, lightning crackling off their weapons. It'd been a long time since Loki had seen his brother wield Mjolnir and it sent a thrill through him. He couldn't help the grin that spread across his face. Thor was back! And he was right back in the middle of the action. Loki supposed he shouldn't be surprised—*he* came back after all, and if he could do it, surely Thor, arguably better in every way, could do it. He'd have to get answers from his brother later.

"Gullveig!" bellowed Thor. "Lay down your arms! Whatever's amiss, better it be settled by words than arms."

Thori squirmed next Loki. "MURDER!"

Loki wrapped his leash tightly around his hand. "Let's hope not."

Ikol hopped around anxiously. "Loki... they're going to see you."

"They won't see me," Loki said. "But fire here? Fire at the World Tree? The All-Mother said that pyromania was spreading, and it was Vanaheim warriors setting the fires. I need to understand what's happening. Especially if Surtur's involved. It's clearly going to be down to me to save the day."

Though he admitted quietly to himself that he wanted Thor to see him saving the day, for Thor to see how much he had changed since Thor's death.

Gullveig shouted back through the thunder and rain that Thor had brought with him. "We wish to scour this effigy of tyranny and submission."

Loki frowned. This was a place of peace. Treaties of peace and the ends of war were made here. How could this be a place of tyranny and submission?

"We will not let you," said Thor, lifting his chin.

"Then let's not waste time with talk," Gullveig shouted back.

The battle was fierce and intense. Axes struck axes, sword against sword, mighty warrior against mighty warrior. Loki could barely make sense of it from the mountain top, but he followed the swirl of Thor's red cloak on the battlefield, saw him engage with Gullveig. From a distance, in the rain, it looked like a slow-motion dance. Then he saw them slow, stop, and exchange words.

Thor spun, looking to mounds of rock on the battlefield.

The rocks exploded into bright fire, so bright it was nearly white.

"Oh no," whispered Loki. He knew where he'd seen that before. On the battlefields of Otherworld.

Ikol flapped his wings and cawed, distressed. "That's Engel fire."

From the places where the rock piles exploded with Engel fire, blazing beasts made of machinery climbed out of the earth, bigger than dragons, ten times taller than Thor and breathing the fire of Otherworld creatures.

Thor called down heavier rains, but it made no difference to the machines. They slugged through the mud, churning it up until it sucked off men's boots and those who fell couldn't get up. They thrashed, caught and suffocated by the mud until their compatriots yanked them free. Faces disappeared between the soot from the machines and the mud they left behind. Destruction was a wide, brown swath of land left in their wake.

On the mountainside, Loki was panicking. "The technology of the Manchester Gods, here. What have I unleashed?"

Ikol pecked at his ear. "What we always have. Chaos."

FORTY-NINE

THE BATTLE was forfeit—both sides withdrew, Vanaheim with cheers over the destruction of the temple—and in the wake of the battle, Loki scrambled down the mountainside to find Thor. Now they were sequestered in Leah's old cave near Asgardia, where Thor sat heavily in a chair that was far too small for him and Loki paced circles around a small fire they'd built, catching him up on everything that'd happened, and why there were machines of fire on the battlefield in Vanaheim.

"So let me make sure I understand this," Thor said, holding up a hand and making Loki fall silent. "In the time since War of the Serpent, you've struck deals with Mephisto, Hela, *and* Surtur."

"Yes, but it was so I could rewrite the Serpent's history to ensure you *were* able to kill him! To give him a weakness!"

Thor ignored this. "You were also complicit in the forging of an ultimate weapon made of raw fear-stuff."

"Also yes, but again, that's not the *full story*," Loki protested. "I used it to make sure the fear-lords would be stuck in a perpetual stalemate over it! To save humankind! *You* save humankind!"

"True," admitted Thor. "It's just that your methodology is so…"

"Clever? Innovative?" suggested Loki.

"Unorthodox," Thor decided. He rubbed a hand over his face. He'd taken off his armor and he looked just like a very tired older brother now, his hair greasy and his face streaked with mud and sweat from the battle. "And now as a secret agent of the All-Mother, you were sent to support the powers of Otherworld against a rebellion but instead you sided with these Manchester Gods and they usurped the true order."

"They're the good guys, I swear!" Loki said quickly. "Trust me, if you met them, you'd totally agree."

"Yes, but you just also said that what we just saw on the battlefield, what we as the forces of Asgardia were fighting, was the same technology as the Manchester Gods created," Thor said wearily.

"Well. Yes," said Loki.

Thor looked up at Loki, a small, patient smile on his face. "Okay. Anything else I should know?"

Loki blinked and looked around. The cave looked exactly as it had the last time he'd been here. "This was Leah's cave. Leah was Hela's handmaiden. Literally, she was her hand. She stayed with me until I was able to find a way to rejoin them. Hela's whole. Leah's gone." He muttered under his breath, "I've been busy."

"Have you done anything solely good? No caveats?" Thor asked.

"I freed the Dísir from their curse?" Loki offered hopefully.

"And now their strength is married to Hela's. Brother, do not mistake her love for order for love itself. She protects the dead. But she'd wish everyone to join them."

Loki could have told Thor that he understood that well enough. He'd spent too many weeks now navigating his complicated debt with Hela.

Thor looked down at Thori, who was gnawing on a bone that Leah had left for him. "I assume the dog is also the product of mischief."

274

"I mean, yes, but not my mischief. Hel-Wolf and Garm of

Hel had some mischief when I was looking the other way. Thori's the result."

Thor turned slowly to Loki. "The Hel-Wolf?"

"Yes," Loki said carefully. "I freed him. Minor detail? I might have skipped that part. It doesn't matter now! Hel-Wolf's dead now. Surtur ate him."

Loki found that his voice was tight and high, caught in his throat, and everything felt wobbly.

Thor wasn't looking at him anymore. He'd turned back to Thori and so he didn't know what chaos he caused when he said jokingly, "Wow, you can't even be trusted to look after a Hel-dog."

Something cracked inside of Loki. Something fragile and mortal, something that had been cracking for a long time, trying to keep himself together underneath the weight of expectations and feelings and hopes and frustrations. He tried to keep the tears at bay, but he couldn't. Not any longer. That dam had broken. The sob that hiccupped out of his chest surprised him and when he sucked in a breath, it only fueled the sobs.

"I was only trying to help!" he tried to say, but it came out as something pining and desperate, a yowl of frustration and pain and suffering, of trying to do good and failing. He fell to his knees. "I am just doing my best."

Thor rose from the chair and came over to Loki, a hand on his back, and then lowered himself to the ground to wrap his brother in his enormous arms. "Loki," he whispered. It was the first time since Thor had died in the War of the Serpent that Loki had heard his name said in such a gentle, loving way. "It will be okay, Loki. We'll make it right together."

"I don't know how," Loki sobbed into Thor's cloak. He was snotting all over it, but he didn't care. He wrapped his arms back around his brother and held tight. "I don't know what to do anymore."

Thor sat back, pressing Loki away from him so he could look into the younger god's eyes. "Well. First things first. You say that this technology in Asgardia is Manchester God work?"

Loki nodded, wiping his face off on his sleeve.

Thor's face was grim, even as he tried to manage a smile. He settled his hands on Loki's shoulders. "Then, I'd love to meet your Master Wilson and his Manchester Gods. It's time for a conversation."

FIFTY

OTHERWORLD HAD changed a great deal in the few weeks since Loki had last been there. A city had built up around Camelot. Iron and steel and smog coated the white castle on the hill. Something twinged in Loki's chest. He pushed it away. He couldn't change what he'd done. Not right now. It wasn't why they were here.

Wilson was waiting for them, sitting on a throne elevated by a mechanical device that whirred, raising and lowering at the touch of a button. He looked stern-faced, almost unhappy to see Loki again.

"Loki. Good to see you. You must be Thor," said the druid, holding out his hand. "It's a pleasure to meet you."

Thor didn't take it. "It's a pleasure unshared."

Loki winced. He hadn't expected Thor to skip the pleasantries and get right to the heart of the matter, but Thor had no interest in dancing through propriety tonight, it appeared.

"My brother is somewhat aggrieved," Thor said lightly. "We saw the fruits of your mechanical loom involved in a certain uprising against Asgardia."

Wilson pursed his lips and said nothing at first, and that pissed

Loki off. He stepped forward, even as Thor reached for his shoulder. "I thought we were *friends*, Wilson. I—I helped you! And this is how you repay me? Us? You let your tools be used to attack us?"

Wilson bowed his head. "My worst fears are confirmed."

He rose slowly from his seat, leaning heavily on his staff. He gestured for them to follow him and reluctantly, they did. They followed him from his throne room across a plaza and into another building that vibrated with the hum of engines.

Wilson gestured to the enormous factory. "The gods of the cities are from Surtur's forge."

"Surtur," said Thor, glancing at Loki.

A troll who worked the factory growled. "Loki freed Surtur."

Perhaps the troll thought that Thor would have blamed Wilson for that. But Thor and Loki both knew with whom that fault lay. Loki hung his head. He'd done so many things for good. Why weren't they turning out that way?

Thor said to Wilson, "You dealt with a devil."

Wilson frowned. "I wanted what was best for the people." He rubbed at his jaw. "Surtur offered us the power we lacked. I needed to give us a future. I had to believe it was possible. He gave us the first city. We grew a harvest and returned him a tithe."

"A tithe?" Thor growled. "That's what he's using."

"I know. I didn't realize—" Wilson began.

"Who you were dealing with," Thor interrupted him. "Surtur only wishes doom. You were an unwitting tool in his mission."

"I see that now," Wilson said, wounded. "The technology is wondrous. I saw it and I thought, *he is a Builder just like we are!*"

"A builder of *doom*," Loki muttered.

"I didn't think it would be to destroy. I thought his fire the flicker of knowledge…"

Thor growled low in his throat, but deep enough to rumble through the room, rattling the machines that lined the walls. It sent a shiver down Loki's spine.

"Surtur is the fire. He is the heart of the fire. And the fire builds
278   until there is nothing left."

Wilson held up his hands. "We're not Surtur's allies."

"It looks like you are," Loki said softly. "You see how it looks, right?"

He'd been on the receiving end of perception before—he knew that perception wasn't always reality. But this didn't look good, for Wilson, or for him.

"We've settled our debts. Our Engels will not march with him. The Manchester Gods wish Asgardia no harm," Wilson insisted.

"You better not," Thor grunted. "Because know this, Wilson. If the Nine Realms fall, I will find sufficient strength to return and to end you, and all of this."

Loki grabbed Thor's elbow, tightening his fingers. "Brother. What's done is done. Threats won't change it."

Thor nodded to Wilson and they turned away. "I must make the rules clear to him, Loki."

"It's as much my fault as it is his," Loki said miserably.

Thor draped an arm over his shoulder as they walked back along the path. "This is dire, but not beyond solving. At least we know who our enemy is now. We'll talk to the All-Mother. I will deal with Surtur. It's good you came clean before it was too late, Loki."

IT MIGHT not have been too late to try and stop Surtur. But it was for Loki. His secrets, his plotting, his scheming, it was all catching up with him. And he had no idea how much it was catching up with him until they returned to Asgardia to find a huge crowd in front of the All-Mother, who sat in their thrones on a dais.

"What in Odin's name is going on here?" Thor asked the nearest man.

He glanced at Thor. "They've evidence that Loki freed Surtur and that the All-Mother knew about the young god's scheming. They're calling for Loki and the All-Mother to be seized. Have you seen the young god?"

Thor's shoulders twitched and he casually stepped in front of Loki, guarding him with his body and putting a hand behind him so he could tell where Loki was. "This is madness! Deposing the All-Mother?"

"It's what must be done!" Volstagg said, pushing his way to Thor. He sounded frantic and desperate. "For the good of Asgardia!"

Thor growled and Loki chose the exact inopportune time to peer around Thor's body. Volstagg stared straight back at him. The man's eyes widened and then he shouted, "Loki! It's Loki! He's here!"

"Seize him!" cried men around them and Thor grabbed Loki, holding him close, turning in a circle as they assessed the threat.

Volstagg would call him out? And betray him? After everything they'd done together in the war against the Serpent?

Ikol cawed at Loki. "He's trying to hide his own involvement!"

Someone took a swing at Loki and Ikol barely dodged it, flapping into the sky and trying to get as much air as he could away from the mob below. Loki was so stunned that he barely heard Thor snapping his name, trying to get his attention.

"Loki! Ready?" Thor adjusted his grip on Mjolnir.

"Ready for *what*?" Loki asked. "These are your *friends*. They're *our* friends, aren't they?"

But they did not look like friends in the moment, and the grim set of Thor's face told Loki all he needed to know. He'd defend Loki against his closest companions and he'd use deadly force if he needed to.

"If you want him," Thor cried, raising his voice, "you'll go through *me*!"

Men, led by Volstagg, lunged at Thor, at Loki, and Thor spun Loki around with one hand and gave him a shove. *"Run!"*

Loki did not need to be told twice. As he ran, thunder crashed above him, nearly knocking him off his feet. It felt as if the sky had split apart. Lightning cracked down and someone screamed.

Loki spared one glance over his shoulder, just quick enough to assure himself that his brother was still on his own two feet. Thor fought off dozens of men one by one, and behind them, defenseless, the All-Mother was led away in chains.

He wouldn't let Thor's fight be in vain. He'd get free of here, as fast as he could.

FIFTY-ONE

THOR AND Loki met that evening in Niffleheim, in a safe house only known to the two of them. Loki was already there with Thori and Ikol when Thor threw open the hatch and hopped down, bringing snow and the smell of pine with him.

Loki was on him in an instant. "I discovered something."

Thor looked weary. He'd been fighting and arguing with his friends all day, people he loved and respected. It drained him faster than a battle with the enemy would. He shrugged off his cloak and helmet, setting them to the side.

"Do I want to know how you discovered it?" Thor asked.

Loki shoved a hot drink into his hand. "Probably not! The general gist of it is—Hela seems unenthused to be our ally. So I had to think outside the box and I think I've come up with an idea of how to save everyone."

Hel, and thus Hela, had rejected Loki's request for aid, but he wasn't about to give up so easily. He'd been plotting and scheming, yes, in the general direction of truth and good. And some of those plots and schemes had caught up to him. But he felt like there were more plots here than he knew of, other hands at play in this game of cards. And some part of him felt like there were too many cooks in the kitchen.

"The important takeaway here..." Loki rushed past the details to keep Thor focused. Sometimes his brother would get bogged down in the means without seeing the ends. "The important takeaway here is that I know a way into the heart of Muspelheim. And this war? It's all about the Engel-power. It's the engine that drives this revolution that threatens Asgardia. If we can figure out how to stop this engine, what monkey wrench to throw into this engine..."

"Then you think the revolution can be stopped," Thor finished, sipping from his steaming mug. He shook his head. "I don't disagree that we need to stop the revolution but sneaking into Muspelheim? That's dangerous, Loki."

"Trust me, brother," Loki said. "You are trained for battle." He waved his hands around. "All those people swinging around their swords and smashing into each other and smearing their sweat on each other. Not my thing. Not my scene. This? Sneaking about? Subterfuge? That's my thing."

He was not wrong. A portal leading to Muspelheim from the base of the Manchester Gods was a challenge for the most legendary of sneaks. Loki would need to inch past the diverse Engels of the new capital of Otherworld, traversing a city that screamed soot into the pastel blue skies of England's dreaming. And he'd have to bypass all those who stood in his way, guarding the portal, guarding the city, guarding the technology that threatened Asgardia's life.

He wasn't concerned. It was just another day.

HE BROUGHT Thori and Ikol with him, because without Leah, adventures and scheming felt a little lonely. And because if he had to crawl through portals and shimmy into spaces not meant for gods of his size, it'd be nice to have two smaller creatures who could help out. It involved putting their faces (and beaks) in a mix of soot and mud, but they'd managed to belly-crawl past the Engels to the base of the Manchester Gods in Otherworld, and right up to the gate to Muspelheim.

It glowed red, so hot it turned white in the center, and flares sparked on either side of it, as though the portal itself was unstable. A thought that Loki didn't want to dwell on for long.

"Alright, it's time," Loki said, mostly to himself. He looked down at Thori. "Thori! Listen. One more time. Sit."

Thori sat down promptly, staring eagerly at the portal.

"Roll over."

Again, Thori rolled over obediently, returning to the sit position and panting, drool dripping from his lips as he looked at the portal.

"Annihilate my enemies!" Loki whispered.

Thori blew out his latest trick, a breath of flame that carried out a few feet in front of him. Loki cheered and knelt, scrubbing at the puppy's head.

"I *like* annihilating your enemies," Thori said with a rough growl.

Loki grinned. "You know, you've turned out to be a cool dog."

"It's like you want to be caught," Ikol said, divebombing at their heads and snapping his beak. "It was hard enough sneaking in here without dawdling. Surtur's left his throne. We must act quickly."

Loki rose and brushed off his clothes quickly. "I had to make sure Thori was ready. It's his first big mission. Now we're ready."

They stepped through the portal together, a boy and his dog and his magpie, and though it'd seemed hot standing next to it, nothing burned them going through. It felt like passing from shade to sun to shade again on a hot summer's day.

They arrived on a cliffside in Muspelheim, the ruins of an old garden around them with dead, petrified trees, pillars of stone and sand, a place that must have been beautiful once.

"Let's see what hell we can raise in Muspelheim," Loki murmured.

IT'D BEEN a while since he had rappelled down a wall for any reason, so it took him a few minutes figure out how to anchor himself without a buddy. These minutes were interesting for Loki—he loved a puzzle—and apparently agonizing for Ikol, while agonizingly boring for Thori. The puppy began to eat rocks and then vomit flame to throw the rocks back up. He did this again and again while Ikol squawked about Thori's poor manners, and Loki tried to figure out how to drill a hole into stone so he wouldn't fall to his death.

Once he was finally set up, he had to convince Thori to ride strapped to him like a backpack.

"It's only for a bit," he pleaded.

"Bite your face off," threatened the puppy.

"I will let you annihilate so many enemies," Loki promised, hands clasped together. "But there are no enemies up here. We have to find them. So you have to let me do this so you can go full annihilation mode."

That was eventually the winning argument. And Loki found that bouncing down a wall with a dog on his back wasn't as hard as he'd thought it would be.

But halfway down the rock-face, Ikol screeched and before Loki could twist and see what he was calling about, an explosion rocked the wall just above them, splitting their rope.

Loki yelled as he and Thori fell down, slamming into the stone, and tumbling head over tail until they hit the next ledge. As soon as they hit ground, Loki shouted, "Thori! Annihilate my enemies!"

Thori rolled over and charged, barking about murder and death and all sorts of violent ends.

Suddenly he yelped, slamming on the brakes and tucking his tail beneath his legs. He trotted back to Loki and hid behind his master, head down.

"Scary lady," said Thori in a hushed growl.

Loki picked up his bow and arrow, holding them up defensively. Then the threat floated down into sight. Dark hair,

LOKI: JOURNEY INTO MYSTERY

pale skin, bright eyes, but she wore a red dress and not a green one.

"I *am* a scary girl," she said.

"Leah?" Loki gasped. "How in the—"

"She's not Leah," Ikol cawed warningly, swooping in and landing on Loki's shoulder.

But she looked like Leah. In every possible way, she looked like his best friend. Same hard cheekbones but soft cheeks, placid expression that knew how to frown more easily than it knew how to smile, eyes that flashed dangerously, hands folded neatly in front of her dress.

"I'm not," said Leah, who was not Leah. "I'm what you made me. Think back. You didn't ever wonder what happened to her?"

Loki blinked, and then swayed on the spot. Ikol had to flap his wings to keep his balance. "You're the Leah I wrote into the Serpent's history."

"You trapped me in that insipid prose for millennia," she grumbled, sounding very much like the Leah he knew. She waved a hand into the air vaguely. "I can see your mind ticking away. I hear your private conversations. Even your familiar is familiar to me. I have provided knowledge of your schemes to Surtur and thanks to that, the Nine Realms shudder. I will destroy all you have ever loved. And now I get to destroy you."

She rose into the air, a power his Leah hadn't had. Her arms outstretched, she continued. "You wrote me a small part. You left me no capacity to grow. Writers lie. You made a lie just good enough to do the job and no more."

"In my defense, I was writing that under a very strict deadline, if you remember," Loki pointed out.

"You're a *terrible* writer, Loki," Not-Leah said. "And I am the lie made flesh. I'm the lie that's finally caught up with you."

Of all the lies to catch up with him, he couldn't be happier that *this one*, the one he'd nearly forgotten about, managed to make its way to him. He exhaled gratefully, shoulders slumping.

"Leah. I didn't know this would happen but I'm so glad it did.

This is much better than I could have ever dreamed up for you. You were my only regret. Now you get to share in the spoils. I can promise you more, Leah."

He *needed* her to believe him. His earnestness was real. Would she believe him? He wasn't sure.

She landed on a rock a short distance away, moving into a fighting stance. "What are you talking about, Loki? You will not trick me."

It wasn't *strictly* a trick. It was sheer relief. He thought he'd missed his chance with Leah. That he'd missed the opportunity to see her in a role that was more than a sidekick, or someone sent to babysit him so he would repay a debt. His hands shook with the emotion.

"I'm not tricking you. Think about it. I've killed my brother. I released Surtur. I brought down Otherworld. Basically, I stabbed a knife into the back of anyone who crossed my path and had them thank me for it."

A bit of an exaggeration, but it was important to share this with her.

"I even made an all-powerful artifact and left it aside for a rainy day. You didn't tell Surtur about that, did you?" he asked quickly.

She blinked. "No, I—"

He exhaled, cutting her off. "Good. Okay, good. We're going to need that eventually."

"Loki," she said, sounding more like Leah than someone who wished his death. "What are you saying?"

He had to turn away from her briefly to rearrange his face into something villainous, something cruel and cold and a bit detached, a version of himself that he rarely wore if only because he hated how comfortable this version of himself felt. But he was afraid Leah would see the truth, even through this.

He turned back to her, a sly, confident smile on his lips. "You know exactly what I'm saying, Leah." He paced among the fire she'd wrapped him in. "You saw me with the real Leah. She—you—were my only friend. And I had to give you up. Hela enslaved you to me and to settle our debts made me find a way to destroy you. The All-Mother blackmailed me."

None of what he said was a lie. It ached, a bit, how true this all was. How much it did cut at him. How much it felt like it scooped him out and left him hollow.

He threw his arms up, adding a little theatrical nonsense to his performance. "Half of Asgard would slit my throat if the chance presented itself and the other half would cheer. And Thor. My dear brother. He brought me back to this world because he *missed me* and then he *left me again with all these people who hate me.*"

He spat the words out with venom and anger and frustration that came from a true, hurt place inside of him. He lifted his chin. "They hated me and still expected me to grow up right, the way they wanted me to grow up, different than the way I grew up before? Why would I want people like that to accept me?"

Leah's eyes were wide and her breathing shallow, like she wasn't sure where he was going with this, like she was hopeful and fearful at the same time.

"Let them burn, Leah. Let everybody burn," he whispered, his own chest heaving. Then he slipped his mask back on. "And then Leah and Loki will dance on the blackened corpses of all those who've done us wrong."

Ikol settled on a nearby rock and rustled his wings, catching Loki's attention. He turned his face to the magpie. The magpie cocked his head. "Loki, why didn't you tell me?"

Loki's laugh came hollow and bitter, a true laugh. "I don't trust you, Ikol! How could I trust you with this?"

The magpie clacked his beak. "Ah. Because I am Evil Loki. Hard to fault your reason."

"Not because you're Evil Loki," Loki said tiredly. "Because you're *Loki.* And I am too."

"No," said this Leah. She looked up to him, her face aglow with light and the reflection of the flames danced in her eyes. "You are

brilliant."

"You trust her?" Ikol asked from his perch.

"Wrong question," Loki said to the side, his eyes watching Leah. "I'll always trust her. The question is, after everything, can she trust me?" He jutted his chin to her. "Please, Leah. Surtur offers you revenge. I offer you all of that and a better life. I'd destroy the Nine Realms to make it up to you."

He sounded desperate and he didn't care. He was desperate.

He hesitated and placed his next chess piece on the board.

"But I can't trick Surtur."

Her answering smile was like the sun coming out on a cloudy day. Blinding, and he was grateful for it. "No. But *we* can."

FIFTY-TWO

HE HADN'T been sure she'd say yes. This Leah was more extroverted than his Leah, more open with her bitterness. But he liked that about her. He liked being able to tell what she was feeling about him at any given moment, even if it was negative. He'd spent too long trying to prove himself to people who seemed to like him on the surface, and then talked about him behind his back. Too long trying to do the good and true things for the good and true reasons, but alongside or for people who would not be good and true in return.

He'd seen Volstagg in that crowd accusing him of turning traitor. He wouldn't forget that.

But now Leah brought him to Surtur who looked shocked to see Loki, and more shocked to see Loki and Leah side by side. The demon king turned slowly, his ember eyes narrowing. Loki's heart beat too fast and for a second, he thought that maybe Surtur had grown so powerful that he could see Loki's fear pounding inside of him, or he could see Twilight's shadow, filched by Leah, tucked away inside Loki's tunic.

And he needed this Leah, this new and unpredictable Leah,

to trust him enough not to spill this secret until the damage was done.

"Leah," Surtur said, his voice a hot rumble. "Why is Loki alive?"

"He has a proposition," she said, her voice cool and lofty. And then, as an afterthought, she added, "I think it has merit."

Which part, he wondered. The part they'd tell Surtur—the lie—or the part he'd told her—the truth? Which would she share with him?

"Another deal, Loki?" sneered Surtur, pulling Twilight out of its sheath. He turned the sword around, allowing the flames to shift, licking upwards, twisting and twining as he rotated the sword. The fire grew, fed by the breeze, and Surtur raised his voice over the roar of the flames. "You think I'd fall for that again?"

"It ended pretty well for you," Loki argued, trying not to look at the sword or show fear. He held up his hand, cutting off the response. "I know. Not as you thought it would, but it ended well for you. Do you really care about the details? I freed you."

Surtur considered this and then inclined his head. "So you did, godling."

He did not like it when those other than Hellstrom called him godling. At least from Hellstrom, it almost felt brotherly. Almost. He swallowed back his distaste.

"We both ended up where we needed to be, and now we can have a little fun."

"I do not believe you are on the side of fire and flame," said Surtur.

Maybe he would be if they were scented candles, instead of sulfur and ash. Something warm and crisp. A label that said, *fresh winter snow* and he was in front of a fireplace with a full plate and Leah next to him and Thori by his feet…

Leah elbowed him. He jerked back to attention.

"I'm not so much on the side of fire and flame as much as on my own side. Loki's side. You may doubt me in many ways, but do you doubt that?"

Surtur studied him, and then puffed out smoke in his direction. Loki coughed.

Surtur rumbled, "Very well, boy. You impress me. What manner of trick do you have in mind? How can you hurt Asgard more than Leah and I already have?"

He did *not* look at Leah. When he'd sensed that more people than he were scheming here, when he'd thought he sensed more hands on the chessboard than there ought to be, it had been her hands. Her moving pieces, and then telling Surtur what pieces Loki had moved. She'd been at points a half step behind him, or a step ahead of him. It'd been her the whole time. He hadn't expected that. It could change everything, if he was careful. If he was cleverer than he'd ever been in this life or any other.

"Let me send a message to my brother," Loki said, bringing a sly smile onto his face.

THE AIR in Muspelheim made it hard to move. It stank of rotten eggs and sat heavy in the lungs. Still, Loki jogged up the path to where a distant figure cut a familiar silhouette.

"Thor!" he called out, relieved that his brother answered so quickly.

"You said *hurry* but I don't think you understand how hard it is to get around here without the World Tree," grumbled Thor. "Fire above, fire below."

"And miles and miles still to go," joked Loki, grinning. He accepted Thor's hand and his brother pulled him up on top of the rocks. They looked out over an ocean of lava and fire that bubbled and gurgled, splashing up on rocks just like theirs. "I know the machine's weaknesses. Your strength in the right place ends much of this. If we can get to the right place."

He pointed across the sea of lava, hoping that Thor couldn't hear his pounding heart. Thor had to trust him. Just one more time.

Thor stared out at the sea. "I don't know if those stones are traversable."

"That's a sixteen-point word in Scrabble," Loki said.

"It means," began Thor.

Loki waved him off. "I know what it means. But it's still true that this is the way."

For a long moment, they stood together, and then Thor said, "Do you know the story of the Scorpion and the Frog."

Loki rolled his eyes. "We're not talking in children's stories, Thor. Come on. Follow me."

He leapt from the rock they were on down to another one in a graceful leap, landing surefooted. He turned around and held out his hand. "See, brother, I am no scorpion. Come on."

Thor hesitated and said, "Reach for me." And then with a giant leap, he sailed into the air. But he had none of Loki's light grace, and his arc began to take him a little short. Loki saw the panic in his brother's eyes, saw Thor stretch his arm toward Loki, but Loki snatched his arm back at the last minute.

Thor fell with a hard splash right into the hot lava. He screamed once, an agonizing, pained scream of a dying man, and then the waves of fire pulled him beneath the surface into the essence of Surtur himself.

Loki's chest hurt and he wanted to fall to his knees and cry.

Forgive me brother. Again.

And then he fled. He fled his brother's death. He fled Leah. He fled Surtur.

He had only one goal and that was to make it to Hel. Come hel or high water.

THOR SANK beneath Muspelheim, the essence of Surtur himself. The heat of the lava and flames ate at his skin, his clothes, his hair. But the worst pain was the image that kept replaying, of Loki watching him fall with a knowing, cunning look in his eye.

If one be a trickster, then the other must be the fool, Thor thought. *I understand now.*

He hated Loki. He couldn't not hate Loki. He'd given him so

many chances, but Loki was who he was, immutable and constant, predictable in his cunning and his evil. He hated Loki for what he'd done and he hated that the Loki problem would fall to those who hadn't wanted him to return, who had blamed Thor for his return and told Thor that he was a fool for bringing the god back, even as a child.

The thick lava engulfed him, filling his lungs. His fight was done. The weight was no longer his burden to bear. His eyes burned and he lifted his face toward what he thought was still the sky, even as he fell beneath the realms.

His final prayer would be a pleading one, a desperate one.

Let those I leave behind match the task of stopping Loki.

And then Thor let the heat and fires take him.

FIFTY-THREE

A YEAR ago, he'd spent time in these borderlands, running between
Mephisto and Hela, trying to play them against each other so they'd
each play into his hands during the War of the Serpent. It'd been
a long time since he traversed these mountains, moving from the
heat and bright red spaces of Hell to the cool, glacier chambers
of Hel. And he'd forgotten how impossible it was to navigate
these borderlands at night, with no lamp, with no flashlight, and
nothing to keep him from plunging over the side. He dared not
light a match. He and Thori climbed along the path that rounded
a mountain, no wider than Loki himself, and steep. Parts he had to
do on his hands and knees.

Ikol flew between him and their pursuers, keeping tabs on the
distance. And this time, when he returned, he cawed. "They're
closing in."

Loki swore under his breath, which delighted Thori who tried
to repeat all the swearwords he knew in order. Loki sighed, "Thori,
shush. We don't need them to hear you on top of their pursuit. It'll
only speed them up."

"There's an overhang ahead," reported Ikol, swooping back

toward them. "There's a place to hide. You'll be found, but—"

"Better than nothing," he said. He checked his pocket. Twilight's shadow was still tucked away in his tunic. "They really want this, huh?"

They'd hopped flaming rivers, climbed sheer glassy cliffs and generally done everything short of sawing off a limb, tying it to a boulder and pushing it down a hill to lay a false trail.

"Who *is* this tracker?" Loki wondered aloud, reaching the outcropping Ikol had identified and breathlessly climbing into the little cave. He stretched out his legs, trying to catch his breath. Everything ached.

"Hel-Wolf," said Ikol grimly.

"Hel-Wolf!" cried Loki and then he clapped a hand over his mouth. He whispered, "My mistakes are hunting me down and my pack of lies are after me. My predicament has become terribly on the nose."

"You're just now realizing this?" Ikol landed beside him.

"We'll never make it to Hela's fortress with the Hel-Wolf on our heels," groaned Loki.

Thori licked at Loki's leg. "Master! Hide in the cave. Give Thori your glove. Evil Daddy dog will follow the scent."

Loki started to pull off the glove, then frowned, pausing. "Thori, if he catches you, he'll…"

Thori wagged his fluffy brown tail. "Murder, murder, murder!"

Tears stung Loki's eyes. "Yeah." He rubbed the dog's ears and leaned down to hug him, but the puppy growled. Loki sat back. "Got it. No hugs. But Thori, I hope you know you're amazing."

The puppy picked up his glove and howled. "Thori Deathripper!" And then he sailed into the night, howling, "Best of all dogs!"

If it worked, he *would* be the best of all dogs. Loki would put up a statue to him in Asgardia. He'd lay flowers at Thori's feet every day. He leaned against the cave wall. His muscles burned and cramped. He'd been on the run for too long now. He'd lost Leah, again, and Thor, again. How many times would he have to lose the people he loved?

He could have sat this one out in a jail cell in Asgardia. He could have let himself be taken that day that Thor and he had returned from Otherworld to a riot and accusations of treachery and treason. He could be sitting in the prison with the All-Mother right now, eating meager rations but safe. Whole. Listening to a war rage outside.

But Asgardia would lose. He knew that. And everything he'd done was to save Asgard. To protect it and keep it whole and peaceful. Now the very way he'd saved it from the Serpent threatened it all over again. He couldn't let his own mistakes hurt people like this. He couldn't stand idly by.

Ikol pecked at his cheek. "The Hel-Wolf followed the pup. Come. We must make haste. Enough delays. Also, stop sniffling."

"He was my dog, Ikol. Why don't *you* ever sacrifice yourself for me? That'd be a nice change." Loki did not stop sniffling. He wiped his tears with the heels of his hands and pulled his sleeves over his fists.

"I literally did that," Ikol said impatiently. "It's why you even exist."

Loki blinked. "Okay, point taken but—"

BOOM! An enormous crash sounded just before the rocks at the front of the cave collapsed in a cloud of dust, and something hulking and large slid into the cave. Loki yelled as something grabbed him by the ankle and dragged him out onto the overhang. He punched and fought, but it wasn't until they were outside in the clear air could he see a familiar outline.

Hel-Wolf stood above him, snarling.

And next to him, Thori wagged his tail, demonic eyes gleaming. "I told you he was here, Daddy."

"That's my boy," the Hel-Wolf said with a low growl.

Loki's eyes pricked with tears. "Thori. How could you—"

"You made me *kneel*!" yelped Thori, his mouth crackling with hellfire.

Loki didn't know if he should laugh or cry. "I made you *sit*!"

"Don't you understand, you ripe little pustule of boyflesh? Like father, like son," the Hel-Wolf snapped.

"Unfortunately true," said a voice Loki couldn't place.

All of them—Ikol, Loki, Hel-Wolf, Thori—twisted, looking for the source of the voice, and saw across the ridge an enormous brown dog the size of a small mountain with glowing red eyes, and on her back, the Dísir. Given how his day was going, Loki didn't know if he should be relieved or terrified. Would they simply fight over who had the privilege to kill him first?

It had been Garm who spoke. Thori's mother.

"Our life would be simpler if that boy pup took after his mother."

The Hel-Wolf snarled. "The mother didn't complain about the father when they met and mated…"

"The mother has awful taste in men and regrets her decisions," Garm said, snapping her jaw at him. And then she launched herself all the way from the other side of the ridge, across the valley, to land on a tiny rock cropping which plainly could not contain them all.

Loki saw the Dísir leap off her back as Garm fought with Hel-Wolf. He waved to them. Worth the risk, he thought.

"Brün! I need—"

She strode up to him, grabbing him by his upper arm and pushing him along the path. "Your needs don't matter. One does not *sneak* into Hel. You should know better. Göndul, take him."

"Wait!" shouted Loki as he was shoved from one Dísir into the next's waiting arms. "You can't do this!"

Göndul laughed, a high, thin laugh that bordered on breathy. "Little boy, I have the weakest arms of the once-cursed sisterhood and I can still tear your head from your body."

"Göndul," he gasped. "Please, it's so important that I go to—"

She shoved him through a portal she slashed open from the air, and he staggered through. With a snap, the portal shut behind him. He straightened up, staring at Hela and Tyr.

298   "I need to go to… right here," he managed to finish saying,

his voice faint. He nearly fell to his knees. "Hela. I know you have said you won't interfere. I know you've said I'm on my own but I need this, I need—"

Hela reached forward and tilted his chin up with two fingers. Her voice was cool and calm. "You want me to unleash you from the story and send you back in time."

He shook from the shock and relief. "Hela, how did you know? I don't understand."

She smiled thinly at him. "Go. Delays are a luxury you cannot afford. You have only minutes to save *everything*."

Green smoke began to gather around her and then it swept across the distance between them, rearing up like a snake. Loki looked up at the smoke-cobra's mouth, and it opened wide, and swallowed him and Ikol whole.

FIFTY-FOUR

THIS WOULD be the second time that Loki rewrote history to get himself out of a jam. He'd need to be careful about how often he used this tool. He wouldn't want this to become too easy for him. After all, it had ramifications and he didn't always see them until it was too late. Like now. But in defense of Loki, who needs no defending to you, no doubt, but perhaps to others, Loki did not use it to write a kinder existence for himself.

Both times, he used this tool to write a kinder existence for someone else.

IN THE minutes before Dark Asgard fell, he ran through the Library of the Serpent, looking for one book. A familiar book. One that already had his hand in it. Ikol helped him spot it amongst the rubble of walls and shelves and broken books, and Loki slid to his knees and pulled the book onto his lap. Relief flooded him. What if they hadn't found it? He banished the thought. He didn't have the time to live in the land of *what ifs* right now.

He pulled Twilight's shadow out of his tunic. The pen gleamed in the dim light.

"Ikol," he said. "How long do I have?"

The magpie circled above him. "Not long enough. This whole citadel is going to fall from the sky, Loki. And if you fall with it, it won't matter that Hela sent you here and you're from the future. You'll die too."

"A deadline," Loki said, forcing cheerfulness into his voice. Then he paused. "A *dead*line. Get it?"

"Write, Loki," said the magpie as the entire floating city shuddered, rocked by earthquakes.

Loki flipped to the pages where he'd written Leah into the story. He reread what he'd written a year ago, when he'd barely known Leah. *The mysterious girl with the green eyes blah blah.* She was right. It was insipid prose indeed. And so limiting. She was always right.

He tore the page out of the book and stuffed in another loose sheet of paper.

He started at the top.

Her name was Leah of Hel.

He wrote of her as he knew her now, after all this time. The handmaiden of Hela who had stood beside him, saved the world and doomed herself. He wrote how her countenance was stern and her words few, but that only made those few kind words more precious than Asgard's entire treasury. He wrote in a frenzied hand trying to express the inexpressible. He wrote how she stood with him in his own messy subconscious. How she forgave him for the order, for holding her binding oath against her and forcing her hand. He wrote how she found Hellstrom and chased him down, how she'd laughed when she put on the Guy Fawkes mask… He wrote how it felt when she took his hand. How much braver he felt when he was shoulder to shoulder with her.

It would not be enough to write her as he saw her. That, too, was so limiting. He wanted to tell them everything. Everything he could.

He was running out of time. He wrote while Dark Asgard's engines shuddered and failed. He wrote while the citadel lurched, sliding from the sky. He wrote as the fall turned bricks into dust around him.

He wrote a lie. That's what it was. But he wrote it so well that he believed it himself. In the end, the lies you choose to tell define you. And he wanted to tell the ones that brought truth and kindness to those around him. Especially her.

He hoped it was enough.

He did not want to live in a world where it wasn't true, these lies and these truths he wrote, where these words were not enough.

"Loki," hissed Ikol.

Loki flipped to a new page. He wrote, *to be continued, however she wishes.*

He slipped Twilight's shadow into his sleeve for later and stared at his final words

She'd finish her own story, whenever she came back.

HE CLIMBED to his feet and told Ikol he was ready, but before they could return to Hel, he felt a tug at his body. Something pulling from a direction he did not want to go. He couldn't stay in Dark Asgard, though, not while it plummeted to earth. His tongue tasted ashes. Sulfur. He realized too late what was happening.

"Ikol," he said warningly, but it was too late.

The world spun hot and bright around him, fire licked at his feet, and in an explosion, he collapsed onto hot, dusty red rock. He grimaced and looked up. Surtur towered above him, Twilight in his hands. Leah stood next to him, looking at her own hands.

This isn't exactly where I wanted to end up, he thought to himself, but it wasn't the worst place.

"What did he change, Leah?" Surtur was demanding. "What is the threat?"

Leah did not look at Loki. She only looked at the lines of her palms that she traced with one slender finger. "He changed nothing anyone cared about…"

Loki's heart lurched.

"Then he dies," Surtur said with satisfaction. "Finally."

Leah looked up. "Until now," she finished.

She shoved her fists out in front of her, green light exploding from them, and Surtur was thrown back, smashing into a rock pillar that exploded under the force of the impact. She leapt backwards, grabbing Loki and shoving him out of the way of Surtur's recoil.

"Leah!" gasped Loki happily.

"Apparently so," she said dryly and she sounded *so much like his Leah* that he wanted to explode from joy. "We're trapped here. You have a plan, right?"

"Of course I had a plan. I had a plan to save you," he protested.

"I'm not feeling particularly saved right now," Leah hissed. She hauled him to his feet and grabbed his hand, dragging him toward a tunnel.

"Not *that* kind of save. Remember? I told you you could have a better life. Here's the better life," he said, gesturing around them at the exploding lava wells and flames filling the path behind them as they ran for their lives.

"You're never going to impress me with wordplay, Loki. You know that, right?"

The cave was cooler than the outside, and the air slicked the sweat on their faces. They both shivered. He started to slow down but Leah shook her head.

"We can't stop here. Do you really not have a plan?"

Behind them, Surtur roared, and things exploded. Rock above and around them trembled.

"I don't really have a plan," Loki admitted. His voice sounded small for the first time. "I ran out of plays. I have no more tricks. It's all out of my hands. Maybe I really did doom everything this time."

He couldn't look at her as they felt along the walls, looking for any way out. "But if I had tried to save the Nine Realms first,

I wouldn't have been able to help you. Not save you. Help you. And I just couldn't leave you."

It was a terribly small admission in a terribly big moment, but he could feel the way it swung between them, a pendulum of feelings that neither of them wanted to catch.

Then Leah said, "You did your best, Loki. Thank you. Better to die as good fiction than live as bad. One way or another, it'll all be over soon."

He looked over his shoulder. "Leah, if I do—"

She cut him off, holding up a finger, cocking her head as she listened. "Shush."

The entire cave exploded around them.

FIFTY-FIVE

WHEN THOR fell into those pools of lava, when Loki tricked him into falling, Thor had cursed him. He'd said things in his mind that he didn't want his brother to know he ever said. Things about how everyone was right about Loki and he'd been wrong. He passed through layers and layers of lava and it'd consumed him and his anger and his hatred.

He had not expected to be spat out in Hel.

He coughed, sputtered, found himself on his hands and knees. The air smelled like death and acid. It was unpleasant at best, unbearable at worst, and Thor could not imagine spending eternity here.

Hel. He'd ended up in Hel.

Hela stood before him, cloaked in green and black, her eyes cold and distant. "So here you are."

He wanted to get off the ground. He wanted to fight something. He wanted to do something. Crush her. But Tyr stood behind her, and it was not Hela's fault that he was here.

"Crushed, broken, drowned in your own arrogance and faith at long last," Hela continued.

He wanted to say that it'd been mostly the lava that killed him, not his own character flaws, but his throat still felt hoarse and scarred, like he'd swallowed lava on the way down. He couldn't form words yet.

She walked a slow circle around him, her heels clacking on the cold stone surface. "Your brother knew you would come here. And as much as I would like to keep you here, there are more important things afoot."

Thor's ears rang. *Loki?* Loki had sent him here on *purpose*? Why couldn't that little conniving snot just share his ideas instead of acting on them in a vacuum?

Hela pulled Thor to his feet and her hand ran down his chest. His armor, his shield, his helmet, his cape, his clothing, all restored to his body in crackling blue fire. He looked around and saw an army amassed around him.

Hela lifted a single eyebrow. "I will empty Hel to ensure all ends as it should."

"My lord," said a soft voice. A woman with a kind face. "I bring you a legion of Asgard's bravest and best—from all eras."

He was surrounded by heroes of old. Heroes of recent times and times long forgotten. People he'd read about in storybooks on his mother's laps.

The woman continued, "I bring you men who will not burn."

"We of Valhalla wish to fight," called another.

"Cavalry's all here, boss. Point us where you need us," said a man, another of Valhalla. He reached out and took the woman's hand. "We're ready."

Thor inhaled deeply and lifted his head. "Well then. Let us all go home."

FIFTY-SIX

SURTUR HAD smashed the cave around them until it did not exist. Until the mountain was gone. Until all that remained was a slippery spit of rock, and Loki and Leah could only stand on it, holding onto one another for balance. The lava sloshed up on their heels and the earth rolled, rocking back and forth. They pressed their feet down for purchase and clung hard, Loki's fingers gripping the collar of Leah's tunic so tightly he thought when he let go, if he let go, it'd be permanently molded into his fist shape.

"Look upon me!" roared Surtur. "For mine is the glory and the embers that smolder at the end of all things!"

"Still think I'm the one with insipid prose?" Loki whispered to Leah.

"Not the time," she growled back.

"I have forged all creation into this very weapon that shall undo it," Surtur intoned, lifting the sword.

He'd grown. He took up the entire sky now. There was no space left in Muspelheim that was not him. There was nowhere else to look or go. This was the end, Loki thought. Surtur heaved Twilight above his head.

"Life becomes death in my hands. The act of living"—he paused for dramatic effect—"SUICIDE!"

"By Odin's socks," said Loki breathlessly. "He's right! How could I have—"

"*Loki*," Leah said, her tone ever suffering.

He turned his head slightly toward her. Their faces were too close. So close. *Wayyyy too close*, Loki thought. But he couldn't take a step back without dying. Couldn't move his face anymore without dying another kind of death. *Trapped.*

"Silence," she said to him.

He could tell by the heat rising in her cheeks that she'd noticed the distance between their faces too. Or, she'd just noticed that Muspelheim was very hot and they were in danger of being roasted like pigs on a spit.

Then Leah's face reached toward him. Their lips brushed.

Now, he wanted to say. *Right now? Are you serious?*

A flicker of light in the corner of his eye caught his attention. He turned away from Leah, his heart wrenching as he did so, and looked up at the sky. A tear opened up against the blazing sky and a white light began as a pinprick and then grew, and grew, until shadows appeared in the white splotch.

It wasn't until Thor bellowed, "For Asgardia!" that Loki realized what was happening.

Thor. He'd made it to Hel. And Hela had done as Loki had hoped she would do. The sky filled with warriors old and new, riding into battle for Asgard.

"Your timing remains impeccable," Loki called to Thor, though Thor could not hear him.

"She emptied the afterlife," Leah said in disbelief.

They gripped each other as the warriors of Valhalla breezed by, the winds around them pulling at Leah and Loki and their precarious perch.

Thor was letting Mjolnir pull him toward Surtur but he flew by Loki first. "I'll deal with you later," he shouted.

"I WAS *HELPING*!" Loki bellowed back.

Surtur chuckled, hot breaths of smoke filling the air. He swung Twilight around toward the warriors. "You are *too late*."

But the warriors of Valhalla were undeterred. They charged at Surtur, plaguing him, but he'd grown to a size and energy beyond their scope. The warriors were no more than annoying pests, bugs that bothered Surtur as he swung at them clumsily, waving his sword about as though he were slapping away mosquitos.

"I am your doom!" he bellowed, slicing toward his foes.

"He is," Loki realized, his heart and hopes falling again. "No amount of clever will save us now."

"Loki, listen to me, this is insanity," Leah hissed. "This is madness. All this blood and thunder. What has it ever done for anyone?"

Loki blink and straightened. "That's *it*! You're a genius, Leah. It's worth a try, anyway."

The battle raged around them and Loki was already plotting again. Leah gripped his arm.

"I don't know what you're talking about."

Loki gripped Leah's hand as they looked at the destruction, at the fallen Valhallan warriors, at Thor striking at Surtur's head again and again.

"Let us go then, you and I."

"Finally, a proper courting gesture," Leah said primly.

He turned to her. "No, not like that—"

But she was opening a portal around them. "I know. Where now?"

HE'D FORGOTTEN that she hadn't gotten to see Otherworld after all the changes Wilson and the Manchester Gods had made to the place. It had changed even in the few weeks since he and Thor were here. It'd jumped from the industrial age again to something sleeker. Shinier. Gone were the steel-covered buildings and the clanky machinery. The buildings that surrounded Camelot and Manchester now were glossy—made of glass and stone that reflected back distorted images of those who stood before it. There were no curves, just sharp lines and angles, infinity pools and windows that reflected the sky.

The sky was still gray and hazy, and there were no trees, no birds, no endless hills of grass. There was no grass at all. No nature and no living beings, save for the Otherworld folk who were coming in and out of the train station and meetings with Wilson.

Still, he loved that in this Leah form, this freer girl, she made the face he suspected she could not have made before. She wrinkled her nose up in distaste.

"I know that they were a better prospect than continuing the ways of the Old Gods," she said to Loki. "But did they have to muck it up so much?"

"I do not think it's mucked up so much as improved," Wilson said mildly, walking up to them on his rock-crunching feet. "You do not like the buildings?"

"I miss the grass," she said simply.

Wilson did not seem to care if she missed the grass. "Loki. I did not expect to see you back so soon. How can we help?"

"The Manchester Gods and the children of your cities feed energy into Surtur's original city. That's how he's gotten so big. I was trying to figure it out, Leah, when we were on that rock. He seemed to be growing exponentially. His master plan. His grand invention. All of that industriousness of his. All that making. That's not what Surtur does. Surtur's not a builder like you, Wilson. Surtur is doom. He destroys things. He un-does. He's an un-maker. Surtur's going to release the process, putting the stored energy back out as all-consuming—"

"Loki, I don't follow," said Wilson, cutting him off. "Please. Speak clearly. Assume I know nothing."

Loki took a deep breath. "Surtur's forged a weapon with all the fires of creation, and when he uses it, he will destroy the Nine Realms. But Otherworld… Otherworld is the center of this Venn diagram." He waved his arms to indicate two overlapping circles. "You see? Otherworld connects to the whole of the Multiverse. It

310

touches every dimension. Every world. Every 'verse that can or will be. He's going to vent this un-making fire through Otherworld."

"It will engulf everything," Leah added.

"Everything burns, Wilson," Loki said, urgency creeping back into his voice. "Everything with a capital E. The Manchester Gods are Surtur's conduit and the link in the chain to the gods with which he threatens the Nine Realms. But if the chain were broken…"

He shrugged.

"He thinks you won't do it," said Leah to Wilson, and Loki could tell this was something that Surtur had told her before she'd been wholly her own person instead of the half-person he'd written her as. "He thinks you won't give up all you've fought for."

"He's played us. He's used us all," Loki said.

Wilson sank to the stairs. "This can't be true. This can't be the end."

"You'll rise again," Loki said softly.

Wilson looked out over the cities he'd built, created from nothing. His expression was unreadable. "It'd be so much easier to be the villain, wouldn't it? But this… This is vile." He got to his feet with his staff and Leah's hand at his elbow. "We will rise again, perhaps. But that we rose at all is thanks to both of you. With our fall, we repay the debt. Poetic, I suppose."

And as he walked away, they heard him say, "Bloody poetry."

"Is he going to do something?" Loki asked Leah, his voice low. "Or is he just going to be angry?"

"Shhh," hushed Leah, squeezing his hand. "Patience."

They followed Wilson to where he stood overlooking the glittering city. When he appeared above them, the Engels—just about everything in Otherworld fell under the definition of Engels at this point, as far as Loki could tell—gathered. They sensed his presence and his need for their attention, or they were just constantly waiting for a speech. Wilson seemed like the type, Loki thought, to give grand speeches.

Wilson threw out his arms. "Fellow Engels! We dance and squirm upon the pin thrust through our chests."

"'Damn poetry?'" Loki murmured to Leah.

She barely concealed her smile.

But then Wilson's tone grew somber. "By sacrificing everything we hold dear, we save the universe. Once again, all hope lies in us proletariats!" And then he added, "And Loki."

Upon the first syllable of "Loki", Wilson's chest burst forth with white light, hot and electric, that spiked out through the air in wild, desperate tendrils. Everywhere around them, bursts of white-hot electric force exploded, popped and fizzled. They spread from the city into what was left of the countryside and into the distance. Burning fires of dazzling heat lit up Otherworld.

"It's done," said Leah softly.

IN ASGARDIA, cities on mechanical legs that bombarded the Asgardian forces exploded in heaps of junk and burning fuel, plumes of black smoke rising into the Asgardian sky.

In Muspelheim, mechanical weapons behind Surtur exploded, and then Surtur's presence began to shrink. The fires around him died down, and the blows of the Valhallan warriors began to take their toll.

And everywhere the machines fell, all heard an echo of Wilson saying, "For the debt to Loki."

Loki.

Loki.

Loki.

The All-Mother looked to the sky from their prison and exhaled. "Our boy did it."

Thor looked to the sky and grinned. "My brother."

ON THE battlefield, Surtur shrieked and raged. "The fuses in all realities!"

He could not grow any longer, but he was still powerful enough without those Engel-engines and fuel sources feeding into him.

And if they killed him without redirecting the energy inside him, he'd unleash it on the Nine Realms and everything would *still burn*. Not ideal, if you asked Loki.

"Crush the Nine Realms!" roared Surtur to his forces. And the forces of Muspelheim rallied to his cry, fighting back ferociously against the forces for good from Asgardia.

Loki and Leah arrived in the middle of this battle, the sound of fury and fire and flame and death filling the air. They'd been there for all of a millisecond when Thor landed beside them and grabbed Loki's shoulder with such force he nearly grabbed Ikol at the same time. The magpie made a rude chattering noise at Thor as he took to the sky.

"*You*," Thor growled.

Loki looked his brother in the eye, and he could see that Thor did not forgive him.

Thor's jaw twitched. "They all said your name. The Manchester Gods and their godlings. Before they fell. Whatever trick or trick-of-a-trick you pulled, it worked."

Loki lifted one of his hands in a weak cheering fist. "Yay Loki?"

Thor shoved him backwards so hard that Loki landed on his butt, skittering across the stones to Leah's feet. "But now we are done, you and I."

A part of Loki wanted to scream *you left me first*. But he swallowed his pride and his hurt. "I did what needed to be done! We both did. Hammer and shadow. Sword and pen. Then I realized only fools try to split the difference."

Thor scowled, maybe realizing that Loki was including him in that *fools* statement. Loki plowed on, pulling free the Shadow Blade he'd tucked inside his sleeve.

"Why not kill them all by using both?"

Thor's face broke into an expression of bright awe. He reached for Twilight's shadow, wrapping his hand around the hilt. It was a pen, and a blade, and Twilight's opposite, mightier than the sword. In Thor's other hand, Mjolnir vibrated with a high-pitched whine. Thor looked at it curiously.

"Mjolnir is drawn to Twilight's shadow." He flipped it around in his hand and thrust it out, dangerously close to Loki. But Thor only had eyes for the shadow. He grinned. "Okay. Now with this I might be able to cause some *real* trouble."

"We don't know what to do if you cause too much trouble, though," Loki said. "If Surtur dies with nowhere to channel his energy…"

"It will not die with him?" Thor asked with surprise.

Leah shook her head. "No. Energy doesn't die. It has to go somewhere. We destroyed the conduits so now…" She shrugged. "There's nowhere to put it." They both heard her unspoken statement. *Except Asgardia.*

Thor growled and slashed Twilight's shadow through the air angrily. He huffed. "We need Odin."

"But—" Loki began.

"I *know*, Loki," Thor snapped. "He's in exile. He put me in jail. You do not know how much it pains me to need him. But you and Leah. You must get him. He is the only one who can harness that power. He did it before, to rebuild Asgardia the last time we faced Surtur. He must do it again."

"Say no more," Loki said, just grateful that Thor still needed him too. "We'll do it, right, Leah?"

She was already opening the portal to Odin's place of exile.

BUT THE time for cleverness was not over, and three clever minds were better than one. With some needling, they coaxed Odin to help them.

"It's everyone's turn to be forgiven," Loki explained cheerfully.

Odin's eye had narrowed. "For what do I need to be forgiven, boy?"

Leah had elbowed Loki and he'd bowed his head contritely. "Nothing. But we do need somewhere for all of Surtur's energy to go. And there's no one as big or strong enough as you to take it."

Flattery always worked on Odin, and it worked here.

Loki prided himself on good timing, but this time, they cut it close, even by Loki's standards. They returned to the battle in the midst of chaos, unclear who was winning, and who was losing. Thor was a blur of Twilight and Mjolnir, striking at Surtur.

Loki shouted, just once, to Thor, who caught sight of him, Leah, and Odin. Thor wasted no time. In the din of battle, he spun and brought Twilight up, driving the blade into Surtur's jaw.

An explosion of light filled the sky—but then Odin was there, white hair flowing, capturing the energy before it could destroy the Nine Realms.

But these details, to Loki, were just that. Details. He'd no concern that once Thor and Leah were both themselves again, both free and back with him in Asgardia, that together they couldn't solve anything ahead of them. This was just the aftermath, at this point. They'd saved Asgardia. They'd stopped everything from burning. The insurrection, the city-gods on legs, the Surtur-fueled pyromaniac rebellions popping up in Vanaheim, the revolt against the All-Mother. All of this ended if the fuel that fueled Surtur was cut off, and they'd done that.

"We did it," Loki said in awe, standing on the edge of Asgardia.

Leah took his hand. "Yes. Yes, we did."

FIFTY-SEVEN

I WOULD LIKE TO TELL YOU THAT THE STORY ENDED THERE. THAT THEY LIVED HAPPILY EVER AFTER AND LEAH WAS UPGRADED FROM A CAVE TO A SUITE IN THE CASTLE AND LOKI HAD DEVISED A SECRET MESSAGE SYSTEM BETWEEN THEIR ROOMS SO WHEN THOR GROUNDED HIM, HE COULD STILL TALK WITH HIS "B.F.F."

I WOULD LIKE TO TELL YOU THAT HAPPENED.

BUT I AM ONLY THE TELLER OF THIS STORY. THIS STORY IS MINE, BECAUSE I WAS GIVEN IT, BUT THE SHAPE OF IT IS NOT ONE OF MY CHOOSING.

YOU ALREADY KNOW BY NOW THAT THIS COULD NOT BE HOW THE STORY ENDED.

IN SOME ways, life did go back to normal.

The All-Mother was restored to their place of power. Thor settled back into his life. Odin—well, Odin was trouble and not everyone was glad to see him back, but they'd needed him, and he'd been willing and able. Loki had a lot more respect for Odin with those facts on the table.

But Loki found himself unmoored. He was lost. Even with Leah. Even with Thor. Even though people saw him as the hero he'd always wanted to be seen as. He felt like he was adrift, and he still had no answers for the things that stuck with him.

He'd wanted to be an agent of chaos in pursuit of truth, and he'd been that. But his misadventures had almost always turned to disasters. It was only with the help of others, like Hela, and the Dísir, and strangely, Garm, that had he been able to right (and write) his own wrongs. He'd failed as often as he'd succeeded. And sometimes he'd done exactly what his past self would have done, pretending that the ends justified the means.

Volstagg tried to give him chores.

"Boys need direction," Volstagg said, his voice rumbling. When Loki didn't have a quick reply, Volstagg tousled his hair. Loki swatted him away, rearranging his locks with quick, deft fingers and a scowl aimed at Volstagg. Loki did not know this, of course, but such an adolescent response soothed Volstagg. The boy was still the boy, even if he was moody and reticent. And it pleased Volstagg to know that somewhere inside of him, Loki had forgiven him. Volstagg was not as faultless as he'd like to seem.

Loki ended up looking for answers, as he always did, in the Library of Asgardia. He bypassed the librarians—lovely though they were, he thought they might think him narcissistic for only checking out books about himself—and took his haul to a dusty space in the back of the stacks where no one ever ventured. Tucked in between books about geology of Asgardia and the meaning of brick patterns, Loki sat the heavy book on his lap, running his fingers over the embossed horns on the cover. He knew those horns. They didn't belong to him, but he felt as if they should. He knew that people thought they did.

He'd flipped through this book before, looking for answers. He doubted he'd find any now. But he still opened the cover and began to read.

He stopped at the same place he always did.

Why did Loki do it? No one knows.

He leaned back against the wall. "Good question."

He knew why *he* did the things he did. Didn't he? He did. He was sure of it. But why had his previous self done what he'd done? Why had he made those choices in that last and final stand?

His fingers traced the ink on the page, until he got to the question mark. He hesitated, and then ran his finger over the marking. Just as it had before this all began, the ink felt different. Glossy and thick. The dot beneath it grew and expanded on the page as soon as his finger touched it. *Not again. Seriously?* He didn't have time for this. And he didn't want this. He didn't want this life to be disrupted. It was finally peaceful.

Loki shoved the book off his lap and scrambled to his feet, backing away. But the dot grew, and grew, as if he'd flipped a switch or triggered something within the ink. It consumed the words around it, the question *Why did Loki do it?* absorbed into the black abyss. The ink spot grew until it swallowed the book and dripped off the pages onto the floor below. The book disappeared, and somewhere, there was a thunk.

The ink spot was a hole. He backed up farther as it grew. Panic rose in him. Would it stop? Would it swallow the stacks? The library? The city? What had he done? The shelves of books about the geology of Asgardia and the symbolism in brick patterns would be no great loss—but the whole library? Unforgivable. Worse than any other crime that his past self had committed, as far as Loki was concerned.

But the ink-spot-turned-abyss stopped just short of swallowing the stacks, though the shelving unit wobbled and swayed right on the edge.

Loki hesitated and then stepped toward it, peering into the darkness. It looked like spilled ink. It moved and smelled and appeared to be liquid. But when he went to touch it, his hand disappeared.

If Leah was there, she'd say, *don't be ridiculous. We cannot just jump into every portal you accidentally open. Even if you know what's down there.* Because she would have amended it to, *even if you* think *you know what's down there.*

But Leah was not there. She was free to make her own choices, and thus was somewhere else, adventuring without him, at least for the day. No one was there to tell Loki to make good choices.

So he made a bad one. He would take personal responsibility for this, of course. It wasn't Leah's fault that he made bad choices. But sometimes, he wished that there was a way to have a seatbelt on his own decision making. Or at the very least, airbags.

He jumped in, tucking his knees to his chest and wrapping his arms around himself like he was cannonballing into the unknown. He landed on soft ground that smelled of recent rain, damp and earthy. He rolled over to his hands and knees and saw Ikol there.

"Magpies gonna magpie," he muttered.

Ikol tilted his head at him, beady eyes bright and dark, and then took to the air, cawing. Loki rose, following the magpie with his gaze, and then Ikol lit upon the pedestal with the horned helmet. His past self rose from the pedestal, ghostly and glowing, oversized and with a cunning look of victory etched on his face.

"Loki," Past Loki crooned. "You can't say I didn't warn you. I *did* say that I was he whom you must not trust. I was *so* close to just playing fairly. But the temptation..." He trailed off, shaking his head.

Loki rolled his eyes. "I doubt you even tried. You wouldn't know fairness if it smacked the helmet off your head."

Past Loki grinned. "True enough, godling of lies." He gestured. "Take a seat. I want to tell you a story."

Loki did not want to take a seat. But he saw little choice. There was no ladder out of the abyss. Past Loki would not let him go until this task was done. He sat cross-legged on the ground, arms folded across his chest. He knew he looked sulky but what was the point of being a Young Loki being lectured by a Past Loki if one didn't get to sulk?

THIS IS WHERE I REMIND YOU, DEAR READER. WHEN I STARTED THIS STORY, I TOLD YOU OF MAGPIES. I TOLD YOU THAT THE

SEVENTH MAGPIE TOOK A FEW DETOURS, NONE OF WHICH WERE NECESSARY TO KNOW ABOUT AT THE TIME. WE'RE COMING BACK TO THAT NOW. I DID SAY IT WAS IMPORTANT.

The seventh magpie, it came to me. It came to my window, a stained-glass thing with a portal through the bottom of the question mark etched into its panes. It was a scrawny bird. It'd been too long in the air and it hungered.

"WHO ARE YOU?" I asked it. A silly question to ask birds, but I knew it was the right question to ask.

In the language of birds, it answered, "I carry a message."

I remember that I inclined my head, indicating that it carry on.

The bird hopped farther into my mess of an office. "Watch Loki. Tell his tale. Eventually he'll construct a device that threatens the universe. He'll think he has it safely stored away. When he does so, wait until the next major war in the Nine Realms and then tell Mephisto all about the buried weapon. Sign the message from his old, dear friend, Loki."

The bird looked as sour as I did at the time. Magpies are no more word-carriers than they are carrion-eaters. And I do not take orders from magpies, or their masters.

"WHAT PRICE DO YOU OFFER ME?" I asked the magpie.

The magpie considered this question. And then it cawed, "You desire tales. Have this one. It will be the greatest that Loki has ever wrought. And only you will know it."

The magpie took flight again, exiting through the question it had used to enter.

So, you see, it was never Young Loki's story to give away.

And it wasn't quite mine either.

Loki of old has been here the entire time, picking at the pins of this lock to unlock and lock the doors of his own creation.

IN THE abyss where Young Loki sat at the feet of the Past Loki, Past Loki lounged on a ghostly throne, casual in his delight.

"So," he said. "That happened. The day came. Surtur's flames of rebellions went up and the Teller did exactly what I told him. He sent word to Mephisto about the predicament of the fear-lords. A single crown for seven heads and seven minds who'd never agree on who the wearer should be. It was a perfectly self-enclosed self-perpetuating system. A *nightmare* of a system, if you will. And perfectly poised for—what's the mortal word for this? *Disruption.* When an external force acts on a system."

Young Loki's mind raced. "No, the fear-lords are bickering with Nightmare still. That's where I left them."

Past Loki's smile was gentle and cruel. "No, little one. Mephisto played his hand well. Especially with Surtur gone. The fear-lords would never have bent a knee to one of their own—but to an outsider? They were almost eager for the organization, the control they gave him, the power they gave up. He would take Satan's throne. Hell on earth. Hell everywhere."

"That's not possible," Loki managed to say. His hands trembled. His words wobbled.

"He will take that seat today," Past Loki said pleasantly.

"Then it's not too late," Loki said, head jerking up to look at his past self. "I can still change this."

"Oh, it is far too late," Past Loki said. His tone was amiable and Young Loki wanted to smack him. "I mean, maybe not too late for eventual victory but for billions of lives? It's definitely too late. Unless…"

He looked thoughtful for a tad too long.

Young Loki wanted to wait him out, but he couldn't stand it. Every moment they bickered with each other here was a moment wasted. "Unless *what?*"

Past Loki bent over him, grinning. "The crown he'll wear is the crown of your thoughts, little Loki. Your thoughts and your dreams. If those thoughts ceased to be… the crown would too. The part of me you carried in your head, it is not you. If you let it overwrite your mind, you will no longer exist. And neither will the crown Mephisto will wear to bring chaos and hell to every realm."

Loki saw now what his past self had done. He'd found a way to come back. To change the Loki who *was* into the Loki who *had been*.

And it'd been the plan from the start. The first meeting between them. Ikol. The debts to Mephisto and Hela. Leah. Surtur. Nightmare and the fear-lords. He'd been trying to right wrongs and bring peace and stability to Asgard, to make up for past wrongs that weren't even his wrongs, and it'd been futile. He hadn't even known it.

"There must be another way," he murmured.

"Probably," agreed Past Loki. "But you're out of time. This is the only option left to you. You delay a day, Mephisto takes the throne and worlds suffer torment unimaginable to man. Yet, sadly, easily imaginable to hellspawn."

"You didn't want to change after all, did you?" Loki said quietly.

Past Loki tilted his head quizzically. "That isn't true. Change is *all* I desired. For me to change. Not you. After all, Loki would only sacrifice Loki... to save himself."

Young Loki rolled his eyes, irritated. "Is wordplay trickery as annoying when I do it?"

Though she was not here, he heard Leah say simply, *yes*, in his mind.

He wished she was here. He couldn't see his way out of this. If he wanted to do the right thing, if he could *only* do the right thing, then he'd save the world, but end himself, and give himself back to this Loki, who would *not* do the right things going forward.

"If the world will not let one change, it's near impossible to do so," Past Loki said, like he'd seen all those times when everyone thought that Young Loki was him, and did not see Young Loki's desires to change for the better. "With your innocence, you reestablished my name and now I have a chance to be something else by taking your place."

"But will you?" asked Young Loki. "Will you be someone else? Does *something else* suggest something better? Or just *change* in any direction? You want my good name. I won't give it up without—"

"I can give you a chance to say goodbye. A gift. Three conversations, none of which can reveal the truth. Three private conversations. If you transgress, you forfeit all immediately."

Loki scowled at his past self. "Must you make everything, including annihilation, into a game?"

Past Loki shrugged, but he looked smug.

Loki looked down at his hands, his feet, the dust beneath them.

"This I swear, but," he said quietly, turning back to Past Loki, "I played the game. I played it as long and as hard as I could."

"You did, Loki," said Past Loki, for the first time his expression contrite and solemn. He laid a hand on Loki's shoulder. "But the house always wins."

FIFTY-EIGHT

BENEATH EVERY slap of his feet on the stone road out of Asgardia, Loki heard the infernal ticking of a clock. A countdown, and he didn't know when it ended. He didn't know how much time he had left to stop this disaster. He only knew that every second counted.

If he knew how much time he had, he might start thinking of ways around it.

He'd set that crown aside for Nightmare, to keep the fear-lords preoccupied. But Hellstrom had warned him that he'd armed Nightmare. And Loki should have thought about what happened if Nightmare was bested. If Nightmare was outsmarted by someone—someone like Mephisto. Now Mephisto would have access to a crown of fear-stuff, Loki's fear-stuff, and the power it'd give him was unknowable. Great. That was the power of fear, after all. That was why Hellstrom spent so much time digging it out of people's heads to try and save them.

And if Loki did not run *just a little faster*, it might have all been for nothing.

How had he been so stupid?

He skidded down the entrance to the path. Hellstrom was on

his back in the cave. Normally, Loki would have made a dirty joke about that or offered him a shirt, but Hellstrom looked like he was dying, and Loki did not have time to get pulled into a squabble.

"Loki?" Leah stood from where she had been wiping Hellstrom's fever-stricken brow. "What's wrong? Hellstrom—"

"I'm going to Hel."

Her hands were already moving, opening a portal for him. He paced anxiously as it opened wider, her magic brighter and lighter than it was when she was Hela's handmaiden. And unfortunately, slower than when she was a handmaiden too.

"What's going on, Loki? You're being stranger than usual."

He leapt through the portal, shouting over his back, "Monologue, not a conversation!"

He did not have words to waste.

He did not have *time.*

Leah followed him into Hel. He hadn't expected that, but he probably should have. He slid up to Garm who growled, "Greetings, liesmith."

Tears pricked at Loki's eyes and he tried to blink them away. He bowed to the dog at the gates of Hel and then kept going. He found the first Dísir he could find. "Brün, a word."

They stepped to the side, Leah conversing with Garm in the distance, their expressions concerned.

Loki turned his back to Leah. "The curse of the sisterhood when you consumed the dead was that you utterly annihilated them. Could you devour me?"

Brün blinked. She'd filled out since he'd seen her last. Her cheeks were no longer hollowed to the bone and her eyes were real, not glowing, cursed embers. Her hair had even grown below her ears, poking out of her helmet.

"No, that curse was broken when Hela drank from the Grail. The wound was healed, Loki…"

Loki's shoulders slumped and he started to walk away.

"Loki," called Brün.

"Thanks, Brün. Never mind," he called over his shoulder.

One conversation. He'd had one conversation and he was no closer to a solution. His heart ached as he sought out Hel in the inner chambers of her fortress.

She lounged on her throne, her many-horned helmet striking an impressive silhouette against the light that poured through the back of the throne room. On a normal day, he'd point that out to her. They were friends now. Almost.

Leah caught up with him, grabbing him by the shoulders. "Brün said you wanted her to annihilate you? I will happily do so if you don't start talking!"

No one had ever begged him to talk before. Loki felt words bubble up and he ignored them. He pushed her fingers from his shoulders. He stood squarely in front of Hela. He swallowed hard but that didn't stop his voice from sounding tearful and hoarse when he spoke. "Leah needs to be sent away, Hela. A long way from here. I don't want anything to do with her."

"What?" Leah screeched. She grabbed his arm. "Loki!"

Hela did not blink. "I concur. Leah of Hel will be sent to the ancient past."

She reached out her hand and white fire poured forth toward Leah.

Leah gasped. "Loki! What are you doing? What's in your head? Are you possessed? Speak to me!"

He'd given her freedom, and now he was taking it away. He hated himself for it. But he wanted her to be safe. Safe from the Loki who was to come. The one who would look like him and talk like him, but lack the goodness and kindness he possessed. The one who would use her, and against whom she would not know to guard herself, or her heart.

The white light swirled and pulled Leah backwards into time. Her final words to him cut him like a knife.

"Loki, you eternal idiot. At least show me sufficient respect to lie to me. As long as there is a heart in my chest, I will hate you."

The words were muffled. Far away. But he heard them clear as a bell. Tears ran down his cheeks.

And then Hela's court was silent. Empty.

Hela looked at Loki with a gentle expression. She reached out and brushed the tears away from his cheeks. He closed his eyes and sniffled, more tears running.

"It's for the best," Hela said softly. "By the time she grows up, she'll be more than capable of dealing with the likes of you."

Loki nodded. He got to his feet—when had he fallen to his knees? He couldn't remember. Two conversations. He'd one more to go. He couldn't waste time. He wanted to stay here, let Hela reassure him more, but if he'd sent Leah to the ancient past for nothing he'd really never forgive himself.

HE FOUND Thor in the Ruingarden of Asgardia. He loved this garden and he loved that his brother did too. The old palace had once stood on these grounds, but long after the walls had come down and the turrets fallen, nature had taken it back over. Now gardeners nursed the plants to life, bringing moss between the bricks of the footpaths, planting clematis that crawled up the walls, sprouting pink flowers along the way. It was dense, and green and beautiful. It was the opposite of Muspelheim and Hel and the many other places he'd been over the last year.

"Loki?" Thor frowned. "What's amiss? You called me here so urgently that I—"

Loki threw himself against his brother, wrapping his arms around his brother so tightly that he felt the breath knock out of Thor. His brother's arms came back around him instantly, warm and reassuring.

"Thor," whispered Loki. Thor wrapped his brother close to his chest. "If I go bad—"

"Loki," said Thor warningly.

"Just do it. You have to do it. Promise me," he said, so intensely that he had to push out of Thor's arms, lean back to see his brother's face.

Thor opened his mouth and Loki saw the promise taking shape on his brother's tongue. And then something shifted in Thor's expression and he snapped his mouth shut, shaking his head.

"No. Never." He knelt so he was Loki's height. "Brother. What is wrong? I can help. There's nothing we can't solve together."

But this was not solvable. This could not be solvable.

"Nothing's wrong," he muttered. His last words to his brother would be a lie. He hated that. "I'm just scared. We all know how this story ends."

Thor shook his head, his grip tight on Loki's shoulders. "I won't let it. And *you* won't either. I will never give up on you, Loki. You must have faith in yourself."

"Faith?" Loki said, laughing a bit through his tears. He wiped his cheeks and nose off on his sleeve. He should have brought tissues. "In myself? Oh, Thor."

He threw his arms around his brother again and mumbled into his shoulder.

"You really are the biggest, sweetest idiot in the whole Nine Realms."

THREE CONVERSATIONS.

"Well, Loki, are you done?"

The voice floated to him and he was no longer in the Ruingarden with Thor. He was walking down a long tunnel. He hadn't fallen through an inksplot or a book this time. He'd simply appeared at the mouth of the tunnel and his feet began on their own accord.

He did not need to ask whose voice it was.

"Well and truly," he said, though it was a lie. He stopped in front of the pedestal with the horned helmet and the ghost of Past Loki. "So. What's next?"

Past Loki leaned down and whispered, "The. End."

Loki sighed. His past self was without a doubt the more annoying version of himself. "No. What's after *that*? It's only the end for *me*."

"Oh," said Past Loki, straightening up. "Well. From what I understand it'll go somewhat like this. The crown fails. The hell king will be deposed, to the amusement of many. Families will be reunited. Families will begin. Those brought low will start to rise. Those brought high will fall, and gratefully so. A new sisterhood. A new peace. With heroes to watch and protect over it. Forever." He waved a hand vaguely. "It'll all be very wholesome."

Loki nodded, seeing the images flicker by his mind's eye. "Okay."

And then, in a gentle voice that surprised Young Loki, Past Loki said, "And in an ancient past…"

Loki knew what Past Loki wanted him to believe. That he'd be with Leah. That they'd be happily ever after, as they wanted to be, as they couldn't be in this time.

Loki snorted. "No. That's a very pretty lie, but I know it won't be like that at all. I'll be gone forever. It's beyond any of our power to end the story like that."

"It is," Past Loki said with a dramatic sigh. "More's the pity! It is time. Swallow the lie."

Loki reached down, picking up Ikol at his feet. He nestled the magpie in his arms, stroking its jet-black feathers. Studying its beady dark eyes. How many times had he relied on Ikol for wisdom or guidance? How many times had he still failed? Had Ikol been there for him, Loki, or for Past Loki?

"I'm sorry, Loki," said Past Loki.

Loki frowned, looking up. "I'm sure you are. But not enough." He took a step closer to the pedestal and the towering specter of Past Loki. "Because I was thinking. You know that you've lost, right?"

Past Loki looked startled. "No. I will change."

Loki was already shaking his head. "No, of course you won't. They won't let you." He stroked Ikol's head now. "I played and won. I changed. I'm the one who found a way to use my nature for better paths, better futures. You're just being yourself, as always."

Past Loki started to look panicked, but he didn't know where this was going, so he could not act.

Loki smiled. "I won, and you lost. Never forget it."

And then in a move he could not believe he could follow through with, he leaned down and sank his mouth into the back of Ikol's skull. He felt the bird's last gasp of air. He felt the bird's neck snap. He told himself this was not a real magpie, that this was a Loki, and an evil one at that. Still, the bird's blood covered his mouth, and when he lifted his face sticky feathers tumbled from the corners of his lips. He was the Serpent, the broken boy in the stone cell, who belly-crawled to rip out his captors' throats.

There was no echoing scream from Past Loki, just a swelling of green fire that devoured the specter and left the hall empty. The fire did not make a sound and did not emit heat, but when Loki crawled to the pedestal where the helmet stood, it gave way, breaking itself to provide a path.

Loki pulled the helmet down into his lap.

He'd done what he needed to do. He cradled the helmet and whispered to it, "I win."

He had, hadn't he?

He knew he could.

He was out of time, and then he was not out of time. Once he was in the hall, he knew that the time that he needed would always exist. That Loki would not let things happen without his hand on the rudder of this ship.

He'd played his last card so well.

But he felt the way it hollowed him out. It'd taken something from him. Something vital and treasured. He lifted his eyes to the sky of the black abyss.

"Damn you." He closed his eyes. "Damn you all."

ACKNOWLEDGMENTS

This book was a *journey* (pun intended) and I'm grateful for everyone who journeyed with me. It's hard to go on a quest alone, and lucky for me, I was never alone.

Thank you to my agent, Lara Perkins, for being steadfast at my side through all the ups and downs. I'm eternally grateful to Marieke Nijkamp, Dahlia Adler, Ashley Poston, Kaitlyn Sage Patterson, Lauren Magaziner, Katherine Welsh, Bella Angel, and Thea Stout for cheerleading me through the writing.

This book wouldn't have existed without Michael Beale and his vision, wisdom, and patience, and for all of that I am grateful. Thank you to George Sandison for shepherding this project along its path. The journey might have been long and wandering, but we found our footing.

Thank you additionally to Jess Woo, Adrian McLaughlin, Paul Simpson, William Robinson, Charlotte Kelly, Katharine Carroll, Sarah Singer, Jeremy West, Sven Larsen, and Jeff Youngquist, who all helped this book complete its quest.

And thank you to Kieron Gillen, for incredible source material, for a Loki who was deeply lovable, flawed, complex, witty, and clever. Every page was such a gift.

And finally, thank you to Loki. For sticking with me. Through Hel, Limbo, and more.

ABOUT THE AUTHOR

KATHERINE LOCKE lives and writes in Philadelphia, Pennsylvania with their feline overlords and their addition to chai lattes. They are the author of *The Girl with the Red Balloon*, *The Spy with the Red Balloon*, and *This Rebel Heart*. They can be found online at KatherineLockeBooks.com and @bibliograto on Twitter and Instagram.

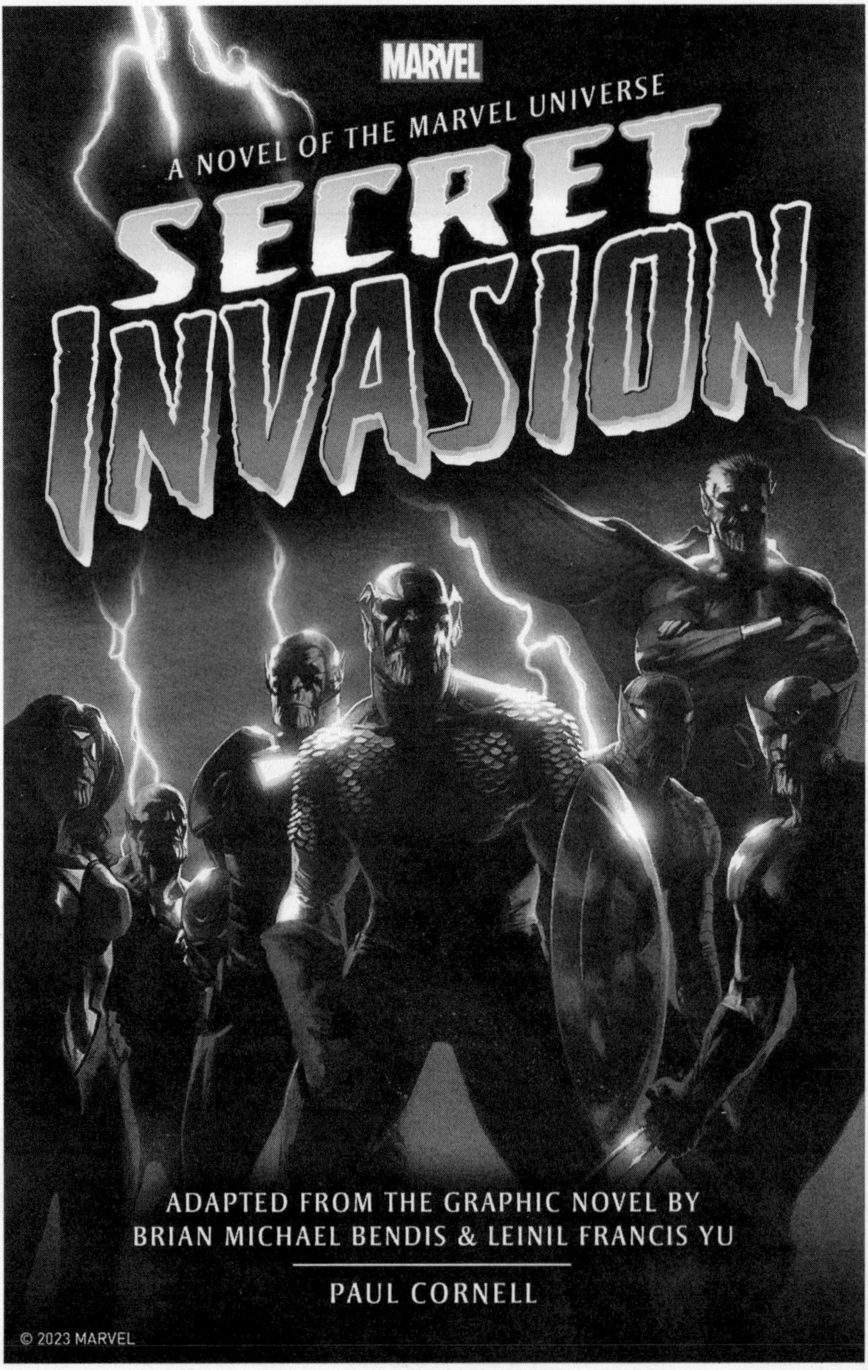
MARVEL
A NOVEL OF THE MARVEL UNIVERSE
SECRET INVASION
ADAPTED FROM THE GRAPHIC NOVEL BY
BRIAN MICHAEL BENDIS & LEINIL FRANCIS YU
PAUL CORNELL
© 2023 MARVEL